ABOUT THE AUTHORS

Bruce Kennedy Jones and Eric Allison first met in a windswept car park in Manchester more years ago than either of them care to remember. They started writing *The Last Straight Face* while Eric was doing time in HMP Risley – swapping material weekly and speaking early every Sunday morning when the prison phones were quiet.

Bruce is now an investigative journalist specialising in crime and Eric, once described by the Manchester police as being 'among the top echelons of British criminals', has since become the prison correspondent for the *Guardian*. *The Last Straight Face* is their first novel. They are currently at work on a sequel, *Fat Blackmail*.

THE LAST STRAIGHT FACE

BRUCE KENNEDY JONES AND ERIC ALLISON

Old St PUBLISHING

First published in Great Britain 2008 by Old Street Publishing Ltd,
28–32 Bowling Green Lane, London EC1R 0BJ, UK
www.oldstreetpublishing.co.uk

Copyright © Bruce Kennedy Jones and Eric Allison 2008

Bruce Kennedy Jones and Eric Allison have asserted their right under the Copyright, Designs and Patents
Act 1988 to be identified as the authors of this work.

A CIP catalogue record for this book is available from the British Library.

ISBN13: 978 1905847 45 7

Printed and bound in Great Britain

10 9 8 7 6 5 4 3 2 1

For Ailsa and Sid

It was a Chinese croupier who found Tomas face down on the steps of Manchester's Royal Infirmary at four o'clock on the Tuesday morning. She'd been kicking around in casualty with a suspect fractured wrist since ten and was making her fags last by smoking them one an hour, on the hour. The paper said she'd thought Tomas was a drunk at first, only he didn't answer when she called across to see if he was OK. Then she saw his shirt was covered in blood from neck to waist and there was a thick sugary pool dripping from the step he lay on down to the next, and the next step after that.

1

I got out of Strangeways at half past eight on the Friday morning and Terry met me at the gate.

He walked up to me, stopped a couple of feet away then shifted from one foot to the other. Either he was nervous or he wanted a piss. 'Hello, mate.'

He'd put on some weight and there was more colour in his face than when I'd last seen him inside eight months ago, but he still looked pretty fit and hard, and his fine brown hair was clean and recently cut and getting flicked at by the breeze. He was wearing crisp designer jeans, ironic seventies shirt and jacket and new trainers. And none of it copy gear, I'd bet.

I looked past him down the slope to Bury New Road. Cars and the good noise of traffic, straightgoers on the pavement doing that brisk efficient stride they use on the way to work in the morning, the quick-step one where they stretch their legs a little bit further, moving with purpose in anticipation of a new day – bang, bang, bang, I'm a straightgoer.

I looked back at Terry. 'Fuck off.'

'What?'

I was already past him and down the slope. I heard him skip shuffle behind me and his breath as he caught up. 'I thought we were mates.'

'We're not.'

'I thought – '

I stopped walking. 'Just fuck off.'

I did the straightgoer stride down the hill, looking for a cab on the main drag. Off the slope by the car lot, I glanced over my shoulder to see the little shit yapping along behind me. 'I just wanted to meet you out of the nick. What's the matter?'

I grabbed his mile-wide seventies collar and slammed him up against the chainlink fence. Then I leant right in so we were nose to nose, and now he was frightened.

'Hey, mate –'

'No. No mate. Not since you stuck us in it.' I shook him with each word. 'Captain Cocaine.'

'I told you, there was no malice.'

I jabbed a finger at the nick. He thought I was going for his eye and flinched. 'Eighteen months. In there. Down to you. Because you took some charlie. Coke, Terry, on work. On a piece of work.'

This time, his nut made the fence sing.

'Going on a piece of work means to burgle and to thieve, Terry. It means chopping up the prize and then going home and spending it out. And living to tell the tale. It does not mean getting nicked and doing time, down to you. And your charlie. Coke to keep you going. Which got found. By filth. And got us nicked. Do you understand?'

He nodded a quick and frightened yes.

'Today is about seeing my son and my daughter, Terry, maybe going for a walk where I want to and smelling air without the stink of piss in it. This is my ordinary world, Terry. Not yours. So fuck off.'

I let go of him. But I didn't walk. Nor did he. Instead, I saw him sold and branded and wearing a scold's bridle.

'I've been chucked out. Janey chucked me out. I've got no money. And nowhere to go.'

So that was it. Girlfriend slings him, he's got no dough, he comes looking for me. I thought it was meant to be the other way round when you got out of the nick. You came out, someone gave you money. Not like this.

Terry's dad was a peterman – a safebreaker – we used to call Yoda, and he'd been a very good friend to me, even saved me from a ten stretch once. Yoda was dead now, so his son had his father's credit and I didn't have the choice. That's why we walked to Victoria station together and went into the buffet and I told him to sit down, and went up to the counter to buy tea and biscuits. Then I looked at the shelves and thought, *All this choice*, so I scooped up a plate and went back along the food counter opening little plastic windows and metal lids and putting food on to a plate, just because I could. Eggs, bacon, sausages, tomatoes, chips, baked beans, hash browns, toast, butter portions, jam and marmalade, more eggs, bacon, eggs, pig's knuckle, hip bone, thigh bone, knee bone, ankle bone.

Now hear the word of the Lord.

I wasn't hungry. I'd had my porridge in the nick. Have your porridge on the last morning, or you'll come back for it. That's what they say. I paid and walked the tray over to Terry. 'Here.' I banged it down. 'Just stay here.'

I looked round for the toilets. A few seconds later I was standing in one of the pissy cubicles going through my cash. They give you a week's social when you get out of the nick. Fifty quid. Leon had sent me in three hundred a couple of weeks ago, and I still had most of that. So I counted out two and trousered the rest.

There was a payphone just outside the bogs. I phoned Carol, an old mate who owed me a couple of favours. Yes, she said, Terry could stay for a few days. Then I went and dropped the dough on him. A tenner slipped off the fold and went on his plate, soaking up the baked beans. He looked up at me like a dog wanting a Bonio. I gave him Carol's address and the SP and told him to behave himself. 'None of your crap,' I said. 'No liberties. Understand?'

He nodded, then looked at the dough.

'A twoer. Against your half of our last parcel.'

'What about the rest?'

'I'll be in touch. If it wasn't for your dad, I wouldn't even be talking to you.' Then I stuck my face in his. 'Taking fucking cocaine on work,' I spat. 'You prick.'

He squirmed in his seat, half-twitched and half-smiled some sort of thanks. Then he picked the tenner off the beans and tried to smile at me again. I made for the door. As I pulled it open I glanced at him. He was sat there licking the sauce off the money.

I did the straightgoer stride again, away from Terry and the station, then I did a left, crossed over, glanced back to check I was alone and doubled back for Marcus's shop and my whip-round from the chaps. Marcus had sent me the postcard saying he was holding it this time round and I was to come and get it. A couple minutes more and I was there: six massive, carved wood thrones and an equally heavy-looking table on the pavement. The street doors were locked back. He was open.

I went in and down a thin gap between a pile of office chairs and a stack of bathroom cabinets. I turned left at the last cabinet and walked past three lifesize copies of the Venus de Milo, except the last one had arms. Marcus popped out from behind this, brushing Brillo-pad grey hair out of his eyes and tugging at one end of a large brown thing.

'Need any help, Marcus?'

He looked over his shoulder, then straightened up and stuck his hand out. 'Do you want to wait in the office a minute? Sort us out a brew?'

Now I could see a young lad at the other end of the brown thing. About twenty, spotty and with John Lennon bins on his nose. A student, probably. Straight, definitely.

'When you're ready, Marcus.'

I slid past him and turned left at a stack of fake Louis XV chairs and ducked into the little cubbyhole of an office. There were two gas burners standing in the corner and, as usual, it was incredibly hot. I pulled off my jacket, tugged out my shirt and flapped it around to get a bit of breeze up my chest. Out in the main shop there was thudding, scraping and puffing as Marcus and the kid dragged the brown thing out on to the pavement. I ferreted around for the teabags and reached a couple of mugs down from the shelf.

Marcus wasn't an out-and-out villain, but neither was he straight; he dabbled, and he'd buy a parcel when there was something going. But he knew most of us and because he was half and half he was usually out, which is why he got given the whips when they came. I turned at a scrape to see him kicking at a stone lion doorstop.

'Leave it open, Marcus. Please. I've lost three pounds since I walked in here.'

He was in a long black winter coat, furry scarf and gloves and showed no sign of taking them off.

'You hot?' The way he asked, you'd think we were druids on Salisbury Plain celebrating the winter solstice by dancing around naked.

'Yes, I'm hot. I'm always hot here. Everyone's hot here. Name me one person who comes in here and says they're cold.'

Apparently genuinely bemused, Marcus stopped prodding the lion with his toe and made a thinking face. 'I can't think of anyone offhand.'

'Of course you can't. Because there isn't.'

He considered this for a second, then shrugged. 'Anyway, I've sent the lad away for half an hour so we can have a rabbit. I suppose we can leave the door open.' He nodded at the CCTV above my head. 'If any customers come, I'll just have to nip and see to them.' Then he went deep inside his coat and pulled out a thick roll of notes. 'Six hundred and forty five.'

'Thanks, Marcus.'

'Whatever, mate. You're welcome. You and a few others, always welcome.'

A beat.

'Jack sends his best.'

'Jack?'

'Jack Keane. He's out.'

Jack Keane. Haven't seen him since . . .

Marcus waved a finger at the dough as it went into my pocket. 'Very generous on that. Sit down.'

I crackled onto an office chair wrapped in plastic as he slid past for the kettle. 'I didn't know he'd come home.'

'Told me to tell you he's away for a couple of days and he looks forward to a drink with you when he gets back. You and Jack go back a long way, don't you?'

'All the way to Foston Hall. Were you ever there?'

'I managed to avoid detention centres.'

'Christmas Day, it was. Jack and me down the block. Other people remember Johnny Rotten, punk and space hoppers that year. I just remember PE at dawn, the kids who couldn't read and the smell of piss. And Jack. How did he look?'

'Fitter than a butcher's dog.'

'He always kept fit.'

'And it's been a long stretch.'

'Yeah, eight years.'

We trailed off. He looked in his mug. I knew what was coming.

'I was a bit surprised to hear about the brown, pal.'

'It wasn't mine, Marcus. I don't go near heroin. Someone planted it on me.'

'Didn't know you had any enemies.'

'Well.' I got up and started to pull on my clothes. 'Thanks for everything, Marcus. Good to see you.'

'And you pal. Are you going to be in the club tonight?'

'No, I'm taking the kids out. Next couple of days, I suppose. Just need to get myself sorted. Fancy slipping back into things quietly. Know what I mean?'

Marcus nodded. 'OK, pal.'

I could have dwelt on the heroin that got me the extra eight months, but instead I went to Market Street and bought kecks, T-shirt, socks, shampoo, soap and deodorant. And a towel and trunks. Then I walked to the metro, bought a ticket to the swimming pool at Sale but got off at Stretford. My licence said I had to check in with probation, might as well do it now.

The place was a car-park from the out and a right feel of the nick on the in, especially the woman on the desk who looked me up and down like a dog screw. Pam Beresford was sick, she said, so I'd be seeing Mr Kingsolver. Just then a door opened and a tall guy in his fifties stuck his head through, calling my name. He waved me in and went through the script at a rattle. I sat and tried to look attentive and nod at the appropriate times. It was all *yammer yammer yammer* automatic parolee supervised till the two thirds point of my sentence *yammer yammer* report once a week for the first couple of months *yammer yammer* Pam ill *yammer*

Kingsolver away next week *bunny bunny* next visit wouldn't be for a fortnight.

A touch.

Yammer yammer behave myself at all times any nonsense and I'd be breached – back inside, that meant – *yammer yammer*. Prick. Then he flicked his hand at the door. The gesture said, *You can go now. And a bit lively*. I split.

There was a payphone outside on the corner, I dropped in some shrapnel and tapped out a number. Lou and Sam had been down to London on a trip with Sara last weekend and we'd not spoken since. I'd been running images of seeing them again in my nut for the last few weeks. The answerphone picked up. Of course, half term, and with Sara at work, they'd be in bed. Where else would two teenagers be this time of day? I left a message and went for the metro. I spent the tram journey on the way to the pool fantasising about wide expanses of blue water, imagining how I would dive and roll at the deep end, changing direction under the surface and swimming round in circles, just because I could.

I pulled myself up and down the bath twenty times in all. There was no rush.

Apart from a loud knot of ten-year-olds in the shallow end, I had the place to myself. I made the swimming slow and powerful, felt the chlorined water splash over my shoulders, face, ears and mouth. I spat water out every other stroke, and kicked harder than I needed to. At each end of the bath, I flipped over on to my back and looked at the foaming wake I'd kicked up behind me.

After I'd done the twenty, I did one more to bring me down the deep end again. Then I dived under the water and kicked my way to the bottom. I swam a full width and emerged gasping for air at the other side, went down again and barrelled underwater, came up for a quick breath, kicked myself back under. This time I went right down to the blue-tiled bottom and rolled over on to my back, holding my nose and looking up. Cheeks bulging with air, I could see vague shapes of light above, hear my heart beating through the blood vessels in my ears. I came up and swam to the corner.

The kids had cleared out and now I had the place completely to myself. I swam a few more lengths, slapping the water hard with my feet and churning up a line of white horses behind me. Then out and into the changing rooms, which smelt of disinfectant. Not the sort they use inside – there was a flower in there somewhere.

A few seconds later I was standing naked under a hot shower, soaping myself up and starting to scrub the stink of nick from my skin. I lathered up face neck shoulders arms stomach arse thighs and legs, stood on one foot then the other, working the soap round ankles, across soles and between toes. The water clicked off and I lathered my ears till they squeaked. I hit the button and felt the water again, then the creamy lather loosened on me and started to slide down to the tray, swirled round my feet and schlepped down the big steel plughole. Head tipped back, I opened my mouth, feeling the shower jet rain on to my face, sluice out my pores, run off my chin and fall on to my chest. Endless steaming hot water. And no one to keep an eye out for.

A shower is a good place to do you if you're stripped off and they're dressed.

A pack of boy scouts ran and skidded into the changing room a few minutes later, and it popped up that if I stayed here much longer someone would try and do me for loitering, so I stepped out of the jets and wound the towel round my waist. Then I went across to my locker, pulled out my gear and the new stuff I'd bought. The kids weren't looking my way, so I squatted down quickly and pulled my money out from under a bench where I'd stuck it in the space between a support and the wall, twisted up in a plastic bag.

There's a lot of thieves about, you know.

Into a cubicle and locked the door behind me. I could still hear the kids outside, but at least I wouldn't be nonced off by Brown Owl.

I towelled dry, then emptied the M&S bag onto the bench and flicked through the stuff I'd bought. I pulled on the socks first. They stretched over my toes – clean, fresh, new. The boxers were snug and the T-shirt was soft, a perfect fit. Strangeways was off my skin.

I pulled the rest of my clothes on, then bundled the towel and bits into one plastic bag and the old underwear into another. I opened up and stepped out. The scouts had gone, leaving berets and green and yellow cravats and woggles hanging all over the shop.

I sat down on the bench for a moment. The fact was that if I wanted to strip off and swim again, I could. If I wanted to go and sit up top and listen to the kids laughing and larking around, I could. If I wanted to buy a paper, and read it or not read it, or go into a shop and change my mind about what I'd come in for, I could. No more doors where someone else had the keys. I was out, I was having dinner with the twins that evening and I'd be paying. There was a half share in a decent parcel coming my way. I had some plots on the back burner, and that would be more money. And I knew more work would be coming my way; it always does when you've got a good reputation. And – without giving myself too much of a reference – I did have a good name. The swim had reminded me I was pretty fit. The divorce had been half civilised and Lou and Sam had taken it well.

The main thing for now was that Strangeways was lifting off me. I walked out through reception and on to the street, jammed the prison gear into a bin on the pavement and walked for the metro. I had an appointment with a brass I knew up in Altrincham called Harry.

Harry was not that pleased to see me. She'd been busy since breakfast, and the punter now sitting in her work bedroom was over-running; he was having a cry because he was cheating on his wife *and* his girlfriend.

'Didn't expect you for another hour.'

'Do you want me to come back?'

'No – kitchen and keep quiet.'

She prodded me in and closed the door. I made myself a brew and spent half an hour taking the tops off her washing liquid and fabric stuff to smell the lemons and flowers, looking in her cupboards and unscrewing spice jars for the thyme and oregano and chillis. I found some coffee beans and dropped them into my palms and crunched them together and stuck my face right in for the crisp bitter scents. I breathed them all in deep – proper smells, healthy smells, not the antiseptic nose of the nick.

'What are you doing?' Harry was standing in the doorway. I'd not heard the front door go.

'Sorry, Harry,' I dusted the coffee bits into the sink. 'You don't get good things inside.'

'I guess not.' She flexed her arm and winced. 'I hate it when they keep themselves from coming. You can feel them tensing up. So they can get an extra few seconds of me touching them. Little tick.'

She took a couple of steps as if to touch me, then mugged she'd forgotten something and swung away to the sink, arm outstretched like a Dalek, and washed her hands with the Fairy.

'How are you, anyway?'

'I'm fine, Harry. Just fine.'

Harry's father and mother were both Thai. Her real name was something that started with Arayatera and went on for about fifteen minutes. She'd been here for a ten stretch and her English and accent were near enough perfect. I'd known her for years, but it still surprised me when I got her wholesome Manchester tones.

'Just fine? Just out of the nick and just fine?' She dried her hands on a kitchen towel, then flipped up a blue pedal-bin lid, balled the paper and slung it in. She folded her arms and leant on the sink. 'You'll be wanting your phone.'

'Did you get the chance?'

'It wasn't difficult.' She went into a drawer and brought out a slim silver model. 'I charged it up first thing and stuck twenty quid on it as well.' It came across with the charger.

'Thanks.'

'And this.' She held out a card with an eleven digit number on it. I glanced down and up again, but I didn't reach out. 'Don't you want it?'

I reeled it off to her.

'I keep forgetting your memory for numbers.'

'Police can't look inside your head.'

'Anything else I can do for you?'

'Just wanted to be in a non-nick place, Harry. For a bit.'

She nodded. Then her eyes fixed on mine and moving slowly, she slid her bare feet the couple of steps she needed to be right in front of me, one foot either side of the chair. She put her hands on my shoulders and bent at the waist, bringing her cheek and neck up close to my face. I felt the warmth of her skin an inch from my nose, breathed in her perfume, strong and sharp. All flowers and fresh air with the edge of alcohol. She moved again, and the motion seemed to release a fresh cloud of scent from her skin. She almost brushed her cheek against mine and I felt her eyelashes tingle against my temple. Then she straightened up and took a couple of paces back, her eyes fixed on mine as she sat down opposite at the table. The kitchen seemed very quiet and restful, the only sound was a gentle ticking from the clock on the wall. She held my gaze a while longer, looked down and the spell was broken. I noticed I was very tired, the swim had taken it out of me. I yawned.

'Sleepy?'

I nodded. 'Just a bit. I had a dip on the way here, to lose the smell.'

'You want to go to bed?'

What was this?

'To sleep.'

Oh. 'No. No thanks.'

'OK, I'll make us something to eat then. Go and lie down in the living room. I'll call you.'

She sat back and stretched her arms above her head. This made her left breast half slip out from under her satin wrap. She looked down, then at me and pulled it closed.

'You'll be needing some money too, I suspect.'

'No. Thanks though, Harry. I've got my whip.'

'You'll be through it by lunchtime tomorrow. Especially if you go and spend it on another tart like me.'

I let that one hang in the air.

'Some of us are expensive,' she went on. 'Pay us enough money, and we'll give you so much time and attention . . .' she tugged at her belt, 'you'll hardly notice we're a whore.' She threw her long black hair up and it fell over her shoulder like a horse's tail.

'Will five hundred do?' she asked. 'I owe you some favours. You haven't forgotten, have you?'

'No.'

'Six hundred with the phone and time on it. Give it back to me when you can.'

It was easier to say yes. 'Thanks, Harry.'

'Don't mention it.'

She went to the corner of the kitchen and, squatting down sideways to me, pulled up the lino and lifted a floorboard. She was a good-looking woman, not much more than thirty. I got a glimpse of her right breast this time as she pulled out a roll of notes from the cash box under the floor, straightened up and stood it on the table in front of me.

'Stick that down your pants or wherever you're keeping your money these days.'

'Thanks.'

'OK,' she said, and shooed me towards the door. 'You know where the sofa is. Go lie on it.'

Down the corridor I went into the living room, took off my jacket and shoes, then lay down on the soft grey sofa, punching a cushion into shape under my head. In the kitchen, I heard cupboards being opened and pans moved around.

Harry was a brass, but she did it solo. That's pretty unusual – even the expensive ones like her usually end up with a pimp. Not Harry. She didn't need anybody for anything. She even ran her own website from the computer squatting on a desk in the corner. She was also a trained kung fu nutter, able to break arms and legs at twenty paces. No need for a maid, then. Another difference was that she planned to get out before she turned thirty-five. Lots of girls say that. What made her most unusual of all was that she probably would.

Twenty minutes later, we were sitting at the kitchen table finishing off the bacon and eggs she'd whistled up. The eggs were slightly burnt round the edge of the whites and the bacon was crispy and done under the grill. The salt came out of a mill and I could feel each individual crystal on my tongue. I clinked down knife and fork and Harry whisked the lot away, replacing it with a bowl of chocolate pud from the microwave. She'd got changed into jeans and sweatshirt and was now leaning on the counter crunching her bare feet as her own pudding heated up. The machine pinged and she sat opposite me again. 'So what are your plans for the rest of the day?'

'Couple of people to see, drop in at my place, then I'm taking the twins out for dinner. What time is it?'

She twisted round in her seat, spoon poised at her mouth. 'Clock says half past. But I keep it twenty minutes fast.'

'Why?'

'Hooker time. The punters always take their watches off. The later they think it is, the more in a hurry they are to leave.'

'Clever.'

'If I was really clever, I wouldn't be a whore.'

I became fascinated by my chocolate pudding.

'Anyway, I'm finishing early today. I'm studying.'

'Studying?'

'Open University course. History of Art. I've told you before.'

'I remember,' I said. 'Can I use your phone?'

'Go ahead.'

I picked up the handset, punched the number in and got the machine. I left another message saying I'd ring again later.

'No one home?'

'Half term. Teenagers.'

'They won't be up yet.'

'Seems not. Thanks for the food, Harry. And the dough.'

'No problem.' She picked up a cloth and started to wipe off the table. When she got to my cup she wiped round it, then lifted it and handed it to me. I carried it into the living room and put my boots on there. By the time I was back in the kitchen she already had her books out on the table and was leafing through a pile of notes.

'Thanks for everything, Harry.'

'I'd like to chat. But I've got to work.'

I nodded and scooped up the bag with my swimming gear. She walked me to the front door, we said our goodbyes and I left.

Harry lived in the Downs, one of the better areas of Altrincham on the outskirts of Manchester. Quiet, broad, sloping streets with trees, leading to parades of shops and restaurants.

I took out my new phone and punched in Leon's mobile as I walked. Leon was my best friend and my teacher. It was Leon who introduced me to proper villainy more than twenty years ago and showed me how to make a proper pound note. He was also my ex-wife Sara's current lover.

The call went straight to voicemail. I hung up. I don't trust answerphones. Come to that, I don't trust texts or emails either. Or most people.

Then I rang Casey, my fence. He'd been shifting the stuff I nicked for years and was currently holding a parcel for me. I asked if I could drop by. He said yes, so I grabbed a taxi at the station and gave the driver the name of a hotel about fifty yards away from the big man's gaff. In the car park, I handed a tenner over the back seat and asked him to wait. Then I went in the main entrance, walked through the lobby and slipped out the side door off-show from the front. A couple more minutes and I made Casey's front door. It started to rain as the hall light went on the other side of the glass, and I saw him glide down the corridor towards the spyhole. He opened up and leant on the frame in outline. 'You were quick.'

'Hello, Casey.'

'We're in the back.' He waved me in, locked up and then sort of danced down the corridor in front of me singing *Fly Me to the Moon* in the club style. Casey was six foot five and a slightly fat version of the wrestler he'd been when he picked up a bronze at the Commonwealth Games sometime in the seventies. He flicked the dining-room door open, spun on the ball of his right foot and went 'Ta-da!'

'Are you taking something, Casey?'

'Just glad to see you on the street, that's all.'

It was getting dark now and the only light was a lamp on the dining table, papers spread its ten-seat length. The room smelt of fresh polish.

'Hang on a minute.' He *dooby-dooby-doed* to the corner, switched on a lamp and spun round. He'd grown a beard. Shaggy, flecked with grey.

'You've grown a beard, Casey.'

'Clever boy.'

'It makes you look like a wino.'

He gave me the sort of look that had probably once been a signal to Giant Haystacks that he was about to start bouncing off the ropes before he was very much older. 'I thought Orson Welles.'

'Sherry commercial Orson, perhaps. Not *Citizen Kane*.'

'I know you're trying to wind me up. It's not going to work.' He launched into the chorus, snapping a finger and thumb in time to some chat about Jupiter and Mars.

'Casey. A man could die of thirst in this house.'

He stopped and looked at me. 'Sorry. Forgetting my manners. Do you want a brew?'

'Please.'

He schlepped out into the kitchen and was back a few seconds later with a tray of coffee. He tried to jive and pour at the same time, but it slopped into the saucer so he gave the Rat Pack moves a body-swerve and settled for humming *Volare* while he served up.

'How was the Big House?' he asked.

'Pretty much the same.' I made space among the papers for my cup. 'Terry was my main problem. On to me all the time. Sorries and apologies right and left.'

'And rightly so. Did you know he was on the charlie?'

'No, so he can't have been on it for long. He met me this morning on the steps. Bird's chucked him out, so he says.'

'Did you fuck him off.'

I took a mouthful of the coffee. It was pus.

'You sorted him somewhere to stay, didn't you?' He chuckled and pulled at his beard. 'You bloody soft lad.'

'I did it for his father.'

'Course you did. You really are a straight face, aren't you? Keep the code, stick to the rules. I think you're the straightest face I've ever known. So what does Terry actually have to do to get struck off your Christmas card list?'

'He's got his dad's credit for now. And that's it. Now, let's talk about something else. How did you do?'

'All right, then. Sixty grand. Cash Wednesday, if that's all right.'

'It is.'

Just then, two small pairs of running feet belted from one end of the house to the other above our heads. I looked up and back as Casey thumbed at the ceiling. 'Au pair's playing with the kids.'

'Au pair? You getting respectable, Casey?'

'Well, wife wanted one. Marta she's called. Spanish. Nice girl.'

Suddenly the beard and Sinatra tribute made sense.

'How is Stella?' I asked tactfully.

'Huh?'

'Stella. Your wife, Stella.'

'Watching telly at the front.'

'Get on with this Marta, does she?'

'Yes.'

'Who hired her? You or Stella?'

'You want more coffee?'

I flicked him a quick grin. 'No thanks, one of those is quite enough.'

The feet pelted back again, and I glanced up at the ceiling. When my eyes flicked down I caught Casey examining me over the rim of his cup. 'All right, Casey?'

'Yes, I . . . er . . . ' He tailed off, then leant across the table and fished a thick white envelope from among the papers. 'There's a grand there. I had it about me when you rang. Thought you might need some exes. I'll take it off the sixty.'

'Thanks.' I stowed the cash and sat waiting for what I knew was coming.

'So are you seeing the twins, then?' he asked after a pause.

I looked at him; he couldn't meet my eye. 'The brown was planted, Casey,' I said. 'I don't know why, but it was stuck right on me.'

'Of course, right.'

I'd known Casey for ten years, and for the first time I was uncomfortable in his company. 'What else did you hear?'

'Nothing more than the spin. I was a bit surprised, that's all.'

'Yeah, so was I. Eight months surprised.' I drained my cup. 'I've got a taxi waiting, Casey. Got to go.'

He walked me to the front. No dancing this time.

The door swung open and there were two screws in the narrow gap. 'Routine search,' said the youngest, a spiny toerag of about twelve. Thin-faced and wearing heavy specs. 'On your feet.'

Just behind him was an older screw called Katz who I'd known on and off for years. He seemed to be on a watching brief, minding the YTS boy. YTS took a couple of paces into the cell then stood face to face with me and said, 'Is there anything in your cell, or do you have anything on you, that you shouldn't have?'

I took in his anxious spotty face and white rubber gloves. 'Of course,' I said. 'I've got a blade stuck round the s-bend of the karsi, and a quarter of blow up my arse.'

What I actually said was: 'No. Nothing.'

And I didn't. Not only was I too careful for all that caper, I only had two weeks left to do.

I emptied my pockets of snout and lighter and pulled my shirt and vest off and handed them to the bespectacled youth who fingered them uncertainly, then handed them back to me. I pulled them back on, then slipped off my strides and skids for their inspection. I wasn't being modest, the routine was for their benefit, so they couldn't be accused of springing a spin just to see you naked. For the sake of a little voyeuristic fun. Not that I have anything against gays, mind.

Strides and skids were fingered and returned. Then socks and shoes came off and went up for inspection. Katz looked a bit weary by now, but the kid was starting to get into it. He checked the seams on my socks and the seams on my shoes. Then he checked them again. Rather disappointed, it seemed to me, he handed them back and told me to take my bedding outside and shake it over the landing. He followed me out as Katz started to run over my peter.

'We're not picking on you,' said YTS. 'This is routine. Just routine.' He made such a point of saying it that I almost expected something to slip out of my blanket and fall the ten foot or so to the suicide net.

Then Katz shouted me in. I turned, went back into the cell, and saw him standing over a sheet of newspaper spread out on the cell floor. On it were the contents of my wastebin. An old *Guardian*, scraps of paper, toilet rolls. Katz looked straight at me. In his upturned palm was a wrapper from half an ounce of snout. In the middle of the flattened foil was a cluster of neat little handmade envelopes about half an inch across.

'What's this then?' he asked.

'We both know what that is,' I said.

'Twelve ninety, boss.' The driver was twisted round in his seat. 'We're here, boss. Twelve ninety.'

I got out and stuck the money through the window. He snorted and drove off and I crossed the road into the cul de sac. My place had been empty while I'd been away and the twins had kept an eye on it for me. The upstairs windows were lit, so the Wessons must be in. I wanted them to think I was still off 'on business', so I let myself in quietly, crept up the stairs to the first floor, opened my flat door double quiet and kept the lights off, standing for a moment to let my eyes adjust to the gloom. There was a pile of letters on the hall table, stacked up neatly by one of the kids. A couple more crackled under my boots. I squatted, dropped them next to the answerphone, called Lou and Sam again and got the machine.

'Lou, Sam, it's me again. Ringing about dinner tonight. It's about half four and I'm at home. Give me a bell as soon as. Bye.' I hung up. There was something wrong here, but I couldn't work out what.

I pushed open the lounge door as the streetlamps came on and window shapes of pale yellow light were thrown across the deck and up the walls.

Everything was the same as eighteen months before: widescreen telly in the window, red leather chairs, red leathertop desk and chair in the corner, white marble fireplace and fake gas fire. Eight twelve-foot shelves down the walls either side of the bay window, some with books, some with pictures, some empty. A club chair by the fire. Low stack of *Cosmo Girl* and *Heat* and other Lou mags on the table. I pressed my foot into the Persian rug, felt it give into the red Chinese carpet underneath. The place smelt a bit musty, but it felt OK.

Leaving the lights off, I went into the bedroom and the bathroom. They were also fine. In the kitchen I put the kettle on and went back into the bedroom to change strides, shirt and shoes. A black leather jacket came out of the wardrobe and I transferred everything from the other. Still in the dark, I went into the kitchen and made black coffee, carried it along the corridor and stopped dead at the hall table as I realised what was wrong. The answerphone light wasn't flashing. I hadn't got a message from the twins.

I left the flat immediately, moving fast on to the main drag to look for a cab.

Buckingham Road is a quiet residential slice of Heaton Moor – speed bumps, bay windows, the lot. I bought number forty-five on a mortgage when Sara and I got married, but it had been in her name for years now. When we split up, the twins stayed with her – she offered them stability. My deal could involve prison waiting rooms.

I took my finger off the doorbell and listened, then rang again. A few steps back and I saw the downstairs curtains were drawn; the bedroom curtains were back, but no sign of life. Back to the bell and I kept my finger on it till the end went white. Certainly long enough to wake sleeping teenagers.

Maybe they were due back from London tonight, not yesterday. But they knew I was out today, they knew we were going out. They wouldn't forget that, wouldn't miss it without letting me know. Lou even left me a message if she knew I'd been away for the weekend, just to welcome me back.

Gas. I'll say I smelt gas.

I nipped down the side entry and dropped over the wall to number forty-five. I found the spare key under the ledge and had the kitchen door open in a few seconds. Inside it looked a bit tidier than usual. Fridge humming quietly in the corner, clock on the cooker green in the dark. Down the corridor to the front room. I paused for a second and let my eyes adjust, then pushed the lounge door open. What I saw in the glow from the street hit me like an iron bar across the face. Breaking the habit of a lifetime, I turned the light on.

The room was completely empty. Not a stick of furniture.

I swung round, slammed on the hall light, took the stairs two at a time and tore the bedroom doors open.

Empty, all of them.

I slapped on the bathroom light and saw empty shelves. I opened cupboard doors, looked in the bathtub. Nothing. Nothing nothing nothing.

I half-ran, half-jumped down the stairs, noticed the lampshade had gone in the hall but the answerphone was still plugged in, shot round the house, looking behind doors, checking in cupboards, like I was expecting them to be hiding. Then I ran round again switching the lights off, slumped in the dark at the foot of the stairs and tried to think.

My ex-wife and children had gone and taken everything with them. And, it seemed, my brain had been replaced with handfuls of cotton wool. Trying to get my thoughts into line was like building a wall with this cotton wool, but whatever had happened here, I'd been turning lights on and someone could have seen and dialled three nines. I was on parole, and not in the mood to argue the toss about whether I had the right to be here or not. Get out, and swift.

I locked the door and stuck the key back, then went over the wall and I was on Buckingham Road again, walking fast. What the hell did I do now? Leon. Try Leon again. Straight to voicemail. What the fuck was going on?

Sara worked about half a mile away on the main drag. I started running, it started raining again and I was damp and sweating as I made her building. There was a courier in leathers just coming out, I slammed past him and took the stairs two at a time to the third floor where Michelle, her PA, was just pulling on a long blue coat to go home.

'Where is she?'

Michelle was in her late twenties and slim with a mop of dyed-red hair. She took a second to recognise me. 'Oh, hello . . . ' she broke off, eyes dancing round the room. Then, 'she phoned in yesterday, said she had to take some time off.'

'They're gone, the house is empty, Michelle, where is she?'

A door opened and a tall meaty neck with five o'clock shadow came out, whisking it shut behind him. 'What's the fucking noise for?' said the neck. 'I've got Japs in there.'

'It's Sara's husband, Mr Bryant.'

Bryant turned, six foot of *I'll deal with this* white-collar aggression. 'Do you understand what a fucking office is? Sara's ill, she's at home and *you* are out of order, so leave right now.'

I was still on prison time, and you don't let someone talk to you like that in the nick. I stepped towards him and he bristled up. Big and beefy, he probably fancied his chances, I could see it running through his brain. *This guy's a villain, probably a bully too, I've heard enough about him from Sara, he doesn't frighten me, the prick.* He jerked his thumb at the door. 'Go on, piss off.'

I made to leave, then swung round and slammed an open palm into his face. The move knocked him back hard against the wall which actually shuddered. I grabbed him by the throat and made a fist. 'Whatever you know, tell me now.' I was thinking nick. I couldn't stop it.

He gave it up in a beat. 'She phoned in sick, then she phoned in again and said there'd been a death in the family and she needed some more time off.' His tongue shot out and worked round his mouth. 'That's the truth. That's all we know.'

It was. Still on prison time, and I knew. I dropped him, his legs gave way and he slid down the wall to the deck.

'I'm sorry, Michelle.'

I took the stairs three at a time going down. If Bryant gave it three nines I was completely fucked. On my kind of licence they hardly needed an excuse to recall you and I'd just given them plenty – they'd have me back inside without the option. I hit the bottom, tore open the door and out on to the pavement. A few blocks down and I slowed, then managed to flag a cab for the centre. It was a black London-style. I slammed the divider shut and called Sara's mobile. Straight to voicemail.

'Sara, it's me. I don't know what's going on, but just call me – please. I'm on this number.' I left it and hung up. The twins didn't have mobiles; Sara was worried about brain tumours.

I called Leon, broke a rule and left a message. 'Leon, call me back as soon as you get this, whatever the time. Here's the number.' I rattled it off and saw we'd hit Deansgate. 'Stop here.'

I chucked some money at the driver and went into a bar. It was heaving and smelt of sex, there were bright lights and loud music, likely lads with gel-chopped number four crops and girls with plunging necklines, pierced navels and strappy sandals. Kids enjoying themselves. Of course, it was Friday night.

I pushed to the counter and got lucky. The barman – who'd been flipping bottles around like a circus juggler – stopped and clanked them down on the metal counter in front of me.

'Beer, any beer,' I shouted.

'These are on promotion,' he shouted back.

'Fine, whatever.' He flipped my glass into a double somersault and I dropped some coins on the counter.

The first drink when you get out is usually very important, you take time over it. Right now, I didn't even notice the label. It was just the rent. I took the bottle and pushed my way through damp bodies to a corner where I could watch the door. A couple got up off a bench where they'd been kissing enthusiastically. I slid into their seat, lit a cigarette and burnt it halfway down on the first drag. I tried to think but I couldn't,

I felt like something had been torn out of me; Lou and Sam were just seventeen and they'd gone. The twins were my life, the most important thing that I knew or had ever known. Even though they lived with their mam, I saw them both as often as possible; they had keys to my place and came and went as they wanted. Sometimes I'd go home and find one of them on the sofa because they'd had a row at school or home and wanted to be away from it all, with me. Or just because we hadn't spoken in a few days and they missed me. And now they'd gone and I didn't know why. What if I never saw them again? The tear inside me got wider. If that happened then my life was over. Might as well just walk out of here and go and top myself now.

No, come on, think. Remember the rules: get knowledge. The first thing was to get knowledge. What did I know from seeing the house? I saw them all dead for a second, laid out on slabs, tags on toes. No, push that down, that wasn't it. And it didn't make sense. Murders would mean police tapes, a watch on the house, a screw at my cell door at three in the morning. No, think about what you saw at Buckingham Road. It was empty, but it was tidy. Looked like they'd packed carefully. And the answerphone was still there to take messages, make people think they were just out or asleep. You'd have to get inside to find the truth.

Who might know? Leon, but I couldn't find him. Had they all gone off together?

Who else? Her friends, they must know – and Steph. Her sister Steph. Steph was very close with Sara, her son virtually lived round Buckingham Road when he was a kid. No way she wouldn't know something.

I pushed out to the street and found a quiet shop doorway just off the main drag. Steph was engaged, so I tried a couple of Sara's friends. No answers. I left messages with my new number on a couple of machines, then tried Steph again. Jan, her husband, answered immediately, like he was sitting over the phone.

'Jan?'

There was a pause. 'What do you want?' He sounded like a man who'd been up all night.

'What's wrong, Jan?'

With the silence, I thought he'd hung up.

'Jan?'

'We don't want to talk to you. We have nothing to say. Just leave us alone.'

The line went dead. I dialled back and it was engaged. What was his fucking game? Well, whatever it was, he wasn't on. I'd lay money they knew more than me right now. I'd find out what their fucking problem was.

Fifteen minutes later I was on their road. I kicked open the gate at number sixty-three, went up the path and buzzed. The door opened and Jan was there in silhouette. Couldn't make out his face, but he was wearing an overcoat like he'd just come in. Steph was slumped on the stairs in a long grey mac. She looked up to see who it was.

'What do you want, you fucking bastard?' Then she screamed and launched herself at me, thudding into my gut and punching and slapping my face. 'Get out you bastard, get out!'

She carried on hitting me, I covered my head with my hands and let her do it, Jan did nothing to stop her. I felt him standing to one side, letting his wife do what she wanted. There were slaps and thin fists on my head and shoulders, the backs of my hands, then it died away and I looked up. She stumbled back a couple of steps, dissolved into sobs and slammed her face into Jan's chest. He stared at me over her shoulder, and now I could see his eyes were red from crying. I took in the hall, saw Tomas's cycling helmet and his bike leaning up against the wall. I started to guess, the question was burbling out, but Jan spoke over me.

'Tomas is dead, and the police say it's because of you. You filthy dirty evil bastard. You killed Tomas, our son. You.'

I was in another cab. Lights people streets shops crowds clubs pubs cars buses street signs traffic lights flicked by the window. From a distance, I heard the driver ask where I was going. I heard myself mumble something to do with the city centre.

These are the facts. Jan and Steph had been out all day. They'd been out because they'd been organising the funeral of their only son,

Tomas. This is Tomas, who used to play football with Lou and Sam and sleep over with them in a tent in the back garden at Buckingham Road. Somewhere I have a picture of Tomas with Lou and Sam and a bird's nest they found when we all went walking in the country one Sunday in spring. Before I made them put it back, I took a photograph. It's about six in the evening, the children are tired after an afternoon's walking and running down hills and chasing each other. The sun is low in the sky and the shadows are long. The twins are seven and Tomas is nine. He's wearing a red jumper Steph knitted for him and he's stood in the middle of my two, giving a gap-toothed smile and holding the nest out to the camera, showing the eggs unbroken.

These are the facts. Tomas said he'd be staying at a friend's Monday night. The police rang the door about six Tuesday morning, Tomas was down at the Infirmary, shot. He was dead by the time Jan got down there.

The copper who stayed with them for the statements was a DC from Bootle Street called Sommerfield. He told them that Tomas had a couple of wraps of heroin in his pocket. Sommerfield said he'd had words with his boss, a chief superintendent called Hamilton Jacks.

Keith Hamilton Jacks. I knew him all right.

Sommerfield said Hamilton Jacks knew I'd been dealing seriously for some time, and that Tomas worked for me. Easy enough to get hold of a mobile phone inside, that would be how I pulled his strings, said Sommerfield. Must have been working for me when he got shot. Post-mortem said Tomas was a regular heroin user. Sommerfield told them that dealers like me try to get their people on the brown to control them. Keeps them on a string, Sommerfield told them.

Jan and Steph hadn't known Sara and the twins had gone, but they weren't surprised. Sara knew about Tomas, and Steph had told her what Hamilton Jacks said. I guess she didn't want Lou and Sam near me any more.

This was when Jan reminded me that I was a lousy father and a lousy human being. Then he slammed the door in my face and I heard them both crumple into sobs as I waded down the path. The noise followed me along the road and stayed in my head while I wandered, looking for a taxi. Now I was thinking of a nine-year-old Tomas playing with the twins. Then the shots came in like a baseball bat and the tears started up. No. There'd be time for that later. Stick with the here and now.

I was in trouble. Tomas was my nephew and Tomas was dead and the police had told his mam and dad that I was involved. And I was on parole and I'd slapped Sara's boss around so the filth could be knocking on my door to take me back to Strangeways any time. I'd be no good to no one back there. I couldn't go home.

We were coming up Portland Street opposite the old Queen's. I told the driver to pull in, chucked a note over the back seat and jogged across the Gardens to Mother Mac's down Back Piccadilly. I bought a drink and sat in the corner watching the door.

Just after nine Marcus came in, still in the winter coat and scarf but with a double-thick black beanie on his head this time. I wove through the boozers and grabbed him at the bar.

'Aye aye. Thought you were out with the kids tonight?'

'Are you driving?'

'It's down the side.'

'Let's go and sit in it.'

Marcus's red Merc was tucked down the side street with a table wrapped in plastic strapped to the roof rack. We got in and he turned on the heater.

'Are you going to the club tonight, Marcus?'

'Later.'

'I've got some proper trouble, Marcus.' I took a deep breath. 'My nephew's been murdered.'

'Oh, Christ.'

'He was shot and dumped at the Infirmary early on Tuesday morning. I need your help, Marcus. I need you to ask around at the club for me tonight, someone must know something. Don't mention my name, don't say he was my nephew, but can you see if anyone knows anything? Names, rumours, anything at all. Please.'

'What's his name again?'

'Tomas Warzyniak, nineteen years old. Royal Infirmary, Tuesday morning, early. The filth say he was dealing brown, but I don't believe that.'

'Was he on the gear?'

'They say so, I don't believe that either.'

'OK, I'll see what I can do.'

I was sweating from the heater, so I cracked the window a couple of inches. 'Have you got a pen?'

'In the glovebox.'

I opened it, found a pen and wrote my new number and Tomas's name on the back of a flyer for a car dealer in Hyde. 'Call me on this number, no other.'

He folded it away in his wallet. 'You should call Jack. If there's class A in there, he might know something.'

'I know what Jack's game is, Marcus. Call me as soon as you've got something.'

'OK, mate.' He nodded outside, it was raining again. 'Do you need a lift anywhere?'

'No. Thanks, Marcus.'

There was one cab left on the rank in the Gardens. I slid back the divider and asked for the Alex Park Estate. 'One of the avenues off Quinney. I'll give you a shout.' The guy clocked me hard in the mirror. The Alex was bandit country. I managed to haul up some calm. 'Just come from the hospital, need to talk to a relative.' Which meant *I'm not at it*.

Fifteen minutes later, we pulled up on the main drag where it cut into Benny's close. 'It's just down there.'

'Yeah, and I'm stopping here.'

'Okay, will you wait then?'

'How long?'

'About fifteen minutes.'

He looked at the meter. It clicked three fifty. 'Fifteen and I'll stop here for you.'

It was only spitting now. I jammed a score through the divider and got out. 'Fifteen minutes,' I said.

I got out and slapped a few paces away from the cab. Then I heard the motor fire and the slag shot off as a waterfall broke on my head, thick sheets building almost immediately to hail. Pressing into the shelter of some bushes, I snapped up my collar and saw a sudden movement down the street. Other side, a few houses along, a guy bobbed out into the light for a moment and it was Tomas, the sharp-boned body, the long hair like curtains. I wiped the water out of my eyes and peered through the hail again. He was gone. The rain stopped.

I jogged the hundred yards down the street and hit the bell. It rang somewhere away in the house and I heard the old guy wheezing and sliding up to the glass. Movement behind the spyhole, then clanking and bolts and keys as he opened up.

'Good to see you on the street again, mate.'

'Can I come in, Benny?'

'Yeah, yeah, course.'

The only light in his lounge was a chipped anglepoise on the coffee table shining on a Swiss Army knife, a tobacco pouch and some rectangles of blow a couple of inches long.

'When did you get out?'

'This morning.'

'And you want something for your head?'

'In a minute. I need a favour, Benny.'

Benny was an obsessive United fan, he listened to or watched every local news bulletin and read half a dozen dailies in case there was something in about the Reds. And because of all the lads in and out buying blow, he had a pretty good idea of a lot of stuff that never made it into the papers, local or otherwise. I told him about Tomas.

'Christ, I'm sorry mate.'

'OK. Have you heard or read anything about it?'

He blew out over his teeth. 'I read something, I think. Couple of days ago, young kid. Shot in the belly, dropped at the Infirmary. I think that was it.'

'Are you sure, Benny? This is important.'

'I know it's important, it's your nephew.'

'I need as much knowledge as you can get, Benny. Mainstream, or off the street. I've got a new number.' I wrote it down on a newspaper and laid it on top of the pouch and cubes of dope. 'Tomas Warzyniak. But keep me out of it, OK?'

'OK.'

'Soon as you can, Benny.'

He wrapped me an ounce and a half of rocky. I paid him and went looking for a cab. Bad area, bad time. *Get out of sight.* I jogged for Stretford, scanning the roads for a paid lift. It started to rain again.

Half an hour later and piss-wet through, I was checking into a B&B on Chester Road round the corner from Old Trafford. The room was a box with a coat hook on the back of the door. I pulled my jacket and shoes off, opened the window, rolled a joint and lit it, then rang Leon again. Voicemail, again.

'Call me, Leon. It's urgent.'

Then I thought of Leon's mam, Judith. He never gave her number out as she was getting bad on her legs and he didn't want her running for the phone. But I knew her well. She answered on the eighth ring. I tried to sound relaxed.

'Hello Judith, it's me. Sorry to trouble you, love. But I got out today and I've been trying to get hold of Leon.'

'I know it was today, I told him to bring you out here to lunch, but it was business he said. It's always business with you, I told him. I asked him who was going to meet you, but he said you'd be happy on your own for a bit. How are you?'

'I'm fine, Judith. It's just that I've been ringing his mobile and getting the answerphone.'

'He's got a new one a couple of days ago. Which one are you ringing?'

'Must be the old one. Can you give me the other?'

'Just a minute.' I heard the phone laid down and a drawer being opened. Villains change their mobiles as often as they can afford it, but normally he'd have told me. 'Here we are.'

I wrote it down, then called it back. 'I'll give him a bell right now.'

'He has it off half the time, anyway. He's a mystery to me, that boy. Always has been.'

'Can you take my new number, Judith? And ask him to call me?'

She wrote it down. It took a while.

'Sorry to be a trouble,' I said.

'Trouble indeed,' she was all mock indignant. 'When are you ever trouble to this house? Goodnight and God bless.'

We hung up and I rang Leon's new number. Voicemail. 'Ring me the minute you get this, Leon. It's urgent.' I spewed my number and hung up.

I'd been tugging so hard on the joint it was nearly gone. And I'd stuck plenty in it. Suddenly I felt dizzy, then the blow whispered at me. *They've all done a runner. Sara, Lou, Sam, Leon. He's taken them all away to his place in Spain. To start a new life together.*

What about the twins?

Plenty of language schools there, probably all been planned for months. That's why he didn't give you the new number. You've been away a year and a half, remember.

Fuck off. They don't need to run from me. Not together. And Leon wouldn't do that to me anyway.

Wouldn't he?

'No,' I kicked at the voice. 'And he wouldn't do it to Judith, and she can't tell a lie to save her life. Except to the filth.'

I laid the spliff in the ashtray, leant back and closed my eyes.

The cold woke me and I didn't have a clue where I was. Then it was, oh Christ blue bed cover grey curtain flock walls single bed Tomas twins Christ no Jesus Christ.

I got up and closed the window, my watch said three fifteen. I picked up the phone to check no one had rung, tried Leon again. Nothing.

I undressed, crawled between the sheets, reached out and flicked off the light. Curling up in a ball, I tried to sleep.

2

The mobile drilled into my skull and red numbers floating in the dark told me it was 07:01. I punched the light switch, grabbed at the phone and pressed answer.

'What the fuck's going on?'

Leon.

'Messages all over, kicking and screaming. What the fuck's going on?'

'Leon, listen. Tomas has been murdered, and the Bill told his parents I was involved. Now, for whatever reason, Sara's decided to believe that and she's taken the twins and gone.'

No answer.

'Leon?'

'What do you mean, gone?'

'I mean they've packed everything up and left. Buckingham Road is empty. They've just vanished. No message, no forwarding address, nothing.' The line went quiet and I thought I'd lost the connection. 'Leon?'

'I'm here. Where are you?'

'B&B in Stretford.'

'What if they're calling you at the flat?'

'I can check the answerphone.'

'Is it on top any other way?'

'It might be.'

That's all we need, I heard him think.

'Where are you, Leon?'

'Newcastle.'

'Can you get back?'

'Three or four hours at most.'

'Usual place. Midday.'

'I'll be there.'

We hung up. I called the machine at home and it was empty. Then I got out of bed, showered quickly and left, leaving my key on the chipped formica counter that passed as reception.

The metal shutter rattled up. I ducked inside the garage, turned and pulled it down to a few inches above the concrete for the air to circulate. Then I switched the work lamp on, stretched for the hook in the ceiling and hung it up.

It was only a lock-up garage, but it was mine and the only bit of me that felt safe right now. Everything was as I'd left it eighteen months ago: boxes and crates floor to ceiling, a three-deep stack of cheap white cabinets, a couple of rolled-up carpets, dozens of flattened cardboard boxes.

No one knew about it. Not Sara, Lou or Sam, not Leon, not Casey, and Christ, not Terry. It was my secret place – a place to hide things, to lay them down. Time was when it would be packed with booze or fags or a lorry load of tights or CDs or DVDs or batteries or engine parts, lawnmowers, hedge strimmers, swimming pool filtration units, copy gear, trainers, running shorts, designer label shirts, boxes of perfume, nicotine tablets, portable TVs, car tyres, seat covers, boxes of sun lotion, catering-size bags of teabags, office-size tins of coffee, boxes of milk powder, baby food, baby formula, baby bibs, stuffed toys, computer games, Playstations, video cameras, sheets of Letraset, train sets, nail clippers, hair dye, false eyelashes, briefcases, eyebrow tweezers, designer bins and football kits, tubs of putty, stuff for grouting, tiles, curtains and shower curtains, boxes of soap, soap powder, tins of tuna, notebooks, pencils, erasers, rubbers, condoms, ink, inkwells, Tippex, Tippex papers, card files, or staplers.

If you can nick it, you can sell it.

Now the lock-up just held the overflow from my flat and a few papers. I rented it under a moody name from the garage round the front and they kept an eye on it for me. The rent was paid in cash and paid in full for the next couple of years. I let out a breath. It felt safe.

I moved across to the desk at the back, feeling and hearing bits of stone and gravel crunch under my feet. It was big and leather-covered, the double of the one in my flat. I sat and ran my fingers under the centre drawer, then traced a line down the edges of the drawers on either side. All the traps were still there, the snapped off matchsticks, the scraps of cotton wool. There'd been no visitors. I pulled open the centre, waded through biros and envelopes to the back and the tiny dip in the lining, sprang the panel and found the black leather pouch. I pulled it out, unzipped and tipped it on to the desk. A couple of passports, a driving licence and a police ID fell out.

One of the passports was a snide – a fake, with eighteen months left to run. I flipped it open and looked at the younger me. I'd been a little beefier when the photo was taken, but my hair and jawline were the same. Still fitted my mug. I'd held on to it as it cost a few quid – and it was on the database along with the driving licence, so it could stand the pull. They'd got me to Italy a few years ago when a piece of work went tits up and I'd gone on my toes for a bit.

I hung on to the fake cop ID and stuck the rest away behind the panel, closed the drawer and slid the broken matchsticks back into the gaps between runner and desk. The rolls of cotton wool went in as well. I arranged a couple more scraps on the edge of the desk to be double sure.

I cracked the police ID and stared at the picture. I'd lost a little weight inside, otherwise no change.

The cab dropped me off near Buckingham Road and I went to work, avoiding the houses where I knew the owners. It didn't take more than an hour before I'd found a real professional prosecution witness cutting his hedge. He was a true pro and I got chapter and verse on Sara's move.

'Nine o'clock Thursday morning,' he told me. 'Big removal van. Plain. Four fellas. Loaded up and left at three fifteen. Kids were helping. The three of them left in her Fiat, following the van.'

'How do you know the four lads were from the removal company?'

'All had the same red T-shirts on. Also,' he shook his head in OAP sorrow, 'their language. Effing this and effing that.'

'I know, terrible, isn't it?'

'Young lads, of course. Do you have children?'

'No. Anyone else helping them shift their stuff? Any friends, maybe?'

'Just the four lads.'

'Just the four, thanks for your time, sir. More people like you around and I'm sure we'd have more villains locked up.'

'Is she in trouble?' He was eager for detail. I made some up.

'No, she's a witness. On the right side.'

'I thought so,' he said. 'Looked a respectable lady to me.'

I thanked the prick and left him on station at his hedge.

I made the meet at ten to twelve. Leon was there already, standing by the roadside with his hands stuck deep in his sheepskin pockets, his big frame looking tight and curved like a shell. He waited for the cab to drive off, then half trotted across the road and we shook. His palm was damp.

'How are Jan and Steph?'

'Bad as you'd expect. I couldn't stay, I wasn't welcome, obviously.'

'They believed what the filth said?'

'Yeah.'

He wiped his hand on his jacket. 'Motor's round there.'

He'd stuck his white XJS on a meter off the main drag. There was his usual thermos of coffee on the dashboard and I could smell the leftovers of his last bit of blow. No surprise, he was as worked up as I was.

'What do you know?' he said.

'They moved out Thursday and they went under their own steam. There was a professional witness.' I gave him the rest.

'You did Buckingham Road as a copper? How long since you moved out?'

'It needed doing.'

'Tell me exactly what happened to Tomas.'

'Shot in the stomach and dumped outside the Infirmary.'

'Oh, Christ.' His head nodded forward into his hands. 'Was he dead when they found him?'

'He was gone by the time Jan made it to the hospital.'

He stayed very still for a moment, then straightened and wiped his eyes. 'What about Sara and the kids?'

'We had dinner booked for last night. Kept getting no reply all day yesterday, so I went round and the place was empty.'

'I had a look on the way here,' he said. 'To check.'

Why did he fucking do that?

I thought of them naked in bed, his fingers paddling in her breasts. I said, 'When did you last see them?'

'Last Friday morning. Sara and I have a bit of a row because I know she's wording the kids against you. That stash of brown they found.'

'Why was she still on about that?'

'Don't know. I ask Sam how you are and Sara just kicks off and tells me to leave. I don't, and she gets even worse. So I reckon I'll go, after all.'

'Go on.'

'That was it. I knew they were away for the week. I called her mobile to apologise, she never called back. Wednesday evening I got her on the house phone, she said she didn't want to talk.'

'She'd have been packing then, if that professional witness is right. How did she sound?'

'I just thought she was still pissed off at me.'

'Or rushed. What then?'

'Got her voicemail on Thursday morning, she didn't call back. I saw she left the answerphone on at the house.'

'So people wouldn't know they'd gone.' I leant forward and picked up his thermos, poured out and drank half a cup of old coffee. 'Let's go back to your place,' I said.

*

Leon lived in a two-up three-down in Audenshaw off Manchester Road. He lived up, his mum lived down. He could have afforded a small mansion in Prestbury, but he preferred to keep his property in Spain. Further from the local cop shop, not to mention the taxman.

'It's Ronnie.' There was a white Volvo at Leon's front door and his cousin Ronnie was helping Judith into the motor. We swung up the drive and stopped. 'Mam's going to Auntie May's for a couple of days. I wasn't due back till tonight.'

'I'll just say hello.'

We got out and I nodded at Ronnie, went round to the back seat and dipped my head in. 'Hello, Judith.'

'Ah, it's lovely to see you. You look well.'

'Thanks. And you?'

'I had a little operation on my knee. Don't know if he told you, but it means I have to be a bit careful for a few days. Have you got the time to come to dinner this week?'

'I'll make some, I promise. I'll see you soon, anyway.' She gave me a papery kiss on my cheek.

'Make sure you do.'

I straightened up. Leon was talking to Ronnie.

'I'll see you inside.'

He nodded and I went down the brick alley to the back garden and in through the kitchen. White and blue tiles inside, white and blue everything. Top of the range cooker, microwave, this, that and the other. I filled and plugged in the kettle, then got the ashtray out of a cupboard and lit up. A couple of minutes later, there was a scrape at the door and Leon showed. 'Mam's gone.'

'Sit down.'

'No, I'll make some tea.' He threw his coat over the chair, saw the kettle was on and came to sit across the table. 'Tell me everything,' he said. 'Don't leave anything out.'

'All right; Tomas was found early Tuesday morning outside the Infimary, been shot. Steph gets a visit from the Old Bill and gets up there, Tomas dies.'

I stopped for a second and went on with an effort.

'There's a DC there taking statements, guy called Sommerfield. He tells Jan and Steph that his boss knows me. Detective Chief Superintendent Hamilton Jacks.'

'Do you know him?'

'Yeah, I know Hamilton Jacks all right.'

'How?'

'Doesn't matter for now. This Sommerfield says his boss Hamilton Jacks reckons I'm dealing – and that Tomas is working for me. So Tomas is my runaround. And he must have been on my business when he got shot. And that's it. That's what they believe.'

The kettle clicked off and Leon sprang at the counter. 'And that's why Sara and the kids have gone?'

'Can you think of another reason? Sara believed the shit, or maybe the filth got to her as well. Anyway, they went.'

He sat down and pushed a mug across at me. 'Why didn't she call you, or tell you?'

'Christ, I don't know, Leon. I thought she still trusted me, I still trust her.'

'Came on the back of the brown in your cell.'

'But she knows I don't go near class A, she knows it's not my style. We were together nearly twenty years, what made her think I could do anything to hurt Tomas?'

The bird's nest again, showing the eggs.

'And she didn't tell me, either.' His mug clanked down on the table.

'Fuck, what a mess.'

I wasn't sure which one of us had spoken.

'All right,' he said after a moment. 'Start at the top. What do we know already? What about this cozzer Hamilton Jacks? Is he haunting you?'

I was looking at my watch. Tomas would never know the time again. A day passed.

'Hamilton Jacks?' Leon asked again. 'You said you knew him.'

'I dealt him a blow once, though he couldn't have known it was me. You know Jack Keane?'

'A bit.'

'I got him and his firm off a charge. It would have been fifteens all round if they'd gone down. Hamilton Jacks was the Old Bill heading up the case, and it would have been big glory for him if they'd gone away. Ten years ago. Jack Keane was big news, even then.'

'What did you do?'

'It was a Strangeways thing . . . talking of which I need to check on Terry. Make sure he's not wandered.'

Leon nodded and disappeared into his mug. Two rings and she picked up.

'Is he there, Carol?'

'No, he's just popped out for fags. Shall I get him to call you?'

'No, it's all right. I was just calling to check that he's behaving himself.'

'He's behaving very well love, and we're getting on very well, as it happens.'

A beat.

'In fact, we're getting on that well that I don't think he'll be too bothered if you don't call him back.'

'Thanks, Carol.' I pressed off. Carol always had been pretty game. We went back a while, as it goes. I met her when she was a housekeeper at the Midland Hotel and she'd slipped me out some pass keys and also marked the cards when any wealthy jewellery-jangling out-of-towners were on the plot. Leon had been in on the coup and the three of us had a good earner out of it. Leon was speaking now.

'How's Carol these days?'

'She's fine. I put Terry in with her. Janey's slung him out, so he says. He was on to me straight out of the nick.'

Leon grunted and flicked the lip of his mug. He wasn't really interested in Terry. 'Can this be anything to do with the brown in your cell? Have you been getting up anyone's nose? I mean, more recently than this copper Hamilton Jacks?'

'Nobody I can think of.'

'Any idea who might have stitched you up?'

'No more now than when it happened. I put the word out strong.

Nothing back, and I put up a oner for any knowledge. That's a lot of dough inside right now.'

'I know.'

'No con with anything to say makes it pretty certain it was a screw did it.' I swung round sideways in my chair and looked out of the window on to the back garden.

Leon drummed his fingers on the table. 'What I don't understand is this,' he said. 'If Hamilton Jacks thinks you had something to do with Tomas, why didn't they nick you when you got out?'

'Now you mention it – doesn't make sense.'

'Unless they know it's bollocks.'

'And Hamilton Jacks just wanted to make trouble. Christ, that's an evil thing to do.'

'Got to be more to it than that. The brown in your cell, your nephew murdered. Where's all this coming from, mate?'

'I don't know, but I'm going to find out.'

Leon drummed some more. I could tell he was sorting through his words. 'Don't you think you'd better get out, mate? Just till we know what's going on.'

He had a point. I didn't know where the blows were coming from. Maybe I should split. But I wanted my children back.

'Whatever's going on,' he said, 'we ain't got the full picture. What if this copper Hamilton Jacks is gunning for you, some kind of revenge plot, huh? They're a big firm, the filth. Go down to London. You've got friends there. Just for a few days. I'll sniff around.'

I didn't have a few days. 'No, Leon. Tomas has been murdered. If I don't find out what's going on, I may never get my kids back. I can't have them thinking I've got anything to do with this.'

'I still think you should go.'

'No.'

He held my gaze for what felt like a day. 'All right. All right, mate. But let's stick to the rules on this. No rushing in. Try and be calm.'

'I'll try.' I swung back in my seat. 'OK, let's start with Sara. Where's she gone to? Her parents are dead. I still know most of her pals, and as she's apparently running from me she won't have gone to stay with them. Can you think of anyone? Anyone I don't know?'

'One or two.'

'Can you go and see them? It's Saturday. They might be in.'

'All right.'

'I need money, Leon. Can you help me out? I've got dough from a parcel due in the next couple of days.'

'All right.'

'And I'll need somewhere to stay. I've sacked the B&B. Can you get me into that place you use in Prestwich?'

'Yeah. If there's a vacancy. No problem.'

I saw him in bed with Sara. His hairy belly sliding against her flat stomach.

'And a car. Can you give Dougie a call, see what he's got?'

Dougie Sanders was a part-ex dealer who kept back and knocked out minters to the chaps from time to time. As a favour, and for a drink on top.

'Anything else?' he asked, suddenly looking pissed off.

'What's wrong?'

He went across to the window and stared out at the garden. He blocked out most of the light. 'I'm not your Joey, you know. This concerns me as well as you.' He was very quiet, very lonely.

I spoke to his back. 'Sorry, mate.'

'Yeah.' He was still looking out at the garden. 'You're always sorry.'

He turned.

'OK. A flop and wheels. And Sara's friends. And the money.' He opened the freezer and reached in for the plastic tub of cash.

There were two lads wiring an estate agent's board up outside number forty-five. I glanced at the sign as I went past, then found a quiet phone box and dialled the agent's number. When they picked up, I asked vaguely if they had anything for sale in Heaton Moor. The girl on the other end said they had a few houses in my price range, and reeled off a few street names. 'And we have one in Buckingham Road,' she added.

'I know it. Any chance of a view in the next hour or so?'

'Should think so, it's empty. I can meet you there in twenty minutes.'
She gave me my old address, I gave her a false name, and we hung up.

Half an hour later I was back in the empty front room. The estate agent was a slim twenty-something called Annie with tied back brown hair and a severe blue suit.

'This is the living room,' she said unnecessarily, though she couldn't have known it. 'Double reception, nice and bright, bay windows and gas central heating installed.'

I nodded and we moved into the kitchen.

'Just been fitted,' she lied. I'd had it put in a good three years earlier. 'Then there's the garden,' she said, opening the door. I stared out on to flowerbeds I'd laid, bushes I'd once kept trim. Then it was upstairs and round the twins' and Sara's bedrooms, the bathroom, the spare room. I looked for signs, saw nothing. Not even a scrap of packing.

'Has the place been on the market long, Annie?'

'About two weeks,' she lied.

'Anxious to sell?'

'She might take an offer. She's already bought I think. Certainly had somewhere to go to.'

'Somewhere nice?'

'Leeds, I think. I'm not sure. I didn't take instructions. Have you been looking long, Mr Drake?'

My name was John Drake. While I was dealing with Annie.

'It's my first day up here, I'm looking for me and my sons. I think I'll make an offer on this, Annie.'

She looked very pleased. I gave her a figure a few grand off the asking price.

'I've not even found a hotel to stay in yet, Annie, but I'll give you a ring first thing Monday morning. Can you get an answer by then?'

'I don't know, Mr Drake. I sometimes leave a message and she gets back to me later. That's what we've done before. I ought to tell you that she is looking for the asking price. She'll probably say no to your offer, she's turned a couple down already. Not quite as much as yours, but not far off.' After only two days I reckoned she was probably lying again.

'Well, see what she says. I've got a mobile in the meantime.' I scribbled it down on the back of her card and handed it across.

'They're not usually in on a Saturday.'

I was in the *Evening News* lobby on Deansgate and dealing with a bottle-blonde teenage idiot. She'd looked up from her copy of *Take a Break* as I walked in and sighed loud enough to rattle the windows. Now she was playing gatekeeper.

'It's important,' I said. 'I need it for tomorrow.' I'd told her I was after a report on the Reds I wanted to get framed for someone's birthday piss-up.

'Well, they're not usually here.' She couldn't be bothered to lie outright, but she still wanted to get rid of me. Not *usually* here.

'Not usually. So could you try them for me? On the off chance.'

'They won't be in.' Her two inch nails gave a quick drum on the counter top.

'But could you try? Please.'

She sighed theatrically, picked up the phone and tapped out an internal number with some difficulty. She could hardly hide her disappointment as it picked up the other end. With another sigh she filled out a visitor's pass and rammed it into a plastic wallet. 'Second floor. He'll meet you at the lift.'

The doors slid open and here was a nine-year-old in white shirt and black trousers that stopped just above his ankles. 'Hello, Mr Mason. Library was it?'

'Thank you for letting me in.'

'No problem. I was bored shitless and desperate for someone to talk to. I'm Simon.'

We shook. 'John Mason. Thanks again.'

Simon led the way down the corridor, speaking over his shoulder. 'Anything to liven it up on a Saturday. So bloody bored here on my own.'

We went through a set of double doors and then left through some more. The shelves and filing cabinets in the next room said 'library.' He waved at a table.

'You can sit there. Last two weeks, was it?'

'Please.'

'Cup of tea?'

'Thanks.'

'Be right back.'

I ripped my jacket off and sat. There were papers cut and half cut up, scraps of newsprint and several pairs of identical long blackhandled scissors. There was a thud at the end of my table. Simon with a stack of the *Manchester Evening News*.

'Here you go. Last two weeks' editions, some of them, anyway. Be right back.'

I smiled thanks and pulled yesterday's off the top, watching his ankles out of the room. As soon as he was gone, I stood up and counted my way down the pile to the previous Monday, split the stack and flipped through the early edition. There it was, page two, news in brief. Tomas dumped at the Royal Infirmary, but no name yet. Later edition had a longer piece, still no name.

'Here you go.' Simon dropped another stack of papers next to the first. 'Find it?'

'Not yet.'

'Big Red is he?'

'Yeah.'

'I'll fetch your tea.'

I flicked through the next couple of editions and found a piece across two pages from Thursday. I'd normally have read the paper in Strangeways, but it was the night before I got out and I was busy. 'MURDERED TEEN WAS HEROIN ADDICT.' Family snap of Tomas, all the rest. I couldn't read it now. I folded the three issues and rolled them into my jacket, then flicked to Wednesday and pulled out the edition with the Liverpool match report just as Simon reappeared.

'All right?' He gave me a mug. I took it and scalded my mouth in the hurry to be gone.

'Yeah, this one. How much?'

'Nah, just take it. No problem.'

A phone rang and he picked it up looking surprised. I waved and mouthed *I'll find my way out*, stuffed a tenner in his shirt pocket with a wink, then picked up my jacket with the other papers rolled up in it. The girl on reception didn't look up as I left.

Back on the street I darted into a bar a few doors down, bought a drink and sat in a quiet corner. Shorter pieces first. The news in brief must have been written on the back of a tip-off from the station that sent the jam butty to the Infirmary. The later edition filled in some detail: a Chinese croupier had found him. She'd been kicking around in casualty with a suspect broken wrist, gone out for a smoke and started screaming. The paper said he'd been shot once in the gut and apparently died from loss of blood.

I discovered a longer news piece on page four of the third paper. This one had a couple of quotes from Keith Hamilton Jacks as the cozzer in charge of the investigation and a couple more quotes from neighbours about what a nice lad Tomas was.

I flicked on through the papers. There was a picture of Hamilton Jacks. First time I'd seen what he looked like, despite our association over Jack Keane's firm and the Turk. About fifty, very fit-looking, nearly white hair swept back. Hard as well, with hooded eyes looking like a pair of slits in the snow. Hamilton Jacks.

A few minutes later, I was back on the street punching in Andy Chen's number. Andy was an ex-boxer I knew. He'd been on my wing in Strangeways until about three weeks ago and I knew he was a pal of Jack Keane's. If this was about the Turk, I needed to speak to Jack urgently. Andy picked up, and yes, he had seen Jack since he got out.

'Can you get a message to him to call me? I've got a new number.' I spewed the mobile. 'It's urgent, Andy. He needs to know that.'

'I'll tell him.'

My phone rang as I hung up. It was Leon with an address in Prestwich.

'You're in for a month.'

Leon jangled a set of keys under my nose then dropped them on the kitchen counter. I looked round the open-plan living stroke kitchen area.

'Fancy a brew?' he said. 'They leave the makings out like a hotel.'

'Thanks, yes. It looks good, Leon.'

It was a service flat in Prestwich, about fifteen minutes cab from the centre. Bland and empty, but also safe and away from my normal patch.

'You're Martin Doyle, you're a mate of mine and you've just left your wife. Not that the bloke was arsed. Paperwork in the kitchen drawer, agreement, local map and agents' details. I'm Joseph Carlton, Mr Doyle.'

'Thanks.'

The kettle clicked off. Leon brewed up and we sat in the lounge – everything shades of grey and blue with low chairs and an MFI table in the corner.

Bottom line was Leon had got nowhere. No one in, no one answering. 'I tried Sara's phone again,' he added. 'Dead. Phone company said it was disconnected at the customer's request. Did you have any luck?'

'House is on the market. I rang the estate agent and got her to show me round Buckingham Road as a buyer. She said Sara's in Leeds.'

'Where she went to university.'

'I know. I'm going to look at schools there from Monday. She won't want them out of class for long.'

'She won't have them in school yet.'

'I've known it done. And she's got friends in the local education mob.'

'Friends who could pull some strings? Bit far-fetched, isn't it?'

'You got anything better to go on?'

'I suppose not.'

'I've got to find them Leon, make them understand I had nothing to do with Tomas, make sure they're safe. Did you get a chance to look at a car?'

'A Rover. It'll be ready tomorrow morning, Dougie has to do the paperwork. Four and a half and a monkey on top for him.'

'Thanks.'

'Anything else?'

'I went to the *Evening News* and checked the papers. Some background, maybe something worth following up, I'll have to go over them again.'

'Well, I dropped round on a couple of our – her – friends. If they knew anything, they weren't saying. One of them got a call to say they were leaving Manchester, and that was it. She didn't seem to know any more.'

'Who was that?'

'Harriet Gribbon.'

'Harriet never liked me. No point in trying to get more out of her. Sod it.'

'So what do we do now?'

'I've put the word out on Tomas already, any rumours, anything off the street. We'll have to see what comes back off that.'

'Jack Keane?'

'Left him a message. But it'll depend how long he's been out.'

'Someone like Jack, doesn't matter if he's in or out.'

'Yeah, maybe.' I sighed and my head dropped.

'You look whacked, mate. Better sack it for today, try and get some sleep. I'll see if I can raise a couple more of her friends.'

'Yeah, go easy, though. We don't want to leave too many footprints.'

'No, we don't.'

'And thanks for the car, Leon.'

'It's only money.'

I saw him to the door, then rang Marcus. 'Any news for me, Marcus? Anything about the lad, Tomas?'

'There weren't many in last night, chief. No one to ask. There's a big school on tonight, so I'll be dropping in for that. Maybe I'll get lucky this time. You all right?'

'I'm OK, thanks. Soon as you know anything, eh?'

'I will.'

We hung up, and I chucked the phone on the sofa feeling pretty shit. I hadn't expected too much off him, but nothing at all was a right downer. I dragged myself across the road to the nearest late store and bought some food and the paper and was pissed off to find someone had rung while I was out. The message was Andy Chen saying Jack would call me tomorrow when he got back. I rolled on to the sofa to think.

Half an hour later I was on the main drag, flagging down a cab and asking it to take me to Buckingham Road where I stood in the shadows opposite and stared at number forty-five. We'd been happy there for a while. Christmases and holidays came back. First bikes, first day at school, new blazers with long sleeves so they could grow into them. Big new satchels. It was starting to rain. I read the board again.

The estate agent was next to a bank. I'd half bussed it, half walked. The house details weren't in the window, which was well lit. I needed to know where they were, and there was bound to be a file somewhere inside relating to forty-five Buckingham Road with contact details, so why not screw the gaff now? I looked up. Bog standard ADT alarm. Maybe it was a key in the panel job, rather than an entry code. Maybe I could turn it off. If not, maybe I could find the file in the time it took the security firm to take the shout.

The impulse was gathering speed. The files would be in alphabetical order, by name, or address. Wouldn't take long to dig Sara's out.

How do you know that? the voice spat in my ear. *Have you ever screwed an estate agent's before?*

No, but there's a first time for everything and everything's in alphabetical order in an office.

Tackle? Who did I know nearby to get turtles, torch and a bar from?

I thought of a mechanic, from off a council estate at the back of the old cinema, about half a mile away. He'd do. What was his fucking name?

I'd cab it down there. No, I'd walk. The cab firm was too near to the screwer.

You mug. You fucking mug. Less than forty-eight hours out of the nick, your head right up your arse and you're standing here, seriously contemplating screwing a gaff without tools or transport. Mug.

Then I looked up at the bell again and thought, *Fuck it, why not?* The clanger's certain to go off, but if anyone bothers to report it, Old Bill will contact some security firm to find a keyholder. The worst way, that'll take twenty minutes. I'll be in and out in ten.

Half an hour later, I was at the back door. Elvis the mechanic had been out, but his missus had let me into his tool shed. I'd picked up a torch, a decent-sized tyre lever, some bits of wood for wedges and a half-clean black wool skullcap, then walked hard through the sleet keeping the parcel low on my inside and ready to dump at any sign of a uniform. My socks were on my hands for gloves and I was carrying the bar and the rest of the bits rolled up in a newspaper.

The agent's yard was split from a back entry by an easy wall. Over it, I pushed at the door and felt bolts top and bottom and the strength of the mortice in the middle. Firm enough, but they'd go, so I squatted and got to work with the jemmy. The bottom of the door proved friendly; I did the lower bolt in a couple of minutes and had four wedges in place up to the mortice. No bell yet, which meant that the system relied on pick-ups and not contact pads.

The skull cap was wet with rain and sweat as I worked the bar well in, stood, gripped the end and gave it a fierce pull. The lock went with a crack. I stopped to listen, then twisted to check the windows behind for signs of the local neighbourhood watch. No sound and no lights. Usually I'd wait a while now, plugged into a police scanner to pick up any trouble coming my way. Not tonight; I laid the bar on the deck and pushed hard against the door with my back. The top bolt held, but there was more than enough give for me to get inside. I snatched up the bar, shoved again and squeezed through. In.

I saw the glow from the pick-ups – one in each corner – a millisecond before the clanger went off. Loud bastard as well, some fucker would report this all right, to get it shut up if nothing else. The torch came out and on, a quick scan showed me a utility room. Boxes, a sink and a karsi leading off. Two strides took me to the middle door, locked. A swift kick saw it off. Now I was in the main office.

Filing cabinets to the right, desks to the left. Files first. Would Sara's details be under her name or address?

I jemmied the top drawer open in a couple of seconds. What's the matter with these people? Common sense says that you need a fairly serious tool to get into the fucking gaff, so what's the point of these Mickey Mouse boxes?

The files were in address order. A to F under my fingertips. No need for the torch. The Indian across the road was lit up like the Taj Mahal, and the office was bright with blue and red neon.

Bentley, Bramhall, Brunton. No Buckingham. Was there something like a new business file? Rest of the cabinets, or the desks? I glanced at the labels on the filers and made the desks favourite. There were three. I tried them, all the drawers were locked. Didn't they trust each other or something? I got to work.

It was in desk one, second drawer down, slim file, '45 Buckingham Road' on the front. Two A4 pages, easily readable in the flashing neon. Sara Harpur – she was using her maiden name again – then the asking price. Set of property details. On the second page, one line: *Client now away. Speak to Annie for details.* Then underlined, and in capitals: <u>DOMESTIC</u>.

That was it. Clever clever Sara. She knew I'd come this way. This was a waste of fucking time. I dropped the file back and slid the drawer shut.

Just then I heard a rattle at the front. I strained my ears to pick up through the clanger – some fucker was trying the front door, and hard. I dropped down behind the desk, sod it, I'd not been in the gaff five minutes. Fuck my luck.

The bottom half of the window was blacked out with the property display board. I scampered across on hands and knees using the desks as cover, I needed a look out. If there was only one of them, chances were they wouldn't fancy the back on their tod. I slid up to get my eyes over the glass. Bollocks. There was a fucking jam sandwich with its light still flashing on the other side of the road. Outside the curry house, the blue flasher was all mixed up with the neon signs. That's why I hadn't noticed. No sign of the cozzer, presumably still in the doorway.

Fucking police. What were they doing showing up at a clanger?

Down and across to the connecting door, fast. Through it, scraping on my belly now. If the cozzer was on his own, he might not fancy the back either – they're not all heroes, the boys in blue. In any case, if I moved swift, I could still be off the plot before he made his move.

Into the back room and up on my feet. Then another noise came through the clanger, the squawk of a police radio from the fucking back yard.

'I'm in the yard, Phil. Back door's been forced. I'm going in, over.'

Crackle crackle.

'No, you stay there in case they try to get out your way.'

More crackle. Then radio silence. The door – still attached by the upper hinge and upper bolt – started to give towards me like a giant catflap. An arm came through; a couple of grunts and the gap widened. I was just a few inches away. I reached up for the top bolt, gripped it, and began to inch it back. When it came out, the hinge should give way and the door and the filth would both hit the deck. I'd jump over and leg it.

The top of his head slid into view. He was having to shoulder his way in, as I'd done. The bolt was sticking now, forced by the pressure. I gripped the jemmy in my left and held it near the bolt. He was almost in. Blond hair reflected in the neon light, and he was starting to turn.

I banged the bolt hard and shifted as fast as I could, but the door twisted off its hinge, flipped over and knocked me on the deck, the cozzer rolling on top. Fuck fuck fuck. I was proper winded and I needed air. I managed to wriggle out from under on all fours, head well down. The copper scrambled to his feet and snapped on his torch.

'How many of you, shitbag?'

'Just me.' I kept my head turned away from the torch's beam.

The kick came in hard on my left shoulder. *Fuck.* 'There's plenty more where that came from. Now get up, slow.'

I shifted onto one knee, socked hands down flat like a runner on the blocks and apparently doing what I was told. Then I sprang, slamming into him head on. He went straight down, torch beam twisting crazily. I leapt over him, he swung at my leg and grabbed on, I went with the move and crunched down hard on his shoulder. He screeched and let go instantly. I tumbled over him and out the back.

'He's fucking done me, Phil.'

Shit.

Slaps of running feet coming from the left. I took off to the right. There was a 'Stop police!' above the clanger, then something heavy bounced off my nut and tanked to the floor. He'd thrown his truncheon, fuck it, keep going. I tore off the socks and jammed them into my pocket, skidded round a corner, sprinted hard away from Kingsway, hurdled a low wall into a churchyard, then stopped for a quick shufti back. Nish – the bold Phillip must have gone to his mate. Good for you, Phillip.

The sound of the first siren wailed up a few minutes later as I ran across the darkened lot of an office car park. It was quickly joined by another and then another. They were coming mob handed, as you'd expect when you'd done a cozzer. Which is why it's usually a mug thing to do.

Then again, the whole fucking venture had premier-league mug written all over it. No time for that now, though. Survival was the only concern. Old Bill would be fanning out and looking for a guy on his own, I had to get off the street. There was a pub up ahead, a Boddington's house, big and sounding lively. Slowing to a walk, I pulled the skull cap off and glanced down in the light from the windows. I was wet, but then a lot would be. A quick brush and in, heading straight for the karsi where I towelled my hair with paper, smoothed it with my hands, and dabbed at my jacket. Trainers off, I sat on the toilet, wrung out and pulled on the socks, then went to the mirror. I'd pass.

Buy a drink at the bar and look round – the house was buzzing and mainly young. I leant into my pint; the copper hadn't got a good look at my boat, I was sure of that, but he'd have got my build and dress. I considered my next move. I could phone Leon, I could phone a taxi. Taxi meant a local one, and the driver might be questioned later on who he'd picked up from the area about this time. No, Leon was the best bet.

'Minibus for Ruby?'

There was a geezer shouting in the doorway. A group of lads, six or seven handed, was stood near me. One of them waved, then turned to his mates. 'Mulligans, yeah?'

Nods all round. They were going into town looking for action. I jumped in.

'Any chance of a lift, lads? They're not even picking up. Must be the rain.'

They turned as a group, Ruby shrugged his shoulders at the rest. No one cared. 'Yeah, sure. There'll be room.'

They were out in force when we passed the estate agent's a few minutes later – two cars and a van, entry cordoned off with blue and white police ribbon. Nice, I thought. Some bastard could mug an old girl on the way back from bingo and she'd be lucky to see a car at the scene. Give a cozzer a sore shoulder and half the fucking force turns up.

The minibus didn't even get a second glance.

An hour later and I was piss-wet through again. Out of courtesy and cover, I'd bought Ruby and his crew a drink before I went looking for a cab. And because of the rain, had no luck. Now, trudging up Bury New Road with Strangeways on my right looking shittier than ever, the stupidity of what I'd done was hammering into my nut. After a near miss with the opposition, the relief would normally be sweet. Not tonight.

The warmth from the central heating hit me as I twisted the key in the front door. I knew I hadn't left it on. Must be Leon. He had a spare twirl.

I pushed open the lounge door and found him sat with his coat off. A bottle of brandy, a jug of water, two glasses, two spliffs and an ashtray on the table.

'You're wet,' he said.

I grunted and made for the bedroom. A minute later, half rubbed down and with a towel round my waist, I dragged back in and slumped into the other chair. Leon pointed at the booze. I nodded and poured three fingers, neat. He passed me a joint and we both lit up.

'Why are you here, Leon? It's pretty late.'

'I thought you might need something to help you sleep.' He was on edge. 'I tried a few more people. They don't know a thing, or they're saying they don't.' He tugged on his joint. 'What have you been up to?'

I told him, chapter and verse. When I'd done he stared at me for a minute. Then he dropped his spliff in the ashtray and laid his palms on his forehead, slid them over his scalp and locked the fingers behind his neck. 'What the fuck have you done?'

I didn't need to feel any worse about it. I said nothing.

Leon looked up. 'I told you to get out this afternoon. Things were bad, now they're worse. Why didn't you listen?'

'You know I can't, Leon.'

'*You know I can't, Leon.* Twenty years I've known you, and this is the first time I've known you this stupid.' He slammed his fist down and the bottle and glasses jumped. 'She's left me as well, remember?'

'No, Leon.'

'It's not just about you, for fuck's sake. I knew Tomas. I know Jan and Steph, and Lou and Sam. And Sara. What's your problem?'

'You better stop now.'

'You stop. I swallowed your orders today: do this, Leon, do that, Leon. A motor, a service flat, like I was your runaround. I stood for it because you're just out and all the rest. And who was I taking orders from? Huh?'

I was naked and wet and tired. I let him have his say.

'Thirty-six hours you've been out. Let's see what you've been up to.' Now he started counting off on his fingers, the prick. 'Two assaults, one on a cozzer; one impersonating a police officer; and one burglary. In two days, less. This rate, you'll be lifed-off by Tuesday. You better go. Manchester's not safe for you as it is, and certainly not with you running around like a prick.' He took a good inch from the top of his drink.

'I'm not going anywhere,' I said.

'Well, you're on your own, then. If you want to carry on running amok, you're not taking me with you.' He leant back into his chair.

'Let's talk about this tomorrow.'

'I think you should go tomorrow.'

There was a long beat. We relit the joints. Then he reached forward and filled my glass again. I drank it down without even noticing the burn. OK, he was mostly right, but I could still have killed him.

'I'm exhausted, Leon. Slept badly last night. Tomorrow, eh?' I tried a smile.

'You bloody look it, too.' He shook his head and got up. 'Come on.' He stood me up, walked me into the bedroom and pulled back the covers. I dropped the towel and rolled in.

'Here.' He pressed something into my hand. 'It's a sleeper.'

I nodded and saw him from the end of a long velvet-lined tunnel. He moved into the living room and the lights went out. Then he was at the bedroom door.

'I'll see you tomorrow. Call me as soon as you're up.'

'All right.'

I heard the doors closing and swallowed the pill. Sometimes sleep is the only comfort. I turned over on my side and stared ahead into the darkness, then felt the chemicals take hold and drifted away.

3

I was sitting over coffee and brandy with Sara in a French restaurant near the airport. We'd been together about eight months by then and doing OK, though I had been skirting round the hard bits. Like what I did to earn a pound note. We were talking about us. Or rather, I was.

'Look, Sara, I'm not much good at chat like this.'

I stopped for a second to swipe away a massive dragonfly that had settled on the table and seemed to be checking the bill the waiter had just brought.

She tilted her head. 'Are you asking me to move in with you?'

The dragonfly was back, circling the table at head height. It seemed to have got bigger. I swiped at it again.

'Don't say anything, not for the minute. There's something I need to tell you. Hang on.'

The dragonfly was about a foot long by now, so I flicked out my tongue, caught it on the sticky surface and rolled it back up into my mouth, feeling it crack against the roof of my mouth. The soft guts slid out and down my throat as I remembered that once you realise it's a dream, you can run it yourself and . . .

Sunday morning in a service flat. I stretched for my watch; past nine. Leon's pill had kept me under.

I flopped back on the pillow. Dragonflies, lizards and Sara. What was all that about? Then I remembered my row with Leon the day before and saw her sweating under him, arm thrown round his neck, pulling him tight into her.

*

'I don't love him and I know it won't last forever.'

I'd done about five months on the last one when Sara asked for a visiting order. We often discussed the kids and money, the divorce had been half civilised. This I hadn't expected.

'I'm thinking about starting a relationship and I think that perhaps you ought to know about it.'

'Why are you asking?'

'It's Leon.'

'Leon?'

'He's taken me out a couple of times. You know, dinner, the theatre.'

'He told me you'd gone out.'

'That was just friends. Now I'm thinking about taking things further. I know he'd like to, though he hasn't said anything.'

She'd said she'd had it with villains. And he was fifteen years older, though he looked after himself.

'I don't love him, and it won't last forever. But I do like him a lot. As for what he does for a living, well, at least he's always around, which you seldom were.'

She'd come because she knew Leon would feel awkward if it developed. I said Leon was a good man who thought the world of Lou and Sam. No reason at all why he and Sara shouldn't do what they wanted to do. That's what I said, anyway.

'Tell me again why we're going to see this Uncle.'

We were in Leon's motor headed for Chinatown. He'd rung just after I got up and said he'd sorted a meet that might answer a few questions.

'Because he knows everyone in the heroin game and he owes me a favour.' With a quick shufti left and right, he shot across a junction. 'And all this is down to drugs,' he said.

You don't talk meets on the phone so I hadn't got the detail until now, and I didn't like it. 'What do you mean, all this is down to drugs?'

'Are you still asleep or something? First there's the heroin in your cell. Then Tomas gets shot, he's on the gear and the filth say you're involved. Put all that together, and it starts to look like a message.'

He pulled up at a red and shook a sharp no at a couple of squeegee merchants.

'I went round to see him yesterday and gave him the full SP about what's been happening to you.'

'You what?'

'Come on, what do you think I am? This guy doesn't tell himself anything he doesn't need to know. He said to drop in on him this morning – oh, come on, Grandad.' My seatbelt tightened as he overtook the half-timbered Morris.

'What about Dougie and the car?'

'It's sorted. I picked it up and left it at the water park for you this morning.'

'Thanks. So your brilliant solution to all this is to go and see a big time drugs dealer who may well have indirectly supplied Tomas with his smack anyway.'

'We need any knowledge we can get. I'll go on my own if you want.'

I drummed the dash. 'Let's just get on with it.'

We fetched up in a car park round the back of the Piccadilly Hotel and walked down pissy concrete steps onto Portland Street and on into Chinatown. I wondered how he'd felt when he went to Buckingham Road and found it empty. I thought about him taking the stairs two at a time and switching on lights. Just like I'd done. Everything like I'd done. I thought of him between her legs again. Then her on top, sweating and arching her back.

We were outside Uncle's cash and carry. Half ten Sunday morning and busy as you like.

Unfamiliar spices and meat smells, steam and chatter drifted out, and I got the feeling of hundreds of people inside crawling around like ants. I craned my head back, looking up at the building. It was painted red and white, white for the brickwork, red for the windows and doors. Inside, everyone was Chinese, staff and punter alike. Chattering couples and groups pushed past me on their way out, all clutching carrier bags white like the building, printed with a big red flower on the side.

I haven't travelled enough, I thought. *Never been to Hong Kong, China, Singapore. Taiwan is just somewhere plastic toys get made.*

Leon was already inside, speaking to a girl on the front desk. She was nodding at him, then glanced out at me and picked up a phone. I watched her in profile for a few seconds, then thought I might as well put myself on show, so I went in and stood next to him, hands stuffed in pockets. The girl was talking into the receiver in Chinese. She nodded again and put the phone down. 'He's at the Everybody Happy.'

'The Everybody Happy?'

'It's a restaurant. He owns it. Sundays he takes Dim Sum with the family.' She stretched her arm out and the elbow bent sharply the wrong way as she pointed. To Leon she said: 'Right, then right again.'

Then to me: 'Dancer. Double-jointed.'

'Thank you,' I said.

'You're welcome.'

Leon led the way out, we turned right and right again and found ourselves in a street of Chinese restaurants. The Everybody Happy was the biggest, with its entrance down a set of grey stone flags. Inside, all the small tables you'd expect had been taken away and replaced with three large ones, each feeding around forty sitting shoulder to shoulder. One table was young men with *tasty* written all over them. Another had women and little children, all shouting and balloons and chatter. The third was a mix of older people.

'Stay here. I'll just go and chat up our man.'

Leon edged his way round a table towards a guy in his late fifties. I assumed this was Uncle. A full head of slicked black hair, grey suit, white shirt open at the neck. He was in the middle of words with a much older geezer, but he broke off when he saw Leon move on him. They exchanged a couple of sentences, and Uncle threw me a glance which was less than friendly. Then he stood up and waved me across. The two of them moved to the back of the room and a pair of double doors into the kitchen. Uncle slid through first and Leon held one open for me to catch up. It was huge and busy, steam, shouting and stainless steel.

'Looks like we have a guide,' said Leon.

A nine foot Chinaman motioned for us to follow him along an aisle packed with paper packets, tins, boxes, catering-size this and catering-size that. There was a brown door at the end next to some deep freezes. The guy knocked, opened up and waved us in. There were a few racks of files and an old-fashioned adding machine with a paper roll on a desk in the corner, three low chairs round a table in the centre. Uncle was already sat pouring tea. He stood up smartly and took Leon's hand firmly in both of his. Then he turned and shook with me coolly and quickly.

'You want a brew?' His voice was Mancunian cut with nothing. I must have looked surprised. 'Not Charlie Chan enough for you?' he asked.

I opened my mouth, I think to apologise. He waved it shut.

'Leon should have told you. Always surprises people. I just look so fucking Chinese, don't I?'

'Milk,' I said. 'No sugar.'

He motioned us to sit down and finished pouring. He handed one cup to Leon using both hands, pulled one across the table to himself and nodded at me to take mine. Then he put an ashtray in front of me.

'You smoke,' he said. 'I can smell it on you. Please feel free.'

I nodded and lit up. He settled back.

'OK, here's the deal. Leon sees me yesterday, tells me you are a good friend of his and that you've got problems. He gives me some details and he asks me to make some enquiries.'

He sipped from his cup without taking his eyes off mine.

'Well, I asked around and I've got a few answers. I shouldn't think you'll like them. I certainly didn't.'

The white noise in my head cleared. 'What are they?'

Uncle put down his cup on the table. He ran his middle finger around the rim for a beat or two. Then he said; 'Luckily for you, Leon's a very good friend. Otherwise, you're not sitting here. But I tell you something. If Leon's wrong, and if what I hear is right, you're fucked twice. Once by someone else, and then once by me. Clear?'

A day went by. 'Go on.'

'As I say, I ask around. And the word that comes back is that you're a grass.'

I stood up for the fight. Uncle sat back and rolled his eyes. 'You want trouble, I can have five men in here in two seconds. Why don't you just sit down and listen?'

Leon hadn't moved. 'You'd better, mate.'

Calling him a grass is the worst thing you can say to a straight face. I sat down with an effort. Uncle went on. 'A grass. Informer. Police informer.'

'That's enough.' I snapped my head round at Leon. 'We're going.'

Leon shook his head again. 'Listen to him.'

'Did you know anything about this?'

'No, that's why I'm listening. You do the same.'

I turned back to Uncle with another effort. I felt every muscle in my neck pull as I did. Uncle poured himself more tea.

'Now to the police,' he said. 'There's a filth called Keith Hamilton Jacks, a chief superintendent. He's heading up the investigation into your nephew's murder. But he's also been interested in you for a while about your drug dealings. The word is that you're trying to push your way into the class A market. Well, that's normal business. But the word is you've been grassing people to make your way clear, and that's what I've been told. Now, I don't know how the heroin got into your cell, but I do know that your wife and children have been told to stay away from you. And I also know that Hamilton Jacks wants you very badly. There's nothing he won't do to put you away. Nothing. Of course, that may all be part of your game as well.'

He rang his cup with a metal spoon, then dropped it in his saucer. 'Here's some advice, and it's good advice. Get out of Manchester. Not tonight, not tomorrow; today, now. Walk out of here and keep walking. Your nephew was on your business when he was shot. If you don't go, you'll be next. And don't go looking for your wife and children. They don't want to know you any more, so you forget about them. Cut your losses and go.' He held my gaze for a beat then sat back.

'And now I've told you all that. I've forgotten about it. Anyone finds out I've spoken to you or that you've met with me, I will have to reconsider my position with my good friend Leon. Please understand I cannot be any more help to you.'

Then suddenly, he went very Chinese. 'If all this wrong, and you are good man, I wish you well. Time you both go now, time you go very quickly.' He looked straight at me.

'Particularly you.'

'Who's your friend Uncle been talking to?'

We were sitting in Leon's motor overlooking the lake at the water park. My new Rover was dark blue, two spaces down. The rain was drumming hard on the roof. I was still reeling.

'You go to see him yesterday, when you leave he picks up the phone or goes and sees someone, and suddenly I'm a grass. Now who's told him that?'

'Don't know, mate.' He sounded uncomfortable. Grassing is like being accused of rape. Your very closest friends check their memories, even if they don't want to. Just in case.

'I've never grassed anyone, never thought of grassing anyone, I won't have anything to do with a grass. I've marked plenty of people's cards if there's a grass on the manor. I wouldn't break that rule, I wouldn't think of breaking it. Now, who's saying I have?'

'There's no blots on your copybook. I know that.'

'So who's he talking to? And what's all this crap about me getting into the class A business? The filth tell Steph and Jan, now Uncle's got hold of the same bollocks. Do you think he's got a cozzer in his pocket?'

'He's got enough money.'

'He says Hamilton Jacks wants me bad, that he's been interested in me for a while about my "drug dealings". What drug dealings? Where's that come from? What's his fucking game, Leon?'

The rain had died off and the sun came out, bouncing off the wet bonnet.

'Shall we stretch our legs?' said Leon.

We got out and walked slowly towards the lake. The rain had kept most people away. There were a couple of drenched walkers under a tree on the other side and two kids skimming stones, otherwise we were alone. The grass flicked our legs as we walked, leaving little stripes of wet around our knees.

'You told me you dealt Hamilton Jacks a blow once,' Leon said after a while. 'You going to tell me about it?'

'All right then, yeah.' I sighed loudly. 'It was all of ten years ago, Leon. You were off in Spain buying your first place and I got nicked for a gaff in Cheshire. Remember?'

'I remember the nicking.'

'No bail, so I was lying down in Strangeways and going nowhere for a few months. Fast forward six weeks or so and a firm of blaggers comes in. There were four of them in for a pounce on a wages van, couple of hundred grand. A passing taxi driver volunteered to get involved and ended up shot in the leg, so Old Bill put a lot of weight on the job and the four got nicked in a flop in Ashton-under-Lyne. Dough was recovered, but guns and kit had been dropped elsewhere. There's a bench over there, seems dry enough. Shall we go and sit?'

The bench was under some thick evergreen. We flicked what water there was on to the deck and sat. Leon unscrewed his thermos and gave me a coffee in the cap.

'Thanks. Anyway – guns and the rest dropped, so Old Bill only had half a case. The word was that all the firm had stayed schtum in interview and were going for trial. They were all Cat A, all on the book with a screw trooping around behind them. One of them, and acknowledged to be the guvnor, was my old mate Jack Keane.' I stopped and thought about being called a grass again.

Leon nudged me. 'Go on.'

'Yeah, well, with a screw on his back all the time I didn't get much chance to catch up with Jack, just the odd word in the canteen queue, that sort of thing. Then one day a stiff gets slipped under my door over lunchtime bang-up. From Jack, asking me to put my name down for the Methodist midweek service the following night. "Make sure you're near the back," it said. So the next evening, there I am standing in the pew in front of him, belting out *Hills of the North Rejoice*, and he's hissing in my ear drum. He wants a favour, he says. He needs to get someone over the wall.'

'Oh, was that all? Piece of piss, then.' Leon actually laughed.

'That's what I thought.' I cracked the briefest of smiles and a few scraps of my tension lifted. 'Anyway, the script was this: the flop where they'd been found with the money was down to one of Jack's four – a Turk, twenty-five years old. College boy who'd dropped out to make a living on the pavement. And of course, in law, anything found in a person's gaff is down to the owner. If the Turk could do one from Strangeways and get back to Istanbul or wherever, the rest of the firm could put the dough from the blag on his toes. They already had a builder straightened to say he'd asked Jack to get a few lads together for a couple of days' work in Bury. Jack would say he'd collected two and was calling on the Turk to see if he fancied it. It was half feasible, and they were desperate anyway. The alternative was fifteens all round. Jack was on the book so there wasn't much he could do. He needed someone sound to put the escape together and asked if I could get the Turk out.'

'You could have got yourself a right trade if you went the other way.'

'It was a big mark of respect and I knew it, and I owed him from Foston Hall and after, so I gave it a lot of thought. Spent a good few nights lying on my bed and thinking over all the angles. The main problem was that the Turk was on the book with the rest of them – double bars, light on all night, hourly check, screw in constant attendance when he was out of his cell.

'But we had one big advantage, and it was this: the Turk wasn't a proper villain. Half the time they upgrade people to the book in Strangeways just because the facilities are there. And things were quiet then, no cop-killers, no serial nutters. Just Jack and his crew. That's why all four of them were made Cat A, and Cat A was now full. Their trial wasn't for another six months, so there was a good chance that some proper villains would come inside in the meantime and go on the book – and that made the Turk favourite to go downstairs. Then he'd lose the screw and all the rest of the cobblers and we'd have half a shout.'

'Half a shout if you were lucky.' Leon stretched out the thermos and I held my cap under the lip. 'More coffee?'

'OK, but half a shout is better than none. And there were still a lot of *what ifs*. We needed tungsten blades to cut the bars on his cell and they were impossible to get. He'd have to drop down out of the cell. There were the dog patrols, once an hour at least. And then he had to get over the perimeter wall, and he'd need help outside, a passport to get out of the country, and a flop to keep his head down until the scream was off and he could move.'

Leon smiled and took a sip of his coffee.

'Well, it was a bad summer that year, it was pretty wet. I was sleeping badly, and I'd been watching the night patrols from my cell for something to do. I noticed they usually skipped them when it was coming down heavily. So if the weather kept on being crap and we chose the night, the Turk probably wouldn't have to worry about the dogs. But the main thing, and the biggest reason I thought we might have a chance was this: Big Norman, Norman the Dummy. Ever meet him?'

'I've heard you mention him.'

'Dead now, God rest his soul. He was in for ringing motors. Made a beeline for me the first day I came in. Script was that he was the censors' trustee, a redband; he swept the floor and made the tea for them. A sound member wouldn't normally get that job, but the screws thought Norman was retarded. Wasn't me who called him Norman the Dummy. Just because he spoke a bit slow. Anyway, he had a scam going. It wasn't just the cons' mail that came into the censors' office, there was a whole lot of other stuff as well – admin for the works and the other departments, you name it. Because the screws were lazy, the letters used to pile up in a tray Big Norm had access to, so he had the odd bit of contraband sent in under false names and whipped the envelopes when the coast was clear. He fancied me enough to put me in on the swindle, so I started getting a bit of blow sent in for the pair of us. Now I needed something else, so we made a meet and I propped him about getting some tungsten blades sent in. He went for it, and we were in business.

'Passports I could sort – someone was slipping them out of Liverpool for me in those days. Just had to get a smudge of the Turk and a new DOB over to the guy who did them up in Kirkby – remember him?'

Leon nodded.

'Well, that bit could wait until he was over the wall – if the coup didn't work, he wouldn't be needing a passport for a long time. So I got Jack to put down for the dentist and squared it with the medical orderly to put me on the same day. By rights, Jack's screw should have been next to us, but I knew he was a lazy bastard like all the rest. Sure enough, he preferred drinking tea in with the medical staff. I filled Jack in with the details and told him to sort the outside personnel for the night and get fifteen hundred to Quiet John to pay the passport guy.

'When the time came, Jack would need a couple of his lads over by the croft and waiting on B wing yard, on top of the tunnel. Then they could sling a rope over on a whistle from the Turk and haul him up. It was still very fifty-fifty, but with Norm and the blades and the weather, you might put a few quid on it now. Jack went and had his teeth cleaned with big thanks all round.

'Anyway, a few weeks later, there was a massive haul of smack at Birch services on the M62. The mob who were pulled for it got the full Cat A treatment and the Turk went downstairs on normal location, along with a couple of others. We waited till the long range forecast was rain for a few days, and the blades came in.

'I was fucking sweating it on the night, Leon. Up on my bed staring up at the stars, it was fucking cloudless. Then at two, dead on, it started to piss down. Even with the storm, I could swear I heard every stroke of the hacksaw as the Turk did the bars. I couldn't have done of course, he was right away on the other side of the nick, but I was bricking it till dawn. And then they opened us up for breakfast and it was all hands on deck. One Turk short, and the whole place on lockdown. He flopped down on a place I'd sorted for a couple of days, the passport came across, and he decided to give the Crown a full body-swerve and legged it to Istanbul.'

I stopped because I could feel Leon's eyes on me. I turned and he was shaking his head. 'So that was you? Even made the English language rag in Marbella. And you did it. Bloody hell, mate. Only bloke ever to get out of Strangeways.'

'Not quite. There was a geezer in the eighties who legged it on a forged bail warrant when he came in on remand, but – er – yeah. The Turk was down to me.'

'Fucking hell. And what happened to Jack?'

'They got the result. Dumped it on the Turk and walked four months after I walked from Chester Crown on my bit of bother. Big Norman didn't stop smiling from the day the screws opened up A wing that Sunday morning and found the roll was light by one.'

Leon emptied his dregs on to the grass and screwed the cap on his thermos. 'And I take it they all lived happily ever after?'

'All except Keith Hamilton Jacks. Detective sergeant then, he'd done all the graft on the pull and thought he was set up for a big piece of glory. Shall we walk a bit?'

We cruised round the lake. The walkers had gone while we'd been talking and the two kids were playing *Star Wars* fighting with a couple of branches for light sabres.

Leon was looking thoughtful. 'How could Hamilton Jacks know it was you that put the work together?'

'I've been trying to work that out. There was a big party at the Midland when Jack and his crew got off, everyone invited, including me.'

'So?'

'Officially, the bash was a fundraiser for some washed-up alkie who'd played for City. Plenty of straightgoers to hide us in the forest – one or two telly celebs, some City and United players, a few page three girlfriends, even the odd councillor. But off in a side room there was this other party going on, with me as the guest of honour. Quiet John was there, so was Sandra – the then Mrs Keane – and one or two others, people off Jack's firm. And Sara, of course. The inner circle. And that's where it happened.

'It was getting late, I had to be up by five, and we were about to say our goodbyes when Jack raps his knuckles on an ice bucket and calls for a bit of hush. "Listen," he says. "I've got something to say before the party breaks up." Then he walks across the room and puts his arm round my shoulder, smelling of cigar smoke and booze. "All right," he says. "I want to see everyone fill their glasses. Go on." Faces and heads did as they were told, and then he says, "This is the man that made it all possible – why I'm here, all the rest. It's all down to him." Then he raises his glass. "No, no," I say. "Here's to the idle screws, Jack. It was down to them, not me."'

'He said that?'

'He was pissed. I remember Sara shooting me a look that said, *What's he playing at?* And then they all drank to my cleverness. That must be when it got out.' I stuck a fag in my mouth and lit up. 'It's always worried me. Seems I was right.'

'And years later – I mean ten whole years later – Hamilton Jacks tells Steph and Jan that Tomas's death is down to you?'

'The simple fact he stuck it on me at all means it's a possibility. I've had nothing else to do with him.'

'Yeah.' Leon wasn't convinced. 'So who's calling you a grass, then? Is that Jacks as well?'

I stood up. 'Guess it could be.' I'd suddenly had enough of trying to piece everything together. 'Come on, I think it's going to rain again.'

We headed for the cars. 'So what do we do now?' asked Leon.

'I need to speak to Jack.'

From the outside, Bowlers didn't look much different from the rest of the Lego warehouses on what was once the biggest industrial estate in the world. Hidden round the back of the *Daily Telegraph* plant, it only stood out because of the traffic – taxis and everything from rollers to bangers held together with string, all spilling the punters on to the space outside the foyer.

I'd called up after I'd left Leon at the water park, and yes, there were fights on tonight. There was a good chance Jack would be here, and I couldn't sit around waiting for him to call. My ticket with the working stiffs and non-faces cost me a score. Jack, of course, would be way up the front if he was there, probably ringside. I'd have to catch him at the bar.

The second fight of the evening was already half done when I sat down. The programme told me it was a featherweight bout between a local lad and a scouser. Not a bad scrap – plenty of atmosphere, considering. The next two were bill fillers, with none of the contestants looking up for it. Then the lights went up and an interval was declared. I stood and scanned the crowd. Mostly young men, not many over thirty. Casual dress, with the odd sharp suit here and there and a few trophy birds in tow. I never knew a married man take his wife to the boxing.

I didn't recognise Jack at first because he'd shaved his head. It was the movement of his crew I noticed. There were about half a dozen of them and they seemed to move from the ringside as one, with Jack at the front walking with his shoulders as he glided through the crowd, breaking stride to gladhand some face or other, or share a joke and a nailed-on grin with someone else. He was in a black knitted shirt, open at the neck, understated cream suit with low-placed buttons, middle one done up to make a deep sharp V of black down his body. His retinue of smartly dressed faces and truck-wide minders seemed to know just when he'd stop and start, there was no visible ripple of them coming to a halt or seeing when he shifted again; they just moved like they had the one shared mind and it was leading from the front.

The firm passed through the crowd to a set of double doors at the back, guarded by four fit stewards who checked the punters' wrists as they went through. I threaded after them, tucking in just behind and saw them flash their lurid green wristbands at the sentries. Jack was without, but the stewards still let him through with nods of deference and a few words of recognition.

I gave it a minute, then walked up to the minder who'd spoken to Jack and pointed to my bare wrist. 'I'm with Jack Keane, mate. Band must have slipped off.' The guy tapped me on the shoulder, then he flashed a grin.

'No sweat, pal. In you go.'

I stepped through. The room was busy with drink and chat. There was a long buffet on the right with a couple of cooks dishing out food. A cramped bar to the left and a big video screen at back showing Sky and Barry McGuigan rabbiting to a presenter ringside. Then I saw Jack again. He was sat at a long table with a reserved sign and plenty of booze, talking to a couple of his faces. His nut was tipped to one side and his right hand was spread out on the cloth in front of him, long and brown and broad like a display of expensive cigars. The years and the nick had been kind to him. He was tanned and he looked well and fit and hard. And prosperous. There was obviously still plenty of money in heroin, and he'd always left taking the stuff to the punters.

I waved at him and for a second he looked puzzled, then he pushed his face into a grin and waved *Come over*. As I moved, he said something to the face on his left. The guy looked at me, then he left his seat for a spare space at the end of the table, not looking entirely happy with the move.

I went across and he stood and we shook.

'Jack.'

Then he grabbed me in a Brando bear hug, burying his head in my shoulder and clamping the breath out of me. I still caught a tang of expensive cologne and sweat. 'Good to see you, son,' he said, coming up for air. 'Been a long fucking time.' He pulled me down into a seat.

'I'm sorry, son, I had a message you called. Only just got back, had to come straight up here. I was gonna ring you tomorrow morning.'

He always called me son. I stood for it. I owed him.

'Good to see you, Jack.' And it was.

'And you, son, and you. Have a drink.'

The cloth was crowded with bottles of Dom Perignon crunched into silver ice buckets.

'When did you get out?'

'Friday, Jack.'

He grunted, stretched across me, popped open a bottle with his shovel of a thumb, filled a glass and pushed it across the table. A few drops spilled over and ran down the stem. 'Cheers,' I said.

'Absent friends.'

We drank, he knocked half his back, then rested the glass on the cloth in the crook of his thumb and forefinger.

'It's been a while, Jack.'

'Yeah. Still, we always picked up again, didn't we?'

'Yes.'

'Ever since Foston Hall.'

'Yes.'

'Did you know it was a woman's nick now?'

'I'd heard.' I took another sip of the booze. Very cold, very quality. 'Where were you?' I said. 'On the last one, I mean.'

'Here first, of course. Then Walton, back to Strangeways, Garth, Risley, then Sudbury.'

'You're looking well.'

'Eight years of weights, son.'

'How was it?'

'How do you think? Did all the courses and gave all the right answers at the start, so I went through the system sharpish. I was working outside at Sudbury, digging little old ladies' gardens for a few seasons. Then parole on the eight, at the halfway mark. You know how it is.'

'Yeah. You look well though,' I repeated. I could tell he was waiting for me. 'OK Jack, this isn't altogether a coincidence bumping into you here. There's something going on. The cozzer Hamilton Jacks is making himself busy.' I felt the hate like I'd opened a boiler room door.

'That prick.'

'Yeah. Him.'

'What's going on?'

'It'll take a while.'

'It's all right, I can miss the first fight after the break. I know the result already. Where are you sat?'

'In the hall with the stiffs.'

'Wait here.'

He stood and moved to the end of the table and had a few words with the guy he'd ordered to shift when I arrived. He nodded at Jack. He'd obviously said yes, but once again, he wasn't pleased. Jack came back down my end.

'He'll go with the punters. When we're done, you can come and sit with me, ringside.'

I gave him the tale from start to finish. All I left out was Uncle's name. He stared at me when I was done, then flicked his gaze away and back before speaking.

'Sorry about your nephew, son. Are you sure it was Hamilton Jacks who's after you for this?'

I pulled out the cutting from the *Evening News* and passed it over. He scanned it quickly.

'Hamilton fucking Jacks, eh. What about that?' He looked at me. 'So what do you want from me, son?'

Now I felt I was walking on eggshells. It's a straight face rule that you don't criticise what another man does for a living, and I was here because Jack did class A for a living and I hoped he'd be able to point the way towards why Tomas got killed, or at least the country he died in. But Tomas would only matter to Jack because he was my nephew; in Jack's game people got shot and sometimes people died. The booze on the table, the ringside seats, his understated cream suit, his deferential retinue and all his respect from the other faces – it all came to him because there were smackheads lying on their backs in Moss Side and Stockport, Newcastle, Liverpool and beyond, rattling and shaking, trying to focus the scraps of their scag-fried brains on what they'd sell or who'd they'd thieve from for their next bag.

'Tomas was a good kid, Jack. Lou and Sam loved him, and if they think I was connected with what happened, I may never see them again. I don't want any revenge, I just have to find out so I can tell them. Can you help me with whatever knowledge you can? It's your world, Jack. I need a lift, some pointers, anything.'

Jack shifted forward a few inches and took off his wedding ring. It was a simple gold band which he laid on the cloth. I never wore one.

'I'll see what I can do. But, listen, this is no offence to Tomas, mate – but we're talking lowlife here.'

'Can you help me, Jack – yes or no?'

He picked up a drinks coaster and weighed it in his right hand, then started to flip it from broad finger to broad finger like he was rolling a roulette chip. 'I'll ask around.'

'I also need to know who's calling me a grass, Jack. Can you ask around there as well?'

'That's an evil thing, grass-calling. But for what it's worth, I've not heard a word said against you.'

'Thanks. And last: what do you know about Hamilton Jacks?'

'He's nicked me twice and the cunt hates me.'

'Is that all?'

'He's just another fucking ambitious cozzer.'

'He must be after me because of the Turk. I've never met him otherwise.'

'How would he know about the Turk?'

'The booze-up afterwards Jack, the celebration for you walking. Was there anyone there you've ever had a question mark about since?'

He drummed a brief, irritated tattoo on the tablecloth.

'No. No question marks. They were all my firm and Quiet John. Quiet John's dead, and the rest are sound. I've always been lucky with my friends, son.'

'So you don't know anything else about Hamilton Jacks?'

The coaster flipped over his thumb and started its journey back again. 'I will ask around, but look; if Hamilton Jacks worded your nephew's mam and dad – for whatever reason – the chances are he's also putting it about that you're a grass. And as for your Tomas, if Hamilton Jacks has the horn for you already and finds out the lad's your nephew, then maybe he just took a chance to make mischief and stuck it on you with his mam and dad.'

'Maybe.'

'Are you going to do anything about him?'

I didn't answer. Jack stopped rolling and leant in closer.

'Do you know how many unsolved police murders there's been in the last century?'

'No.'

'I do. One. Think about it. The weight they put on a cozzer being killed.' Jack snapped the coaster in two, then four and dropped it on the cloth.

'Are you sure you're not seeing a connection where there ain't none? Maybe the gear in your cell was some Nazi screw you upset somewhere down the line. Kept a few wraps back from another find. Easy enough.' He stretched for the bucket and filled our glasses again. 'And your old lady fucks off, well they do that, don't they?'

The sound of booing came up from the auditorium. Jack turned his head for a second, then looked back at me and jerked his nut towards the noise.

'Fucking pansies. Now a woman, she hits you where it hurts. You know Sandra divorced me while I was away?'

'No.'

'After everything I did for her and that bunch of parasites she calls a family.'

He put his glass down and moved it a couple of squares on an imaginary chessboard.

'Hamilton Jacks put the cuffs on me for the last caper, with the lad Sonny Jim. You met him.'

'I remember.'

'Wasn't his fucking case, either. Bastard walked all over the drugs squad to nick me personally. Prick.'

He looked at his watch, then slid his wedding ring back on his finger and pulled a business card out of his breast pocket. Video shop in Blackley.

'That's a better number to reach me on, but I've got yours anyway. I'll start tomorrow, get back to you as soon as I can. You still in Chorlton?'

'Not just now, keeping away for a bit.'

'Quite right too. Now come on, son. I don't want to miss the next fight.'

We pushed into the main hall and sat ringside as the music came up – *Eye of the Tiger*, one of them always uses it. He had to push close and shout the rest.

'This is light heavyweight. A Wigan boy and one from here, and it's a real needle match. Wigan's wife fucked off with the Manchester lad a few months ago. Take it from me, this fight will not go the distance.'

He was right, it was war from the first bell.

The Manchester kid did well at first – he pinned his opponent in the corner of the ring, raining in blows to the head and body, every thud of the glove sending a fan of sweat up and out into the air. But halfway through the third, Wigan started to come back. His handful of travelling supporters started to scream their man on, and the aggro spilled out into the crowd. A fight broke out, and the stewards – a right bunch of heavies themselves – waded in, putting their weights between the two sides and handing out slaps all round.

By the start of the fifth, it was clear that although he'd lost his wife, the Wigan boy wasn't about to lose the fight. The local lad was trapped in the corner now, leaning back on the ropes and stanchion and the front row was being spattered with blood every time another punch landed on his mess of a face. One or two of the punters were shouting at the referee to end it, but mostly they were baying for more. This was no longer a contest and it should have been stopped. I turned towards Jack to tell him what I was thinking. 'Jack,' I shouted. 'Jack.'

He didn't hear me. His eyes were bright and staring and he was half crouching forward out of his seat, fists clenched, pumping at the air to the beat of the blows landing above us.

Then, rather than words came the thought of Jack kneeling, on the canvas in front of us, licking the blood off the fallen fighter, long slow sensual tongue strokes like a cat licking salt block.

I'd had enough. I leant into Jack's ear and shouted I had a meet on and had to go. 'I'll ring you, Jack.'

He thumbed up at me and I split as the towel went in from Manchester's corner. It occurred to me as I'm sure it must have occurred to Wigan – now bouncing around on the apron and punching the air for the cheering mob – that if Mrs Wigan had fancied the Manchester boy on his looks alone, she might be having second thoughts when he got home.

There were no cabs to be had outside, so I walked. It was starting to rain again.

*

Nine years ago.

The door swung open and there was a young Asian guy, suited and booted, in the frame. About thirty, thick hair, shot cuffs, gold tiepin and an aftershave that could blister paint. 'Who are you here for?'

'Mr Webster.'

'John Webster?'

'I never learnt his first name.'

The Asian smiled widely. 'Jack told me you'd be on time. On the stroke, he said. Come in.'

He pulled the door right back, and I could see it gave into a wide whitewashed corridor. I stepped in and he locked up behind me.

'I'm Sonny, Sonny Jim, Jack calls me, and I'm very pleased to meet you.'

A well-manicured handshake, another wave of aftershave.

'The place is empty. Follow me.'

We did a couple of corners into the main showroom – hundreds of jeans and shirts in clear plastic bags on racks running from here to Stockport. A few lights so we could find our way, otherwise dim enough to hide in. Sonny twisted left and we clanked up a dozen or so steel steps leading to a cabin with a commanding view of the schmutter house.

'This is my office,' he said as we echoed up. 'I like to keep an eye on my investment.'

A brown slab of a desk dominated the room at the top and Jack Keane was leaning on it. Tanned as usual, with his wavy brown hair combed forward. He unfolded as I came in. 'On the dot, just like I said. Didn't I say he'd be on the dot, Sonny Jim?'

'You did, Jack.'

Jack was doing some kind of Father Christmas act. He shook my hand, then kept hold and pulled me and Sonny together. 'Shake, both of you.' He laid his paw on top of my and Sonny's clasp. 'We're trusting each other with years of our lives.'

Then he let go and marched back to the desk. Sonny dropped me with another puff of scent and said, 'Drink? Beer or tea or coffee?'

'No thanks.'

'Let's talk.'

Jack waved us down into a couple of armchairs. It was Sonny's office, but he was in charge.

'I'll come to the point.' He was talking to me first. 'Me and Sonny have been getting a nice few quid out of the blow game for the last couple of years.

'Sonny no one knows about. Just me, and one other member. And now you. Now, here's the deal: I've not been on the pavement for eighteen months, son. And I don't intend to go back. This is the game to be in. This is where the money's going to be in the future.' He paused, looking like he was holding for a photo. Then he went on.

'We're going to expand, start a new operation. It's the future, son. A new source, and it's all ours. New buyers, too. I'm not going to sack the old business, but this one's going to be a lot bigger. I'm talking serious money. With you on a full whack. I know how to pay back favours, son, and I owe you.'

It was a good plot. The blow was to come in via a very safe route and stored in one of Sonny's slaughters. Jack wanted me to run the distribution chain through Liverpool, Newcastle and maybe Glasgow – and to collect the dough. I could use my own couriers, have as many cut-outs between me and the dope as I wanted.

The key to the whole operation was Jack's new source: he was talking about each of us clearing around a hundred grand a load – with regular shipments. Serious money; it had to be half a ton a time for blow.

'Do you want time to think about it?' Jack was looking very smug.

'No. Sounds right to me. You've done well with the source, Jack. Good blow's hard enough to find, especially in the kind of bulk you're talking about.'

'Hold up.' Jack was looking confused.

'What?'

'I think we've got our wires crossed a bit here, son. I'm not talking about blow. I'm talking about brown. Heroin, direct from Pakistan. I thought you'd got that.'

My head clouded over inside. *Fuck*, I thought. *Why didn't I tipple?*

Why didn't I stop him before he gave me the full story and pictures? Fuck.

I thought of the look on Sonny's face when I knocked them back the next minute, knocked them back because I wouldn't have anything to do with the brown. Jack tried to persuade me into it – I couldn't tell if he was trying to save face with Sonny or if he was really trying to talk me round. Didn't make any difference, it was still a no.

'You know I've forgotten all this, Jack,' I said at one point. He was OK about it, Sonny not. Too late now, anyway.

Jack saw me back to the door.

'Sorry, mate. I'm sorry.'

'It's history,' said Jack. 'Forgotten. Be lucky.'

They weren't as it happened. Six months, and it was on top. Jack was nicked first, Sonny Jim and the rest of the firm a few days later. Fifteens all round, eight with parole. I was away on my toes when it happened, they were all locked up by the time I heard. Hadn't seen Jack since, until tonight. But we went back a long way.

4

Monday, nine o'clock. I was at the Queens Hotel in Leeds under a moody name and ringing a corrupt brief.

'Hazlitt and Partners?' The girl on the switch was in my ear.

'Mr Hazlitt, please.'

'He's away for a couple of days.'

'Does he have a mobile?'

'Can't give it out. He doesn't like it.'

I gave her my number and hung up. Morrie Hazlitt had never represented me but he knew me and my game. He'd suss this would be about an earner. He'd be in touch.

I'd woken at five and decided to head for Leeds, to look for the kids. Took me five minutes to sling some stuff together and get on the road. I was checked in for a couple of days – Manchester was only about forty minutes down the motorway and I could whip back if anything came up. They were the most important thing, anyway.

My phone rang. I answered and got heavy traffic noise, then Morrie's voice.

'Long time since I heard from you, sir. What can I do for you?'

Over the roar of the motors, Morrie told me he was on his way to Huddersfield for the magistrates that morning, representing two lads who'd turned over a Yorkshire tommers.

'I'm going for an old-style committal. Might get it struck out, I told them. More chance of Huddersfield Town winning the European Cup with ten men.'

'When are you back?' All I got was the thunder of an HGV as

it overtook him. 'I said, when are you back, Morrie?'

'Tomorrow.'

I shouted did he want dinner that evening, got a yes and we made a meet. Then I sat at the desk with a Yellow Pages and a streetfinder. I lit up and cracked the A to Z.

Annie the estate agent said Sara was in Leeds. She'd been at university here and still had some friends local, but I didn't think she'd flop on them – that would make her too easy to find. And I knew she had a long stocking so she could afford to rent. The twins were the key. She wouldn't want them out of school long.

I flattened the book at the area map of the city and scored out the south side and a couple of other areas I knew she didn't like. Then I opened the Yellow Pages and flipped to Letting Agents, picked up the room phone this time and dialled.

I was now a potential punter in the same income bracket as Sara. I was looking for a three bedroomed house, on a short lease, around the north of the city – Headingley, Roundhay, Oakwood – and I wanted to be near at least one good school. Probably because I was at a half-decent hotel (and let the drum-letters know that by getting them to ring me back) the agents indulged me. By half two I had a good idea of where Sara could afford to dwell and the schools she'd be looking at. Then I thought of Lou and Sam walking into some classroom on their first day; saw thirty odd pairs of eyes look them up and down for the first time. I said, 'I love you both, you know that, don't you? That's why I'm here.' A hoover started up in the corridor.

Two schools kept going straight in at number one according to the drum-letters, so I decided to take the biggest, washed my face with cold water and left.

School number one was about half a mile west of Roundhay Park. Only the one entrance, which was a touch. I joined the motors already parked up outside the main gates, cracked the window and opened a newspaper for cover. It was twenty past three.

Dead on half past a trickle started, building quickly to a wave of green and grey blazers and skirts. These were the lower years. The twins were older, and in any case, by the time you hit seventeen it's considered most uncool to steam out of school like an express train. The uniforms dried up and a few older ones cruised out, girls in pairs and the odd couple wrapped round each other. Then I thought I saw them. My two, bobbing along in the centre of a knot of other kids; Sam's tight black curls and Lou's looser waves because she'd started pulling her hair straight when she was four. He was head down, ferreting around in his bag; she had hers tilted, talking to a girl in a baseball cap on her left.

I gripped the doorhandle just as a bus spluttered to a stop right beside me, trapping me in the motor. I wriggled over the handbrake and passenger seat and pulled myself out kerbside, snapping round to search the two of them out through the bus windows. All I could see was traffic and bobbing heads, more buses, kids getting on and off, dozens, scores of them, where were Lou and Sam?

The bus pulled away and I jumped back into the motor, wrenched myself behind the wheel and fired the engine – just as a long white van pulled up and boxed me in again. I cranked my window furiously and shouted up at the driver. 'Fuck's sake, move. I'm in a hurry!'

A spiny lad looking like a rat in a donkey jacket felt brave enough up behind his wheel to shout back, 'Think I'm gonna fucking fly across this lot? Cunt!' He flicked a V sign and pulled away.

I sank back into the car and breathed her name. 'Lou.' I knew it was them. I couldn't be sure it was them. But I knew it was them. I looked at my hands and noticed the dirt under my nails and a tiny red scratch across the back of a knuckle. I couldn't think where I'd got it.

I sat in the car till gone five, just in case one of them came back. Then a caretaker from central casting – short grey overalls, tab stuck to his lower lip with glue – appeared in the pool of street lights, clanged the gates shut and locked them from inside. A few seconds later, the playground spots went out.

I drove to the hotel, showered and went out to meet Morrie.

The brief was sitting in the bar when I showed, wearing grey pinstripes and dandruff snow on his collar. He saw me and unrolled his six-foot-plus frame from the leather upholstery. 'You're looking well sir,' he said.

'All right, Morrie.'

We shook and went into the restaurant. As the waiters fluttered around bringing menus and wine list, I tried to make small talk.

'How's it looking for your lads?'

He shook his head slowly. He was concentrating on the menu. 'No,' he said. 'Just as expected. Excuse me, sir.'

He wasn't going anywhere, just focusing on his nosebag. He said he never did business over food, so I had to sit through forty-five minutes each way of slack-jawed chomping before he waved in a brandy and took a half smoked cigar out of a red leather case.

'Now,' he said. 'You wanted to talk about something.' He sparked up, sucking noisily.

'There's a cozzer who seems to have it right in for me Morrie,' I said. 'I need to know why, and anything else you could find out about him.'

He sucked a bit more, looking at me over the smoke. 'What sort of thing? Asking specific questions draws a lot of attention. Too much for you, I'd have thought.'

'Get what you can. Is he bent, is he straight? Does he like a drink, a bird, a bet. If he does, who does he play with? Is he married? And I want to know where he lives.'

More sucking and smoke. 'Are you planning to hurt him? His family?'

'No. You've got my word on that. And I'll pay well, as usual. Are we on, or do you want to think about it?'

He took his time. About four seconds. 'Five hundred plus the dinner.'

Corruption. I love it.

'So who is it?'

'Jacks,' I said. 'Hamilton Jacks. Detective Chief Superintendent.'

Morrie looked smug. 'Keith Hamilton Jacks. I know him. Or rather, I know of him. Do you know the Bull in Hale Barns?'

'Yeah.'

'If you can be there tomorrow evening about six I should have something for you.'

The waiter chose that moment to bring the bill. Perhaps because he looked more affluent, he laid it in front of Morrie. With a discreet cough, the brief slid it across the table to me.

An hour later, I was at the hotel hitting Leon's number. He picked up on the first ring. No *hello*, just: 'Any luck?'

'Maybe.' I told him what happened at the school. 'But I can't be there tomorrow afternoon. Can you sit on it at three? I've got to pick up that parcel and I've got an urgent meet out of town at six.'

'No problem. I can do lunchtime as well.'

'Are you sure, Leon?'

'I told you, we're working together on this and as it happens, I've got a quiet day, OK? Do your stuff and we'll meet in the evening. Get me on the mobile.'

I gave him directions to the school and hung up, feeling troubled.

I sacked it at nine fifteen next morning. Complete waste of time. There was a light drizzle so most of the kids walked with their hoods up and heads down. By ten I'd gone back to the service flat in Prestwich, dumped the Rover and got a cab across to Laurie's car shop. If Morrie got me Hamilton Jacks's address, I was going to sit on the place. The Rover was down to me, so it couldn't go on show. I needed another motor.

Laurie ran a small car hire outfit. Most of his trade was straight, but he did the odd rent for a bit of work. Of course the ID had to stand up in case it went reels and the smoker had to be left behind. Any screw-ups there, and it wouldn't be long before he'd be on an insurance blacklist. But Laurie knew the game. If it came on top he developed sudden short term memory loss and just couldn't remember what the hirer looked like.

The cab dropped me off at the chainlink fence that ran round the yard. There was a Portakabin office with a few steps leading up. Laurie must have clocked the motor because he leant out the door and waved me in.

'Ah. Ahhhaahhhahh ah,' he said as I came up the steps.

'All right, Laurie?'

He stuck out his hand. 'Very well, thanks.'

Laurie was tall like a crane with thinning hair he combed over Bobby Charlton-style. I followed him as he loped through the outer office past Hattie on reception and into his room at the back.

'You'll be having a cup of tea?'

'Thanks.'

He selected a couple of comic mugs from the line of comic mugs on the shelf. He took Bart Simpson, I got Buffy the Vampire Slayer. 'So, how've you been?' he asked, standing my tea in front of me.

'Well, I'm just out now. So you know how it is.'

'Ah, right, right.' Laurie didn't. But he made the effort to empathise. I asked about a car.

'It's only to look at a bit of work. Ninety-nine per cent certain the wheels will be back safe and clean. I'm a bit short of spare ID, though.'

'No problem, there's an Escort you can use. One and a half a week, eh?'

'You'll take a oner on top?'

'Ahh. Aahhaa. I've told you before,' he flicked a grin. 'You will never embarrass me by giving me money.'

I stood up. 'Another thing, Laurie. Do us a favour and don't mention you've seen me. Keeping a low profile at the minute.'

I unrolled the cash on to his desk. He stood and trousered it, then unhooked the keys from a board on the wall behind him. 'Never saw a thing.'

Like Dougie the car salesman, Laurie liked being close to villains. So do a lot of straightgoers, I've noticed.

'Au pairs. Leg over. Yes or no?'

Casey was standing at his dining-room window looking out at the garden and tugging at his beard.

'What do you mean?'

I'd come about the dough for the parcel, but he'd insisted I stay for a brew. Now it seemed he wanted my advice.

'I mean. If a twenty-two-year-old Spanish bird strokes your leg and says she wants to see you naked, do you say yes or no?'

I didn't need this. I was busy and counselling my fence was not on the agenda. I looked at him over my cup – OK, he was in pretty good shape but he was still a dad and not about to trouble Brad Pitt in the handsome shop. I'd seen Marta the au pair pruning a pear tree in the garden when I parked up. She was whip thin and a right looker.

'Are you sure you heard her right, Casey?'

'Yes, I did.' He cleared his throat. 'Last week, she'd just come in from a night on the town, I was locking up. We were sat down in the front room having a bit of a chat, then she ran her fingers up inside my leg and sort of danced them on my crotch and said, "Do you want to go in bed with me?" Been thinking about it ever since. Can't get it out of my head.'

'She'd probably just had a few. Has she ever come on to you before?'

'Never. Not a thing. Jesus, look at that.'

I went and looked over his shoulder. She was now bent over tugging at some weeds.

'She's a pretty girl, Casey, but I wouldn't risk it. What about Stella?'

'What about her?'

I went back to my seat. 'Your wife. Stella, your wife.'

He broke away from the window and made like he was thinking. 'What if she does it again? The crotch dance, I mean.'

'Make sure you're not alone with her as much as possible, she'll get the idea. That you're not interested.'

'Blimey, mate.' He was looking out the window again and his tongue was hanging down to his belt. I bolted the rest of my brew.

'Don't mess with other women, Casey. You'll end up without the house, sitting outside in the car at weekends and blowing the horn for the kids to come out and see you.'

I picked up the briefcase he'd given me – thirty-nine grand in tens and twenties. The other twenty to come next Friday. 'I've got to go now.' I left him to it.

I called Harry from the car. She took a few rings to answer.

'Can I drop round?'

'Not now. Busy with a client. Come at four, not before, yeah? Got that? Not before.'

'Sure, Harry. Whatever you say.'

Someone must be having the full executive relief treatment. I gunned the Escort and pulled out. Well, bugger. She was just round the corner and all I wanted to do was drop off the dough I'd borrowed from her when I got out. OK, I'd go to Amy's now and stick this briefcase down. I swung the car towards Ladybarn.

Amy was my safe house. Sixty-eight years old, she was a Czech who'd once been called Agnieszka and had dyed black hair that fooled nobody. As usual, she greeted me like I was the second coming and fussed me into the back room. Rynka her Jack Russell leapt and yapped round our ankles as she put the kettle on. Christ, no more tea.

I used to do business with Amy's husband. He was called Conrad and he'd spied for the British during the Cold War. When things got too hot for them in the East, they split for England, only to be fucked off by their spook handlers. 'Ten years I work for them, OK?' Conrad told me once. 'They teach me lie, cheat, steal. And I risk my life, Amy does same, OK? Then the British fuck me off. Now I cheat and steal from country who taught me. One good joke.' Conrad was dead ten years now, too young at sixty.

Amy kissed me three times. 'You hungry? You must be hungry. They never feed you in prison.'

'I'm fine.'

'No, you thin again. You need eat more. You want your doings?'

'Please.'

She waved the dog out of its bed into the garden and I shifted the basket, folded back the carpet and felt for the canvas bag under the boards. I stuffed in most of my cash from the Casey parcel and all of Terry's. I didn't intend to declare the accounts to the boy for now. I wanted to know what he was sticking up his nose first. I put everything back and gave Amy a oner.

'Bingo for a week,' I said.

'Bingo? No, no need.'

'Come on, Amy. Just a couple of nights out. As a thank you.'

'I have pension. You a friend of Conrad, why take money like this? No.'

'Because your pension's rubbish and you're doing me a favour. All right then, if you win on it, we can split the prize.'

'Now this is small gamble. Investment. OK.'

She always said yes eventually. Not that she was in it for the dough; she was more sweet on being part of the game.

Leon rang as I was parking up for Harry's.

'Anything?' I barked into the mouthpiece. A bunch of background noise but nothing else. 'Leon?'

'I'd have called you if there was. What makes you so sure about this place, anyway?'

'I saw them, remember?'

I felt him shrug down the line.

'If you say. Well, there was nothing. Couldn't have missed 'em either. Only a few came out, all older looking. Sixth formers probably. No sign of our two.'

Our two.

'And there's something else,' he said. 'Forgot. Terry rang Judith's. Could do without that, mate. Don't want her bothered. Have a word will you? He wants you to ring him at Carol's.'

'I'll deal with him.'

Harry had been edgy because her last client was a copper. His name was Dave Craze, a detective sergeant and a regular john, pleasant and with good manners. He even got a discount for being a regular, she said. And for the manners. 'I assumed you'd rather not be within a hundred miles of the police.'

'No. Thanks, Harry.'

She stuck the roll of notes I'd given her into a blue and white china pot by the sink. 'Tea?'

I'd planned to shoot straight off, but now I changed my mind. 'If you're not busy.'

'Not until the phone rings.'

I stared at her back as she brewed up. She was wearing a silk wrap that stopped just below her buttocks and a pair of high heels. As she poured the milk out she kicked the shoes off and shrank about three inches.

'The living room's warmer.'

We drank our tea in a comfortable silence. I drained my cup and sat looking at the leaves at the bottom. Harry was looking at me. 'What's on your mind?'

Your copper Dave Craze. 'Is he friendly, your policeman?'

A look of complete irritation flicked across her face. 'He's a pleasant client,' she snapped. 'Why do you ask?'

I gave it a couple of beats and then told her a bit of what was going on. I filled her in about Tomas, the children, the brown in my cell.

'That's a lot of grief.' Harry was curled up on the sofa now, all painted toenails and perfect make-up. I noticed the cut line of her lipstick and wondered how she applied it. Not the way Sara did, with quick broad stripes in the hall mirror on the way out the door.

'Well, go on,' she said.

'Is he chatty, this Craze?'

She sighed. 'He is quite full of himself, yes. Likes talking about his work, what he does, who he knows.'

'Any idea which station he works?'

'Bootle Street. He's seen me in a hotel near there a couple of times. In the afternoon.'

'His idea or yours?'

'I know it's Bootle Street. He's been seeing me a couple of years.'

I went for the bite. 'Harry, I know this is a big favour, but Bootle Street is running the investigation into Tomas. Your copper might have heard something, and I need to know where they're going on it. You could say Tomas was a friend of a friend's, someone's mam's worried about their own kids, that sort of thing.'

'You're pushing it a bit now.'

'I know, Harry. But no one's died before.'

She drummed the side of her cup. 'He said he'd be round again at the weekend. He might come before, he might not come at all. But he usually shows once a week at least. I'll see what I can do.'

Her phone rang and she went to answer it. I took the chance to bell Terry for a meet. We spoke briefly. He sounded like a man who wanted his dough. I rang off as Harry appeared at the door.

'It's all right, Harry. I'm just off.'

'Half the punters out of the small ads don't show. You can stay and go if he appears. Or hang on while I do him. Just keep out of sight.'

'No. It's all right.'

She swept up the mugs and walked me to her door. As I stepped out on to the landing, she touched me on the arm. 'I didn't mean to be rude before.'

'I know. It's a lot to ask.'

'I'll do what I can. You're a good man.'

Where did that come from?

'At least, that's what whores like me always say in the movies.'

I went down the stairs wondering how the copper Dave Craze could afford to see Harry once a week at one fifty a throw. Six hundred a month on a sergeant's salary, now where was that coming from?

Back in the smoker, I drove for the hotel where I'd arranged the meet with Terry, thinking he would probably kick off about his dough when we got face to face and he got nish. Well, fuck him. As long as I had his money I had his attention, and that meant I knew where he was. Right now, that's how I wanted him – on a very short leash. And here's why.

Twenty-one months ago.

I was lying on a bench in a police cell in Oldham going nowhere. Terry was in another peter down the corridor. He'd shouted to me a couple of times when they first locked us up, but I'd blanked him. It was an old trick – stick a couple of guys into separate cells and hope they'll show out to each other, giving the listening filth new knowledge in the process. He should have known that. What was the matter with him tonight?

We'd been here since midnight after we got pulled at a roadblock on the Huddersfield-Oldham road. The roadblock was down to a robbery at a jewellery exhibition at the Huddersfield Hilton. We knew this because we'd been sitting up behind a house a few miles away which we were about to burgle. I'd been plugged into a scanner listening to the police bands when D-Day broke out – armed robbery, guard shot, all hands on deck. It would mean the plot would be crawling with filth, so we buried our tools under a water trough and came away.

We took the scanner to know what was going on up ahead and wiped the memory when the jam sandwich came in sight across the road. The button boy got some bunny about us having come from a mate of mine's where we'd talked greyhounds. Everything was sweet until he blimped Terry and saw the boy was sweating buckets. Then he told us to pull off, locked us in their motor and him and his mate gave my Saab a spin. One of them seemed to find something on the deck inside, but I couldn't see too clearly from where we were sat. Ten minutes later we got driven across to the station and locked up. I was expecting the trip because the Saab was down to me, and they'd get my pedigree when they called it in. I didn't expect to be here twelve hours later.

Now there were keys outside, first to the corridor gate, then to my own peter. I sat up as the door opened. No uniforms this time, two plain clothes. Button-popping fat with CID slapped all over them. One leant near the door, the other sat down on the edge of the bunk, a raised block of solid wood, mattress on top. He took out a packet of Benson & Hedges and offered them. I shook no. He lit his own, then studied my face before speaking in a slow, deliberate, almost pantomime Pennine accent.

'Nah then, lad. Tha's probably wondering what this is all ab'aht.'

Surely he didn't really speak like that. No one spoke like that any more.

'Well, I'll put you in t'picture, lad.'

Jesus, he did speak like that. I felt laughter starting up inside.

'When those uniformed lads stopped you, they were looking for a firm that had committed a very serious robbery in which shots were fired, over Huddersfield way.' He took a deep, theatrical drag. Then he went on.

'But you probably know about that, don't you? Probably heard it all on that scanner of yours before you wiped t' memory.'

I said nothing.

'He were nearly going to let you through, was t'uniformed, but there were something about your mate that bothered him, which is why you and your pal were put in't police car.' He dragged deep again and flicked the ash a yard across the floor.

'And look what they found.'

He pulled a small round tin from his jacket pocket, opened it carefully and held it out towards me. I glanced down at it briefly. He licked his pinkie and dabbed it lightly into the tin, then lifted it up again so I could see the white powder speckling the tip.

'You'll know what that is, eh? Our button boy did. They're not all as thick as pig shit up here, *tha' knows.*'

I sensed what was coming. And he was playing up the yokel bit. Which meant he was enjoying it. He brushed the coke off his finger back into the tin, then stuck it in his pocket.

'Oops, where's me manners? Ah'm Detective Sergeant Busby, and this is Detective Constable Breadcake. They call us B and B. For Bastard and Bastard.'

Breadcake laughed at this. I flicked a glance across and back.

'Our lads thought they'd got themselves a pair of drug dealers. That's why they called us in. I didn't think so, though. Not once I'd done me homework. Not thy line of country, is it lad?'

Busby turned his head towards Breadcake before he went on. 'We know what's going on in our lad's head now, don't we mucker?'

Breadcake nodded.

'He's thinking there's nowt down for us two here. If the charlie belonged to his pal, then his pal will stick his hands up to it in court, leaving our friend here wi' nowt but an interrupted weekend to show for our pains.' Busby turned his head back to me and the panto accent evaporated.

'Well, listen to me, you prick, and listen good. I don't know what you and your coke-sniffing pal were up to last night, but sure as shit you weren't over Milnrow talking about fucking greyhounds. You were at it, and you were at it on my fucking patch. Well here's a newsflash. You're not coming out of this one smelling of fucking roses. Because when me and my partner searched that Saab – registered to you – for the second time, we found the following items.' He dug in his pocket and read from his notebook. 'Two crowbars, two screwdrivers, two pairs of gloves, a torch and a roll of Fablon adhesive.' He looked up.

'All these items are obtainable from B&Q stores. And we've confirmed that it is not possible for B&Q to tell us where, when and by who they were purchased.' He dropped the menace and went on, comfortable by now that I had his drift.

'Inside your motor there was also a transmission detecting device known as a scanner. This scanner had been tuned in expertly to receive police wavelengths in the immediate trans-Pennine vicinity.' He shut the notebook and dropped it back in his pocket.

'You'll be charged with going equipped and you'll eventually be tried at Oldham Crown Court by an Oldham jury. Most people around here don't take the view that all coppers are bastards. It'll be you and your mate's word against me and my partner.' He leant in, stinking of fags.

'You're going down, you little prick, and you can take this message with you. Tell all your Manchester burglar mates to keep off my fucking patch. If they're nicked up here, they'll go down as well. Whether the evidence is there or not. You'll be in court Monday morning.' He smiled again. I let him play out his part. There was nothing else for me to do.

'Don't forget to tell your pals to keep off the grass.'

With that, they went away.

Fifteen months we got. Six and a half with remission and the month we did before bail. I got done for the brown in my cell, so I did eighteen. The CPS dropped the charlie on condition we pleaded guilty to going equipped. If we fought the going equipped, they'd do us for possession as well. Juries don't like class A in that part of the world, and they certainly don't like their filth being accused of a fit up, so we'd have sunk without trace. Eighteen bloody months. Eighteen fucking bloody months.

The Posthouse was crowded with suits, checking in after a hard day's repping. I saw Terry curled over an empty glass, pushed through the knots of drinkers and tapped him on the shoulder. He looked up, the aggression in his eyes fading as he saw it was me. 'All right, mate?'

'All right, Terry. Drink?'

'Cheers.'

I bought a pint of lager and a beer. He grinned 'ta' at me, I lit a fag and put the packet on the table. Without asking, he took one and lit up, then laid the lighter on the pack, very gently.

'How's Carol?'

'Sweet, yeah, sweet. Thinks a lot of you.'

'Janey?'

'Left a message on the machine this morning,' he said. 'Couldn't leave her a number, though. Obviously. Going to try her again, maybe slip round tonight.'

I assumed he was lying, just saying what he thought I wanted to hear. 'Well give her my best. When you slip round tonight.'

I pulled a copy of the *Evening News* out of my jacket, folded it tight and laid it on the table. 'There's a twoer in there, against your half of the last parcel. All being well, you'll get the rest in a few days. I'll give you a bell at Carol's when I've drawn. If you're not there, leave a number. I don't want Judith bothered, though. All right?'

He snapped the paper across the table. Here it came. 'No offence, mate, but I'd have thought that parcel should be well sold by now. It's been over a year. Nearly two, as it goes.'

'Remember the scream that went up at the end of that bit of work? The prize was warm. Very warm. The fence knocks it out when it's safe, not before. He knows his job. End of.'

'But I'm right on my arse. That's why I phoned Leon's. Why couldn't

I have collected it while you were in? If I'd had my dough, maybe me and Janey would still be together.'

Fuck this. '*If* you'd collected the dough, it would have been well ironed out by now – up your nose along with my fucking whack. You know you don't meet the buyer. That's the rule.'

'But if –'

'If your auntie had a pair of bollocks,' I hissed, 'she'd be your uncle. How's this for an if; *if* you hadn't stuck that charlie up your nose going on work then we wouldn't have been nicked eighteen months ago. End of story.'

He didn't look happy, but then he had no right to be happy. A year and a half of my life pissed away down to him.

'I've had nothing but blow since I got out.'

'Not interested. If and when I decide we go out again for a pound note, you're getting piss-tested. By me. And you won't be able to swing the ones I'll arrange for you. Do you understand?'

'Yeah.' His eyes went down, his finger traced a pattern on the moisture on his pint. I almost felt sorry for him again. He really was still a kid, even though he'd be twenty-six next month.

'All right,' he said.

I managed to crack out a thin smile of encouragement, I didn't want to force him away from me. I didn't need any more enemies.

'Finish your drink, Terry. I'm going to find a cab. I'll be in touch as soon as I've collected the dough.'

Outside the hotel, I crossed the road then turned and watched the door for a few seconds to make sure he wasn't following me. Then I walked about half a block away from the Escort, checked for him on the pavement again, turned off the main drag and threaded my way back to the motor as quick as I could.

Morrie was sitting in the far corner of the Bull, apparently working his way through a pile of papers. His cigar was dead and there was a nearly full glass of red wine.

'Same again, Morrie?'

'No, thank you. Enough points on my licence already. Couple of bags of crisps, though. Salt and vinegar.'

The bar was sparse of punters. Two minutes later, I was back at his table with my orange juice and his snacks. He tore one bag carefully down the plastic seam and laid it on the table. Then he talked, licking his fingers in between each crisp.

Keith Hamilton Jacks, he told me, was a rising star in the firmament of filth. Chief superintendent in the Regional, and not long from being made assistant chief constable. He was a jock, which was a little bit unusual. There had been a time in the sixties when a Scots mafia ran the CID, and if you didn't wear a kilt on Burns night you had no chance of rising through the ranks. Not these days, though.

'Thanks for the history lesson, Morrie.'

Hamilton Jacks was married with two kids, reckoned straight, not a gambler and didn't have it with birds. He wasn't even a mason.

Morrie kept what he thought was the best bit till last. He must have smelt the monkey in my pocket and wanted to make it quite clear he was worth his fee.

'He's got a thing for a villain called Jack Keane. Ever heard of him?'

Hello. 'I know *of* him, Morrie,' I said carefully.

'Mr Keane really ruined his day some years back. He and his firm walked out of a courtroom on a charge of robbery with violence. I remember the trial quite well. Hamilton Jacks was the then DS who nicked them. Never really smiled again till he did Mr Keane for something else a year or two later. He's quite obsessive from the sound of it.'

'Go on.'

'A young gentleman of Turkish extraction was arrested with Mr Keane and his – er – colleagues. Somehow, the Turk managed to escape from Strangeways and did what they used to call a home run during the war.'

'A what?'

'A home run. Remember the film? *Escape from Colditz?* British prisoners of war all lined up on morning parade, commanding officer marches up the front and says, here's a postcard I think you'd like me to read out. There's a picture of Piccadilly Circus on one side, on the back it says "Home Run, Wish You Were Here. Love Uncle Ted and Auntie Jo." Or in this case, some nice scenic shots of Istanbul and all the best from Uncle Achmet.' He rasped the *ch* sound of Achmet and looked me straight in the eye.

'My firm represented said Turk. Or at least, we did until he escaped. Anyway, a couple of months later, when it came to trial, Mr Keane's firm said it was the one with the swarthy complexion and jellabah that done it, and walked free from the court.' Morrie smiled.

'But Hamilton Jacks had his day. He pulled Mr Keane for importing heroin. Mr Keane went down for fifteen years.' Morrie rustled about in his file as he spoke and, glancing theatrically from side to side, slid a photocopy across the table.

'That's Mr Hamilton Jacks, sir. His address is on the back.'

It was a copy of an article from the *Manchester Evening News* dated a couple of years before. Jacks had been fronting some kind of crime initiative, and he was pictured with a couple of mums from an estate in Didsbury. The accompanying article went on about how Josie Marples and Val Abels could now dance in the streets day and night since new foot patrols had chased the muggers away. I flipped the sheet and read the address in Morrie's tight neat copperplate.

A salty forefinger slipped over the top and tapped the paper. 'He's a zealot. That makes him very dangerous, my friend.'

'Thanks, Morrie.' I slipped his envelope across the table into one of his files. His eyes never left my face.

'You told me you weren't going to hurt him or his family. You'll not let me down, will you? I can only go so far.'

'My word on it, Morrie. My word.'

'Good. Then our business is concluded. Let me go first. I've a meeting at seven thirty.'

'Mind how you go.'

'I'll drive carefully, sir. I always do.' He gathered up his papers, dropped them into his briefcase and left with a nod.

*

I was firing up the Escort when the phone went off. It was Marcus sounding like thermal underwear was on a special at Argos.

'Got something for you, mate.'

'Go on.'

'Not over the dog. Can you come down to the shop?'

I drove quick as I could without drawing attention and tucked the smoker in front of Victoria station. The shop was dubbed up and I had to bang on the woodwork to be let in. I started stripping off as soon as I was in the office. 'Christ, Marcus, this is beyond a joke.'

'Do you really think it's that hot?' He was making yet more fucking tea and he had his coat on and buttoned right up to the neck.

'And you don't?' Down to my vest and strides, I sat and took the mug he handed across.

'Just the way I like it, that's all. You want any sugar in that?'

'No, I don't. Thank you. Now, before I get dehydrated, what's the news?'

He sat opposite me and spooned two sugars into his own. 'The club was dead over the weekend. Nothing saying, nothing doing. But obviously, I knew this was important so I didn't leave it at that. I rang around, said your Tomas was friendly with one of the lads who used to work for me. Kept you out of it. Anyway, I called everyone I knew who might be able to help, anyone who might have a line into a copper. I had a bit of luck.'

'Go on.'

'Well, it's a funny one. There's a lad I know runs a salvage yard over in Failsworth. And he has quite a lot of Bill through there.'

'Lots of them do. Leaning, getting a few scraps about what the car thieves are up to. Maybe poncing a bit.'

'Yeah. Anyway, I asked this lad if he'd heard 'owt. He said he was expecting some copper this afternoon, one he knew well enough and the guy works the Infirmary beat. Said he'd see if he could get anything. He called back me this evening, and then I called you.'

'And?'

'The copper he was expecting is a button boy, young lad, only signed up a couple of years ago. Turns out him and his mate were in the nearest car when the Infirmary put the scream out for your Tomas. So they attended.'

'Go on.'

'The copper – a lad called Stefanowitz, and remember that name – says there wasn't much to do when they showed; Tomas had been taken into casualty already. They just put some tape out and secure the area. Stefanowitz and his mate toss a coin, the other guy gets to sit with Tomas, or at least go inside and hover around, and our man stands in the car park minding the site and waiting for the plainclothes boys to show.

'Well, time goes on and about half an hour later, a couple of DCs from Platts Lane turn up. Platts Lane is Stefanowitz's own station as it happens. OK, fair enough. He gives them the SP and they schlep in to have a look at Tomas. And then, about ten minutes later, a second motor shows and another copper gets out and comes across asking where Tomas Warzyniak has been taken.'

'He said *what?*'

'Exactly. Stefanowitz says *Who?* and the copper says the lad found shot an hour ago, Tomas Warzyniak, where is he? He knows your Tomas's name. And that's the first time Stefanowitz has heard it. And Stefanowitz remembers it very clearly because his own dad's Polish –'

'And Warzyniak is a Polish name. Didn't Tomas have any ID on him?'

'No. And nothing over the radio either.'

'Who was the new copper?'

'Well, that's the thing. Our lad recognises him because he gave a couple of lectures while he was at police academy or whatever it's called. Superintendent by the name of Keith Hamilton Jacks.'

'Hamilton bastard Jacks.'

'You know him?'

'Sort of. Go on.'

'What's even odder is this – it ain't even Hamilton Jacks's patch, according to the lad. Jacks is from Bootle Street, Divisional HQ. Miles off the plot.'

'And yet he turns up at five in the morning knowing that Tomas Warzyniak has been shot and dumped at the Infirmary. Only no one has said it's Tomas who's been shot, because no one knows.'

'Is any of this making sense to you?'

I tipped back my chair, looking at the ceiling. 'Hamilton Jacks is leading the investigation into Tomas's murder,' I said.

'How did he swing that?'

'Not how, why. Why take over a murder from well off his own patch? And how did he turn up knowing more than all the coppers on site?'

I drifted off. The office was so hot, the sweat was running down my spine in rivers.

'Are you all right, mate?'

'Yeah, fine. I owe you one, Marcus.'

'Glad to help. Any time.'

I stood to pull my shirt and jacket on. 'If anyone asks, Marcus, you haven't seen me since I collected my whip, all right?'

'Of course. How bad is all this, mate?'

'Bad enough. This Stefanowitz, is he bent?'

'He's probably a bit fifty-fifty.'

'How do you know?'

'Like you said just now, sometimes the car squad gets kind of lively, don't they? If there's going to be a sweat on, it's nice for the salvage boys to know in advance so they can tidy up a bit. If Stefanowitz is in there at all, and expected, well . . . You want an introduction?'

'Not just yet. I'll be in touch. And thanks Marcus. I appreciate it.'

'Be lucky, uncle.'

On my way home I drove past Hamilton Jacks's house. It was in a cul-de-sac off Barlow Moor Road behind the Princess pub. Good alarm, satellite TV, a grey Mercedes estate in the drive. I did a wide arc, headlights picking out the high wall at the back of his house and a big black and white cat clawing up the base of a telegraph pole. It jumped at the light and shot off into the bushes. I pulled up round the corner and let the motor idle for a moment.

Hamilton Jacks. Whoever Morrie was talking to, it seemed that Jack Keane and the Turk were part of the cozzer's personal myth; one of those cuts on a trunk that stripes a tree for ever. And now Marcus tells me the copper turns up at the Infirmary knowing it was my nephew on the trolley, before anyone else. How the hell did he know that? What the fuck was going on?

I rang Leon and we made a meet near Strangeways. Then, still deep in thought, I pulled away and pointed the car towards the nick.

Leon's Jag was parked up when I arrived. He flashed at me and opened the passenger door. 'Nothing at the school this afternoon,' he said as I slid in. 'Do you want a cigarette?'

'You would have called if there was. No, thanks. I saw Morrie about Hamilton Jacks.'

'Did you?' He opened his window and sparked up.

'Whoever he was talking to, the Turk came up.'

'Oh yeah?' Leon smoked in silence for a moment. 'I've never known a copper plot up like this, mate. Ten years.'

'Jacks turned up at the Infirmary knowing it was Tomas on the slab. And he was first past the post knowing who he was. Hospital didn't know, cozzers didn't know. But matey boy does.'

'Jesus. How did Jacks know it was Tomas?'

'Beats me.' I turned over some of the options in my head and got nowhere. 'There's a fuck of a lot more to this than we've spliced together so far, Leon. The Turk, Jack Keane, Tomas, Sara and the kids going. And Hamilton Jacks in there in all of it. What's his fucking game? Has he been keeping a tab on all my family? Leon?'

He didn't answer. I twisted my nut right and saw he was looking troubled.

'Just as well you're out of your gaff, mate.'

'Yeah.' I lit up and forced my thoughts in another direction. 'Are you busy tomorrow, Leon?'

'I can make time.'

'Can you do the school again? Morning and lunch.'

He tapped the steering wheel for a couple of beats. 'I can, but I think you've got your priorities mixed up. There's two of us, we could be sitting on two schools every day. You want to find the kids.'

'And you want to find Sara.'

'What's wrong with that?'

'Nothing, but she's running from you as well.'

'Only because of you.'

'You don't know that.'

'Well, what other reason is there?'

'I don't know. Maybe there's something you haven't told me?'

'That's a fucking liberty, all I want is this sorted out. You fucking withdraw that last utterance.'

'All right, withdrawn.' I tapped his arm. 'Sorry, Leon. It's just all getting a bit much, that's all.'

We sat in miserable silence for a few minutes. I was about to split when he grunted and leant across me to the glovebox. 'Here you are.'

He pushed a small, paper-wrapped box into my hand. I unscrewed the brown bag and took out a travelling alarm clock.

'Got it at my gadget stall up on Suedehill. Left mine somewhere while I was away last week. Thought you could do with one, too. Only four quid each. Bargain.'

'Thanks.' I stowed the clock away in my pocket.

'Tells the time in various time zones,' he said. 'And it takes three wallops on the button to turn it off. So you can't sleep through it. And, *and* it has a solar panel to keep the battery topped up. So it'll last for years. I should have bought a dozen.'

I smiled. 'Thanks, Leon.'

5

I was on the field opposite Hamilton Jacks's drum by seven the next morning playing fetch with Rynka when a black Granada pulled up outside the cozzer's house. The dog bounced up and I squatted to take the ball out of his mouth, using the move to slip a pair of racing bins out of my jacket. I got the busy as he hit the street – hard face, grey hair, a couple of files clamped in his fist. Two brisk strides and he ducked in the motor. Thank you, Morrie.

I gave it a few minutes, then whistled the dog up and walked him to the pub car park where he took a piss on the telegraph pole at the back of the cozzer's drum. I watched him prance around it for a bit, then clipped the lead on and dropped him back at Amy's. I grabbed four and a half grand for Leon, drove back to Prestwich, stuck some clean clothes in a carrier and split for Leeds.

'Do we know anyone who can tap a phone?'

We were sat in Leon's jag in Sainsbury's car park just off the ringroad. He'd seen nothing at the school, morning or lunch.

'Why?'

'Hamilton Jacks's house. Unusual to have overhead lines in a built-up area, I could see his line clearly. Do we know anyone?'

There was a young mum struggling to get four bags of shopping from her trolley into the back of a tatty hatchback while keeping her toddler from jumping out of the child seat and making a break for freedom. Leon sat watching them for a minute, and I knew he was wondering if I'd really thought this through. I filled in the silence by pulling out the brown envelope of cash and handing it across. He grunted thanks and stuck it inside his coat. Then he sighed deep and long.

'I do, as it happens. Geezer by the name of Grundy.'

'Grundy. Born on a Monday,' I said.

He turned. 'What?'

'Solomon Grundy, born on a Monday, school on Tuesday, married on Wednesday, took ill on Thursday . . . ' I trailed off.

He shook his head. 'All I know is that you talk a lot of bollocks sometimes.'

'It's a nursery rhyme,' I said.

'Yeah. Well, this Grundy used to be a telephone engineer. He can tap a phone.'

'Can you get hold of him?'

'What do you think you're going to get?'

'Information.'

'The cozzer won't use his home phone for business.'

'He might.'

'It's a fucking huge risk. Especially for might.'

'It's worth a try.'

He nodded, but I could see he'd not bought it. 'All right, I'll call Grundy when I get home,' he said.

We arranged to speak later, I got out of his car and he left. I gave it about ten minutes and drove slowly to the school and got nish.

Grundy lived in a two-up two-down off Matthews Lane. Leon had called and said he'd agreed a meet at nine. We rang the bell at five to. Grundy opened up looking more like an English teacher. Tall and greying, tweed jacket with leather patches on the elbows. Turned out he had to be dressed respectably for the function he was due at shortly.

'Just as well you're early,' he said, waving us in and down a bare floorboarded corridor to his lounge. 'It's my daughter's parents' night at school. Wife went earlier. I've got the last appointment. We'll have to be quick. What do you want?'

I gave him the SP. He chewed his lip for a minute and said, on account of me being a pal of Leon's, he'd do it for a couple of hundred quid, but on one condition.

'If it comes on top while I'm hooking the phone up, I want to say that you told me . . .' Here, he stabbed a nicotine-stained finger in my direction. 'That you told me the house belongs to your ex-wife. And it's all down to a domestic. That way I'll get a slap on the wrist, no more. Domestics ring true. Ex-wives can be funny things.'

He glanced across at a framed photo on the mantle. It showed a younger Grundy, stripped to the waist on a beach. He was holding primary colour buckets and spades in one hand with a toddler in the crook of the other arm. A pretty brunette had her head on his shoulder, and there was a girl of about eight or nine standing in front.

'She's doing her A-levels this year. Wants to go to university. Wife wants her to get a job.'

He wasn't talking to us any more. Then he snorted loudly, and for a second I thought he was going to lose it, so I tried to bring him down. 'Won't come on top that time of the morning.'

He snorted again, eyes still on the picture.

'What sort of ladder will you need?'

'Nah – still got me boots.' He broke away from the picture and pointed to a heavy pair of spiked leather boots lying in the corner on top of a pile of newspapers. 'As long as I can find the line easily, I'll have the job done in about fifteen minutes.'

'Do you need anything else?'

'Voice-activated tape-recorder, some wire and a few other bits and bobs. Call it three and a half hundred and I'll do the shopping.'

Leon got his roll out before I did. 'Three five oh,' he said, counting the fifties out. 'Can we do it tomorrow?'

'Small hours,' said Grundy. 'Call me tomorrow about six in the evening to confirm. Talk about dogs, afternoon for morning. Normal style. You never know who might be listening.' He chuckled, and his face lit up for a moment.

'Now get out, the pair of you. Want to make sure I get a good session with the English teacher. Not too happy about what he wrote on Katie's last essay. Tomorrow at six, Leon.'

The sun was very bright the next morning and it made spotting the twins more difficult. But at half eight, I saw two lads tapping a football on the opposite pavement. About twenty yards away, one looked up.

It was Sam and I scrabbled for the door.

Then the kid turned full on, and it wasn't Sam. It could have been his brother, though.

This cheered me up for some reason, like a horse running well in one race making you fancy him for his next. Daft, but there you are. I nipped back to the hotel, collected some laundry and found myself a service wash. I was back at the school for lunch, and again later that afternoon, but the sky cracked as I parked up and it pissed down solidly for the next hour, which meant hoods up or caps on and heads well down. Lou, Sam or twenty of their clones could have come out and I wouldn't have known.

I called Leon at half six and we talked about dogs. 'Will it be running, do you think?'

'At three tomorrow,' said Leon. 'Same track and meeting starts at twelve.'

Tomorrow meaning tonight, same track meaning Grundy's house. Three meaning when we were to do the tap, twelve meaning when I was to get to Grundy's. But who was the dog? Me or Grundy? Didn't matter, I suppose.

Leon was speaking. 'You won't need me to be there for the race, will you?'

'No. It only gives 'em three for the price of two if there's a problem.'

'OK,' he said. 'Take it easy, then.'

'I will.'

I sat with Grundy in his back room till half two, then I drove us on to the plot. We left the Escort a few streets away and walked to the car park. The lights were long off in the boozer and the patch was in total darkness.

It was a pleasure to watch Grundy go to work; the guy was a real pro. He was up the pole in about two minutes flat, and spent another ten perched on the cross joint. I stood by some bushes a few feet away, watching the road and listening for cars travelling slowly. Then I heard movement above – Grundy was coming down, stopping every few feet to staple a skinny cable to the side of the pole. At the bottom, he wired the lead up to the tape recorder, stuck it in a plastic bag and buried it in some loose earth about a foot away from the base. A dead fifteen minutes from start to finish.

In the car on the way back to his gaff, he went over the details again.

'I'm finished now,' he said. 'Unless we're unlucky and some real eagle-eye spots the wire running down the pole, the tap's safe. It's as thin as fuck, so I don't see it happening. But anyway, there might be an engineer doing some work on the line, who knows. You'll need to change the tapes every couple of days. You saw the machine I stuck on?'

'Yes.'

'Right. When you're finished with the tap, just yank the wire hard from the bottom, and the connection will come away at the other end. That's it. I've used flimsy gear on purpose so it doesn't give you any trouble when you do.'

'Thanks . . . ' I paused. 'I never got your first name.'

'Grundy's the only name I've got. Never use my Christian name. Even the wife calls me Grundy.' He snorted noisily. 'Never liked my first name.'

A beat. I had to ask.

'Is it . . . ?'

'Yes, it fucking is.' He twisted round to look at me. 'Yes, it fucking well is.'

Solomon Grundy
Born on a Monday
Christened on Tuesday

I wanted to ask him what day he was born and christened, but it didn't seem the right moment. Instead, we drove on in silence for a few minutes until with an effort I asked:

'How did the teachers meet go?'

'Bollocks. The man's a cunt. Knows nothing.' He snorted. 'I helped Katie with an essay on *The Great Gatsby*. Have you read it?'

I shook my head. He snorted again.

"Spent about three pages on images of seeing. Fucking book's full of gear about the way people see what's right and what's not, all that style. Teacher said that was old thinking. I bloody told him . . . '

He twisted sideways and jabbed his finger at me. 'I bloody told him, there's nothing wrong with that thinking. The whole book's about what appears to be right and what actually is right. Whole bloody book. Gatsby sees the wrong thing about Daisy from the moment he meets her. Teacher told me I was wrong. Bollocks.' He swung and fixed his eyes on the road ahead.

'Nothing ever looks the way it is,' he said. 'Like my wife. Out selling cosmetics she told me. Turned out she was selling sex aids for some fucking sex company. Like tupperware parties, but with vibrators, fruit flavoured johnnies, all that style.' He turned back.

'They gave her fucking custody of the kids. Can you believe that? Are you married?'

'No.'

'Good fucking job. Good fucking job. Just here. I'll walk the rest of the way.'

We pulled up at the kerb and Grundy got out and walked away, hands deep in his pockets, collar turned up.

I lit up a cigarette and nodded at Grundy's back. 'He's got problems,' I said. 'Bad divorce,' I replied.

I crawled into bed at the hotel at five, two hours before I had to be up for the kids. I couldn't raise reception, so I fiddled around with the alarm clock on the bedside table and set it for seven fifteen. At least I could get some kip later in the day.

6

No matter how tired I am, I always seem to beat the alarm. It's probably the nick: I always want to be up before unlock, otherwise it seems as if they're making you get up.

I felt pretty good considering I'd only slept a couple of hours. *Shit.* There was daylight creeping around the heavy hotel curtains. It was quarter past fucking nine. Shit fucking shit. I'd set the alarm for seven fifteen. Look again, I didn't switch it to alarm mode, bastard.

'This would have been the morning and I've missed them – fucking hotel.'

I got to the school for twelve fifteen without shaking off the feeling that I'd had my chance this morning and blown it. I waited for the lunchtime out, then spent the afternoon cruising streets in the area on the off chance, thinking about Lou and Sam and their enforced new life: did they have any new friends to hang out with, had they learnt Leeds yet. Back for three. Several hundred kids skipped out of the gates like they were paroled for the weekend. I called Leon and told him nowt, then pointed the motor towards Manchester. It was Friday, so I tuned into the local traffic news before I hit the M62. Sure enough, an excitable traffic-copter girl came on shouting there was a 'Two! Mile! Tailback!' on the road up ahead. I came off the motorway to avoid the traffic. It was a mild evening, so I dropped the window. A couple of miles on, there was a sign for Flockton, followed by a smaller one saying 'Prison'. What nick was that? Oh yeah, there's a detention centre at Flockton. Sounds like Foston. Foston Hall. Foston Hall Detention Centre.

I cranked the window up. The air didn't seem fresh any more. I tried channelling my thoughts elsewhere, anywhere – people, places, Leon, the cozzer Hamilton Jacks, the tap on his house, air, fire, water, oh Sara. Too late. Go on, then. I pulled into a layby and wound the window back down, lit up and looked blankly into the night. Go on. Just let it be quick this time.

There was a high desk out of Dickens with a squat thug of a screw behind it. He had short aggressive grey hair, and his face was formed from chunks of angry red gristle posing as cheeks, nose and mouth. The copper uncuffed me and made me stand behind a white line painted on the floor as he handed over my paperwork. The screw first looked down at the green and yellow sheets and then looked up at me. 'Full name.'

I was fourteen years old and so nervous I couldn't speak. I opened my mouth, but all that came out was the usual – the stammer I had in those days. It wasn't the sort that stuck on a consonant: my problem was getting the words to start in the first place. I managed to force my name out, then I stopped. I was trying to say 'Sir', but it just wouldn't come.

The screw looked at me and started to shift. He got down from behind the desk slowly, then walked round it and towards me. There was no rush. This was his fucking manor. He was the master here. As he moved, he raised his right fist back level with his shoulder and I saw his arm was thick as a thigh. I'd never seen thicker, hairier fingers or bigger knuckles on a clenched fist. Then he smashed it right into my nose and I was too paralysed to ride it. I heard the crack like a brick across my face and I went down, eyes stinging. The screw was speaking. 'From now, in this place, you will address every adult you come across as "Sir", do you understand that, you little piece of shit?'

Half an hour later, they'd locked me in a cell off reception for the night. It was the first time I'd been behind a door. I felt torn up, empty and frightened. They'd given me five minutes with my mam after the court, and that was it. She hugged me tight and whispered she loved me in her light Scottish burr, then they took me away. I looked round to wave and saw her starting to cry, then someone closed a door between us.

They'd turned the light off in the cell already. It was December, and it felt cold and smelt damp. I crawled under the newspaper-thin blanket and started to sob quietly. All I could think of was this: if that screw was confident enough to slug me in front of two cops in uniforms, what was coming now the law had gone? I chewed the edge of a nail and shivered into a couple of hours' sleep.

There was one barred window up above the bed and grey light woke me for dawn. I noticed a warm feeling somewhere round my middle. I was that grateful, I wriggled about in it, thinking maybe I'd dreamt the court and the rest and I was back home. Then I realised I was lying in my own piss.

I fell out of bed, stuttering terrified half words under my breath and flipped the mattress. It was so thin the piss had gone right through. Sweat broke out down my back. Looking round there was no radiator and no pipe. Jumping on to the bedframe, I opened the window and dragged the mattress up against the sill, wettest side facing out, then spread the sheet out on the bedsprings. I had no hope of removing the evidence altogether, but maybe the air would clear the smell of my piss. Maybe.

My pants came off and I flapped them round to get them dry or at least to smell less of piss. My crotch was damp and cold, I was getting . . .

The sound of the twirls in a lock sent me jumping into my kecks and hopping across the stone floor for the mattress and sheet. I dragged the mattress on to the frame, then threw the pissed sheet on top and lay down, snapping the blankets over me. Then the light was switched on from outside, my door opened and two screws appeared. One was about fifty. He stayed by the open door, hand resting on the key in the lock. The other – younger and nastier-looking – came in, carrying a yellow plastic tray with a mug, bowl and plate on it.

'This is your breakfast,' he snapped. 'You've got fifteen minutes to eat it, get dressed, fold your bedding and be ready to move.'

He bent with a grunt and dropped the tray the last few inches on to the deck. The mug rocked and spilled tea on to the yellow plastic. Then they left and locked me in.

I gave it a couple of seconds and picked up the tray. Tea and porridge. They tasted exactly the same – grey – but at least they were hot. I ate quickly, then pulled my trousers on and folded the sheets and blankets to hide the wet patch. The two screws came back a few minutes later and shouted in to pick up my kit and tray and come out. Outside, the older one pointed at a trolley for the tray and a bin for the sheet. Then the other screamed and I was in trouble.

'Back in here you little shit.'

I trotted in obediently. As I got level, he grabbed me by the collar and dragged me into the cell.

'Look what the dirty little bastard's done.' He was half talking to the other screw, but most of it was ritual preparation for the beating I knew was coming. 'He's pissed his fucking bed.' He twisted my collar till it was cutting into my throat.

'Pissboy. Little pissboy. Little piss*dog*. Well, if you're going to behave like a dog, you'll get treated like a dog.' His grip tightened on my neck and I felt his other hand on the back of my head. He was going to rub my nose in it, I started to flail at him wildly. Then the other screw said 'Stop'.

He came in and told me to go outside. I waited, rubbing my neck. A couple of minutes and the dog left and the older guy walked me down to reception to get my prison kit. One good man.

That wasn't quite the end of it. For the next six weeks I was put in the pissbeds' dormitory, though no one actually ever pissed the bed in it. This was hardly surprising as the night screw woke us every hour on the hour from lights out at half eight to lights on at six and marched us all to the karsi where we'd stand and piss or force a few drips out or stand and strain and do nothing and this was the worst.

The sequence stopped. I smoked a couple more fags, turning things over in my mind, then drove for the flat in Prestwich.

The next morning, we were playing Wimbledon at home and usually I'd have been going to watch the game, but those were normal times. Instead, I got up, showered, made black coffee and called Annie the estate agent. She said Mrs Harpur – Sara's maiden name – had turned my offer down. I offered the asking price and told her I'd call back Monday for her reply.

I kicked around the flat for a couple of hours, then went up to Old Trafford for half one and ended up walking with the crowds round the ground. The twins were big fans; maybe they'd come back for the match with their mates. I had nothing better to do, anyway.

As usual, the streets were full of red shirts, scarves and hats, like a council flower bed on the move. Small crowds and streams bobbed and flowed into each other and on into the ground. Then the pavements cleared for kick-off and I went and sat in the motor to listen. We hammered Wimbledon 5–1. I went back to the ground a quarter of an hour before the final whistle, picked a gate at random and watched the stream come out. Then I dragged round all the food stalls and hotdog sellers till dark, just in case.

Leon's alarm woke me at ten that evening. I say woke – it fucking catapulted me out of my sleep. It would have woken my mam and she'd been dead ten years, God rest her. I dressed and drove for Hamilton Jacks's house, stopped round the back of the pub and had a good shufti round, then nipped into the shrubbery tugging at my flies. Squatting at the pole, I changed the tapes, scraped back the soil and split. Back in Prestwich, I slid the cassette into the machine. Three out by a woman, another by a young lad to his pal to arrange the return of some porn. No Scotch tones. Nothing to indicate Grundy had made the right connection. Then a woman rang to ask if they could they make Sunday lunch that week.

'Fraid not. Keith's on duty.'

Keith's on duty. Keith Hamilton Jacks is on duty. Nice one, Grundy. I made tea to celebrate. A working tap on the enemy and he didn't know where the fuck I was. Well done, Grundy, my son.

Then the mobile rang and it was Jack Keane.

An hour later, I was sat looking at a pair of kings, pair of queens and two jacks. The game is Kaluki and I've got a trio of fours, so virtually any face card gets me down. The Vietnamese guy to my right – Mickey something or other – is, I know, holding pictures. But he won't let go because he's sussed that I'm looking for them. It's 501 up and I've got 420 on the board, having already bought myself back in the game.

Jack had told me that he was in a game upstairs at a pub round the back of the Britannia in the city centre. He had some news and did I fancy slipping down? I went, and took my dough with me. Grotty little dump, but the action was serious – Jack was rolling up what looked like a couple of grand as I showed. Someone was leaving, so I sat for a new game with Jack, the Vietnamese guy and a geezer introduced as Clarry.

Right now it wasn't going too well. I'd had a lot of lousy hands. But then my luck turned – Mickey threw me a red queen, I took it and came down. The move sparked off more action and Jack won the hand, knocking Mickey out. Just the three of us left. Then I got a terrific hand – two threes and a joker. I called up in three plays, doubling Jack's score to 348 and putting Clarry out of the game. Jack was still favourite, but it was game on. Then Jack made a rick, switching from attack to defence and coming down early. I got another great hand leaving me needing one card after just nine plays. He put me up on the tenth, with a jack, if you please. Kaluki. Game set and match. I almost felt sorry for him. Almost.

I shuffled my winnings together and I was seventeen hundred in front. Jack looked at his watch.

'No offence, gentlemen, but I'm calling it a day. I'm meeting a Kate Moss lookalike in an hour.' He glanced across at me.

'I'll come with,' I said. 'Only called in for a coffee, as it happens. Thanks, lads.'

Two of the guys who'd been side-betting sat down and there was a new game on before Jack and I made the door. Out in the street he led the way to a very new looking BMW two-seater.

'I've got my own wheels, Jack.'

His keyring bleeped and the locks slid open.

'I've got . . . hang on.' He took out a black metal mobile and slid it open. 'Hello?'

His head dropped down and he spoke quietly into the mouthpiece.

I couldn't hear the words, but from his tone I guessed it was Kate Moss. With a little click of his tongue, which could have been a blown kiss in a softer place, he nodded and snapped the phone shut. 'She's going to be late. Forty minutes. She's a woman, it'll be an hour. Well, she's given us a bit longer any road. Got something to tell you.' He pulled open his door and nodded at me. 'Hop in, son.'

I slid into the passenger seat. It smelt new, all lemon and laundered. He took out his pack, offered me and we lit up.

'Any news on your missus and kids?'

'I'm working on it. You said you had something for me.'

Jack cracked his window about an inch at the top, took a drag and flicked some ash out through the gap. 'There's something I found out,' he said. 'Thing is, I don't know if I should be the one telling you.'

I was breathing shallow. 'What is it?'

'Did you know your mate Leon was having it with Sara?'

And I breathed deep again. 'Yes. She told me.'

'You're not bothered?'

'No.'

Jack took another pull at his fag. 'Your business of course, but my first reaction was that you didn't need to look any further for the guy mixing you the bottle.'

I flicked into the ashtray. 'How did you find this out, Jack? They didn't exactly advertise their relationship.'

Jack glanced away, then back to me. 'No offence, mate, but I'd sooner not say. The guy wasn't up to mischief when he told me. I was just asking around, like I said I would. He saw them in a hotel up in the lakes.'

'Second weekend in February. I knew.'

Jack shrugged. 'Sorry mate. Didn't want to make trouble.'

'It's all right.'

'Have you got anyone in the frame yet?'

'No, not yet. I've run the rule over everyone around me and they all come up clean. Apart from Terry.'

'Terry?'

'Terry Grant. Yoda's son.'

'Yoda Grant? The peterman?'

'Know him?'

'Yeah, did some time with him once. Parkhurst.'

'Did you ever meet Terry?'

'No. Yoda died in Parkhurst. Ghosted me out the day after.'

'Well, I've been grafting with the boy about three years.'

'And what's the question mark on him for?'

'We were nicked badly.'

'Who gets nicked well?'

I gave him the tale: Terry, coke, Breadcake, Busby. 'It was a blatant fit up, Jack.'

'Do you think this cozzer Hamilton Jacks has you flagged?'

'What do you mean?'

'On the computer. The local yokels don't just get your pedigree, they get a note saying call DCS Hamilton Jacks.'

'And then?'

'Yokels call him up and he tells them what a bad lot you are. Then he says how about giving you a little present, and the three of them plot up. And by the time they've finished, the country boys are owed a big fucking favour by a big fucking man in the Manchester Regional. That would certainly explain your long wait in the cells, wouldn't it?'

'And now he knows where I am, he could organise the brown in Strangeways to keep me in for longer. It's possible.'

'Well, whatever, he's got the horn for you, son. You better be very careful.'

I tapped my thumbnail against my teeth. 'Jack. Apart from you and me, who knew for sure I was involved in the Turk?'

'Only Quiet John. And he's dead now.'

'Yes, I know. I need you to think, Jack. This cozzer is after me, and the Turk is the only harm I've done him. How did he make the connection?'

'If he did, I don't know.'

'Well dredge your memory and think about it.'

'Did Sara know?'

'What about Kate Moss?' I said.

I heard the rustle as he looked at his watch. I felt the draft from his window catch the back of my neck. 'Kate, yeah. But I do have a few minutes left, and I will think about the Turk, all right? But, before I go. About your nephew. I know a young kid who sells brown at street level. I've put him to work on getting some knowledge. He grafts in Wythenshawe, which isn't a million miles off your nephew's plot.'

'Thanks, Jack. I appreciate it.'

We shook across the handbrake.

'I'll be in touch, cock,' he said. 'Soon as I hear something. Mind you take care, all right?'

'And you Jack. Be seeing you.'

I got out and went to find the Escort. Behind me, I heard him fire the engine and glide off.

Twenty-five years ago.

I was down the block at Foston Hall. Like a frightened little dog, I'd bitten a screw's ankle for kicking me. As it happened, he kept quiet about the bite when I came up in front of the governor. The charge ended up being Dickensian as the building: 'Making han hunprovoked grab at my leg and calling me ha cunt.' Five days all round. I got beaten and slapped on the way down and they slung me in – no bed or mattress, just a concrete box with a chair screwed to the floor. I lay down on the deck and stretched out. My head was throbbing but it could have been worse. There was no blood, anyway.

'Are you all right, son?'

Someone across the corridor. I sat up.

'I heard the cunts giving it to you. OK when they're mob-handed, ain't they, the cowardly twats. Like to see one of them come in here and try it. Any one of the bastards, big as they are.'

'Shut your fucking mouth, Keane. I won't tell you again.'

'What if I don't, screw? You're on your own at the minute so you won't come in, that's for sure.'

The pain started to go as I realised. I warmed up so much, it was almost sexual. All we had to do was say no.

'Jack Keane, Manchester, Collyhurst. Second time down here. Got fourteen days for smacking that cunt Frazer right in his big fat mouth. Called me a shitbag once too often. What about you?'

I shouted across and gave him the details. He shouted back.

'It's a shithole here son, but there's one thing you can stand on. They may give you a good hiding for stepping across the line, but they won't kill you – it's all short sharp shock in here. There's lads go home every day. Makes it hard for them to keep a death quiet.' Then he roared again. 'What do you say, screw?'

No reply.

'You ain't got much remission to gain means you ain't got much to lose. Plus, the governor don't like to take all a lad's remission. Makes the system look like a failure.'

This was someone who knew how it worked, how to knock against it. Someone who knew the way out. Maybe someone who wanted to be my friend.

We talked long into the freezing night, me and Jack Keane. Mouth pressed up against the slit between door and wall, then ear pressed for the reply. We both got slapped around for the talking. 'So fucking what?' we shouted, and carried on through my second day and night. We became intimate, like lovers. That's not too strong a word, we were so close. I had never experienced anything like it. The older boy was warming me with his words, he was gathering my tired little body up and letting it rest against his far tougher hide, protecting me in what he said and how he said it.

My fourth day, Jack's last. It was Christmas morning, something I'd forgotten in all the excitement. The wake-up call came at seven, Sunday time.

'Happy Christmas, delinquents. Pack your kit, Keane.' There was none for either of us to pack. 'And make your bed up. You can have your Christmas dinner on the wing.' Then the screw rasped through my door. 'And you, you can keep your mattress in today as a Christmas box from the staff down here.'

Then Jack shouted, 'I'm going nowhere, screw, unless the lad across the road comes up with me. That's the end of it. You dragged me down here and you'll have to drag me back up. I ain't going on my own.'

They must have gone for a governor. The screws didn't have the arsehole – let alone the authority or compassion – to do me a favour without checking first. A couple of hours later, some senior screw came to my door and told me that I was getting a break because it was Christmas Day. I was going back up on to the wing.

You never forget something like that, and I never forgot Jack Keane. My game stopped being his game after a while, but the bond was always there. If he asked and I had it to give, I would. And so would he. Those days down the block always sat in my head. Jack Keane made me, or he started to that day.

I drove back to the service flat slowly and found I couldn't sleep. The late movie was *The Wicker Man*, which I watched for the twentieth time. Edward Woodward as a Christian copper and a good man. The witches burn him at the end.

7

I was pulled up across the road from a Catholic church in Withington. I've never really gone in for confession, but Sara was always quite firm on the gas and gaiters front. She'd insisted the kids were baptised and she used to do mass occasionally while we were wed. I knew this was a gaff she'd used, maybe she'd come here today. Odds were a hundred to one, plus, but it was a time for long bets.

There was quite a wind on as the Godbotherers streamed out of the building and milled around on the pavement. A few of the women wore hats, and they were hanging on to them with one hand and trying to keep their skirts down with the other. I scanned every face as they exchanged words with the padre and drifted off down the road. Ten minutes and the bodies dried up. The priest bobbed back inside to take his frock off, came out, locked up and crunched down the gravel sparking a white-tipped fag. Like I said, a hundred to one, plus. I twisted the ignition and drove across to see a mate of mine who owned a car body shop in Stretford.

Dud the body shop guy had bed hair and was still in his slippers. About five and a half foot and blinking sleepily, his face normally had the look of someone who spent most of his life under a car and didn't bother to wash too well in between. Today he looked well-scrubbed.

'Did I get you out of bed?'

'Out on the piss last night. Got company, but she's still in kip. You want something done?'

'Not work.'

He nodded me in and locked up the yard gate behind me. We chunked up the iron stairs to his flat above the workshop and sat in the kitchen. I told him about Tomas, Sara and the kids but not the cozzer Hamilton Jacks. Dud cut open the odd safe or made a special tool when you asked him, but he was half straight and the filth made him jumpy. I was here because the kids were friendly with his younger brother Gerry.

'Very sorry to hear about your Tomas, mate.' He stood a mug on the table.

'Has your Gerry heard anything?'

'If he did, he didn't tell me.'

'I know it's a long one, Dud, but could you get into your Gerry, see if they've been in touch?' I wrote my mobile on a linen off a pile on the deck and pushed it across. 'This number, no other.'

'Dudley . . . '

I turned at the light scouse voice. She was standing in the doorway, streaked blond hair down to her shoulders, athlete's body and totally naked.

'You coming back to bed?'

She tweaked a small brown nipple at him. Then she noticed me. 'Didn't know you had company.'

She leant into the woodwork and stroked the washboard she used for a belly. Even from here, she smelt of sex.

'When you're ready kid,' she said, and dipped away.

After a second nailed to the after-image of her bum in mid-air, I turned back. 'That was?'

'Bird I met last night.'

I nodded and stood to go. 'Soon as you hear from Gerry, eh?'

I left and drove back to the service flat in Prestwich, thinking about straightgoers' lives and how they could just stop work because they'd met a bird in a club. Even without all this kind of shit, I never did that. I couldn't guess what I'd missed.

Then next day I was over to Leeds for the school run. Nowt. I had nothing better to do, so I spent the evening cruising the streets, slowing at any group of teenagers and staring at any tall elegant woman in her thirties walking out of a late-night store with a pint of milk or a packet of fags.

After a sleepless night at the Queen's came another morning and afternoon at the school gates. And nothing. I drove back to Manchester and called Annie. She told me Sara had accepted my offer for Buckingham Road.

'I'll need your solicitor's details, Mr Drake. And have you got a landline for me yet?'

'Not yet, Annie; and I still need to sort a solicitor out.'

She went chilly as nun. 'I see. Well, Mrs Harpur has asked me to organise a holding deposit from any buyer, Mr Drake.'

'Holding deposit?'

'To take the house off the market. Mrs Harpur told me she's been messed around by a couple of buyers in the past. She suggests three thousand.'

'Fine,' I said, trying to sound upbeat. 'How shall I get it to you?'

'As soon as you get your solicitor's details across to me, then they can deposit it with hers. She's instructed me not to take the house off the market till then.'

'Fine, I'll call you tomorrow.'

We hung up. Previous buyer my arse. Sara guessed I'd come this way. She wasn't going to give up her solicitor let alone anything else until there was another brief in the frame and money on the table. She always was smart. And funny and beautiful, I thought. Well, I'd hire a brief as John Drake if I had to. Whatever it took to keep this line going. I stood up and slung the phone on the couch. Maybe Morrie could deal with it for me.

The phone went off again. I groaned and clutched it up. It was Harry, saying she'd seen the copper Dave Craze.

Harry opened up in jeans and jumper. It was the first time I'd seen her without make-up and she looked like a child. A child who'd been crying.

'You all right, Harry?'

'Go into the lounge.' She didn't smile, she didn't welcome. She just took a step back for me to get past and locked up.

The flat was cold and the kitchen sink was full of dishes with empty wine bottles on the table. She took a long time locking and bolting the door, and I was sat down before she came in. The room was untidy, which was odd: books and papers in rough piles, files spread across the carpet and a laundry basket spilling clothes on to the floor. She padded in and sat across the low square table. It was bare except for a yellow envelope, the kind you get photos in.

'You look like you've been crying.'

She wouldn't meet my eyes, just sat clicking her nails and staring at the deck. Then she sighed and looked up at me. 'He came last night. Rang about six, asked if I wanted dinner. He takes me out sometimes. I said no, why not come round. I'll cook for you, I do sometimes. Part of the service.' She twitched me a fake smile and went on.

'For the money, he'd normally stay three hours. But when it came to it, I said stay for a bit, we're having fun. And we hadn't . . . done anything, you know. He'd had quite a bit to drink. Well, he likes to talk anyway. Boasts a lot, actually – the job, what he's doing. How he's going to be promoted. He's very ambitious.'

She looked at me directly for the first time. Then she went on.

'I asked him about work, just in general and I got what you wanted, all about Tomas, all of it. He's on the investigation, so I didn't have to pump him that hard. Not much to tell anyway, they're not getting anywhere.' She twitched a smile again. 'We were both quite drunk by now. But then he says, there's more to it than the boy. And then he clams up. Come on, I said, you've got me all interested, you can't just leave me hanging on, but he wouldn't. Just sat there grinning and shaking his head. So I said, if he told me the rest I'd do something for him I'd never done before.'

'Harry –'

'Shut up. If you want to hear, shut up.' She pressed a finger in the middle of her forehead and rubbed it hard. Then she straightened and looked right at me. 'His boss is a man called Keith Hamilton Jacks. Do you know a gangster called Jack Keane? Yes, you do, don't you? I can see it in your face. Eight years ago, Dave's boss put Jack Keane away for heroin. Biggest bust in the north ever, Dave said. They wrapped the whole firm up, the price on the streets went up for nearly a year it caused such a famine. Well, maybe he was boasting again. Boasting for his boss.' She laughed like it was a joke.

'But there was one person they didn't get. No proper proof, but Hamilton Jacks was obsessed and he's wanted this guy ever since. And now – with Tomas – he thinks he's very close to him. And then Dave told me who it was Jacks is after. And it's you.' She folded over and sobbed miserably. I was cemented into my chair. I couldn't have got up for a thousand quid. She wiped her eyes and sniffed.

'What did you have to do?'

'I kissed him. To get what you wanted, I kissed him. And when he'd finished I went to kiss him again, but he wouldn't let me.' She flicked the yellow envelope across the table. 'Look at them. They're of Dave and me.'

I flipped back the cover and slid out the photos inside. They were Polaroids of Harry and a guy in his thirties, short black hair and a moustache. From the angles, they were mostly taken with a timer. All different places, different seasons. In a park, on a balcony, by some water. In hotel rooms, her perched on his lap or lying in his arms. Everyday couple photographs. You wouldn't have known the difference.

'Don't ever believe we can't have feelings,' she said. 'Not just for a good *punter*, either. Real men go to whores as well, there are worse things than paying for sex.' She sniffed again. 'He won't ever see me again, now. He told me.'

I put the photos back in the envelope and closed it up. 'I'm sorry, Harry.'

'You didn't have anything to do with that heroin, did you? Or your nephew?'

'No.'

'No. Well, I hope this was worth it.'

I followed her to the door, she unlocked and unbolted and shut me out. I walked down the stairs and drove for Prestwich thinking that I had never understood anything that had ever happened to me in my life.

8

eon's alarm threw me against the wall at four thirty the next morning and I was on Hamilton Jacks's plot by five, wondering if I was the only face in town who didn't have a direct line into the Greater Manchester Police. Fringe merchants like Marcus and half-straights like Harry could ask around and get breaking news but I had to scrabble around in the dirt and freezing cold before the birds were up for a tape recorder tap to the filth. Well. Harry seemed to have paid dearly for what she'd got me. I should stop whining. I reburied the machine and skipped back to the Escort. Twenty minutes later, I was sitting on the sofa in Prestwich. I pressed play.

Jacks had taken a call from another copper around ten. I guessed it was ten because I could hear the news starting in the background. Unless it was the Sunday night, in which case it would have been later.

The first time his voice came on, I stopped the machine and wound it back to listen again. Definitely Scotch, but going easy on the haggis and kilts. Educated. I let the tape run on. The other filth had a message from Chester House, GMP HQ. Seemed that Jacks had a meet booked with some high-ranker the next day (today, if the tape was Monday) and the head honcho had brought the meet forward to three.

'That's a fucking nuisance,' said Jacks. 'I called a meet with a snout for the afternoon. Now I'll have to bring that forward as well.'

And he used his own phone to do it. Past ten at night, who wouldn't? Two rings and a deep Manchester voice rattled up. No name, and Jacks didn't give his either.

'Can you make that two o'clock tomorrow? My timetable's been altered.'

The other end was silent for a minute before giving it a deep but crackily grunted 'Yeah'. I didn't recognise his voice. But then Jacks dropped a bollock.

'I hope to Christ it's not another gay film,' he said. 'Half the fucking cottagers in town were there for the last one. I don't want some sissy boy giving me a tug.'

They hung up and I was turned right on. If this was last night, Jacks was meeting his grass this afternoon at one of the two cinemas in Manchester that showed wall to wall porn.

Fucking bloody hell, Grundy my son – right in my fucking lap!

Could be that some of Hamilton Jacks's dirt on me was coming from this same grass. Even if it wasn't, I could identify him and expose the bastard round town – that would be a right fucking kick in the nuts to Jacks.

I grabbed the *Yellow Pages*, dialled the two venues and listened to their recorded info lines. Both were showing films that afternoon.

I was outside the school in Leeds by eight, calling Leon.

'I need a meet.'

'Place? You do have one in mind I hope; I'm still half asleep. Can't make decisions yet.'

I suggested a café we knew in Beswick. 'Can you do it?'

'I reckon.'

We rang off. I watched kids go in and out of the gates for the next hour, then drove. Leon was already in the car park, leaning back against his driver's door and nodding into his mobile. He raised a hand at me as I drew up. I got out and lit up.

'Tony, something's come up. I'll call you back. Yeah, later. Bye.' He snapped the unit shut. 'Fucking timewaster. So, what's all this about?'

I told him Jacks was meeting a grass at either the Continentale or the Cine Club.

'Well, it takes all sorts,' he said. He didn't look quite as chuffed as I felt.

'Listen, I'll cover one – '

'And I'll cover the other? Do you know for sure the call was made last night?'

'No. I'm taking a flier.'

'No. *We're* taking a flier.'

'If you don't fancy it, Leon.'

He shook his head sharply and took a sovereign out of his pocket. 'Heads you take the Cine Club.' He tossed and caught it, then slammed his palm down on the back of his hand. 'Heads it is. Where's the Continentale?'

'Other side of the university.'

'I'll look it up.'

'The meet's set for two,' I said. 'And this is what Jacks looks like.' I gave him Morrie's clipping. He stared at it for a minute and gave it back.

'You showed me already. I'll remember him.'

'If there's nothing by two fifteen, then spew it. Whichever one of us cops – if we do at all – turn his phone off in the cinema in case – '

'In case Jacks turns round and makes us? Give me some credit.'

'Just thinking aloud.'

He rolled his mobile in his palm. 'I'm not sure you're thinking straight.'

'What do you mean?'

'I mean this. Jacks is meeting a grass. Fine. Cozzers meet grasses. We don't have to monitor it every time it happens.'

'We don't usually know.'

'I thought we had bigger things on our plate. The twins, for starters. You'll miss a shift for this. So will I.'

I could tell he wanted a row. Come to that, só did I. But I wanted to put the tail on Jacks more than I wanted to scream and shout.

'Just do this for me, Leon. I fancy it. I don't know why, I just fancy it.'

He looked away at the main road again, and stayed like that for about a minute. Then, hardly turning his head, he said:

'All right. I suppose we can always stick his name out over the tannoy.

If we know him. And if the meet's today. I'll call you later.' He slid into the Jag and split.

I waited for a few minutes then drove back to the service flat.

The Cine Club is in Oxford Road almost opposite the Palace Hotel; I was there by one forty. There was a handy bus stop a few yards down on the hotel side, so I loitered under the shelter and behind a newspaper. It came on to rain, so it was heads down and collars up and I couldn't see any faces. But I did see half a dozen geezers and two couples stroll in. I assumed they were couples, anyway. Long hair and high heels on one of the two in each case. This place, you couldn't assume anything to be that straightforward.

At two minutes to two, Hamilton Jacks's Granada pulled up near the lights and the busy rolled out. I counted twenty, splashed across the road and followed him in off the street. Steep stairs just inside and I glimpsed the cozzer clip through a green door up top as I came in. I counted twenty again, then nipped up and through into a foyer about eight foot square. A fiver at the tiny ticket window got me an old-fashioned bit of red board with ADMIT ONE stamped on it, John Bull-style, from a pretty young crustie in a red top. She was reading *The Ragged Trousered Philanthropist*.

The flick was in Italian, and – from what was going on as I took my seat – unlikely to appeal to homosexual tastes. There were about a dozen punters on site, at least two having a discreet play in their strides. I sat close to the back and made out the cozzer ten rows in front, three seats in. The seat next to him was taken.

Hamilton Jacks moved about ten minutes later. I slid down and put my hand to my forehead, fingers outstretched as he passed me. Then I just sat and waited.

The snide must have been enjoying the sex on show, because he didn't shift until the first movie ended, about half an hour later. Then he moved swiftly. I waited till he'd gone past and the doors squeaked shut, then zipped out and got him as he made the street. He was tall and grey-haired, wearing a Bogart mac with the collar up against the rain, and seemed to be walking with a slight stoop. I kept well behind up Oxford and along Portland Street, where he broke into a trot as the rain came on heavier. He went left in front of the Plaza Hotel and on through the bus station. Piccadilly was half empty, so I held back for a second and sweated, then twisted right and ran hard round the Gardens, making the cab rank on the corner as the grass ducked into the first hansom. I scrawled the car number on a snout packet and checked the time. Then I found a payphone and rang the club, asking if Ken was in. 'It's urgent, thank you.'

I'd known Kaluki Ken for years and he was always in the club during the day. Played cards all and every day and drove a cab every night. Fuck knew when he got his sleep.

'Hello?'

'Ken. You well?'

'I am. Didn't know you were out, though.'

I gave him the cab number, the place and the time. I said I wanted to know where the fare had been dropped and there'd be an earner in it for him if he could deliver. He told me to ring back in a couple of days. I hung up and called Leon.

'You should have been at the school today, you should have been looking for the kids. Not had us running around town chasing a grass. Or, more likely, our tails.'

'My choice, Leon. They're my kids.'

'Oh, do me a favour.' He looked round the pub and dropped his voice. 'Now it's all "they're my kids". So why am I involved, then?'

'I didn't ask you to get involved, Leon. Remember, I was away.'

'This is about me and Sara isn't it?' He was spitting, I saw the flecks jump over his teeth and hit the table. 'I thought I felt sorry for you,' he said. 'I was wrong.' He picked up his car keys.

'I'm not going to fight you in public. But this is going to be sorted between us. For the moment, my priority is to find the kids – and that would have been my priority whether I'd been seeing Sara or not. I'm in Leeds on business tomorrow. I'll do the three shifts and then assume you're doing Thursday. All right?'

'No, Leon. I'll do it all from now on.'

'Suit yourself. I'll be there anyway. Maybe they'll nonce us both off.'

Then he split and I sat feeling like a fool. After all these years, we could have ended up scrapping in a boozer like a couple of mugs. Sure he'd been out of order with all that snide but I could have allowed him that, this once at least. Instead I'd gone on as if he was interfering, not helping.

I went out and found the Escort, fired up the engine and drove, realising I had nothing to do and nowhere to go. I tried Carol's, got no reply. Then I rang Dud the mechanic to see if there was any news from his brother Gerry. He told me he'd not heard back. Still on the chase round for knowledge, I called Benny, the dope dealer in the Alex Park Estate to see if he'd got anything for me. An answerphone clicked in. First time I'd found him not at home in years. The message started with a few seconds of a Bob Marley track which dipped under Benny's voice asking you to leave your name, number and order. He couldn't have made it more blatant if he tried. I left a few words asking him to call me, chucked the phone onto the passenger seat and stopped at a red. The service flat seemed about as inviting as a cell in Strangeways. Not for the first time in my life, I reflected that I had hundreds of contacts and acquaintances and very few friends.

The lights were green and the queue shifted. It was thick, early evening traffic, so we moved slowly. I was sick of the service flat and sick of the flop in Leeds. And I was sick of being alone. I decided to book into a decent hotel and take a long bath, then ring an agency and spend some time with an upmarket hooker. I had enough money on me. I swung off the road into a side-street, went left and left again, then drove for the city centre.

The Midland Crown Plaza on Peter Street used to be the plain old Midland before it changed hands. They'd tarted it up and stretched the name, but it was still the grandest flop in Manchester. I checked in as John Drake, went up to my room and turned on the bath. The bathroom was standard hotel issue, but it was big and clean and stocked with thick white towels, shampoos and soap. I called down to room service for the most expensive sandwiches on the menu and a copy of the *Evening News*. If there's one thing Manchester has plenty of it's hookers, and they all advertise in the local rag.

Then I picked up my phone and belled Annie, my friendly neighbourhood estate agent. Some youth answered and said she was on another line. I gave the Midland's and my room number and asked for her to call me back. The room phone jumped a minute later. It was Annie, sounding far more friendly than last time. Carpet treaders don't normally dwell in a hotel like the Midland. 'Mr Drake! I was just thinking about you,' she lied.

'Annie. Just checking in about Buckingham Road. I've had a recommendation on a local solicitor. I'm hoping he can fit me in first thing tomorrow morning. Then I'll be handing matters – and the deposit, of course – over to him.'

'That's great, Mr Drake. I know Mrs Harpur is keen to move things on.'

She's opening a door for me. Don't push at it too hard, or she'll slam it shut again. 'Already bought somewhere, has she?'

'Well, that's what I thought at first, but it seems that she's renting in the short term. The place was empty when she gave it to us. She said she thought it would sell quicker chain free. Quite right of course.'

'Still, quite a big step to move on the off-chance. Is she moving for work or something?'

'I'm not sure, to be honest. I know she's in Leeds with her children right now. I think one of them might be going to the university next year. Maybe she just wants to be closer for that. Will you be at the Midland for long?'

'I'll be here for the time being. I'll call you with the solicitor's details tomorrow.'

'Look forward to it.'

'Goodbye, Annie.'

The sandwiches and coffee arrived. I ate slowly, staring out of the window. I thought Annie was going to deal me up something there. Well, you can't have it all.

After a while I undressed, tuned the hotel box to Radio 3, and sank into the still-steaming bath. I dozed for a while then towelled off and rang down for more coffee. When it came, I took a cup over to the window and looked out over the city. It was getting dark fast, and the hum of rush hour motors was building by the second as more straightgoers joined the queues of traffic on their way home.

9

A swim in the Midland's curious kidney-shaped pool the next morning did nothing to lose the depression I woke with. I went back to my room and got dressed, then dragged myself down the corridor for breakfast, pressing the call button for the lift like I was winching the bloody thing up the shaft with my finger. I was the last into breakfast. The Swiss-German queen hovering by the door wrinkled his nose as I sat down. *Late straight*, his face said. He came and hovered at my table. I asked for coffee and a full English and he evaporated.

I picked at my breakfast, feeling lousy. I'd checked into the hotel for a distraction but in the end I hadn't even called a bird. I just did the same sad stuff I would have done in Prestwich – ate, drank and watched telly till late. But the change of surroundings had done nothing for my mood, and my brain was still wandering places I'd rather it didn't go: Tomas lying in a pool of blood on the hospital steps; his mam and dad, red-eyed and broken, blaming me for his murder. Here comes the darkness.

Back in my room a few minutes later I drew a cigarette down to the filter in four drags and stubbed it out. This was no good. Do something, anything. My mind flipped to Sara, then her boss Bryant and the way I'd got hold of him the first day out. I should have checked on that bit of fallout already. I picked up the mobile and dialled Sara's office. Michelle the PA answered.

'Michelle, it's me. Look, I'm sorry about the other evening. I was having a bad day, I guess. I need to know, did the boss man call the police after I got a grip of him?'

'He was going to, but I talked him out of it. I told him it would cause Sara more trouble.'

'Thanks, Michelle. Have you heard anything from Sara?'

'No, we haven't. Please don't call here again.' The line went dead.

I was back in Leeds by four at the usual hotel, and ringing Leon. I'd checked out of the Midland at half eleven, picked up the Escort and dumped it with Laurie. Now I didn't have to sit on Hamilton Jacks's house I could use my own wheels again. I cabbed it back to Prestwich and packed. I'd spent the drive across brooding on Leon lecturing me yesterday and the fact he was in Leeds on school duty doing my job, sod it. Now he answered and said he'd got nothing. I said I'd go the next day. Our talk was strained

I spent the evening cruising the areas they might be living. Maybe Lou or Sam would be out on the streets, popping to the chippy or some late-night store. I slowed the motor every time I saw a group of teenagers hanging around, but all I got was hostile looks. Eventually I gave up, bought some fish and chips and ate them standing by the car, feeling heavy and thick-gutted. When I got back to the Queen's I was tired; I slumped in a chair and the depression rolled straight in again. It took me two hours to get to sleep.

I was at the school the next morning as the trickle started, building to a flow over the next twenty minutes. Parents dropped children off, kids waved goodbye, men and women ruffled hair and picked bits of fluff off embarrassed children in outsize duffel coats; kids came in one by one and two by two, pairs of girls larked around listening to the same MP3, lads tapped footballs to each other along the pavement; children pushed and elbowed and shouted, ran around the playground and laughed with and at each other. Then it all dried up and I was left alone. My eyes ached with staring at the crowds.

I left the plot and killed time by buying a coffee and reading the *Guardian* in a layby on the ring road. An article on the probation service reminded me that my probation officer would have sent an appointment to my gaff in Chorlton by now. I rang the office to find out the SP. The line went quiet while a cheery young girl checked.

'We've sent you a card. You're due in to see Pam at ten tomorrow morning. Is that OK?'

'Fine. Thank you.' I hung up. No point in not going. It would bring heat I could do without.

Lunchtime, I was back on stakeout duties. A couple of times, I had to give one lad or girl a second coat: similar build or hair style to either Lou or Sam. My pulse quickened, then slowed when I saw the full face. Maybe I'd missed them already – hard to see when they were in groups and heads down. But clocking situations and people was meant to be my game. Hmmm.

I cruised the grid in the afternoon and got back by three for the flood. Nothing till four, and I was just about to call it a day when I saw two girls drift out of the gates and turn left towards me. They were talking with heads down, both around my Lou's age and the one nearest to me had her build and hair. She threw her head back and laughed and it was her.

Oh Jesus.

I ducked and fiddled with my seatbelt till they passed, then I read the street behind me in the mirror. I didn't expect Sara to be picking her up at seventeen, but even so, I looked, then pushed the motor forward and did a lively three point turn. By now the girls were almost at the end of the road, and I drove steadily down after them. They turned left again, towards Headingley and the city centre. Nosing out of the road flashing left, I saw the girls had split up. Lou was on my side and stood alone at a bus stop, while her mate had almost reached the other kerb for the one opposite. I did the left and looked away as I passed. She was still busy calling across to her pal. I'd have just been another car, if she noticed me at all.

A block down, I pulled off in front of a blue Fiat and killed the engine. A bus juddered past going north, and the other girl got on with a wave. Without even stopping to lock the Rover, I made the pavement and started walking towards Lou. She was still gazing towards the stop where her pal had been.

'You selfish bastard. We never believed you were selling heroin. We knew you'd never. But you were in that lousy prison, otherwise it couldn't have happened.'

She'd mostly stopped crying now. She broke down when she saw me on the pavement, cried her way into my arms and flopped down the street beside me as I steered her into the motor. But when I got in and tried to hug her again, she'd fought me off and screamed all sorts at me, words I'd never heard out of her mouth before.

'Don't give me all that you've-always-been-straight-with-us crap. Don't you think it would have been better for Sam and me if you weren't a thief?'

I went to speak, but she waved me shut with the back of her hand.

'Nice, isn't it, going to school, knowing that this could be the day your dad gets arrested again. That's always assuming that morning wasn't the one the police had already chosen to knock down the door and drag you out in handcuffs again. That's a nice everyday thought for a child, isn't it, Dad?' She screamed again, 'Why couldn't you have stopped being a thief?' She broke down into sharp, painful, sobs. 'We never believed about Tomas, never – '

'Lou, I didn't know – '

'But if you hadn't been a thief, they couldn't have told us you had something to do with him being killed. Leaving our friends, school, house, everything. Do you think that's normal? Running out at a day's notice? And it was *your* fault.'

She started sobbing again, and I just sat there wretchedly. She didn't want to look at me, wouldn't let me touch her. She turned away, shoulders pumping up and down with her crying. After a few very long minutes, she faded into sniffs. Then, with a huge sigh, she tugged at her hair, fished a pack of tissues out and blew her nose.

'Where are you living?'

'Service flat in Prestwich.'

'I thought you'd moved. I rang your number all times of the day and night. You never picked up. I didn't leave a message, just in case. Is it safe?'

'I think so.'

'For messages on your machine. But not for you.'

'No.'

'Are the police after you?'

'Not in the usual way.'

She laughed loudly. 'Am I supposed to feel better the police are after you, *but not in the usual way*? Oh, Dad.'

'Is your mother expecting you?'

'She's out. If we're late, we're to leave a message on the answerphone. She's getting us both mobiles this week, so she can find us easily. Since Tomas, she gets hysterical if we're a minute late.'

A beat.

'Let's talk about that first.'

'What if I want to go home?'

'I can't make you stay.'

She sighed again. 'There's a phone on the roundabout.'

Crucified by guilt, I drove us down to the box. 'Lou . . . '

'I'll think of something. I'm your daughter, remember?'

I stayed put when she went to phone; that way she knew I wasn't chasing her new number. When she got back, I asked if she was hungry.

'I guess.'

'Fish and chips?'

'All right.' It was grudging, but her tone was slightly less hostile.

'I know a good one, proper fish and chips. It's near.'

'All right.' She was staring ahead again. She wasn't about to make anything easy. I slipped into drive and we moved off.

The sit-down part of the gaff was just opening when we showed. We got a table in the corner and as we ate, Lou told me the rest. She repeated they all believed the brown in my cell had been a fit up.

'But then Tomas got killed and everything went wrong.' Her eyes filled up. She put down her knife and fork and put her head in her hands. I knew not to touch her. After a few moments' silence, she picked up the fork and speared a bit of fish.

'Auntie Steph rang the hotel while we were in London, a few days before you were due out. We came straight back.' Two plainclothes had turned up at Buckingham Road the next evening, saying they were part of the murder team and that my name had cropped up. Sara should have known this was bollocks. If I'd really been in the frame, they wouldn't have said a word. The police told her the same pack of lies they told Jan and Steph – that I was dealing and that Tomas worked for me.

'We were all too upset about Tomas for anything new to go in anyway.'

'Just a minute.' I pulled out the Hamilton Jacks clipping and slid it across the table. 'Recognise him?'

She glanced at it and nodded. 'Yeah. He did most of the talking.'

I took the sheet back and nodded go on. I was glad she hadn't looked at the other side. I didn't want to have to explain his address being there.

The phone calls started later that night. Three of them, between nine o'clock and eleven. A Manchester voice, hard sounding, telling Sara what a slag I was. Saying that it might be her son or daughter next time. Well, that had been it. Sara hadn't waited for another bell or knock at the door. They'd stayed up all night packing and got a removal firm to take the furniture across to Leeds next day and put it in storage. They followed, booked into a hotel, and two days later they were dwelling in a rented gaff. Lou didn't say where. And I'd been right about the school. Sara had friends, she'd pulled some strings to get them in.

Sara wasn't much interested whether I was involved in the smack or not, said Lou. But she'd lived in Manchester long enough to know that people did get killed over class A, plenty of people. So she was taking her kids out of it. And she'd do it right – she'd seen me disappear often enough. Yes, the police would find her, if they were looking. And maybe I would, she reckoned. But she'd make it hard for the kind of people that killed Tomas.

Leon came into all of this. It wasn't that she didn't trust him. But she knew what he was and where he went, and she'd decided that her kids had come close enough to villainy in their short lives. So she left Leon as well, without a note, without a word. That's how it's supposed to be when you're a mother. All that matters is your children.

'So what's happening?' she said. 'Why are they saying these things about you?'

Why indeed. Best keep it simple.

'I don't know yet. But I'm pretty certain that copper in the picture, the one who came to see you, he's mixing me a bottle.'

'Why?'

'You remember Jack Keane? Uncle Jack?'

'Is he the one that gave us White Bear and Brown Bear for our seventh birthday?'

'Mr White and Mr Brown. That's him. I did him a favour once and the copper got burnt fingers as a result. Might be that he wants some kind of revenge.'

'On us? Ringing Mum, making threats?'

'I don't know about that . . . '

'What about Tomas?'

'I don't know, Lou. But I'm finding out. I'll find out.'

I paid the bill and we split. I told Lou I'd drive her to the centre and put her in a taxi. She was silent on the way, and my mind was running over what she'd said earlier. As we came up to Roundhay Park, I said, 'Can you spare me another ten minutes, love. Before you go.'

She turned her head to me. The smile was very brief. 'All right.'

I pulled across into a layby where pedlars sold ice cream in the summer. We both wound our windows down and sat in silence. There was a smell of cut grass from the park. I lit up and smoked for a minute. Then I flicked my half-burnt fag in an arc towards the roadside. It made a tiny red curve in the sky like a minute comet, fell to earth and went out.

I turned to Lou and reached across for her hand. I squeezed it for a moment, then let go. She'd returned the pressure.

'Lou, virtually everything you said before was spot on: I have been a lousy dad to you both. What I'm going to say to you now will sound like mitigation.'

'Go on.'

She knew what mitigation meant. I remembered her nine years old and looking it up in a dictionary, running to me and saying 'Look, Daddy, all you have to do is say sorry and they'll let you go. You don't have to go to prison again.' God forgive me.

'Lou, I've always tried to be straight with you. But that's not enough. Being straight hasn't stopped me from being selfish.'

She nodded, but she kept her eyes to the front.

'By the time I met your mam, I was a villain inside and out; villainy dominated my mind. There wasn't even the option of another option. It was what I was. A good father would have turned the game in when you and Sam came along. He would have stopped running the risk of being away from you. I didn't. I just carried on. I justified it in my mind, of course, but I knew I was letting you down. So I can't plead ignorance. I told myself that with the dough I was going to get, I'd make sure you got the very best of everything.'

She was still staring ahead, but I knew she was listening.

'The truth is, you could have got the really important things if I'd been skint, as long as I was there. But I wasn't, was I?'

A prison visiting room, her and Sam just five and the screws shouting 'visit over' and neither of them understanding why they had to go and I had to stay.

'Most people would use the fact that I did carry on thieving when you were born as sure evidence that I didn't love you enough. If that's all it does take for a guilty verdict, then I'm convicted now.'

'I'm listening, Dad.' Her voice was hard.

'Lou. I can't feel any more for anyone than I feel for you and Sam. That's all there is to it, but I need you to know. I need you to tell Sam that.' My throat was dry. I cleared it and went on. 'But you should build your lives around your mam. She has to be your rock for now.'

'We don't have a choice.' She held my gaze for a few seconds longer than I would have liked.

'Tell Sam what I've said, Lou. I need a channel open between us. I need to know you're OK.'

There was silence again, so long that the blood started rushing in my ears. A day passed. Then: 'We'll adapt, Dad. You didn't have to ask. But I'm glad you did.'

I guess I got off lightly.

I pulled into a services on my way home and belled Leon. It hardly rang before he picked up.

'I've spoken to Lou. I know where they are.'

'Thank God.' From the other end of the line, I felt him shed about ten years. 'Are they all right?'

'They're fine. She's got my number, they're getting mobiles and she's going to ring me with the numbers. So we can keep in touch. Listen, do you want to come round? I'll be back in about an hour.'

There was a long, contented sigh from the other end, then he said, 'Fine. I'll see you there.'

I drove back into Manchester feeling I was lying back in a warm bath. My children were safe and secure. For the moment, nothing else mattered.

I was back in the service flat talking to Leon by half eight. As I told him about Lou, I swear I saw some of the lines fade from his face.

'And she looked all right?'

'Yes, she looked fine. Beautiful and well.'

I was standing in the kitchen brewing up a second cup of tea. He was leaning against the counter, arms crossed. 'And Sara's OK?'

'Yes, Leon. Far as I know.'

'She can take care of herself.' He loved my wife all right.

'Lou sends you her love,' I lied.

'Did she? Did she say anything else?'

I looked at his face. I thought about how he had no one but his mam, and then I made up some words. 'She talked about you a bit, said how much she and Sam liked you. That they miss you as well. She wanted me to tell you that. It wasn't anything to do with you that they went. She wanted you to know.'

'It's just because I'm a villain.'

'Same as me.'

'Yeah. Same as you.' He sighed deeply, and another line went. 'Well, at least Lou had a word for me now.'

I was glad I'd lied. I was sure she would have given me a message for him if she hadn't been listening to me. She'd probably give me one next time. Leon saw me tip the kettle and shook no before I brewed again.

'I think I'll give that one a miss. I ought to be heading back home.' Now he was making like he was in a hurry.

'Leon, listen,' I said. 'About that row we had . . . '

'No,' he said. 'Don't spoil it. They're safe and that's all that matters. Everything else tomorrow, OK?' He was at the door now. 'Need to get off, anyway. Got a meet in the morning, about one of my gaffs in Spain. It's local, as it happens, so I'll be through by lunchtime and we can talk then. I'll call, all right?'

'OK, Leon. Goodnight mate.'

I saw him out the street door and went back inside where I crumpled on the sofa. There wasn't anything pressing to do before tomorrow morning, and I felt exhausted.

I wondered what Lou would tell Sara about me. Or Sam. Had she told her brother already? Or was he out? He'd know tonight, that was for sure. What if Sara overheard them talking, went into one and made them all move again. To get away from me? What if . . .

I yawned, and felt the calm flood through my entire body in waves. I hadn't realised how wound up I'd been. I turned on the telly and watched half a minute of some programme about skirts before I realised it was in Italian. Then I noticed the little logo in the top left-hand corner and realised the video under the telly was actually a decoder. The flat had cable. I hit another button and some American talk show host appeared. A tickertape across the bottom of the screen said: I'M LEAVING YOU FOR MY PHONE SEX LOVER!

I thought I'd only been away eighteen months.

I button-punched a few more times and found what I was looking for, the sports channel. An announcer was giving the SP for the evening's programmes. This would include a documentary about United and the Munich air crash. Then tractor pulling came on.

Suddenly livened up, I pulled on my jacket and nipped round the corner for a Chinese.

10

Leon's alarm threw me against the wall and demanded a fiver at eight o'clock. I stretched over and punched it, then fell back into a doze. A few minutes later, it went off again. I groaned back into the light, groped from under the covers and knocked it onto the floor. Bugger kept going. With a loud *sod it* I rolled out of bed, scrabbled and picked it up, stabbing the button. Still going. Then I woke up properly and sussed the racket was someone else's. And it wasn't stopping either. The thoughtless bastard.

I hustled myself into the shower, my clothes, and then out of the house. I had plenty to do, starting with an appointment at probation. Then Casey for the rest of the dough, and go see Benny in the Moss to hurry him along about Tomas. And the Jacks tape would need changing tonight.

The other bloke's alarm was still screaming as I slid behind the wheel of the Rover. Someone was going to be late for work.

Driving on the mirror, I joined the stream for town. A few minutes and the traffic thickened and slowed to a stop-start pace. By the time the flow was passing Strangeways, we were almost at a standstill. Heavy plant noise up ahead. Roadworks. This was bad. Whipping past the joint I could deal with, but moving so slow got the anxiety fluttering around in my gut. I opened a window and thumbed the lighter in. A couple of seconds and it clicked out. I sparked up, saw the red circle and felt the heat on my face.

I couldn't stop myself. Never can. Neck and eye muscles pulling taut, I glared up at the dirty red tower, one of the few parts of the nick left after the riots. It dominates this part of Manchester and sticks in your head when you pass it, like staring at the sun. It always nauses me because I know what's going on in there, out on the wings and down in the seg unit. The violence and the hatred.

There were horns up my arse. The traffic was moving and I hadn't noticed it. I joined the flow past the *Manchester Evening News* Arena, then on up through Ancoats and into Stretford knowing I was clean. I still didn't want the Rover on show near the probation office, so it got tucked up in a side street behind the Arndale.

I'd been thinking about this appointment. First, there was a chance that it would be on top, down to my getting a grip of Sara's boss on day one. That would mean Old Bill sat waiting for me and straight back to Strangeways without the option. But if Michelle the PA was telling the truth that wasn't an issue. Second, there was the estate agents and the run-in with the filth. But I reckoned it was a million to one against the filth thinking it was anything other than a local burglar who could have a fight. So I felt safe on that.

The third point-of-grief was that Pam would be wanting to do a home visit quite soon and I could definitely do without that. I took out my phone and weighed it in my palm for a minute. Then I belled an old pal who ran a pub in Winsford. This lad owed me a few favours, so I called one in.

Pam was an attractive woman in her late forties, and a bit of a hippy. Mother Earth, Grateful Dead, *Lord of the Rings*, that kind of style. I'd also got the impression from the nick that she'd be saving most of her time and energy for the younger villains on her books; the ones where she might make a difference.

Today's interview went OK, as it happened. I told her that I was working in a pub in Winsford, and was grafting all the hours that God sent.

'Oh dear,' she said. 'That'll make a home visit awkward.'

'You're always welcome at the pub. Boss knows the score.'

She wrote down my spiel in a hardback A4, but I felt pretty safe. If she showed at the pub my pal would say that he'd given me a few hours off. She looked up, and for a second I thought I'd spoken aloud.

'Strictly speaking, you should come into the office once a week,' she said. 'But it is at my discretion, and I don't want to risk upsetting your work, especially when you've been so quick to find a job.' There was the slightest inflection on *quick* as she spoke. Maybe she knew the score as well.

'I'll send you a card in a couple of weeks. Then we can fix up a chat.'

I left. She was all right, for a Care Bear. I hadn't minded lying to her though.

The big man opened up in his dressing gown fifteen minutes later. Casey was eating a bowl of Rice Krispies and looking hungover. It wasn't a pretty sight.

'You're looking hungover, Casey,' I said. 'And you're in your dressing gown and eating a bowl of Rice Krispies.'

'Come in.' He coughed at me chestily and led the way to the dining room.

'Stella and the kids are away.' He sat down heavily at the table and the chair creaked alarmingly. 'Marta stayed on here.'

'I think you told me.'

'Took her out for dinner last night.'

Here it came. He'd taken Marta to a trendy Italian in town. They'd eaten and drunk till midnight, then Marta suggested going on to a club. To Casey, club meant *the* club and nothing else. Marta had different ideas. She'd dragged him along to a place called Monica's Skirt down in the gay village. Inside, so Casey said, there were a lot of teenagers waving their hands in the air and hugging each other.

'Hot as fuck, mate, hot as fuck. And packed. Fucking packed teeth to arse. And the drinks. The prices. Tenner for a couple of lagers. A tenner. And people kept hugging me. Why was that?'

'Either they were dippers or it was the drugs. It makes them very friendly.'

'What does?'

'E. Ecstasy. MDMA. Keeps them dancing all night and makes them all lovey dovey.' Casey was tugging his beard at me. 'The twins are teenagers, mate. I like to know what's going on.'

'Oh. Right. That's it, then.'

At some point, Marta had grabbed him and pulled him on to the floor for a bit of arm waving. Feeling well out of place but wanting to impress, he'd gone along with it. Various kids danced up and started some kind of hug-in and Casey had misread the signals from Marta.

'Thought she wanted a bit of the other.'

'But she didn't.'

'No. She didn't.'

Marta had slapped his face, taken a cab home and locked herself in her bedroom. When Casey got in and went up to see her, she'd shouted a washing line of Spanish abuse through the door and that was it. She was still in bed as far as he knew.

'I'm fucked if she tells Stella.'

'She won't.'

'Should I sack her?'

There was a loud noise from upstairs. We both looked up at the ceiling and heard Marta rip open her bedroom door. Then she stomped down the corridor and into the bathroom. Another door slammed shut.

'Sack her? What for?'

'Nothing. I just can't have her grassing me to Stella. The kids love her, mind. Oh bugger.'

The toilet flushed upstairs, the bathroom door went, there was more stomping, then Marta slammed her bedroom door. Creaking floorboards, then one big squeak as she threw herself back into bed.

'I thought you said she'd asked you to sleep with her.'

'That's what I understood. I must have misheard. What shall I do?'

I tapped my fingers on the table. 'Sacking her would be the simplest option. It would get the trouble off your doorstep. But you'll need to come up with an excuse to tell Stella. And what if Marta comes round and tells her anyway? You can't be in all the time. And as you said, the kids love her.'

'Bugger.'

'Best thing to do is apologise, Casey. Say you'd had a few, whatever, say it won't happen again. Tell her you don't want to cause trouble, and you don't want her to cause trouble. Then give her a large cash bribe. About a grand.'

'Fuck. She only gets forty a week.'

'Your choice.'

'Thousand quid. Expensive bloody feel. All right. Can you do us a favour? Go up and tell her I need a word. I don't want her to think I'm giving it another go if I knock on her door. She's on the first floor, door at the end of the landing. Could you?'

'Casey, I'm a thief, not a counsellor.'

'Please, mate.'

I shook my head at him, went along the hall and swung round the banisters to take the stairs two at a time. At the top, I went up to her door and knocked on the woodwork.

'No!'

Sod this. 'Marta – '

'No! I call Stella! I call the police!'

Sod this again. I didn't have time for all this crap. I opened up and went in. She was sitting up in bed looking red-eyed. Long shiny brown hair, dark eyes and clear olive skin.

'Who are you?'

'I'm a friend of Casey's. He asked me to come up and talk to you.'

'Fuck off, friend of Casey's.' She wriggled down into the bed, slammed her head on the pillow and turned her face to the wall. A couple of seconds later, she sat up again. 'You still here?'

'Casey wants to say sorry.'

'Too late. I going tell Stella everything.'

'Did he hurt you?'

'No.'

'Did he touch you in the wrong place?'

'No. But I understand what he want.'

'Did anyone else see anything?'

'No. I just felt it. On my, on my . . . ' She slapped her backside through the duvet. So that was it. Out of order of course, but not the crime of the century.

'Right. He wants to say sorry. Please come downstairs and talk to him.'

'No.'

'He's really sorry, Marta.'

'No.'

'He wants to give you some money.'

She held my gaze for a couple of seconds, and I immediately understood that this was a stand-up for cash. She threw back the cover and swung her feet over on to the floor. She was wearing a sweatshirt, trackpants and thick woollen socks. 'Go downstairs and tell him I come.'

I sat in the kitchen and listened while Casey and Marta traded horses next door. Casey went in at five hundred. Marta said she also wanted two extra nights off a week and her boyfriend being allowed to stay overnight.

'But you don't have a boyfriend.'

'When I get a boyfriend. And not you, Casey, no chance.'

Casey was in no position to negotiate extra nights off. He KB-ed the boyfriend and offered seven hundred. She asked for a grand. They finally settled on nine hundred sheets. She also wanted the rest of the week off until Stella and the kids got back.

'But they're expecting you to go up and join them tomorrow.'

'You make some excuse. I go to see my friend in London. Don't worry, I come back Sunday night.' Casey had no choice, so he gave her a yes.

'OK. I make my packing, you should give me the money before I go.'

I heard her leave the dining room and go upstairs. I went in. Casey was sitting at the table, looking out of the window and shaking his head. His Rice Krispies had long turned to mush.

'Sorted?'

'Seems to be. Thanks, mate.'

'We've got business of our own, Casey.'

'Oh bloody hell. Sorry.' He went out and reappeared a few seconds later with a cheap briefcase like last time. 'Twenty grand. Please check it.'

I opened the case and flicked the bundles. 'That's good, Casey. Thanks.'

'Thank you. For, er . . . ' He gestured vaguely upstairs.

'Forget it.'

I rang Leon from the Rover, rehearsing a few words in my nut. I really had to clear the air after that row. It was important. He didn't pick up though, and the voicemail didn't click in either. The dash clock said eleven fifty. Not quite lunch, I guessed.

I rang my answerphone in Chorlton for something to do and picked up a message from Lou giving me her and Sam's new mobile numbers. I rewound the machine and scribbled them down on a scrap of paper from the glove compartment. That was quick. Sara must have been out shopping yesterday. Thinking of Sara reminded me of the estate agent and the stroke with the house, so I rang Annie. She'd just gone out for a sandwich. I left a message that I was withdrawing my offer on Buckingham Road because I had to go abroad on work. No need to carry on being John Drake now I'd found Sara and the kids. Chucking the phone on the passenger seat, I drove across to Amy's and laid the dough under the dog's bed with the rest. I was out by half twelve, tapping Leon's number into my mobile as I pulled away from the kerb. No reply and no voicemail.

Back to the service flat and across to Mr Rauth's for some lunch. I stuck his chicken casserole in the microwave, then sat and ate it in front of the news. After five minutes fingertapping and staring out of the window, I called Judith.

'He's not back, lovey. I was expecting him for lunch, but it'll have to go back into the oven now. Never mind.'

I hung up. The chicken was hanging around inside, so I opened the window. That bloody alarm was still going off. I banged on the radio so I wouldn't hear it. It wasn't that loud, but it was pissing intrusive. One fifteen.

Five past two and now out of fags, I schlepped across to Mr Rauth's again and bought eighty. That alarm was still at it, I felt like finding the bloody house and caning the fucking door. And to fuck me off even more, my own alarm went off as I stepped inside. I chucked the fags and kicked into the bedroom. Set to two twenty, what the fuck? Must have knocked the dial this morning. I could still hear the other fucking alarm bleeping and jangling away, the same sound as mine.

The same sound as mine.

Oh Christ.

I nearly fell back into the kitchen, tearing open drawer after drawer looking for the sod. Got it – tenancy agreement with the agent's number at the top. I whipped my phone out and punched it in. A young lad picked up. Keeping my voice calm, I told him that I was renting a flat in one of their service blocks, and that the people upstairs were a bit noisy. Did they have a place in another block? Yes, said the lad. And the other block was only on the next corner, but they couldn't show it till Monday because they had two people off with the flu. He gave me the address.

I slammed the phone down, shot back into the kitchen, upended the dustbin across the floor and scrabbled around amongst the crap for a used prepay card. Somewhere, somewhere, fuck. Got it. Snatching turtles and jacket, I ran out the front door and on to the street and twisted right at the corner. The alarm got louder, as I knew it would. Gloves on and up the drive; the hedge was high enough to hide me from the road. I glanced round at the front door, then loided it with the phonecard. This hall was the same as my block. The alarm clock was screaming from above. Urgent and loud enough to throw you against the wall when it blew. Two steps at a time to the first floor, a door with a large brass 3. I glanced up and down the stairs and kicked it in.

A quick shufti told me I could use the window for an offmans – it couldn't be more than fifteen foot down – so I shut the door and took the bedroom first. Blankets on the deck and Leon's brown leather holdall on a chair. I punched the alarm, then went back in the lounge to case it with my ears ringing.

Behind the sofa there was a table draped in a cloth. Behind that, on the wall, about head height – a red smudge. Christ. I dragged the table away and found Leon, slumped on the floor. He was in jeans and a thick grey jumper. His feet were bare. His eyes were open. He was looking straight at me.

'Leon, mate.'

It was like I was trying not to wake him. I pulled off a glove and touched his cheek. Cold. He'd been dead a long time. Pink blotches on his jumper; I pulled it up, saw the stab wounds. There must have been twenty: stomach, chest, neck, shoulders. The blood had dried now, or been soaked up by the wool. His hands were striped. Defence wounds.

I straightened and stretched the glove back on. Whatever had happened here, I couldn't be in the frame. I shot into the bedroom and went through his jacket and bag. Nothing with my footprints. Then into the kitchen: three mugs and a pint of milk on the side, that was it. A quick glance in the drawers and cupboards brought nowt, just cutlery, plates and more cups. Same style as my flat. Check round the lounge again. Nothing. The place was clean. There was a phone on the table. I checked it was connected, then cradled the receiver and knelt down next to him.

'I'll look after your mam, Leon, I promise. And I'm sorry about the thing with Sara.' I reached over and closed his eyes. 'So long, mate.'

Then I stood and dialled three nines. I heard the operator answer and laid the receiver down on the table. Tinny and distant, she asked again what service I wanted. They'd trace the call and send a car. I only had a few minutes.

I was back in my lounge in time to see the police car sweep past. Not long after I saw the ambulance whip by and imagined the green-overalled paramedics taking the stairs two at a time, checking Leon's body, the coppers unrolling the blue striped incident tape across the doorways, getting on the radio for the plainclothes to attend, the detectives arriving. Later there would be forensic men with their rubber gloves and white overalls, dusting for prints. And much later, the place would be sealed, maybe with one young uniformed lad on duty outside, stamping up and down in the cold, waiting for someone to come and relieve him in the morning.

It took a few minutes to empty my flat. The clothes and gear from the bathroom went into a holdall, the food and drink from the fridge went into one plastic bag and the contents of the kitchen and lounge bins into another. Five minutes with a damp cloth got my dabs off any surfaces Old Bill were likely to dust.

The filth would be round for sure. Both blocks were owned by the same landlord, and both were service flats. And Leon had sorted the place for me. No way did I intend to be available for interview when they started doing their homework. The snide name, along with the knowledge that I was a known associate of Leon's would be enough for them. And once I was on a lie-down, fitting me up for the murder wouldn't take much doing. I'd broken in to start with. And there was a copper out there who wanted my arse. Fuck knew what Hamilton Jacks would do when Leon's death filtered through to him.

The thief's instinct for self-preservation also called the cards for fronting Judith. No way could I go round. The police had been on the plot in minutes, the ambulance told me they'd found Leon almost immediately. There was no ID in his jacket, but the law would make him pretty quickly anyway. Chances were that they wouldn't swoop on his home drum straight away – once they'd made Leon as a villain, the filth might choose to sit on the discovery for a while – but I couldn't take the bet: I'd be no use to anyone locked away in a police cell.

I thought of Judith, waiting for Leon with his dinner still in the oven. I couldn't just leave her like that. Then I remembered Leon's cousin Ronnie. He was straight – in the rag trade with a warehouse near the nick – but he knew Leon's game and he knew me and he knew we were very close. I'd go and see him.

I made two trips to the car, checking out Leon's block as I went. Two police cars and an ambulance on the drive, but no one making themselves busy on the gravel. I went back for the bin bags and slung them in the back with the rest, then I took off for Ronnie's gaff in Empire Street. He was in with two Asians, I told him it was urgent. He gave me a right look, but said they were just winding up. 'Wait outside for a minute, would you?'

The rag trade went on in the warehouse – racks of clothes trundled in and out of parked-up vans, a radio cranked up to eleven, blue-overalled lads shifting boxes of gear from one bay to another and larking about in between. Then I heard the goodbyes as Ronnie ushered his visitors out. He turned to me.

'This had better be important.'

I waited till he'd closed the door and got back behind his desk. Then I told him about Leon and he started crying. I had no time for this, but I gave him a few minutes to straighten up. Then I asked him to go and see Judith straight away. I didn't have to justify making myself scarce, he knew what I was.

'You'll need to go now, Ronnie. I don't want her to hear it from the police.'

'Yeah, yeah.' He was standing up, shuffling papers into the desk and locking the drawer.

'I'll give you a couple of hours, then I'll ring you there.'

'Why?'

'To see how she is.'

'What if she blames you?'

I looked at him. I couldn't think of anything to say. He shook his head.

'You better get going.'

'Ronnie – '

'Just go, for God's sake.'

I drove using busy roads, forcing myself to concentrate on traffic lights, junctions and crossings. Up through Collyhurst, Failsworth and then Gorton. I turned left up Hyde Road, fuck, the nest, you mug. Fuck, how could I forget? Go and clear the place before the filth do.

The nest was the Wilmslow Love Nest, a cottage he'd bought for when he wanted to go case with a bird. But it was more than a shag flat, it was for work as well. Leon kept stuff there; stuff that I would now have to shift.

It took me twenty minutes to get down. There was a space on Bollin Walk a couple of streets away, and I made Leon's terrace on foot – a row of eight tiny two-up two-downs with a church at the bottom. The nest was the last, at the far end. Down the side and into the yard, where I felt below the kitchen window for the twirl. The back lights said next door was out, two down was in and three down was out. I twirled the lock like I had the right.

The kitchen was dark. I pulled the blinds and flicked the light on. Then I slung my jacket on a chair, pulled on my turtles and went under the sink for the Phillips that dwelt there. Could have found it with my eyes closed, it was in the same place it always was.

I opened the upright freezer and rifled through the ice. Too much, have to take some shit out. A bag of prawns, a small chicken and two stews in tubs that Judith had cooked and labelled. At the back there were two loaves of bread, one brown, one white. The brown was heavier. I opened the wrapper and prised the first two slices off the top, then upended it over the sink and knocked it on the side. Four wraps of notes dropped out, and got stowed in a plastic bag from a drawer full of neatly folded plastic bags. I stuck the frozen stuff back and the kitchen was done with.

I shot into the lounge. There was a small antique writing desk slotted into an alcove. I lifted the brass well out of the inkholder and pushed down hard with my thumb on one of the four studs that held it in place. A shallow drawer slid out into the space underneath. I lifted it out completely and laid it on the blotter. A thick bundle of documents tied with pink ribbon, like a lawyer's brief. Top page written in Spanish. And a bound notebook, slightly larger than A5. They only got the briefest of glances – it was enough they were in the drawer and well off-show; they were going.

The drawer clicked itself shut, the inkwell went back in smoothly. Tell 'em fuck all.

I went upstairs. His bedroom was off the tiny landing, and the door was open – bed neatly made, hospital corners and counterpane hanging down at sharp right angles. Then I saw a rumpled set of sheets, sweaty and twisted, and Sara lying cradled in his right arm. He was lying back with closed eyes; she was looking into the distance, relaxed and content.

With an effort I tore my eyes away and went to drag the pine blanket box across to the trapdoor. I climbed up on it, bumped the hatch open and racked down the metal ladder. Up into the loft, find the light, bend at the shoulders and then inch along the rafters to where joist and roof meet. There I crouched and felt for the slot in the padding between the joists. Got it, roll it back, and there were fifty of them. Plastic wrapped bundles of fifties – probably a grand apiece. I stuck the lot into a carrier, then prodded round to make sure I'd missed none and finally stuffed back the cladding. Crouch and scuttle to the trapdoor, twist the neck, drop it onto the deck below and follow it down, then pull the trap shut behind me. Finally, I dipped into the bathroom and used the Phillips to whiz the bath panel off. Nish. Back went the panel. Tell the bastards nothing.

I'd just done in the bathroom when I heard a knock at the front door. Fuck. Better get it though. The lights were on, it would look more suspicious if no one answered. I jogged downstairs, stuck the money and turtles behind a cushion, turned the main light off and a lamp on, then opened up. I half recognised the guy on the step. Him and his mate were gay and lived two doors down.

'Oh, hello. Is Leon around?'

'No, not at the moment.'

'Oh, right, it's just that I noticed his guttering at the back was leaking last time it rained. He's not been around much last few weeks, so I thought he'd like to know.'

'Thanks. I'll leave him a note.'

He nodded goodbye and I closed the door.

I was done. I stuck the carriers in a holdall I'd found, switched all the lights out and left, sticking the twirl back under the kitchen sill. My eyes bounced all over the terrace as I went for the car – no curtain flicks or net twitching that I could see. Couldn't feel anyone in the shadows.

I fired up and drove aimlessly, turning left or right at random and with no idea of where I was going. After about half an hour of this, I decided to make for Hayfield and the hills. Phone box first, there was no signal round here. Ten minutes further down the road I clocked one and stopped to call Judith. Ronnie picked up.

'How is she?'

'Upstairs having a lie down.'

'Why, did she collapse or something?'

'No. She took it very quiet. Said nothing for a couple of minutes, then she asked about you. I said you were taking care of yourself.'

'Was that it?'

'No. She got me to call her sister, my other aunt. Lives in Kersal. Asked if she could take a taxi down and sit in with her for the night.'

'She there yet?'

'She's on her way.'

'Tell Judith I called. I'll call again in a day or so.'

'OK.'

'Tell her I called.'

'I said, OK.'

I hung up and stared through the glass at a chip shop just down from the box. Two lads and a girl were mucking about inside as a Chinese guy wrapped their food. One of the boys was waving the vinegar about like a Star Trek laser gun and the other two were holding their hands up in surrender. The guy laid their third parcel on the counter and they left, their breath making clouds as they laughed down the street. I'd sit and speak to Judith again one day soon. I'd make sure that she had whatever she could do with.

I stopped a bit further down at a walking gear shop. It was just closing, but the guy let me in.

'Thanks,' I said.

'I want your money.'

I bought walking boots, thick socks, a thick jumper, and a cheap cagoule. I gave him his money.

The Royal Hotel's car park was big. Plenty of residents, plenty of passing trade. It made me feel a lot safer. I asked for a room with a proper bath. Not a shower. The girl on the desk got a moody name and no, I wouldn't be taking dinner, but could she sort me some sandwiches and a bottle of wine. She could.

I took my things and Leon's up to my room where I whipped the side off the bath and hid his stuff behind it, then screwed it back.

And went out to buy brandy.

Back in the hotel, I ran a hot bath and rolled a joint. I smoked it in the tub, then I just sat feeling numb. Twice I let some water out and some hot in. After about an hour, I towelled dry and rang down for the food and booze.

I ate slowly when it arrived, but knocked down the booze a glass at a time. Just before nine, I booked an alarm call for the morning, then carried on with the drink and the dope. When the wine was finished I used the same glass for the brandy. That bottle was done by eleven. I passed out soon after.

11

My head was pounding as I left the hotel and took the metalled road out of the village for the old quarry and Kinder the next morning. A few hundred yards along the river, I turned and struck up a steep slope for the hills. The going got stiff and my breath came in rasps. Each step made my hungover nut thud harder. Usually I'd stop a time or two for the view, but today I was here to push myself. I was already sweating heavily, despite the chill wind whipping me across the face.

I levelled off and cut right to join the footpath to Jacob's Ladder – a set of stone steps set into the hillside, once a pack route from Manchester to Sheffield. My breathing got easier. No, this had to be hard. I forced myself up to a trot, grunting so loud that the dirty grey sheep grazing either side of the path jumped and darted away.

An hour later and with Edale Cross in sight, I sat down against a gorse-covered slope and lit one of the joints I'd brought with me. The only man-made thing in sight was a drystone wall. I'd brought Leon and Jack Keane here once, years ago. I remembered Jack slumping down on the grass for breath and asking if I did this often. 'Bloody hell, son,' he said. 'I thought I was pretty fit. Am I, bollocks.'

That was the only time Jack came, but Leon got into walking after that trip, and we'd rested here a hundred times. One time, he'd pretended he was too knacked to go on. 'Leave it out,' I'd said. 'Next time we'll have you going the distance. Not just this bloody stroll.' The next time.

When I'd finished crying, I took a drink of water, splashed a little around my eyes and carried on up the hill.

It was a steady climb to Edale Rocks and we'd usually stick to the path, part of the Pennine Way. I took the hardest route and started walking across the moor instead. A few paces and the going got tough again – up and down and across dozens of gorse-topped trenches, all gummed with boot-sucking peat. Good. I was here to test, to break hard sweat and to make my muscles work till they hurt. I had to flush something out of my body to make my mind balanced again, and this was it. I imagined the sweat pouring out of the pores across my forehead, scalp, down my back, out through soles and palms. The splashes of salt water were pitted with tiny black crystals, washing them out of my body, cleansing it of all the grief and fear that had swamped me since I found Leon slumped under the swab of his own blood. I walked on faster and harder, pushing myself and straining up and down the trenches until my lungs were heaving, pushing against the bars of my ribs.

I stopped at the top of the Downfall to eat the sandwiches I'd bought in the village and splashed my face with some peaty river water. Then I did a mile or so back on the path and began the descent down Williams Clough. It was steep and the river running down next to it made the going slippery, so I had to concentrate on where to put my feet. By the time I made the reservoir half an hour later, the need to push myself was over. I sat down and sparked another joint.

From here, I could see nearly all of where I'd walked – from the scar of the quarry car park to the slopes of Kinder Low and the dark ridge of the mountain itself. I imagined looking down on myself and saw a dot in the gorse; just another bit of punctuation in the world. Alone again without him, but I could deal with it. I'd left the sharp end of my grief in the hills, now it was just the pulse of sadness.

I looked at my watch for the first time. Three. The dark was already beginning to show.

Half four and I was running a bath at the Royal. There was no weed and no booze this time. After a good soak for my legs, I dried off and rang down for a call and some food in two hours. I hung up, lay back, and dozed off in a second.

My eyes snapped open at a gentle knock. 'Yes?' I swung my feet on to the carpet and shook my head.

'Room service.' Muffled voice from the other side of the door.

I padded across and put my eye to the spyhole. Round red waistcoat and huge curved red bowtie. Looked like room service to me.

'You ordered dinner, sir.' The bubble man through the fisheye carrying the concave tray was now looking deeply pissed off. 'Shall I leave it outside, sir?'

'No, just a minute.' I pulled on the hotel bathrobe from the back of the door, rifled my jacket for change and opened up. Two quid didn't seem to cheer him up much.

'Thank you. Please sign here.'

I scribbled on the ticket he held out to me. Still half asleep, I'd forgotten what name I was using, so I made it illegible. I pushed it back at him and took the tray. 'Thank you.'

After I'd eaten I put the tray out in the corridor, doublelocked the door and checked the chain. Straighten the bed, flatten the counterpane even and smooth. No more putting it off now.

I took the Phillips to the bathroom, screwed the panel off and tugged the holdall out. Unzipping it on the bed, I lifted out Leon's books and papers and laid them gently on one side. Then I tipped the bag upside down and let the bricks of cash fall out.

The main parcel from the loft contained fifty grand – or at least fifty similar-sized bundles. I counted five at random, and they each came to a grand. This would have been his parcel money. A handy stash in case a decent prize came on the market. When a firm nicks something, they usually want their dough a bit lively. A man with this kind of readies could make himself serious money. The other cash, from the freezer, would have been for day to day. And being Leon's, it was neat and tidily bound. Another four grand.

I shuffled the cash back into the holdall and started to flick through the papers. Mostly in Spanish, but the English pages told me it was legals relating to his two flats and a house in Marbella. All rented out with a Madrid account looked after by a local lawyer whose letters spoke good

English. Someone would have to make contact with her at some point. It wouldn't be me, though.

The book from the drawer was a yearbook, and I moved to the chair and the stronger desk light to go through it. There wouldn't have been a lot in it for anyone else – Old Bill for instance – but I recognised a few bits of his personal shorthand as I flicked the pages. Code for something bought or sold, meetings, a line through the weekend in February he'd taken Sara to the lakes. And a date circled from a couple of weeks back with a happy little smiley face next to it: Friday October 9. The day I came out. No words, just the happy face.

'Didn't bring you much in the way of happiness, did I Leon?' I said quietly. 'I'd have done a lot of people a favour if I'd stayed in the nick.'

I closed my eyes for a moment. Outside, a crow cawed and for some reason I imagined it as a Disney character, flapping lazily across the sky, bowler hat jammed down on its nut, puffing at the cigar stump in its teeth. I opened my eyes and shook my head. You're safe here. Go on. See if he can help you.

The day before I came out, he'd had a meet in London. A short entry: *BF3 11am*. This I recognised. BF meant bed factory, which meant hotel. BF3 was in London, the Imperial at the top of Southampton Row, a few minutes' walk from the British Museum. No indication of who he met. My second day out, he called me at the B&B. Said he was in Newcastle. Nothing but a squiggle on the page for that day, nothing I could make out. The next couple of sheets were blank.

I sparked up again before I turned to yesterday, Friday 23rd. The day he died. What if there was nothing. There had to be something. I need some help on this, Leon, I need a lift.

I flipped the page and there it was: *SLF, 9am*. And next to it in brackets: *Fishcakes*. Fishcakes? No idea, but I knew what SLF meant: South London Face. Most of the villains we knew in the Smoke dwelt south of the river. We only knew one or two from north of the Thames. I fancied fishcakes was something he'd made up on the spot, but it didn't matter now. The SLF did.

I pushed back into the chair and forced myself to picture the flat where I'd found him. Leon was booked to meet a face, maybe more than one, from South London, on the morning of the day he was killed. He died before eight – I knew from the alarm clock – and so his killer or killers had left before then. When I found him, he looked like he'd pulled clothes on to answer the door. Maybe he was asleep when the knock came, maybe he was just up. Whatever, he'd pulled on strides and a sweater and gone barefoot to the door. And answered it to two visitors. Three mugs in the kitchen. One for Leon and one each for the newcomers. They were expected, but they were early.

It was possible that the SLF had turned up when Leon was already dead and just turned round and run. But there was only one meet in the diary, and you don't book two close together, anyway. Means there's a risk of one face bumping into another by chance, no villain likes that. I started again.

Two people showed early, half seven maybe. He brought them in, went into the kitchen, put the kettle on, got the three mugs out. Then he came out into the lounge and something happened and he ended up dead.

I flicked through the last ten weeks of the year. Nothing, but there was a slight bulge on the inside cover – a small cardboard square tucked under the endpaper, about the size of my thumbnail. A SIM card, the bit that stores info and gives a mobile phone its identity. The day I got out, Judith had given me his new number. This must be his old SIM card. Like most villains, Leon changed it like he changed his socks. You normally destroy the old one swiftnick, so this probably had some numbers on it he wanted to keep and hadn't got round to transferring. He wasn't on the same network as me, so I'd need to buy another phone and check it later. For now I slid it back, closed the book and lobbed it on the bed.

'Who was it, Leon? Who did we both know?'

Everyone Leon knew down south, I knew. And I knew more faces from that end of the country than he did. If a new name had come up, he would have asked me to check him out. He hadn't, so that meant whichever SLF he was due to meet his last morning was probably someone I knew as well.

I shut my eyes and went through the London faces I knew who weren't doing time or retired. There were four of them. Davey Hollerbach and Ken Crago, a bit of a firm from Battersea. Louie Fenton, an ex-blagger from the Walworth Road area. And then there was little Johnny Jones from Catford. I thought of Leon sitting against the wall, head on his shoulder and eyes wide open. Who had he looked on last?

I stood up and went to the window. It was quiet across the carpark and I could hear the river Kinder running down past the hotel. It would be here long after any of us were gone. I shook my head and tried to concentrate. I couldn't see how his death was connected to everything that was happening to me, but I didn't think it was out on its own either. Leon didn't have any enemies, he'd never fucked anyone, he wasn't looking over his shoulder. I was in grief, he was my best friend. It had to be down to me, somehow.

I went back to the desk, picked up a hotel pad and started to make notes. Look at the background first.

Ten years ago, Hamilton Jacks nicks my old mate Jack Keane and his firm for robbery. I spring the Turk, Jack walks, the cozzer gets sick. He hears I got the Turk over the wall, so he starts to keep tabs on me as well.

He doesn't have to wait very long for Jack. Two years later he's got him and Sonny Jim, and according to Harry's copper Dave Craze, he thought I was the third man in their heroin game. So that's why he's linking me to heroin. But how did Hamilton Jacks know it was Tomas lying in the Royal Infirmary?

Never mind the why, just fix on the route that's brought you here. I turned a page and started again.

I remembered what Jack suggested in his car after the card game. When Terry and me got nicked in Uppermill, local yokels Breadcake and Busby look us up on the computer. There's a flag on my record saying call Manchester and speak to Hamilton Jacks. They call up and end up with a plot and a serious favour now owed them by a very senior Manchester copper.

And Hamilton Jacks, who's been obsessed and waiting for this for years – he knows where I am now, so plotting up on me is easy. The brown in my cell would have been a piece of piss to sort out. The filth are in and out of Strangeways all the time, interviewing and taking statements. The cozzer could have propped some lackey to do it any day of the week. And then he gets really lucky. Tomas is shot, Hamilton Jacks takes charge of the murder and cocks up a story on the spin of a coin to black me up. Threatening calls to Sara and the kids and they split. He's done his homework, so he knows the twins are the most important thing in my life. He knows losing them would fuck me good style. And with me on the back foot running around town with my head up my arse, he reckons I'm easier to frame up for Jack Keane's heroin trade. But why – why all this? After all these years, why doesn't he leave it? I remembered what Morrie said: *He's a zealot. That makes him very dangerous.* Maybe Jacks was one of those psycho coppers who just couldn't let go.

Maybe.

But what about Leon?

I noticed I'd been drawing an oval in the middle of the page for the last few minutes, going round and round so hard I'd torn through the paper. I flicked to a clean sheet and sparked up again.

Leon didn't fit into any of this, not obviously. But he's a known associate of mine, and easy to find when I dropped out of sight. If Hamilton Jacks couldn't get at me, maybe he put a sting on Leon instead. Maybe the meet was a set-up that went wrong, some undercover copper went in, lost it and stabbed him. Maybe Jacks was running around on the cover-up right now, changing notebooks, pulling records, marking cards. Maybe. Try another route. I wrote TOMAS at the top of the page.

Why was Tomas killed? It came out of nowhere. He was a smackhead, and nobody knew. OK, that happened. He got shot as a result. That happened as well down in smackland. Maybe he'd fucked the wrong dealer for dough. Or some other kid wanted to make a name for himself. Maybe Benny had something for me on Tomas by now. Or Jack Keane. It was Jack's world, after all. All those undead in Manchester, Birmingham and Liverpool. Planet Smack.

I heard car doors slamming. The bar must have shut up downstairs.

I could connect Hamilton Jacks to most of what was going on, even if I couldn't fit the bits to each other yet. That made him the key. In my position, a lot of villains would have thought about going straight to a copper they knew. There were half a dozen firms I could think of with a filth straightened out. But Manchester was too hot for me right now. My brain went south.

SLF the diary said. Leon had been meeting a Londoner. This took me to Monty. North London boy, old enough to be my father and a good friend. In the business a long time and knew most of the moves. There weren't many serious faces trading with Manchester. He was one, maybe he'd know some of the others. At least he might be able to help me narrow down my shortlist for the SLF.

That wasn't all.

I needed a gun. I could buy one up here any time, but I wanted one that wouldn't carry any footprints, before or after it was used. I'd need it for whoever did for Leon when I found him. One from out of town would be safer. Another good reason to go down to Chalk Farm and see Monty.

I took my notes and went to the bathroom. Bending over the karsi, I burnt the papers and flushed the ash away.

I checked out early the next morning and drove into Glossop to use the phone. There are some calls you can't make on a mobile. Judith answered on the third ring. I stumbled out a few words but she cut in. 'Now listen, be quiet. I've seen Leon. He looks lovely. I can't have him till after the post mortem. Then I'm going to bury him in the grave I bought for myself.'

'Oh, Jesus.'

I thought I'd left it all in the hills, but it started bubbling up again.

'You're not to worry about me. You're not, all right?'

'I don't know when I'll be back, Judith.'

'I'll have my sister with me a few days, and you know Ronnie's been here. It's you I'm worried about. You should be taking care of yourself.'

'Is there anything you want?'

'I said you look after yourself. I know how it is. I know you'll have things to do. Just be careful. All right?'

I hung up. She hadn't asked why it had happened. I was grateful.

Just in case there was a tap on her line, I drove a couple of miles to a motel and belled London from there. Monty picked up and I asked him to drop into the office. Fifteen minutes, he said. I bought a tomato juice at the bar and sat down with last night's *Evening News* off reception. The inside front page carried a short piece, naming Leon as the man who'd been found dead with stab wounds in Prestwich on Friday. No mention of his form yet, just name and age.

I phoned the office on the stroke of fifteen. In Monty's case, 'office' was either of two call boxes next to each other in Belsize Park, a mile from his flat in Chalk Farm.

'What,' he rasped as he picked up, 'what was all that bollocks about you being nicked with scag in your peter?'

'It's a long story, Monty, I'll tell you later. I've got another one to tell you first.'

'Go on, then.'

'I need to come and see you, stay the night if that's OK. I'm assuming it's not on you at the moment.'

'No, it isn't on me at the minute and what are you doing asking permission? You've always got a flop under my roof, how many more fucking times? Where are you?'

'I can be on the motorway in twenty minutes,' I looked at my watch. 'I'll be down about five.'

'You'll be down about four,' he said. 'The clocks went back last night.'

We hung up. I went back to the Rover and changed my watch to lose an hour. I'd lost an hour and Leon'd lost the lot.

This is all my fault.

It is not your fault. You didn't kill Tomas, you didn't deal brown in the nick, you didn't put it on yourself.

You are a villain. You bring grief. That's what you do.

It is not what I do.

Pull up the anger. Hate, it'll keep you going. Hate Hamilton Jacks, whoever did for Leon, the screw who found the brown, hate all the way back to Foston Hall, just find some hatred and stoke it up.

It worked, eventually. I silenced the other voice and sat alone in the Rover again. I drove south.

I'd met Monty fifteen years ago on C wing in Strangeways. Then as now, he was a very heavy armed robber at the back of what he'd called 'a fucking civilised three. I'd have knelt down and kissed the judge's arse for a seven.' We'd got on well and kept in touch. We'd done a little work together, but mainly he found me new outlets for the prizes that came my way. I also asked his advice sometimes. Monty had been born into the game over half a century before and he'd stayed in it ever since.

I made Haverstock Hill by four and belled him from a box to check that nothing had come on him since the morning, then walked the rest of the way to Chalk Farm. His intercom crackled at me twenty minutes later, the street door released with a clack and I took the two flights of stairs to the top landing. Number 6 was open, and Monty and his young Japanese wife Noriko were standing in the doorway and there was music coming from inside. Frank Sinatra in duet with his daughter.

And then I go and spoil it all
By saying something stupid . . .

The world was getting weirder. I shook Monty's hand, Noriko kissed me and led me into the lounge as he slotted back the bars.

'You're as cold as cold can be,' she said, and rubbed my cheek. 'Into the bath with you. The water's ready.'

Monty moved past me and for a moment they stood next to each other, like a pair of bookends. I'd never understood how they ended up together. He was a tough – and, to be honest, ugly – ball of a man who seemed to attack everything in life like he had an axe in each hand. She was a stunning slender graduate half his age who'd come to London to learn English and married him instead after they met in a bar down the West End. She ran her eyes over him as he spoke now.

'Do as she says, mate. Into the bath, and take these with you.' He produced a glass of wine with one hand and a burning spliff with the other. She brushed his shoulder with long blue fingernails and hustled me into the bathroom with her smile. When I came out an hour later, there were smoked salmon sandwiches, salad and cheese on the table. And a tray of sushi.

'I'm trying to broaden his food horizons,' Noriko said as I sat down. 'Waitrose sells this on the Finchley Road, so it's hardly Japanese but, hey, it's a start.'

'Fucking fishbait,' said Monty, filling my glass. 'Keep telling her she's in England now, look what I have to put up with.' He nodded at a pile of brightly dressed dolls in the fireplace. 'Look at that, it's like having a fucking baby round the place.'

It took me nearly two hours to tell Monty everything. When I was done, he nodded us onto the sofas, swilled some more wine and thought for a minute.

'Was he into the blow, your mate Leon?'

'Not usually. But he mentioned one of his places in Spain the night before, just before he left. Maybe someone was looking for storage.'

'Would you have known if it was a deal over here, rather than Spain?'

'Yes. He'd almost certainly have offered to cut me in if there was room.'

'OK, go on.'

Noriko cleared the plates and went into the kitchen as I told Monty the four names I'd whittled Leon's meet down to. He knew three of them a bit, and Johnny Jones he knew of. Then I told Monty I was going to kill whoever had done Leon and that I wanted him to get me a gun, one from down here, one without a history. 'How long will it take you to get it?'

Monty rubbed his teeth with the tip of his tongue. 'How long you been out, mate? Ten days?'

'Fortnight.'

'And what you done since? Chased your arse from the sound of it. And now you want a shooter. Jesus. We're good pals, am I right?'

I shrugged him a *yes*.

'OK, so listen. Forget about going back up north tomorrow, with or without a piece. Stay down here instead, for a day at least. I'll need to do a bit of running around myself.'

'I want a gun, Monty.'

'I'll get you one, if that's what you want. Just let me ask around first, eh?'

Noriko came back with another bottle.

'Thank you, sweetheart. See, she knows what I'm thinking, mate. Don't even have to ask.'

Noriko smiled and stood the bottle on the floor in front of him.

'OK, let's have another drink and talk about something else,' he said. 'Then you go to bed and get some fucking sleep. I'm going to be out early to see a few people. I'll be back by noon and we'll talk some more, all right?'

I was very tired, and I trusted him. I'd go along with all this, till noon tomorrow, anyway. Nothing would bring Leon back, whatever I did. Monty opened the new bottle and Noriko laid her head in his lap.

'Why don't you tell us that story about Ron and Reg Kray?' she said.

He started an anecdote about the night Peter Cook opened his club in Soho and the twins tried to shake him down for protection. It was a good tale and Monty was a good talker. That and the booze made me forget. For the moment.

The flat was empty when I showered at half nine the next morning and decided to go out for breakfast. Before I split, I spent a couple of minutes examining the massive iron bars Monty had for when they were indoors. About four inches deep and a couple more thick, there were three of them stood up against the wall to drop into steel slots bolted direct into the masonry either side of the front door. Most heavy guys have something like this – gives you half a chance of going out the window or destroying evidence if Old Bill come breaking in at five in the morning. Thirty seconds can make the difference between going on your toes or going away.

I checked on the car, found a coffee shop and got back by eleven. I was looking through Monty's collection of early editions of childrens' classics when I heard his key. He showed wearing a steady fella car coat and flat cap and looking like a fit pensioner. Nothing to suggest he was still one of the heaviest robbers in London.

'Any luck, Monty?'

'I'm just going to have a rinse.'

'I'll get you some coffee.'

'Cheers.'

I heard water run in the bathroom then movement in the lounge and found him drying his face on a towel.

'Where's Noriko?' I said, and stood his mug on the table.

'Flower arranging class down Marylebone High Street. Japanese thing, don't ask.' He took a mouthful. 'That's better. Did you sleep all right?'

'Thanks, yes.'

'You were fucking dead to the world when I looked in.'

'I didn't hear you.'

'Nah. Must have been around five. Only time to move on wheels in this town, especially if you want to catch some faces before they're out and about. And another thing about leaving your drum early, it's the only time of day down here you can guarantee it ain't on you, and that you ain't bringing it on some other face you're gonna see.' He sounded like he was just getting into his stride, but he caught my look, changed gear and got to the point.

'I had four to see, three on that side of the water, one on this. I caught the trio over there still in kip. Fortunately, the guy on this side is a spieler and seldom moves before midday.' He cleared his throat, phlegming and rattling. Half a century at twenty a day.

'Now. You may have had a result. It's a small world down here when you're talking about serious people, and they're very parochial. They think Watford's next door to Scotland and they like sticking to their manors. And people talk, as we both know.'

Rattle and phlegm.

'Johnny Jones is in the Scrubs on remand. Ken Crago is on holiday in Florida and he's been there for two weeks. Davey Boy Hollerbach was propping up the bar of his local last night and he'll be there again tonight. But . . .' Here he paused to suck on his fag. Coming to the punchline. 'But Louie Fenton hasn't been seen since Wednesday night last week. Leon died on Friday morning, correct?'

I pushed away the image of him slumped against the wall and nodded.

'Right. Louie cancelled a meet for Saturday afternoon on Saturday morning. Word is, it's on top for him.'

'I haven't seen Louie for a few years, Monty. But murder ain't his style.'

'Doesn't mean he did it, mate. But for now, it's enough he's gone to ground.'

'Can we find him?'

'I've put the word out, that's all I can do for now. There's a bit more to come. Hang on, these are cold.' He took the mugs into the kitchen. I heard the kettle click on as he made more coffee, then he was back with the fresh.

'You're thinking that it's down to you,' he said. 'Leon being put under.'

I looked at him miserably.

'If it hadn't been for you and your troubles, your mate might have been here now. You think.'

'He would.'

Monty sat down. 'This ain't an easy game, mate. If it was, they'd all be at it. Leon's beyond our help now. It's done. So we need to put it right.'

I nodded. 'OK.'

'All right, here's the end of it. The last bloke I went to see also does a lot of business up your end. But he's a bit different. He's a brief, or he was. He's still got contact with lawyers and Old Bill, in and out of the Met. And he owes me. I cut a geezer bad once who was trying to put the bite on him.' He stirred his coffee, then tapped the spoon on the rim.

'Anyway, I got him out of bed and he went out and made a few calls. Don't ask me who, 'cause I don't know. But the upshot is this: you're not in the frame for Leon. Can't guarantee you won't get a pull in the future, but you're not in the frame at the moment. So you're OK, for now at least.'

'Are you sure?'

'Trust me. Trust him.' He drained his cup. 'Let's go down the market for a sandwich. And a walk, yeah?'

It was gone twelve and there was a sharp wind getting up. The streets were full of students in goth lite spooking round the late season tourists. We found a stall selling soup and rolls and took the steps down to the canal.

'There's a quiet bench along here,' said Monty. 'Bit more sheltered, too.'

We moved along the towpath and sat. I took the lid off my soup and blew on it. 'How do we find Louie Fenton?' I said.

'Difficult if he's on his toes. Easy enough to find out he'd legged it – sometimes it's like there's only ten people living in this city and I know six of them,' said Monty. 'But the upside of that is they're so bloody little Britain, you can disappear by crossing the river. Leave town and you're Lord fucking Lucan.'

'We can still try,' I said. 'I can think of a couple of places to start.'

'Hang on a minute, I want to focus a bit here. Go back to what you were telling me last night. This Chinese geezer, Uncle; the one that Leon took you to see. He said you were being worded as a grass, correct?'

'Yes.'

'And he's the only person you've heard that from, correct?'

'Yes.'

'Now this is what I don't understand. Lots of gossip doing the rounds about your good self. The brown in your cell even got to me down here. And there was chat about your Tomas too, so you told me. However, no gossip about you being a grass. Except from the Chinaman.'

'I suppose you're right. I'd lost sight of that.'

Monty finished his soup and chucked the cup into a bin. 'OK, now who's he talking to, this Uncle? Did Leon give you any clues who he was plugged in to?'

'None.'

'Well, we need to think about that. Maybe lift this Uncle and liven him up a bit.' He unwrapped his sandwich and tore a bit off, lobbing it into his mouth and rolling it around on his tongue like it was passing an entrance test to go down his throat.

'I think you should go back to Manchester, your own flat in Chorlton. Put yourself on show.'

'Why?'

'Give your friends a chance to get in touch. And the people pretending to be your friends as well. The filth aren't after you for Leon. No dawn raids on the slate. You're safe for a few days at least.'

'What about Hamilton Jacks?'

'Whatever he's doing, it's by the back door. I don't fancy him for a straight fit-up.'

'Maybe he's done that already.'

Monty grunted. 'Whoever got the brown left in your cell could have paid the same smackhead a bit more to kill you. But he didn't. So he's playing a very long game.'

'What about the gun?'

'And who are you going to point it at?'

'Whoever did Leon.'

'And who did do Leon?'

'Louie Fenton knows.'

'Maybe, and if you can't find him?'

A couple of old women in short black coats and hats like turbans walked past us on the towpath. One of them was pulling a shopping trolley. We both gave them our teeth and a 'nice day' as they came level. When they were out of earshot, I snapped, 'I'll find him, Monty.'

'No. You are looking the wrong way. Hamilton Jacks is the root, you said so yourself. Some of it, at least. You've got to concentrate on the copper.'

'This is bullshit.' I stood up and kicked to the edge of the canal. The water was black and hardly moving. It could have been two foot deep or two hundred. A scrape on the gravel and I heard the old guy breathing over my shoulder.

'Waving a gun around is not the answer,' he said gently. 'Not right now, anyway. If we find Hamilton Jacks or Louie Fenton or Uncle Tom Cobley did for Leon, then we'll deal with him. But I'll do it. Or somebody like me who owes me a favour. And when it happens, you'll be fifty miles away with a hundred straightgoers round you to swear it. This prick's hurt you enough. If you end up back inside with a twenty-five rec stuck up your arse, then he's still won. Whether he's dead or alive.'

That night we ate expensively. It diverted me for a while, but the good tastes just reminded me Leon wouldn't be getting any, and nor would Tomas. We were in Covent Garden, somewhere that clearly catered for the rich and the criminal. Some of the starters were a score or more. Monty said that he'd had a touch the week before last. This was the first chance he'd had to christen his good luck.

There was white burgundy with the first course. Then oysters, quails' eggs and smoked salmon. Premier cru claret, tiny trussed portions, decorative sauces, artfully arranged vegetables. Cheese, some kind of port. Then brandy, liqueur, pricey wraps of Italian sweets. Sod the lot of it. By now I was pissed, replaying the conversation I'd had with Monty earlier on while Noriko was getting ready.

'One way or another, we agree the cozzer Hamilton Jacks is the key to some of this,' he'd said. 'So why not have him over?'

'Do you mean screw him?'

'Drugs, drugs, drugs, it's all drugs, your story. Class A makes Old Bill very greedy. The kudos on offer when they make a big bust makes other filth spew.'

'I'm not with you.'

'Set up a nice big drugs bust for the copper, and he'll bite. And we'll do him then.'

'How?'

'Details, details. As it happens, I'm due up in Manchester this Thursday on another matter. At the Britannia, as Mr Alexander. We'll compare notes then. In the meantime, make sure you bell me or the girl daily so we know it's not come on top. Bloody Nora, look at that.'

I'd turned and seen Noriko smiling in the door, batting her long natural lashes in a face like a watercolour. She was wearing a short black dress and tall sharp stilettos that made her legs go on for an hour, a catwalk model about to go onstage.

The bill was just over a monkey and Monty paid it from a toilet roll of tenners, saying him and Noriko fancied a nightcap. I'd had enough, so I took her twirls and left them deciding on a bar. I was asleep before they came in.

12

Back at my gaff in Chorlton, the relief at being back in familiar surroundings lasted about five seconds. That's how long it took to catch sight of the answerphone, flashing so angrily there was hardly a break between lights. The tape rewound for minutes, then dozens of messages from Lou and Sam, panic building with each one until the last scraps which consisted of Lou shouting *Dad!* and hanging up. And then: 'This is Sara. It is now half past four on Tuesday afternoon. You selfish fucking bastard. The minute you get this message, you go out or do whatever you're doing nowadays and call me.'

Coat still on, I scrawled the number that followed on my hand. Then I ran to the nearest phone box. Why didn't I think they'd have heard the news about Leon? Christ. I pumped silver into the slot. Three rings, 'Sara?'

'Where the fuck have you been?'

'Sara, listen – '

'Where the fuck have you been?'

'I had to get away.'

'I know you had to get away.' She was screaming. 'It was Leon, for Christ's sake, Leon. Me and the twins, Judith – it's not just about you. It was in the paper. How do you think we felt, for Christ's sake you fucking lousy pig . . .'

She was somewhere between screaming and wailing now, but she didn't hang up.

'Sara, I don't know – '

'I rang Judith and she said you'd called – '

'She didn't tell me – '

'She's an old woman and her son's been murdered, what do you expect?'

'I didn't know how to get hold of you.'

'Yes you did. You've got a number for Lou. She told me.'

'I had to go.'

'Then why didn't you get one of your precious fucking friends to do it for you?'

'I couldn't.'

'The twins were terrified. How the fuck did you think they'd feel?'

'I couldn't do anything else. I had to go.'

Now she started crying properly. 'Oh God, you bastard. You lousy fucking shit. You fucking bloody fucking criminal shit. You stay away from me and my children.'

'Can I speak to them Sara?'

'They're in the next room. They don't want to talk to you.'

The line went muffled. I stuck more coin in. Then Lou came on. 'Dad.'

'Lou, I'm sorry – '

'Didn't you get our new mobile numbers? I left them on your answerphone. You didn't give me your mobile in Leeds. What is it?'

'Yes, yes, I got your message, I'm sorry, Lou. And I need to change my mobile, now. I don't know what the new one is yet.'

'OK. Call me when you do.'

The line went muffled again. I heard Sara shouting, but I couldn't make out the words. Lou took her hand off the mouthpiece in time for me to hear:

'. . . then this won't happen again, will it?'

Then Lou said, 'OK, just call me when you've got your new mobile.' She hung up.

I dragged my feet back to the flat. Just inside the front door I stripped naked, then stumbled and fell into bed. I wrapped myself up in a tight ball, squeezed my eyes closed and tried to sleep.

*

I got up after an hour trying not to think what Lou and Sam might be thinking about me. Still naked, I went into the front room, tipped open the bag from the mobile shop in London and set the phone I'd bought that morning to charge. Then I flicked through the rest of the instructions and established it would take two hours to juice up. Couldn't examine Leon's SIM card till then, sod it. I took the one I'd bought for myself into the kitchen and switched the cards in my own phone. Then I fetched the pliers out from under the sink and spent a couple of minutes breaking the old one into tiny bits. These got swept off the counter into a screw of newspaper to dump next time I went out. Now no one would know who'd I'd been calling.

I texted Lou my new number, then got dressed and went up to see the Wessons to tell them I was back. She was having a nap, so I spoke to him at his door for a few minutes. No sign in his face he'd been propped about me, and he was a transparent guy so I was probably OK. Then I went downstairs, picked up the screw of SIM bits and pulled on my jacket.

'Now we're on a war footing, don't forget your traps. Even if there's nothing on site, don't forget your traps.'

It was the last thing Monty said to me that morning. I spent ten minutes gloomily jamming matchsticks into the skinny gaps between drawer edge and desk or bedside table and snapping them off. A couple of matchsticks got leant up against cupboard and fridge doors, I left tiny scraps of cotton wool on the edge of the desk, the kitchen counters, the shelves in the living room. The slightest movement nearby would move or blow them off completely. The last was a matchstick up against my front door.

I drove to a quiet phone box in the Volvo hatchback I'd hired on my own brief that afternoon. The Rover might have been clocked around the service flat, and it had definitely been too near the scene of Leon's leaving. I'd stuck it in Amy's garage on the way back that afternoon when I'd laid down Leon's stuff and hired this one, just to be double safe.

The phone box stank of piss as usual. Jack Keane's video shop picked up. A young lad took a message I'd rung. 'Ring back tomorrow. Give it till lunch at least.'

I gave the kid my new mobile number, hung up and dialled Benny, the dope merchant in the Moss.

'I tried you a few times, you been off again?'

'Bit of urgent business.'

'Oh aye. Well, I didn't leave a message, didn't know what was what. Now. One of the lads who sells to me let something slip day after you came, mentioned your Tomas by name. Cut a long story short, hang on.' He stopped and I heard him suck on his inhaler.

'OK, lad put me on to someone else. He's round first thing. Thinks he's just coming to buy, that's all. I reckon he could help. You give me a call mid-morning, yeah? Mid-morning.'

I hung up and got into the motor. I was about to twist the ignition when my phone went off and it was Jack Keane, sounding like he was walking down the street in a hurry. 'Just popped into the shop and got your message, son. I haven't got any knowledge on Tomas yet, is something wrong?'

'Are you clear your end, Jack?'

'Yeah but I can't hear too well, hang on.' The background noise dipped and went.

'OK, I'm in the car now.'

'Leon's dead.'

'Oh, Christ.'

'Someone carved him up on Friday morning.'

'Oh, Jesus. Any idea why or – '

'I'm working on it. I need a piece, Jack. I don't feel too safe these days. Can you get me one?'

'Guns aren't your style, son.'

'Nothing's my style, right now. Can you get me one?'

'What for?'

'For whoever did Leon, when I find him. And to keep me safe for now. Can you get me a clean one?'

The line went silent for a long beat. Then Jack said, 'All right I'll get you one. Where are you?'

'My place in Chorlton. How long will it take?'

'I'll call you tonight or tomorrow.' He sounded troubled. 'My number's on your screen, now. Don't ring me at the shop again, only this one – OK?'

'Thanks, Jack.'

'Sorry about Leon, son. I only knew him a little bit, but I knew the pair of you were close. Are you all right?'

'Keeping it together. Thanks again.'

I drove for the cozzer's house. I stuck the Volvo in the pub car park and made a big fuss of locking the doors then went inside, got a beer and stood at the bar for ten minutes. Then I slid back outside and went to the tree, making out to have a piss. It was half seven and clear for the minute. I dug up the machine, switched the tape for a clean one and buried it again, scraping some twigs and leaves across the turned earth. Then I zipped up and drove home.

Back in Chorlton, I bent at the knees and checked the matchstick against my front door hadn't moved. Inside, I went round for the scraps of cotton wool on shelves and the other matchsticks jammed into drawer cracks. Then I listened to the tape: the calls ran end to end for about five minutes, incoming for Mrs Jacks and the brats but no cozzer chat. It's as well to know nothing as something. I went into the kitchen, stuck the kettle on and leant against the counter waiting for it to boil.

Leon's SIM card, you prick.

I walked my brew into the lounge. The indicator said the new phone was charged. I unplugged it and laid it on the desk, along with the hands-free. Then I went into my bag for Leon's diary, unpicked the endpaper, slid the SIM into the phone, replaced the back, pressed on and the thing bleeped into life. Good. I stuck in the hands-free, lit up and tapped the desk with my thumb, staring at the mobile. Then I pressed 1 and held it down to connect with voicemail. It rang twice and a recorded woman asked me for the PIN number.

Shit shit shit. Shit.

I tried his birthday, my birthday, the year his mum was born, first four and last four numbers in each day/month/year sequence. I tried his last prison number, my last prison number, my first, all my prison numbers, the date I last saw him before I went in, all the dates I could remember of any time we'd really had it off, the year he was born, the year his dad died, a couple of PIN codes on accounts we'd once shared, obvious combinations like 2468 and 1357, the year Kennedy was shot, the Armada set sail, other years: 1939, 1945, 1066, 1492, Bay of Pigs 1962, Woodstock 1969, the Somme 1917, 1914, 1918, World Cup 1966, famous birthdays, famous deaths, the first four digits of his phone number, the last four, the same for mine, mutual friends, Sara's, United player combinations, England line-ups, random numbers, dozens, scores, hundreds of random numbers, my fingers were numb and sticky with sweat.

Somewhere around midnight, I tried Sara's birthday and the woman told me Leon had two messages saved and three new ones. I sat there staring at it in amazement for a few seconds, then I pressed the number to play them.

The two saved messages were both Judith, giving phone numbers of people who'd rung for him.

The first two new messages were from me on the day I got out. The third was not, and had me cracking my spine straight and breathing fast. It was from Friday just gone, the day he died, seven twenty-three in the morning. I crushed the earpiece further in.

Crackle crackle crackle. Background roar. Someone in a car?

I could hardly hear a word.

I ripped a drawer open, found pen and paper and scrawled down what I thought was there. I replayed the message again and again, dozens of times. It was a man's voice. Could have been a Londoner. He seemed to be shouting, he was breaking up all the time. White noise, the odd word, more white noise, a couple of words. I played the message back again and tried to stop my mind making links and hearing sounds that weren't there. It sounded like:

I've come in. No. *I'm coming and . . .*

That was all that was clear. I listened again and heard something like:

Early . . . I'm coming and . . . jacking it . . . in . . .

Or was it:

Burly . . . I'm coming and . . . jacket clean . . . in . . ?

Or:

I'm burly . . . early . . . I'm coming and . . . ringing . . . it . . . in

Early . . . I'm coming early . . .

No.

I'm coming . . .

Then something like *jacking, jacking it in, I'm coming or jacking it, blacking it.* Couldn't be. Something like *I'm coming or jacking it in, I'm coming or jacking it in*, with a big crackle before the *jacking it in*, if that was what he was saying. Please God, give me better hearing, just play it and listen again you prick.

I'm coming or (crackle) *jacking it in . . .*

I'm coming (crackle, probably *early*) *or* (crackle) *be jacking it in . . .*

I'm coming or jacking it in.

What the fuck did that mean?

It was nearly two, my head was throbbing and I felt the unreality that comes with no sleep and too much stress. I tugged the wire out of my ear and put the SIM card back in Leon's diary. Then I set the alarm and rolled into bed.

I was out of the flat by six, and feeling better than I should have done after four hours sleep. The paranoia was right on me though, at least partly down to lack of kip. I'd put the traps down – cotton wool, matchsticks, all the rest – and drove right on the mirror, rearranging bits of white noise and crackle and half words and words in my head from a few hours before. Early, burly, hurly burly, coming, I'm coming, or jacking it, maybe racking it in, racking it up, not coming but running, try to make sense of it, what would it be at that time of the morning? Coming not running, he sounded like he was in a car. Are you sure it was a he?

I parked up near Tib Street and walked through the old market area to the club. I rang the bell for five minutes and was just about to sack it when the hatch snapped open and a face I knew appeared.

'Is Ken in?' The doorface nodded and opened up without a word.

Kaluki Ken.

The name had drilled into my skull the second I'd opened my eyes. Kaluki Ken. Maybe there was a late game still running at the club. If there was, Ken would be there. He didn't get his moniker by being dealt out of schools.

'Just the four of us in the bottom room.'

Coming, running, incoming . . . I'd let my attention wander for a second.

The doorface repeated himself. 'I said, just the four of us in the bottom room.' He was speaking over his shoulder and his voice was half lost in the felt-lined passage.

'Just four. Been nobody in since about two. We've got the spare twirls. You looking to play? Only we're thinking of calling it a draw soon.'

We were in the main room. A table, two more of them and Ken. I waved across, then muttered to the doorface. 'No, thanks. Just on my way home.' Then, to the table, 'Coffee, lads?'

There was a general warble of yes, so I made five cups and put two quid in the honesty box Davey left out when he went home. I started to leaf through yesterday's *Racing Post* from the rack, half an ear on the sound of the cards and the low-voiced comments. Fifteen minutes later, the game broke up. The face who'd let me in asked who was going to dub up. Glancing at me, Kenny said to give him the keys. 'I've got a couple of calls to make.'

I sat down in an ancient leather-backed armchair while he saw them out. The leather felt greasy under my fingertips. I glanced around and was reminded how the club hadn't changed much since Atlee was Prime Minister: the walls still looked like a photographers' gallery with black and whites of boxing champs from Jack Dempsey and Gene Tunney to Randolph Turpin and Sugar Ray Robinson. And stickytopped tables with circle marks from last night's and last year's mugs and cups. Big black ashtrays full to overflowing. I heard the door close and movement in from the corridor.

'How's your luck, Ken?'

'Cab's mine for the moment and I don't owe a tanner to no one.'

Kenny was prone to 'selling' his cab and leasing it back when things weren't going well at the tables.

'Hang on a moment, let me just do this.' He ducked behind the bar, coming out with an old paintbrush and a kid's plastic seaside bucket. Then he moved from table to table, cleaning the ashtrays.

'Davey insists on this. Don't know why, the whole place is one big fucking ashtray.' Then, from nowhere: 'I won a twoer off that miserable get Bernie last night, which is always sweet.' He stopped brushing, but he didn't look round. 'I heard about Leon. It was in the paper. Are you in trouble?'

He made a meal of emptying the bucket into a bin behind the bar.

'No, but I've been keeping my head down. I didn't know you knew him.'

'Only from the tables here. I'm sorry, mate. I know you were close.'

'Yeah, thanks.' I walked my mug over to the bar. 'Any more coffee there?'

He stuck the kettle on and rinsed out our china under the counter.

'I came about that black cab, Ken. Any luck?'

'Got it right here, mate. Had it a few days. Rang your gaff a couple of times, no reply. Didn't leave a message.'

'Keeping my head down, like I said.'

'Course.'

He reached out a William Hill diary and handed over a slip of paper. The address meant nothing to me.

'North of the city,' he said. 'Off Sheepfoot Lane, opposite Heaton Park.' He gave a brief description. Same guy who met with Jacks, no doubt. 'My man's picked him up a couple of times. Thinks he's married, no teapots at home. Seen a missus.'

The kettle clicked off and he spooned out instant coffee, then poured the water on and sniffed the milk. 'Just on the turn.'

'It was all right before.'

He slopped it into the mugs and pushed one across.

'Will your man mention this enquiry to anyone else?'

'No, he's all right. I told him to keep schtum, and he will.' He looked down at his coffee. 'Sorry about the white bits. Tastes all right. Mine does, anyhow. Yours?'

'It's fine. Thanks.'

'Are you all right for dough? I'm in front right now, like I said. Got a couple of grand handy. Sooner you had it than give it back on the tables.'

'I'm all right for now, thanks. Will your man expect a drink?'

'No. It's a freeman's. He was delighted to do me a favour.'

We shook and I left. It was ten to eight.

Back in the Volvo, I drove slowly out of town. Turning left into Swan Street, I carried on across Miller Street, past the CIS building and right on to Cheetham Hill Road. After a few hundred yards, I threw another right down to Red Bank and back towards town. The traffic was building up now, but not enough that I wouldn't have been able to spot a tail, unless they were very many handed. Twenty minutes later and heading north again, I was happy. Never assume that if you're clean in the morning you're sweet for the rest of the day. Sometimes they lose you by design and pick you up later. It's not exactly difficult with cameras on top of every lamp post.

By now the traffic heading out of town was easier and I found the place in a few minutes – a nondescript semi in a dull street. I glanced at it, drove on a few hundred yards to Heaton Park and pulled up for a bit. There was no point in joining the rush hour crawl back. I sat and watched the motors putter by sluggishly, considering the glance I'd got after the porn cinema; the broad shoulders and greying hair, his slight stoop at the hips as he strode through Piccadilly Gardens.

Manchester Central Library, and still only half nine in the morning. The electoral register had a Charles and Irene Pearson down to vote. This might not help. If the stooping face didn't dwell at the address in question, it was all bollocks. And there was no guarantee the cunt was on my case, anyway. I sighed so loudly at this thought, the man on the other side of the table looked up. I shook an apology, took the electoral roll back to the desk and picked the Volvo up off the meter.

It was just gone eleven and I was sitting in Benny's lounge as he brewed up in the kitchen. There'd been a new *Homes and Gardens* development in the last fortnight. Like the club, there were framed black and whites all over the wall. He'd been a singer and compère on the Manchester club scene in the early sixties when that was a big deal. The snaps showed a younger Benny with singers and celebrities, some still famous, some dead. Benny with Al Bowlly, Benny with Colin Crompton and Frankie Vaughan. Benny with a young Max Bygraves. A group of sharp-suited young men round a piano. Benny leaning on the lid, with what looked like – and as I looked closer, clearly was – Liberace at the ivories. Bloody hell, Benny with Liberace.

'Liberace, that one.' He was in the doorway, a mug in each hand, apparently pausing for a rest. I could see his chest rise and fall and there was a whine of air travelling down his windpipe.

'Let me take them for you, Ben.'

He nodded and leant against the doorpost for a second, then shuffled and sat down heavily on the sofa, stuck the inhaler in his mouth and pushed the canister down, leant forward breathing more deeply and waited for the Ventalin to kick in. I sipped my coffee until his wheezing got better and he straightened up.

'Liberace, that one. In the club that night, came backstage after the show. We had Des O'Connor top of the bill. Liberace fancied Des's pianist, came back to squeeze his arse. Nice enough bloke, though. We had them all there in those days.' As he spoke he rolled a couple of spliffs. One he offered to me, the other he stuck in his own mouth and lit up.

'Blow actually helps the chest,' he said. 'Doctor says I'm fucking mad, I don't care. Fucking chest pulled me off the stage, I'm not having it fuck the rest of me life.'

I decided to save my spliff for later.

'I think I've had a result. Just go over to the sideboard, pull open the top drawer, yeah. Bring me the notebook.'

There was a greasy red vinyl notebook on top of some snaps and an elderly porn mag. I walked it across to him; he laid the spliff in the ashtray and breathed out, then cleared his throat. He concentrated on breathing for a few moments more, then swallowed. 'Right, let's see. Here.'

With some effort, he tore out a page. There was a name and address written on it in small neat print. It was the number of a house in Seedley Street down Moss Side, and a name: Sean.

'I was right about the lad this morning. This is the spar of the kid who killed your Tomas. And he was there when it happened.'

I felt my arms round his neck, tightening until it snapped. I'll have you. Benny broke in. 'He's young and he's white. My lad says he's seen him with his foil in the phone boxes, round the rubbish bins, any damn place round here. I don't know, though.' He paused for breath.

I looked up as tugged on the inhaler and the cold damp of prison came in on me. Benny – seventy and gasping for breath, dealing in dope surrounded by kids dealing in hard shit and killing each other for it. My eyes flicked up at the black and white on the wall with him and Liberace. Maybe it was more than the state pension, but still. He was speaking again.

'Name and address there. He lives alone, the kid says. Stroke of luck, that. But you can get lucky sometimes.' He half turned his head towards the showbiz photos. 'Another thing, might be useful. He keeps regular hours, which is unusual. Scores at the same house every morning around eight. Kid couldn't say why, something to do with the guy this Sean buys off. Kid says he's seen Sean round this guy's house a few mornings and always about eight, *Christ*.'

The *Christ* was an intro to more wheezing, serious this time. It went on for several minutes, and finished with him flopping back on the sofa and sucking hard on the Ventalin. He gestured for me to help, so I walked him into his bedroom and on to the bed where he stretched out, rasping hard.

'I'll get you some water.' Going out the door, I knocked something off the dresser. I bent down and saw it was a pile of Christmas cards. He hadn't noticed. For some reason, I took them to the kitchen with me while I ran the cold tap. They were all from a grandson, about a score of them, one for each year. They started in 1979, 'Dear Grandad' spelt out in spiky five-year-old's script, each year his writing getting more rounded and mature. The last date was 1998. Nothing more recent.

He used to be a singer, met the famous of his day. He used to have a grandson who sent him a card at Christmas.

I took the water in and slipped the cards back on the dresser. He was still on his back looking up at the ceiling. 'I'm all right now. You get on. Lock up and put the keys through the door. I'll bolt up later.'

On the way out I slipped two hundred quid into the phone book in the hall. Maybe he'd think he left it there when he was stoned.

Seedley Street was about half a mile away and I drove straight for it. Turning right off Great Western, I came into a set of side roads that looked pure *Corrie*, only tatty and run down. Past a couple of boarded-up houses and into Sean's road. His front curtains were drawn, but the upstairs were open and there was movement as my eyes flicked up.

The road was packed with motors left and right. It was the sort of area where everyone seemed to have two or three cars. Half of them on the drip, some of them hot or just resprayed with a mugshot in this week's *Auto Express*. It kept the pavements locked and that was going to be useful for me. I'd come back this evening and check.

For the moment, I twisted the Volvo and pointed it towards the centre where I stuck it on a meter and went into the Arndale. The woman in Toys4U told me rather sniffily they didn't sell toy guns any more as a company policy, but Twentieth Century Cults a couple of shops down wasn't so bothered. In among the *Star Wars* dolls and racks of American comics was a small display of spy movie gear and I picked up a James Bond Walther PPK for a score and a bag of jumbo elastic bands from the newsagents opposite.

Back in Chorlton about an hour later, I peeled the 007 sticker off the side and stood in front of the bedroom mirror waving the toy around. It looked all right, and he'd only get a glimpse at most. If Jack came through today I'd use that, but this would do otherwise. I stuck it in the desk drawer, binned the packing and rang Carol. It took her a while to pick up.

'Just calling to check on the boy. Everything all right?'

'He's OK, but you just get used to your own space I suppose.'

'Is he giving you trouble, Carol? I'll get him out of there if he is.'

'Just a minute.' I heard her lay the phone down and the sound of a door being closed in the background. She came back on. 'He was OK when he moved in, but I've had to get him to sleep in the spare room the last couple of nights.'

'What's he doing?'

'He's been coming back late, drinking a bit. Cans everywhere, that sort of thing.'

'I'll have him out.'

'No, leave it. I like the lad, I really do. And I owe you the favour. He'll be all right for a couple more days.'

'It won't be for much longer, Carol. Weekend at the latest. Call me if there's trouble in the meantime. I've got a new number.' I reeled it off. 'All right? And you know I appreciate this, Carol. Thanks again.'

'OK. I'll speak to you on Saturday.'

I was back on the Moss by six. I'd spent the afternoon catching up on sleep and ringing a couple of people to let them know about Leon. This time I'd remembered.

Now my mind shifted on to other things. And I was proper on guard – it was dark and this was the frontline. As I parked the Volvo in front of the social club outside City's ground, two ten-year-old lads materialised from nowhere and offered to mind my wheels. 'Just to keep an eye on it, mate,' shrilled one of them, all spiky hair and copy gear.

Keeping an eye was a euphemism for claiming to guarantee that my car would still be in place when I got back. I slipped them a fiver, hoping they were the 'official' minders and not a pair of chancers and walked down to Seedley Street pulling a baseball cap well over my eyes and trying to look like a local. Once on the Seedley pavement, I drifted up the road opposite Sean's house and stopped to light up and get a good blimp at his bricks and mortar. There were lights on up and down, but no movement. Motors outside his gaff like the rest of the street. I turned and walked about ten yards and there were two white vans my side, back to back. I glanced down – enough space between them. Chances were they wouldn't move before tomorrow morning. Useful if they stayed put. All right.

The Volvo was intact when I got back. The two kids reappeared and I gave them another jacks.

'Pleasure to do business,' I said, 'with honest hustlers.'

'Thanks, chief,' said the spiky-haired one.

Then they both bowed to me, they actually bowed, and the other said, 'Tell your friends to look out for us on match days.'

'I'm a Red, lads. I wouldn't be seen dead near here on match days.'

They bowed again and faded away.

I drove home on the mirror, stopping once to bell Noriko and ask her to go to the office. She said ten minutes and I called her from outside the fish shop round the corner.

'I've got a name,' I said. 'Tell him Charlie Pearson. He's got a wife, Irene. He'll know what it's about.'

'I'll tell him,' she said. 'Anything else?'

'Just tell him I'll see him up here.'

'Be careful.'

'I will.'

At five the next morning, I walked naked to the desk and got the Walther PPK out of the drawer. In the light from the street I snapped a couple of elastic bands round the butt, flicked the magazine out and slammed it back in. It sounded real enough and felt heavy. I took a cold shower, dressed and emptied my bladder. Then I drove to City's ground on the mirror and parked up. I sat in the car and smoked a couple of cigarettes, watching the road and the houses. Nothing moved and I felt alone enough. I got out of the motor at six thirty and stuck the gun down my waistband, handle pointing in. The elastic bands stopped it from slipping.

I made Sean's street by ten to seven. The pavements were clear and I could see the vans were still there, back to back. I walked till I was level and with a quick glance all round, slipped down between them and sat on the tarmac, leaning up against the bumper on one side with my legs stretched out under the other. The gun was digging into my gut, so I slid it out the waistband and tucked it in my jacket. Then I settled down to wait. It was dark enough and I was low enough to be invisible if anyone went past on the pavement this side but I could still see the top half of Sean's front door. I was gambling on neither of the vans getting moved and the baghead leaving on time. And plenty else, but I didn't have the choice. My arse was cold already, I shifted and my right hand found something soft on the deck. Looking down, a band of amber streetlight told me it was a curl of dog shit. Swell. I scraped it off on the tarmac and tried to ignore the stink.

With my minces firmly on the baghead's door, and my legs getting numb with cold, I filled the time by whispering some of *Through the Looking Glass* to myself. 'It wasn't the black kitten's fault, that was quite certain. It had been curled up sleeping all afternoon, Dinah had quite given up on washing its face for it.' Lou and Sam loved that book. I'd read it to them slowly when they were six, chapter by chapter each day. Once, in the nick, I'd tried to learn it off by heart, committing a paragraph or two to memory every morning. But they didn't want reading to when I got out on that one.

Seven thirty and it was getting on to that morning twilight. A milk float hummed by and two straight-looking geezers crossed the road, looking like they were on the way to work. There was the odd motor. I cracked my knuckles, checked the gun and stuck my hands under my armpits to warm them up. I was getting very bastard cold. My mind ran over anything as a distraction – black kittens, white kittens, rearranged black kittens and white noise and crackle, the roar of motors, words I couldn't quite hear early coming I'm coming blacking sacking jacking in my head.

Wait a minute.

The door was opening. Someone on the move. Youngish, tall and slim. Short brown hair to go with his mud-coloured fatigues, combat pants, and dirty army boots. Sean the baghead, assuming he was the only one there. And that was the biggest gamble. The guy buttoned his jacket and had a clock round the street. Apparently satisfied, he started for Claremont Road, keeping his head down, the posture of a man who's been pushed to the side of his own life. He was rangy and he had a long stride, but otherwise his body had no health in it. I felt a tingle run down my back and across my arms, imagining the sluggish brown-poisoned blood farting through his veins.

I twisted round on to my knees as he got to the corner and vanished. I counted one two three, couldn't see or hear anyone near me, four, five and I slid up, back against the van. My legs screamed at the movement, shit. I rubbed the muscles hard and with a quick glance each way I broke cover, shot across the road and made the corner. He was about fifty yards ahead at the junction. I moved quickly at first, then dropped back when I'd got his speed and bottled him off for about half a mile to a cul-de-sac at the back of Princess Road. Then I backed off to about two hundred yards from where he'd turned, and waited again.

He was quick, four or five minutes at most and heading back the way he'd come. Now I kept in front, glancing round as a car or walker blocked his view of me and made Seedley Street a minute ahead of him. Counting in my head again, I turned and started walking back a few seconds before he came round the corner. By the time he hit the pavement we were almost the same distance from his drum. Sweet.

The guy's pace picked up as he got near his flop. He probably won't be rattling yet, I thought. Smackheads usually time their treatment better than that. But the chances were that the bag he'd just bought was the only thing on his mind right now. He was certainly keeping his head right down, didn't even look up when he stopped at his door, key in hand. If he had, he might have noticed me three or four paces away. I was level as he opened up and stepped in. Then I twisted and charged into him so hard he pitched forward into the house, straight on to the deck. I stepped inside, pulled the gun and slammed the door shut. He was scrabbling to get up, so I kicked him in his back and he went over again, face down. I crouched and laid the gun barrel at his temple. 'Is there anyone else in the house? You've got three to answer. One, two . . . '

'No, no fucker. Just me. Listen, there's no gear here and no bread, I swear to God . . . ' He trailed off, shaking.

The street door gave right into the living room; there was a door into the kitchen and a yard out the back. Stairs up and that was it. Except that the gaff was hanging and now that I was near, I could tell the baghead was hanging too. I straightened up. 'Stay there. Face to the wall. Spread your arms and legs wide. Slow.'

I flicked my eyes to a cane chair and dragged it across, keeping my eyes on the baghead. I chucked a filthy looking cushion on to the deck and sat. Matey boy was breathing heavily. He rattled something in his throat, it came out as:

'Listen, whatever – '

'Shut up.'

I waited for maybe ten minutes, straining my ears for sound of movement upstairs. Nish. I took in the scraps of silver paper and other discarded works littering the floor next to the sofa. What a slum. The baghead shifted slightly. Something must be starting to ache. His arms, legs, maybe his gut, were twitching for the brown.

'I wonder what you're thinking, boy. What's all this about? Maybe I'm somebody you've fucked.'

He started to babble again.

'Shut up, you little turd. I'll tell you when to answer.' I got up and stepped towards him. Then I put one foot on his calf, leaning to increase the pressure until, with a shout, I jumped and slammed both feet down on the back of his leg. The breath spat out of his body, but he was too frightened to scream.

'Fuck! Fuck!' he gasped.

I took the few paces backwards, then sat again. 'Remember that pain when I start asking my questions. All right?'

'Yes,' he half hissed, half grunted.

'Good. Let's begin. Tomas: the lad who got shot two weeks ago last

Tuesday. Why did you do it?'

'Don't know what you're talking about.'

Maybe he didn't. Maybe this wasn't Sean. I let out a long, exaggerated sigh. 'We both know that's a lie. Is your leg still hurting, boy?'

Nothing from the baghead. Time to test his bottle, or I'd be here all day. I reached over for the cushion I'd slung off the chair then crouched and hissed into his ear. 'I said, is your fucking leg still fucking hurting you little piece of shit?'

I stuck the cushion down on the back of his kneecap – the leg I'd jumped on – pressed in the gun barrel and gave it a good dig. 'The first thing you felt was the stinking cushion off your poxy chair. The second was my gun. Your next lie will make you a fucking cripple. Do you understand that, you little shit?'

He hissed out a terrified *Yes* followed by one of the longest farts I'd ever heard.

'So, let's see if we can get you into the habit of telling the truth for a change. Where's the bag you just bought?'

'It's cheeked up,' he said, jerking his head backwards.

'Right. Put your right hand behind your back and get it. Slowly.'

I stood and watched him reach back, stick his hand down his strides, feel between his arse and pull out a small plastic bag.

'Now throw it behind you.'

It flopped on the boards and I scuffed it across with my toe. Well, he was a smackhead anyway. It was a start.

'That's good. Now. Another easy one. What's your name, and how old are you?'

'Wallace, Sean Sean Wallace. Sean Wallace. Twenty-two.'

Thank you, Benny. 'Well done, Sean Sean Wallace.' I sat and the cane creaked. He flinched in time.

'Here's a few facts for you, Sean. I know you were involved in the shooting, and I knew the kid who was shot.'

He'd stopped trembling; he'd almost stopped breathing. He was expecting the worst now.

'I want to know why. Tell me easy or you can tell me hard. The hard way is this: you lie and I'll leave a pill from this gun in the back of your knee. I'll do it through the cushion, which should keep the noise down a bit, though I don't think many people in this street are going to be dialling three nines because they may have heard a gun go off.'

I gave it a pause, maybe half a minute.

'When I've done that, I'm going to wait, for an hour or so. The cushion will stop a lot of the blood, especially if my foot's on it. But the bullet will still be in there, and that's what will make it hurt. Remember that pain before, Sean? It's going to be like that, only much worse.'

A beat.

'In an hour, you'll really be starting to rattle, so you may feel like telling the truth. If you don't, I'll do your other knee. Then I'll go for your bollocks. Now that's the hard way, Sean. The easy way is that you tell me the truth, all the truth, the first time. Then I leave, and I may even leave you with a few quid. Then you either toot or jack up and get your head together and get on with your life. Now tell me what you know, from the start, about the shooting.'

He groaned and shifted slightly.

'You can move on to your side. Just keep your face to the wall.'

He rolled and started talking. If I'd been police, he'd have talked himself into a life sentence. This is what I can remember. Some of the detail might be out because he gabbled as much as he talked. But this is the main of it.

Sean and his mate, some guy called Carl Raymond, were selling smack together, and Tomas was buying from them. This is Tomas who used to run after Lou and Sam when they were all children together, who got sick at their tenth birthday party and fought with Lou and drew a big curly moustache on her Barbie doll. Tomas bought heroin from them, which he smoked. Cash up front at first, then he got a bit of credit. They laid Tomas on.

So after a while, Tomas owed them money and suddenly this Carl wanted it quick. So they arranged a meet and Tomas showed. He probably expected a bit of a row, but he couldn't have thought it was going to get so heavy and so fast. Neither did Sean – at least that's what he said. He didn't know Carl was carrying.

'Tomas was into us for about one and a half hundred. Carl had this shooter. Fuck knows where from. I'd never seen it before – and he was waving it around to show Tomas he was serious. And then . . . '

He sobbed and I saw it all. I know how spirits stay on the earth when they have unfinished business, and I felt Tomas in the room with me and the baghead and I saw it all. The night-time meet, the shouting and the stretched, drugged-out nerves.

'Fucking went off,' said Sean. 'Gun fucking went off.'

Minutes passed, then I managed: 'Be specific. Where were you?'

'In the motor, at the wheel. We'd had a meet, down at the Croft. Tomas got in the back with Carl. Nearly burst my fucking eardrums. I looked back, and there's Tomas just staring down at his gut, trying to work out what's happened. Carl jumped out the car, ran across the other side of the road, spewed up in the gutter. Then he run back, didn't know what to do.'

According to Sean, he pulled Carl into the passenger seat and the car filled with the stink of shit as Carl crapped himself. Then Sean just stuck his foot down on the pedal and shot out of the place, doing sixty, seventy. After about ten minutes, Carl screamed him to stop on the bridge just before Northenden. Sean said Carl then got out of the motor, walked across the road and threw the gun in the river. He came back to the car, but only to say he was going.

'He fucked off, said he was going up to Wythenshawe. He's got a cousin up there, proper villain, he said. Never seen him again.'

This left Sean with Tomas in the back, so he'd driven across town to the Infirmary and thrown him out, then gone and dumped the motor. It was nicked, anyway. Nothing to bring it back to them.

'So you just left him there.'

'Yeah.' He was afraid again, I could feel it. Then suddenly, for the first time, he got arsey with me. 'I got him to the hospital, didn't I? I didn't just fuck off and leave him like Carl did.'

I let his words hang in the air with the rest. Then I said, 'Yes, you did. That was big of you.'

This was how Tomas had died. And it wasn't down to me. Nothing down to me, despite what Jan and Steph had been told by Hamilton Jacks.

After a few minutes' quiet, I asked another question. Just out of curiosity. I wasn't looking for more angles. 'Why did you give Tomas credit? Guys like you don't, not usually. You're only a rung above any other baghead. You don't have the dough to give lay-ons.'

'No, but Tomas was connected. He gave us a name, Carl checked it with the guy we bought off. He said the geezer was a face, well known. Had a bit of respect.' Then he said a name. My name.

Oh Jesus, Jesus Christ, Jesus Mary and Joseph, Jesus. Oh Christ.

Sean and Carl weren't able to lay on Tomas themselves, but they'd mentioned my name to their supplier. And their man had OK'd the credit to my nephew, who'd used my name. My name. It was down to me.

I felt the silence stretching out in front of me. I licked my lips moist and said, 'Who's your dealer.'

'Ricky Yatnick.' He coughed it out, like he'd swallowed something and it stuck in his throat. 'He lives down the back of All Saints. He works for – ' And stopped.

'Who? Who does Ricky Yatnick work for?'

'Guy called Nathan Chambers.'

Nathan Chambers I'd heard of. Collyhurst gangster.

'Who did you tell about the shooting? Ricky?'

'I had to. We owed him dough. Tomas's dough, some of our own. Maybe five hundred the lot. I went straight round, I was rattling.'

'How quickly?'

'What?'

'How quickly did you go round?'

'After I dumped the car, I needed some gear. An hour, maybe.'

'And what did this Yatnick say when you got him out of bed?'

'He said he'd wipe his mouth, gave me some brown on top. I stopped dealing. That's what happened. I'd had enough.'

So had I. I stood and stuck the gun down my waistband, pretty sure that Sean wasn't about to have a row. A couple of paces and two fifties fluttered to the deck.

'I'm going now, Sean. I'm leaving you the price of a few bags, next to your parcel. For now, I believe what you've told me. If I find out different, I'll be back. None of the names you've given me will know you've spewed. So I suggest you keep schtum about all of this.' I stepped over his body and took a pace towards the front door.

'Stay on the deck and count to a hundred. Then go about your business. If Old Bill haven't got round to you by now, chances are they never will. So mark it down as a good result.'

Then I left, snapping the door shut behind me.

I smelt of Sean when I got home, so I stripped off and stuffed the lot into a laundry bag, then showered on boiling, shampooing and scraping my skull and body, rubbing soap into every crack and sluicing out my pores till my skin squeaked it was clean. The water twisted to freezing until I was gasping for breath, then I got out and made coffee on auto, still dripping and slapping wet prints on the lino. I sat in the lounge to drink it and thought. My first instinct was to find Yatnick and Chambers and front them with a gun that worked. And I had only one question: why did they give credit at the mention of my name?

'No,' I said aloud, 'that would be a bad move.'

Never plot damage when you're angry. Let it settle first.

I made myself busy instead: I wiped the Bond shooter clean of prints, wrapped it in a binliner and went out and dumped it in a bin on a quiet corner. Then I called Noriko from a payphone and got the message Monty would be at the Britannia at seven that evening.

I'd just bought forty fags in a newsagents when my mobile went off. It was Jack. 'We need a meet, son. Got something for you.'

'Where?'

'NCP off Ancoats Road, all the cameras are bust at the moment. It's safe. Half one. Park up and ring me.'

I found a café and ate breakfast without tasting it. Sean would be jacked up and out on his bed by now. I tried to think of something else. A family holiday in Greece twelve years ago. Blue sky, white sand. Sara coming out of the water in a red bikini, one twin on each hand. All three of them smiling, Lou and Sam showing identical gaps in their teeth. I remembered the happiness as I pressed the shutter.

I pulled onto the second level in and saw Jack's BMW. I parked a few rows down and rang his phone. 'Can I join you?'

'Quickly.'

I got in the passenger side. He nodded and reached a shoebox out from under his seat and rested it on his lap. 'Are you sure about this, son?'

'Sure.'

'You ain't never used one, have you?'

'I've never pulled a trigger. But I know how to use it.'

'You're not going after that copper, are you?'

'Stop mothering me, Jack.'

'I'm not fucking mothering you.'

'Look, Leon is dead. In my part of this game, people don't get killed like that. Your game, yes. But someone like me, someone like Leon, we don't expect to die on work.'

'What's different all of a sudden?'

'This is different. Someone's after me and my best friend gets killed. He never fucked anyone in his life, he never had an enemy; he was one of the straightest faces I ever knew, Jack. Whoever killed him, it must be connected to me and I don't know what the fuck is going on right now and I need some protection, so what are you fucking on about?'

'All right.' He ran his fingers over the lid, slipped them under and lifted it off. There was a gun inside, wrapped in oiled brown paper. 'It's a Beretta,' he said, laying the box on my lap. 'Bird's gun, but the best I could get at short notice. Twenty rounds.' He tapped a small box in the corner, like a box you'd buy nails in. 'Most I could get. It's clean. Never been fired.' He dropped the lid on.

'Thanks, Jack.'

'You got anywhere with all this?'

'Don't know.' I looked round the other motors. We were still alone. 'I don't know.' I rubbed my eyes. 'Have you heard of anyone called Nathan Chambers, Jack?'

'I know of him. I don't have it with him, though, he's off my plot. Why do you ask?'

'His name came up. Doesn't matter. What do I owe you for this?'

'Nothing. Just don't use it.'

'It's a clean gun. It's got to be a lot of money.'

'Freeman's, son. Just don't use it.'

'OK, thanks. Did you get anything from your lad about Tomas?'

'Not yet, I'll keep pushing. Let you know as soon as I hear. If I hear.'

'And the Turk.'

'And the Turk.'

'OK. Thanks again.'

I got out and walked to my car. I heard him fire up and back away. By the time I was behind the wheel of the Volvo, his BMW was down the ramp and out of sight.

I took an hour to drive to Amy's, doubling back and checking all the time. She was just on the way out when I turned up. I said I'd leave something in the garden and wouldn't bother her when I came back to fetch it. She had a hedge round the front, so I could bury the shooter in a flowerbed without being seen. If it got found, it wouldn't be down to her. I'd need to test it later, but that could wait. I drove back to Chorlton and spent the rest of the afternoon lying and dozing on my bed. I was too knackered to do anything else.

I drove slowly through the rush hour traffic and called Mr Alexander in his room at the Britannia just before seven that evening.

'Come on up. I'll order coffee.'

I made it just after room service.

'So what's been happening?'

I waited for the door to click shut then I told him about Sean, Chambers and the dealer Ricky Yatnick. I didn't tell him about the gun

I'd left buried in Amy's front garden.

'I've heard of this Nathan Chambers,' he said. 'Not well. Throws his weight around too much for my liking. Never heard any black on him, though.'

'Well, he's involved, anyway.'

'In what? All they did was OK some credit down to your name. And that happens. Then they wiped their mouths of a monkey following an accident. No evidence they mixed any bottle.'

'I don't know either of them. Why did they give Tomas a yes based on my name?'

'Because you're known and you're a face. It happens.'

'Not often. And what about the dealer Ricky Yatnick?'

'You've lost me now.'

'Sean the baghead goes running round to Ricky Yatnick to spew about Tomas. Hamilton Jacks turns up at the Infirmary shortly after knowing all about Tomas being on the slab. There must be a connection there.'

'You tell me where it is, then.'

'Nathan Chambers?'

'And he's connected to?'

I thought of Elvis singing 'Ezekiel cracked them dry bones.'

'I don't know, Monty.'

'Well, nor do I, so let's move on.' He poured out the coffee and passed me a cup. 'News for you. Louie Fenton is still making himself scarce.'

'No word?'

'None at all. And the latest on Leon from Old Bill up here is nothing doing. No clues, no word, nothing.'

'They're nothing without grasses are they, the filth?'

'No. Bit more to come. More coffee?'

'Please.'

He freshened my cup. 'Now,' he said, settling back into his chair. 'Charlie Pearson.'

Monty had been in the game a long time and knew a lot of people. When he'd got Pearson's name from Noriko last night, he'd arranged a very late meet. That meet had resulted in another meet on the way up this afternoon. Monty had been to see a geezer in Birmingham called Haşim, who had traded with Pearson a time or two. Haşim had given Monty the full *Ancient and Modern* on Pearson.

It turned out that for some years, Charlie Pearson had been and still was a godfather figure to a few serious younger faces around town. He used to set up work for them, mainly on the pavement. More recently he was laundering their dough.

'One of these younger faces,' said Monty, 'was a grafter by the name of Keane. Jack Keane.'

With a savage jolt came a sequence: Foston Hall, Strangeways, the Turk, Jack walking. Then the celebration in the Midland. Faces in a row as Jack tapped the ice bucket for silence.

This time, the sequence continued. The Midland, the toast, glasses raised. Jack Keane, Sandra Keane, Quiet John, and now I understood, grey even then and thin-faced, one of the faces stepped forward and took a bow before melting back into the crowd again. Charlie Pearson. Charlie Pearson who had meetings with the copper Keith Hamilton Jacks in a porn cinema in Oxford Road.

Oh yes, Charlie. How long have you been doing this? Close to Jack Keane and the rest, how many bodies have you given up since you started?

Here's to the man that made all this possible.

Nod and raise your glass, Charlie. Best of health and best of luck. Then go out and ring your handler, Keith Hamilton Jacks.

Charlie Pearson. Pearson the grass. Charlie Pearson.

13

A lot of time passed. I remember smoking at least one cigarette and grinding it out and Monty standing to fill my cup. After a while, I found myself over by the window.

'Probably grassed me before the champagne was flat.' I turned and leant on the sill. 'I told you about the Turk, didn't I? The party at the Midland after?'

'You did.'

The radiator had started to burn a line across my arse. I straightened up. 'Pearson's the link. He shops me to Hamilton Jacks for the Turk and everything else follows. Breadcake and Busby, the brown in my cell. Jacks and Tomas, blacking me up to Sara, frightening them out of town.'

'And Leon?'

'Leon never had an enemy in his life. He must be connected.' I looked at Monty again. 'I'll kill him. Kidnap, torture and kill him, the cunt.'

'Who? Hamilton Jacks or Pearson?'

'Both.'

Monty grunted.

'How hard can it be to sit on a house and wait for them to come home?'

'Twenty-five rec apiece. That's not the way.'

'It is. I won't get caught.'

'You're not thinking, mate. Just give me the courtesy of a couple of minutes, eh?'

I forced myself down into a chair.

'I've had this knowledge since yesterday,' he said. 'And the time to sleep on it. I think we can have Charlie Pearson right over – and the copper who's running him.' He outlined his plot and sat back looking smug. If it worked, Pearson would be finished and Hamilton Jacks would be in serious grief. This was the plan.

Pearson, it seemed, was almost certain to be at the fights at the G Mex centre the following night. Monty was attending on a meet, and he'd picked up some extra luggage on the way up. Half an ounce of cocaine. Peruvian flake, ream tackle, with plenty of room for cutting.

Monty would approach Pearson. He'd mention Ha□im and tell him that the Brum had given him Pearson's details; Ha□im had been well primed to give the old boy a glowing reference. Monty would say that he and a kid from Manchester – his northern end – had nicked four kilos of coke off a firm in London who'd fucked him for dough. For obvious reasons, Monty wanted to knock the parcel out up the road. The charlie would be on offer at a price that was certain to get Pearson's juices flowing. Assuming he was interested – and he would be at those figures – Monty would drop the sample on him there and then. He'd tell him to take it as a sign of good faith and a chance to test its quality. Pearson liked a snort, according to Ha□im. Monty would then say that the northern end would be in touch with Pearson in a day or so. If the trade was on, his friend in the north would take it from there.

The northern end, of course, would be me.

Would Pearson be able to resist handing me over to the filth on a plate? And would the copper Hamilton Jacks be able to resist pulling me for dealing class A? Monty thought not. I tried to pick it to pieces.

'The coincidence,' I said, 'will be too much for him to swallow.'

'The copper's greed and excitement will blind him.'

'I'm holding my wrists out for the cuffs.'

'The greed and excitement will cloud their judgement.'

'What about the charlie for the deal?'

'No. Parcel of glucose, whatever we need to work the swindle on them.'

'And what will that be, exactly?'

'Dunno yet. We'll sort the details later.'

This worried me. 'What if he's not at the fight?'

'He's a face and he will be. If not, we'll just think of another way to prop him.'

'And if he doesn't go for it?'

'He will. They will. He's a dog and he'll behave like a dog.'

This was too casual. The idea was crumbling, and I wasn't convinced. 'I'm not convinced, Monty.'

'Listen,' he said.

Monty would tell Pearson that the northern end was in a bit of bother and totally paranoid as well – which they'd go along with, once my name was in the frame. Monty reckoned this would leave us plenty of room to work the coup and live to tell the tale.

'How does Hamilton Jacks get screwed?'

'Pearson goes straight to the copper with the tale. Jacks needs flash money for Pearson to pay you for the coke, so he goes to his bosses for the folding. That's how it works. But there'll be no coke and we'll steal the money – which will put Jacks in deep trouble with the boys up top.'

'The grass will bring snide notes to the meet.'

'No. We'll set it up so that they'll have to supply real money. We'll be turning them on with our promises of four kilos of coke. They'll have to get a hundred grand together to flash for that.'

'And then we rip them off.'

'You got it.' He lit a smoke and rubbed the stubble on the back of his skull.

'All right,' I said. 'There are two main problems, though. First, I've got to mark Jack Keane's card. If Pearson is still into him, then fuck knows what damage he's doing.'

'If he goes for Pearson straight away,' said Monty, 'that will nause our coup.'

'He has to know.'

'You'll only tell him what he needs.'

'I'll just say I'm certain Pearson's a grass. He'll just have to be careful for a bit.'

Monty nodded and stretched. Then he said, 'What was the second problem you mentioned?'

'Just the details. How the fuck are we going to nick a hundred grand off the Old Bill?'

The old boy's smile faded a bit. 'Do I have to think of everything?'

I rang Jack on his mobile from the car on my way back to Chorlton. It was dead. I tried a couple more times, still dead. No ring, no nothing.

He must have changed his SIM card. The kid picked up at the shop and said Jack had to go away for a few days.

'When's he back?'

'He comes and goes as he pleases.' The lad was sounding pissed off.

'Have you got a number for him? Did he say why?'

'No. And no. Well, he said something about woman trouble, needing to have a proper break together. He didn't give me a number, OK?'

'All right, tell him to call me the minute he gets back. I need a meet. Tell him that it's very urgent. Got that?'

I rang off. I could only give the Pearson news direct to Jack himself. Fuck knew who else was snide around him. Back home, I scrambled some eggs and went out at one to swap the copper tapes. No calls at all. I got to bed at two and slept badly.

I was on the meet with Jack.

'Pearson's a grass,' I said.

Jack began pacing round the room, then he started riverdancing up the wall. Pearson came in.

'He says you're a grass, Charlie!' Jack shouted down at him.

'What do you know, Irish!' Pearson shouted back.

I shouted myself awake and found I was lying in sweat. Half six and the paranoia was right on me. Hamilton Jacks, Pearson – what would they do to push me under if they thought I deserved to drown? Even my flat – which had felt clean when I moved back – was now alien and unsafe. A hundred faces were giving me a coat from the dark. Their eyes were unblinking and weird, all black with no difference between pupil and iris.

I had intended to spend the day tracking down Nathan Chambers and Ricky Yatnick, but I knew I wouldn't be thinking straight. There was a gun buried in Amy's front garden. I was clear enough to know I wasn't clear enough to trust myself with it. And I wouldn't go back to sleep now, I felt like I was being watched. Maybe Hamilton Jacks and his crew were out in the street, waiting for me to make my next move. All right then, I'd give them something to get excited about. I got up and set the traps.

Half an hour later, I was walking through Chorlton Village making no attempt to check my behind. If they were out there in the dark and the cars and the stripey workmen hides on the pavement they were going to earn their dough today. I made for the metro.

Half nine found me in Chinatown walking with apparent purpose round the tightly knit streets and pretending to look in jar-lined windows. After a couple of hours, I went up to Piccadilly Gardens and I jumped on the metro for Bury. Three people came with me from the platform, but no one I'd seen before. From Bury metro I went up the hill to the Victoria Hotel, and had lunch. No one came in, but then they'd have all the exits covered. Sod 'em. It was a cold day outside, and I wasn't planning on going anywhere for a while.

There was a minicab dropping off as I came out, I nabbed him and asked for the airport. I couldn't see anything with us in the mirror, but I told him to pull up at a bus stop for Oldham anyway, gave him fifty and said to continue to the airport and pick up a Mr Hanratty who was arriving on the four o'clock flight from Madrid. I got out as a bus showed and jogged up to the top deck. Just me and a pensioner and a dog. Nothing suss on the road behind.

The bus was full by the time we made Oldham town centre. I got off, two young lads and a besuited businessman coming with me. As I cruised up to the market I felt a sudden sweat across the back of my neck; there was someone up my arse.

Some of the stalls were packing up. I drifted along a couple of bric-a-brac jobs and bought a second-hand book; a 1962 Macmillan edition of *Through the Looking Glass*. I found a café, took a seat near the window, and started to read.

The Red Queen was just telling Alice how they took five nights in a row in winter for warmth when I heard the door open and glanced up. The lads from the bus. I recognised them immediately. They were both plastered in designer labels – copy gear I'd assumed – from head to foot. The kit looked so new, and they looked so uncomfortable in it, I reasoned they had to be plain clothes on obs. Particularly as they'd been two places that I'd been and I'd not seen them in between. Well, fine. I went back to reading Alice.

The White Knight showed up in the forest. I vaguely remembered this was Lewis Carroll writing about himself. When he says his goodbyes to Alice, it's meant to be Carroll saying his goodbyes to the kids he's told stories to over the years. Goodbye because they're getting too grown up for a daft old man's tales.

The two young lads weren't talking, and they'd made a single cup of coffee last nearly forty minutes. Definitely Old Bill.

I could see a bus chugging for the stop on the other side of the road. The two coppers were too far from the window to see anything. I slipped some change on the table and got up suddenly, pocketing Alice. I was last on the bus. The two coppers made the door as the bus pulled out, one of them got on his phone as we turned the corner. I stared at the cars following till my eyes hurt.

We went down through Failsworth, Collyhurst, then Ancoats and along Newton Street. I got off at Chorton Street bus station and walked to Stevenson Square. It was getting dark and colder now, but there was a café still open. I bought a *Big Issue* from the bloke on the street, went in and ordered a toastie and two mugs of tea. I drank the first down at the counter and took the other to my table. When the food arrived, I pushed it around my plate and stared out of the window at people hurrying home. This had to stop. All this running and they were still winning the round.

I licked the fork clean and rested it on my right thigh. And stuck it right in, pushed harder, hurt myself as bad as I could. I'd been sleepwalking. Now I woke up.

'Something else, love?'

I looked up, feeling daft. I gestured OK at her. 'No, I'm just going.' I walked my plate and mug over to the counter and split.

I got in at six, stuck the kettle on, laid *Through the Looking Glass* on the desk, shrugged my jacket off and fumbled for the anglepoise in the dark. The bulb blew.

'Shit.'

I changed the bulb then sat at the desk and took a few minutes to look at some of the Tenniel illustrations. Pictures of a land where nothing means what it does in our world, no one says what they mean, and half the people Alice meets can't be trusted. A looking-glass world that reflects everything wrong. All very familiar.

I was set to bell Monty around nine to see if he'd got into Pearson at the G Mex fights. I lay down on the sofa and listened to Leon's phone some more. *Hurly, burly, early, coming, jacking, jacking it in, early, incoming, I'm coming, and coming, and coming.* I wasn't concentrating properly; I went to the window, pulled back the curtains and waved to any watchers on the other side of the road. Then I went for a shower.

At eight I did the traps, desk last. Usual routine: open the drawer slightly and slip a match in the gap between runner and frame, then close up and snap the match off so it's flush with the front of the drawer. The rest of the match went in lower down the gap and got snapped off again. I checked the two bits weren't sticking out, popped the sulphur head back in the box and stuck it in my pocket. Another match got leant up against the front door on the landing. The hall light clicked out as I made the street.

I drove around watching my tail for an hour and fetched up in a layby halfway to Denton just after nine. A mound of shrapnel went into the payphone and I called Monty.

'Hello!' He was shouting above the noise of the crowd.

'Monty!'

'Hang on! Stay there!'

I pumped in another sov while he moved off the crowd.

'All right?'

'Fine. How did it go?'

I heard more roaring from his end, but further off. 'Still can't hear. Hang on.'

Another minute as he moved outside.

'All right, that's better.'

'How did it go?'

'One hundred per cent. Dog's a good bet. We can talk about stakes tomorrow.'

'Good.'

'What?'

'I said good.'

We hung up. Sounded like Pearson had bit, and bit big time. Feeling really calm for the first time that day, I drove to a fish shop on the edge of Chorlton where I sat and ate cod and chips in the car with the window down. When I was done, I screwed the paper up and lobbed it at a bin about five yards away. It went straight in, and I sat surprised for at least a minute.

Midnight and I was listening at the street door for any movement where I wouldn't want to hear it. Nothing. In and close quietly, punch the hall light and up to my door before it went out. The match was just where I'd left it, leaning nonchalantly against the door. I scooped it up and unlocked in one motion, lights on and round the traps. Desk: matchsticks in place, both OK. Into the kitchen, kettle on, ashtray, spark up, lounge, desk. Lay the ashtray down. I switched on the lamp and emptied my pockets, heard the kettle click off in the kitchen and went to brew up.

I made a two-bag mug of tea, and flicked the by now inch-long ash into the sink. It fizzed gently as it hit a few drops of water. Back into the lounge, and mug on the desk. There was folding in my back pocket, I got it out and slid open the drawer to put the dough away. The two bits of match fell out. I bent and slung them into the clean white china ashtray.

Something was wrong.

The world switched off around me. I heard my own blood pumping through my ears with an urgent insistent thump. I picked up the two bits of matchstick.

I'd started to breath through my mouth. Very gently, I dropped the two tiny bits of wood into my left palm. The fag went into the ashtray. I pulled the anglepoise further in and bent closer.

The two pieces of match were a slightly different tone. One was faintly grey. I tried to fit the two bits together. They wouldn't go. I turned the grey fragment and tried to fit them together the other way round. Splinters of match met other splinters when they should have found a tiny wood socket. I remembered the sulphur end in the matchbox, laid the two sections on the desktop, opened the box, and saw the fragment lying among the rest. I took it out and laid it next to the others. Too long.

I had to make sure. I knelt, then lay on the floor. After a few minutes feeling about under the drawer unit, I found a gap between carpet and skirting board, slid my fingers into it and there was a tiny splinter. Fingertip and thumb brought out a snapped section of matchstick. White wood. Not greying, white.

The three white pieces fitted together, as I knew they would. Sulphur end broken off, middle snapped both ends, and the last section, snapped one end only. They lay there in the pool from the desk lamp. The rest of the room faded away.

Someone had been here while I was out. Someone who knew me, someone who knew my style. Someone I'd taught.

'This is a good move,' I told him. 'Snap off a match in the gap between the drawer and the runner. Then if they're on the deck later, you know someone's taking a serious interest in you. A serious interest.'

'Fucking smart,' he said.

We'd been drinking and on the blow. I felt like sharing a secret with him.

'No one notices a match against a door,' I said. 'But it tells you if someone's been in while you've been out.'

'Fucking smart, you're fucking smart mate,' he slurred.

He'd remembered the match at the door when he let himself in, and the rest of the traps around the flat. He forgot the matches in the desk though, he didn't see them until they fell out and then he only found one. So he took a match from the box in his pocket, slipped it in the gap and snapped it off. Snapped it off so I wouldn't know he'd been here.

Terry slipped the match into the gap and snapped it off so I wouldn't know he'd been here. Little discs slipped into round sockets in my head. Terry put the brown in my cell. Terry was fucking me. Terry.

An hour later, or a minute, I was sitting on the couch, not knowing how I got there. This half trance thing had happened before, usually in the nick and only when things were really shit bad. My mug squatted on the coffee table. I touched it, still hot. Hadn't been away for long.

What now?

My head flicked through all the work we'd done together, all the times I'd helped him out for dough, a bed for the night, whatever. What the fuck was his game?

He hadn't crept my gaff hoping to nick something. He'd know there wouldn't be anything here to steal; not his money, not mine. He knew I didn't keep anything warm around me. So maybe he wasn't hunting alone. Maybe whoever was pulling his strings had sent him in to put something down rather than take something out.

Like a bug, for example.

I took the place apart. I unscrewed the phone mouthpiece and the earpiece, looked for replacement sockets on the wall plugs, ran my finger along skirting boards to see if the dust had been disturbed as he slid something behind the wood. I checked all the appliance plugs to see if they'd been opened or changed, felt around the insides of lampshades, looked under desk, chairs, mattress, tore off pillowcases and put them back on, then tore them off again to check.

Nothing on show. If there were sound detectors, they were well hidden. And if they were here, they wouldn't pick up much unless I talked in my sleep. OK, then, I'd stay put. I wouldn't give them the satisfaction of moving out tonight. Bed at two thirty and slept immediately: quite a surprise.

My bones and body were aching. It was six eighteen, and I was driving round in circles looking for a tail. I rang Monty just after seven.

'You're early. I ain't dressed yet.'

'I'm not bothered.'

He was in shirt, strides and bare feet when I knocked on his door a few minutes later.

'I ordered breakfast.' There were two plates and the rest on a table. He'd already begun eating and now he sat down again. 'All right?'

'No.' I told him: matchsticks, Terry, Judas. He had a forkful of egg halfway to his mouth when I started. Never made it. He clinked it down on his plate, then rocked back on his chair as I gave him the full SP.

'Fucking hell, mate. That is a bad business.' He breathed out over his teeth.

'I want to sweat him, Monty. Will you help?'

'Do you want him hurt?'

'I don't think he's working alone. I want to know who's pulling his strings.'

'Do you want him hurt?'

'I want him to talk.'

Now he picked up a triangle of toast and took a bite. And kept his eyes on mine. 'We need to get him on site,' he said. 'Can you pull him out of this Carol's?'

'All I have to say is that I've got the rest of his dough waiting for him.'

'Where does this Carol dwell?'

'Salford.'

Monty looked at his watch, I looked at mine. Twenty to eight. He wiped his lower lip.

'I'm going to use a call box downstairs. Have some coffee.' He split.

I poured myself a cup, moved to the window and looked out over Piccadilly Gardens. Five floors up, the commuters were indistinct enough to look like a gently flowing mass rather than a crew of bad-tempered individuals stamping or gear-shifting their way to work. I focused on a short queue of motors at a traffic lights, imagined the stressed-up men and women sitting behind the wheel, tapping their fingers and tugging on a cigarette or thinking about giving up. This was a life I'd rejected years before. But with Tomas and Leon dead, Sara and the kids in hiding, enemies I didn't even know I had two weeks ago – well, it didn't exactly advertise the road I'd taken.

For some reason I thought of the twins' seventh birthday. A pile of aunties and uncles round, Sara's family, several thousand kids hyperactive on chocolate overdose. My mam still alive, doing the granny bit. Everyone was out that year, and even Jack Keane showed up with a pair of teddies in shades – one white, one brown. 'White Bear,' he'd said, 'and Brown Bear. That's their names.' Lou asked why they didn't have real names. 'Those are real names,' he said, winking at me over her head. 'Mr White and Mr Brown. They're very special bears.'

Monty's keycard slid into, teased, then opened the door. He was breathing heavier than usual. Excitement and exertion, I assumed. Fit as he was, he was still gone sixty. Probably ran up the stairs two at a time instead of waiting for the lift.

'Coffee,' I said.

He took a gulp, then: 'Here's our MO. When we're done here, get on the phone to this Terry and agree a meet before he moves this morning. You need to pick him up, drive around a bit, stop off for a takeaway coffee, a piss, any fucking thing, just make sure you're driving up Withy Grove at nine forty-five. You know where the second-hand bookstalls are?'

'Yes.'

'Right. What car are you driving?'

'Dark blue Volvo.'

'OK. I'll be standing there and showing out. Stop and wave me over. I'll ask for a lift. I'll get in the back, behind your Terry. Make sure the cunt sits in the front, right?'

'Monty –'

'In the front. And I'll take it from there. We'll need to be over and done with by two, whatever happens.'

Eight forty. Carol picked up.

'He's still in kip,' she said. 'Still in the spare room.' No hello and no small talk. I heard her shift around or sit down. She spoke again, this time her voice was much lower. 'I don't want him here any more, I was just suffering him until you got in touch.'

'What's the problem?'

She sighed into the phone and said, 'Did you know he was on the gear?'

'No.'

'Well, he is, I found it yesterday. The rest I can deal with, but I don't have it with smackheads. I told him to go, today or tomorrow. No later. But go.' Then she added. 'Don't say I told you, unless you have to.'

'I'll deal with him now. I promise there'll be no comebacks on you. Where will you be the rest of the day?'

She rattled a mobile at me. I scribbled it on my wrist to be sure. 'Try me here first. But I'll have that with me otherwise.'

'Thanks. Can you get him out of bed and put him on, Carol? And if anyone calls for him, just tell them he's gone out. End of story. OK.'

'OK, love.'

I heard her put the phone down, move across the room and shout for him. Then she shouted again, voice rigid with exasperation. Clattering and thuds as she ran upstairs. A few minutes, then bare feet thudding down and the phone being scraped off the table.

'Hello, yeah?' He sounded rough.

'I've picked your dry cleaning up.'

'Oh, sweet.'

'Get dressed and get a move on. I've got something to look at when we're done. Pick you up in the square round the back of Carol's in ten minutes.'

I was in a box round the corner. I made the square in two. He took another five. Fuck, he was keen. And rank, as I nosed when he got in next to me. He smelt dirty and musty.

'All right, Terry?' I cranked my window to lose the stink.

'All right, mate. Yeah, all right.'

I felt sick. It wasn't the smell. It was the knowledge that he was a Judas.

The motor was idling, so I slipped into gear and headed north. He switched the radio on, then bent in and started fiddling with the dial. He lost Radio 4 and found some pop, then sat back and nodded his head in time to the beat spewing out of the speakers. There was something different here, I just couldn't put my finger on it. He hadn't lost weight; his shirt and black jacket looked tidy enough, considering he'd just flopped out of his pit. Got it. It was the constant movement, the scratching and face touching. Nod, scratch, rub his cheek. He was on the gear all right. I wondered if he'd had the time before he left. No, he'd been too quick. I changed down and took the chance to tug my jacket away from his seat. It was brushing against his thigh. His betrayal naused me.

'Carol been treating you all right?'

'Yeah, she's a lovely lady. I'm grateful you sorted me to stay. Thanks.'

'What about Janey?'

'She's been ringing up and mithering me, asking for dough.'

'And?'

'Well, I'll go and see her today, yeah? Make her happy.' He half turned his head and smiled at me. He looked relaxed, his voice was relaxed. He just thought he was off to get his money.

The dash blinked nine forty-seven as we crossed at the Corn Exchange and headed up Withy Grove. I looked to my right as casually as possible. 'Hold up, Terry, there's a mate of mine showing out. I'll just see what he's after.'

I indicated and pulled over, leant out the window and shouted over at Monty. He looked up and came across, weaving his way through the motors to Terry's side. The boy racked the window down and he stuck his head in.

'This is a surprise,' I said.

'It's a fucking stroke of luck,' he grated.

'Terry, this is Billy.'

Monty glanced at him. 'Hello, Terry.'

'All right?'

'Can you do me a big favour, pal,' he said, looking back at me. 'Somebody's let me down and I've got to be up near the Embassy Club in ten minutes. Can you give me a lift?'

Look at your watch, look at Terry, then shrug. 'We're a bit pushed, but yeah, jump in. I can spare ten minutes.'

The kid leant over and opened the back. Monty levered himself on to the seat. We drove on.

The Embassy Club is a drinker once owned by the comedian Bernard Manning, and it was easy enough to get to from here. Monty rabbitted on about this and that. He looked calm in the mirror. Past the lights at Queen's Road, he motioned to what looked like a carwash. 'Just pull on to the forecourt there mate, that'll do me nicely.'

We pulled in to what was in fact a derelict car wash, just where the motors used to roll out. The doors were gone – now it was just an open space either end of the tunnel. As there was nowhere else to go, I drove into this cavern, wondering how the fuck Monty had sorted this plot out in the last hour. We were off-show from the road, the exit was on a slope, and the back end of the car was in shadow. An ideal place for what was on the cards. Of course, Monty had made this move before. Been down here previous with violence in mind.

What was the outcome last time?

We stopped and Monty bounced out. Seeming to button up his top smother, he stepped up to Terry's door and stuck his thumb up at me in thanks. Terry half clocked him, perfectly normal. The next move seemed normal as well; Monty opened Terry's door, bobbed and stretched his left hand across the lad at me to shake. Then he shot his right behind Terry's head, grasped the hair on the back of his neck, jerked his nut against the dash, kneed him in the ribs, swung a leg over and finally slammed his entire body weight down on the kid's back, forcing his head under the glovebox and his body on to the floor. A Stanley knife appeared in his right hand. He slid the blade out with a tiny *snick*, then lowered it so it was nearly touching Terry's right eye.

'Struggle and you lose an eye. Got that, cunt? No ifs and no buts, just don't fucking move.' He manoeuvred himself into the passenger seat, keeping the Stanley at Terry's eye and resting his right boot on his back. He twisted round and his eyes were bright and shining. 'Door,' he hissed.

I strained across, getting a nose of Monty's sweat and Terry's fear. I fingered the handle towards me and slammed it shut.

'Mirror OK?'

I glanced into it and nodded.

'Right, let's go. Head towards where you and me last saw Tommy Hanlon, remember?'

I gunned the motor. Tommy Hanlon was a face who'd died a long time back, we'd both gone to the funeral. Where had that been, the crematorium? No, a cemetery – but which one? Phillips Park. I swung right on to the main road and glanced across. He nodded.

I took the long way round. I didn't know how this was going to end. The state he was probably in, Terry was unlikely to work out a route from his position, but I couldn't be sure. We went down Grimshaw Lane and on to Briscoe Lane to the north of the graveyard. Monty started giving it lefts and rights with sharp jabs of his free hand until we finished up in Clayton, down a set of backstreets I'd never seen before.

'Slow down. Just here.'

It was a pub with a small car park and beyond that, a high brick wall with gates round a yard. The gates were open.

'In here.'

His blade was still horizontal at Terry's eye. I fancied I could see the boy blink in the shadow. I swung into the yard and stopped the car in the only space available – on the left, behind the wall and next to a four wheel drive.

'Hop out and close the gates, eh?' Monty said. 'There's a bolt on the left.'

I slid out. The windows overlooking the car park got a quick coat of eyes but they were empty. Of course, Monty had been here before. He'd have sorted everything.

I crunched through a patch of gravel, swung the gate closed and bolted it. Back to the car and I bent my head in. Monty motioned for me to open his side. As I pulled the door, he jerked Terry's top and shirt up and over the kid's head, then he rested the Stanley on his spine and hissed, 'That's the blade. Don't fucking move or I'll cut you. Understand?'

Not a word. Holding the knife steady, Monty swung his leg up and levered himself out of the car in a couple of seconds. Then he grabbed Terry and pulled.

'Out. Make trouble and I will kill you.'

He took a step back. Terry had been crunched up in a tight foetal position for nearly half an hour and he moved like he was aching all over. His left leg came first, toe scuffing the tarmac, then he sort of wiggled out – backside, right leg, body and the rest next. He reached for the handle as he came and heaved himself up, half flopping over the open door and groaning quietly.

Monty laid the Stanley on his back again and looked at me. 'Door behind you.'

It was black and paint-chipped and the handle turned easily. It opened into a short corridor. I heard movement and the sound of the car being kicked shut, then Monty again.

'Light switch on the right.'

I found it, a weak single bulb a couple inches above my head.

'Coming through.' He armtwisted and pushed Terry past me then snapped. 'Down on the floor. Hands and knees. Right down. Then lie down.'

Terry went on all fours like a dog, then he lay on his belly.

'Stand on him, mate. Make sure he can't move.'

I kicked the door shut and stuck my heel in the small of his back. Monty moved down to the end of the passage and turned on a light. Then he motioned me away, dragged Terry up by the arm and pulled him out of sight. Following, I saw the pair of them standing on the last of six stone steps. Monty thumbed me down and past him, then he let Terry go and said, 'OK. Pull the jacket off your head. Slow.'

The boy reached up, and gingerly pulled his jacket down. Even in the feeble yellow light, I could see the sweat on his face. He blinked, and it occurred to me he hadn't made a sound since we pulled him at the car wash. Here I got the proof that Terry had betrayed me. If I'd got it wrong, there'd be shouting and screaming, protests. I could only see guilt.

Monty stashed the blade and nodded at him. 'Up to the barrels. Squat.'

There was a line of aluminium barrels resting on a gantry. Terry trotted up to them and dipped down on his haunches, hands hanging limply between his knees and his eyes now switching away somewhere into the mid-distance. I heard the wheeze as Monty opened his mouth to speak again but I turned and shook my head. I took a few steps towards Terry, a couple of wet foot slaps told me Monty had followed, the low wheezing told me he was about half a yard behind me. Now I looked down on the boy, wondering how to lead in.

'All right,' I said. 'Let's start.' I fished my smokes out and tapped one up. 'I'm in no hurry,' said the gesture. 'This is all just dotting and crossing.' This was the second smackhead I'd shaken down in two days. Getting to be a habit.

'Take me through it from the beginning, Terry.' I kept my voice low as I sparked up. 'First off, who is it? Who are you making yourself busy for?'

Monty coughed quietly. I looked round and he pointed at his mouth. I nodded. 'I knew your old man,' he grated. 'And I think I'd be doing his memory a favour by putting you away. If I had my way, you'd be at the bottom of the Irwell with a bullet in your head and some butcher's weights round your ankles. One lie from you and that's what happens.'

Terry slumped back on his arse, back against the barrels. Then he started to sob. He was a child, told off by his mam. 'They said you were a grass. I swear to God, they told me you were a grass. That's why I did it. Not for the smack. Please. I wouldn't have done it otherwise.'

I took a punt. 'How did they recruit you?' I was still gentle and even quieter. You're just telling me the details, Terry. No need to worry about sticking someone else in. I looked at him very deadpan. We have all the time in the world.

He looked at me and back at Monty. Then his eyes flicked around the cellar and I could see he was working out if he had any chance against the pair of us. But there was only one way out and he'd have to get past the two of us first. And we were well ahead on points. No, the odds weren't good. I could see it click on to his face.

'All right,' he said. 'It was about four months in on the last one. You were blanking me, Janey had the hump, I was doing my time bad.'

I sat down on an upright barrel. Monty did the same, arms crossed over his chest, head slightly to one side.

'I remember,' I said.

'I'm out on the exercise yard when a guy I know called Reg Hebble comes across and says someone wants to talk to me. Then this big black geezer called Nathan Chambers appears. Big sod, grey hair. Hands like fucking hams.'

Hello – Nathan Chambers? That would be Ricky Yatnick's main man, who was Carl Raymond's main man. Carl, Sean's friend. Carl, who sold gear to Tomas. Carl, who killed him.

'After a bit of chat, Chambers comes out with this: he says you're a grass. A fucking grass. I told him straight off, no way you could be a grass, told him you hated them, wouldn't piss on one if he was on fire. Then I fucked off.'

The way Terry told the story, that would have been the end, but Nathan Chambers stopped him after a couple of paces by simply calling out Janey's name. And her address, and where she worked. And what a nice girl she was, and how – and this I could hardly believe – and how it would be a pity if something happened to her. So Terry had come back and he'd listened while Chambers had lied to him.

The bottom line, said Chambers, was that I was a grass and that I'd caused a lot of trouble for some of his friends. Now they wanted some of their own back. Terry had fallen for this, he said, because his head was up his arse. Any other time, any other place, he'd have fucked them off. But not this time and not this place. All Chambers wanted for now was to mark Terry's card. And he dropped some charlie on Terry, there and then. Terry reckoned later this had been laced with smack. Right or wrong, he'd gone on the gear soon enough afterwards.

Chambers had worked on him. He'd supplied him with charlie, then brown. And Janey had been looked after as a result, this Terry knew from her letters. Little packets of cash dropped through her letterbox every Friday, and after a while, weekly bags of coke as well.

'Why did you stand for all this?' I said. 'Only an idiot would buy it.'

'My head was up my arse.' He was giving it a bit of attitude now. 'And after, it was the gear.'

They had him on a string, pull and he came jogging. He confirmed he'd stuck the wraps in my peter. Idea was to keep me in for longer. And of course, it gave them more time to work on him when he was out, alone.

When Terry had got out, he'd met another, older, white geezer. This one seemed to be head boy; the one pulling Chambers' strings. The description Terry gave of the white guy was tall, greying, in his fifties, maybe late fifties. And walked with a slight stoop. Sounded like Charlie Pearson to me.

'He never gave you a name?'

'No.'

'Think. Chambers. Did he ever mention the white guy's name?'

'Never.'

'You mean he just rings you up and says this is the voice of God, let's go to work?'

Terry was trembling now and his voice climbed a notch or two. 'He never told me.'

Real mind games. Even hiding his name from the boy. Must have freaked him out, what with the gear he was on and everything.

I asked him who suggested a spin of my flat. Tall, greying, stooping geezer went into the frame. Terry, of course, had a set of twirls. Partners always do, you may need to whip round and clear the place after a nicking.

'What was your brief?'

'Check you hadn't changed your locks, have a look round while I was there.'

'Looking for what?'

The boy shifted and wouldn't look me in the eye.

'Speak up,' rasped Monty.

Terry gathered himself together. 'Any diaries, papers. Anything with appointments in them. And they wanted me to check the layout of your place. See what the offmans was like from the back windows.'

'Did they say why?'

'No.'

'Did they ask you to put anything down?'

'No.'

'Are you sure, you little Judas?'

'I'm telling you the truth, now.'

'When did they tell you to go in?'

'Yesterday. Chambers rang me at Carol's and rushed a meet. They told me to sit on your place and go in as soon as. I nearly bottled it when you came to the window and waved in the evening. Thought you knew.'

'I felt your eyes. Thought I was just being paranoid. How did they find you?'

'They gave me a mobile for a bit. And the meets were regular, next meet always set up. And Chambers gave me a mobile number yesterday.'

'You got it with you?'

'Somewhere.'

'Turn your pockets out.'

He stood and emptied his jacket and strides on the top of a beer barrel and picked through the debris of Rizlas, tobacco and other shrapnel. There was a square of neatly folded lined paper among the junk. I flattened it: a mobile number and 'NATHAN' in a script I didn't recognise.

'All right, sit down, Terry.' I felt like I hadn't smoked since the Relief of Mafeking. I pulled my pack out again and offered Monty. We both sparked up and I drew the fumes down very deep. Then I stepped back to the stairs and motioned to the old guy. 'We need to talk,' I hissed.

Monty nodded and glanced up and around. Before his eyes had finished the sweep, Terry started to bay like an animal, an awful, tearful, drawn-out moan that echoed round the cellar. Our move and muffled voices must have made him think that now he'd spewed, he was going to get it there and then. I looked over to see him clench his fists and start beating the deck on either side like a pair of kettle drums. 'I know what I've done, I'm sorry, I'm sorry, I'm sorry. I'm so sorry. Please don't kill me, please please please please . . . ' Now he was slapping the sides of his head with his palms, harder and harder, in time to his words: 'Please please please . . . ' He spread his arms out and wailed, head back, mouth open like a big gaping O, then trailed off into an eddy of indistinct whimpering.

Monty snorted to the echo and stamped to a shelf where he took down a transistor radio and stuck it on the floor near the barrels. Then he yanked the kid to his feet, marched him across, upended a black plastic bucket and pushed him on to it. Last, he jammed his cigarette under Terry's snout. 'Get a hold of this, and stop your fucking moaning, you cunt. For all you fucking deserve to, you ain't gonna die. Not here anyway. Now just listen to this radio. We want to talk.'

He jabbed a button: talk emerged, sounding like a phone-in. He bashed it again. Music this time, pop music. Clearly not sure that this wasn't some kind of stroke, Terry took a trembling drag. With a grunt, Monty swung back towards me, stretching out his hand as he came. I held out my pack, he snatched one and lit up. We moved away, though I stood so I could watch Terry over his shoulder.

'I can't hurt him bad, mate,' I said.

'I'll fucking do it, then.'

'No.'

'Cut his feet, that'll keep him off the case for a while.'

'No, I know his mam. But I do need him off the street. For all his penance and promises, if a bag of shit got waved in front of him, he'd do it again.'

Monty had drawn his cigarette halfway down in a single tug. The length of ash looked solid, red and angry. 'I'm assuming the tall stooping white guy in Terry's tale is – '

'Charlie Pearson. Certainly sounded like him.'

Monty sucked on his fag again. 'Wonder what they wanted with your flat?'

'If we assume Pearson's working for Hamilton Jacks and the cozzer is behind all this, then I'm guessing he had a fit-up in mind. Plant it, raid me, nick me.'

'I don't know if that's the start and finish of it,' he rubbed the back of his head. 'But if it's Old Bill at the back of all this, get out today. Not tonight, today. Soon as we're done here.'

'I know. But we need to deal with Terry first. He'll go Judas again in a moment.'

'So what's your bright idea?'

'I need to make a call. Can I leave here and come back, or do you need to see the guvnor first?'

'Don't worry, he won't move from the front until we've gone.'

I looked at the rows of barrels.

'If there's a problem with them, it stays a problem. He'll serve them bottles.'

'All right.'

I took the steps outside and rang Casey on his mobile. Fences are pretty much backroom guys, so this was going to be a big favour, but my list of straight faces was very short at the moment. Sometimes I felt like I was the only one left. 'Casey, it's me. Are you clear your end?'

'Uh huh. Just doing some paperwork.'

'It's about Terry. He's gone Judas.'

'Christ, not another. Poor Yoda.'

'He stuck that brown in my cell, Casey. He's working with a copper's grass to put me away.'

'Where did all this come from?'

'I'll give you the details later. I've got him here, Casey. He's right on the smack.'

'Good enough for him.'

'No. I want him put down for a few days. Not hurt. But he'll need a couple of serious minders. Maybe a bit of methadone to keep him from screaming or throwing himself through a window. I'll pay whatever it costs.'

There was a long long pause. Then Casey cleared his throat and said, 'I'd laugh if it wasn't so serious. You're too fucking straight, you know that?'

'I could do with a bit of help here, Casey.'

'I don't really know about that, mate. I'm not really a frontline guy. I don't get involved.'

'It'll only be for a few days. You must know a couple of heavies.'

'You're pushing it here, you know that?'

'Sorry. There's not many people I can trust right now.'

A beat, another long one. 'Yoda would be proud of you. And Leon.' He sighed. 'I'll call you back in fifteen minutes.'

'My number's new. It's on your screen.'

'OK.' He hung up.

I checked the time and went back to the cellar. Monty was sitting at the foot of the stairs reading a newspaper he'd found somewhere. The radio was off and Terry appeared to be asleep, curled up on the floor next to it.

'He's akip,' said Monty. 'Couple of minutes after you went up, he asked to turn the transistor off and just lay down.'

'Must be all the excitement.'

'Any luck?'

'I think so. Someone's calling me back. I'll go up for it.'

Monty glanced across at Terry and flicked his paper down. 'You got any fags? I'm out.'

I gave him one and we lit up.

'Wonder what Hamilton Jacks has on Charlie Pearson to make him dance so enthusiastically?' I said.

'And Nathan Chambers.'

'I don't think Chambers knows it's police involved, I reckon he just thinks it's a bit of private enterprise by Pearson. Chambers is just a minor player here, helping his mate out. He probably thinks I *am* a grass.'

'What makes you so sure?'

'He happened to be in Strangeways when we were, so Pearson propped him. What do you think keeps Charlie dancing, Monty?'

'Fucked if I understand how a grass's mind works. They think as high up as the gutter. I'm sure it's not the money, though. Or the threats. Mate of mine was stuck in it by a supergrass back in the seventies. I was helping out with his case, I saw the guy's statements. All the detail this grass was dealing up, he was doing it □cause he liked it. I think they do in the end, being at the centre, spooning out grief where they fancy it, when they fancy it. Lot of power in that.'

The phone started ringing as I emerged into the car park. Ex-wrestler Casey knew some big, heavy guys, just like I'd thought he would. He'd called on a kid with *Good Housekeeping* muscles of the month. This kid had done a bit of pavement work, but was keeping his head down at the minute, said Casey. And the weight trainer had a mate – one without form, but with access to a high-rise flat in Benchill. Very high. So there'd be no jumping out of windows, at least not to talk about it later. The pair would want handy money, but would keep Terry secure and furnish him with methadone.

'We can meet you in an hour tops,' said Casey. 'Car park opposite the animal enclosure in Wythenshawe Park. Entrance off Wythenshawe Road, pitch and putt, bowling green, car park. On the right.'

'Thanks, Casey. Grand apiece for the lads with a monkey a day for refreshers.'

'I'll tell them. Just make sure you give me full story and pictures later.' He rang off.

I could afford to be generous with dough. It was coming out of Terry's corner of our last parcel. He'd had enough charity off me to last him a lifetime. I went down and gave Monty the script. 'And I think we ought to do Pearson swiftnick,' I said. 'Whatever him and Hamilton Jacks have in mind, we need to head them off at the pass.'

'I've got to be in the Smoke tonight and tomorrow. But I can be yours in a couple of days.'

'OK, I'll kick off up here. Now we need to tidy up a bit. Terry will have to call this Nathan Chambers.'

We shook the boy awake and frogmarched him upstairs. Monty had the Stanley out again, although Terry didn't look like he'd need it. When we were outdoors, I turned to the lad and said, 'Listen up. You need a story for your new pals, so this is what you're going to say. Tell them I've given you some of your money today and you've hooked up with a bird you used to know. You're taking her away somewhere exotic, like Blackpool. If they complain or create, just say the line's bad and hang up. Got that?'

'What's going to happen to me?' Little frightened boy again.

'I'm going to put you down somewhere safe for a while. And for your father's memory, there'll be someone to look after you. And that's more than you deserve.'

I hit 141 on my phone – didn't want him clocking my number – and dialled Nathan Chambers off the paper from Terry's pocket. I held it next to Terry's ear so I could hear both ends of the chat. It rang twice and went to voicemail.

'Leave him a message,' I hissed.

Terry ran through the script and sounded convincing enough to me. I pulled the phone away and pressed off. 'Very good. Now: one more thing. What did you tell this mob about Carol?'

'Bird I flopped on.'

'No connection to me? Sure?'

'None.' Then suddenly, he yawned. Like a big cat, he looked like he just wanted to sleep. Monty snicked the blade away and we moved for the car. Without being told, Terry crawled under the glovebox and we covered him with his jacket.

'Do you think Chambers will buy all that?' said Monty as he rested his boots on the boy's back.

'No reason not to. I rumbled Terry by chance – no one's going to suspect that. Gives us a couple of days at least.'

I fired the Volvo and drove, keeping well under the limit. The few smokers in the animal car park twenty minutes later were empty, except for one ancient Renault. Four equally ancient senior citizens were emerging from this as we pulled in, bowling bags heavy with woods. Aside from that, nothing to report.

Casey was stood next to a plain white transit. One thickset guy in the passenger seat, about the size of a baby elephant; the other lad was in the back. He was bigger, said Casey. Terry could go straight in the van. Monty stayed in the motor till I gave him the office, then got out and pulled the boy after him. There followed the most bizarre sight on an already weird day, when he shooed Terry across the car park like he was a small flock of geese. Head down and feet dragging – almost sleepwalking in fact – the lad stumbled across the tarmac and tumbled into the back of the van.

'I don't think he'll be any trouble,' said Monty, with a nod at Casey.

'Did you know his father as well?' said Casey.

I watched as they closed up, then went back to the driver's door. The big man was leaning against it tugging his beard.

'Thanks for this, Casey. And stop tugging your beard at me,' I said.

He shook his head. 'After this, I'm going to be round your house tugging my beard at you all day. This is five Martas, I'm telling you.'

'We'll see. But thanks anyway.'

'I assume you're going to fill me in on all this sometime?'

'Yeah. Full story and pictures.'

He swung himself up into the cab. 'Be seeing you.'

The van pulled out and I joined Monty in the motor where he was smoking and scowling at two small boys standing on the back seat of a Nissan who'd just shown up with their mum.

'Why are you doing that?'

'I want to make them cry.'

'You're joking.'

'No.'

I drove him back to the Britannia and let the engine idle outside while we sorted a couple of details. He was due to call Charlie Pearson at the Shakespeare in Fountain Street that evening. Apparently the grass used it as an office.

'Then we'll know for sure he's bit,' he said. 'Call me at nine tonight. I'll have spoken to him by then.'

We shook, then he bounced out of the motor and jogged up the hotel steps. It was just coming up to one. I decided to call Carol.

'Oh, it's you.'

'We need to talk,' I said.

'No doubt.' She sounded pissed off. I felt my guts rumble. Time for a peace offering.

'Have you eaten, Carol?'

'No. I need to go to the shops. I was just waiting for you to call.'

'Fancy some fish and chips?'

'Not really.'

'I mean at Harry Ramsden's.'

'Oh. À la carte. You sure know how to treat a girl.'

'I'll meet you in the car park. Get a cab and have a drink. I'll pay for it.'

'It's ten minutes walk. Save your dough.'

The sun had come out by the time I arrived at the restaurant, so I leant on the railing looking over the River Irwell to wait. I'd been on since five that morning and Carol wasn't a social engagement, she was part of the day's graft. I looked down and thought of a much cleaner river in Italy.

I turned at some steps. Carol was wearing a white T-shirt under a light brown suit that showed off her good legs. Somewhere out there was a softer life, one where men and women just enjoyed each other's company and each other's bodies in warm rooms with R&B on the speakers. I thought of her in bed with Terry. I hoped she'd taken precautions. Smackheads like him could carry more than a dose of the clap these days.

'Hello.' She sounded a lot better off the phone. She pecked me on the cheek. Awkwardly, I kissed the air to the left of her face. Then I got looked at like I was some alien from another planet. 'Prison didn't do you too much harm this time, did it?'

'I wasn't in long.'

'Eighteen months is long enough. Come on.' She linked her arm through mine and we went inside. We ordered, the wine came, and I asked her about Terry's smack-taking. She said that she was pretty certain that he hadn't been absolutely bang on it when he'd first arrived.

'He was too good in bed for that. When they're heavily into the gear, that's all they're interested in, the gear. Take it from me.'

'So what occurred?'

'Well, he got weird and I stuck him in the spare room. I found a spoon and some silver paper yesterday morning, so I fronted him.'

'And?'

'Screaming row. He'd never seen the stuff, blah blah. Lasted a couple of hours. Then someone rang for him and he went out. Came back after I was in bed.'

'He had a busy day yesterday,' I said, thinking of the spin on my flat.

'Hmm. Well, I do like him. He begged me not to tell you that he was on the gear. I half thought about keeping it to myself, I felt sorry for him. But you always feel sorry for people like that, don't you? And it gets you nowhere.' She filled her glass to the top and drained it in two mouthfuls. Something harsh reasserted itself under her face. 'Got a fag? I've left mine at home. Trying to stop.'

We lit up in silence. Terry said he'd told his new friends little or nothing about Carol. But they did know her address and phone number. For this reason, I filled her in on some of the story. Like how Terry wouldn't be coming back.

'He's not been hurt. But there's a couple of naughty people who may be round asking after him.'

'Naughty people? Don't you mean the filth?'

'No. My lot. Terry's been very naughty himself. Some of his new pals have already done me a serious mischief, and they're looking to do more damage.'

'Like what?'

'It's more or less sorted. We all just need to be double careful for a few days. I'll give you the office when the scream's off. In the meantime, can you pack up Terry's scraps and bring them out to me? I'll drive you round and wait up in the car.'

'Yeah. Of course.'

'And if anyone comes round just tell them that Terry's done a runner on you. Say he suddenly had dough around, OK? Do that for me?' I scribbled on a beer mat and handed it across. 'My new mobile. If you get any problems, ring me right away. I'm sorry for bringing troubles to your door like this, Carol.'

She smiled. It wasn't the widest one I've ever seen, but it was there. 'Doesn't matter.'

In the motor on the way back to her gaff, I gave her a thousand quid. The dough was given and taken without embarrassment. Carol was OK. I pulled up in Sainsbury's car park. She got out and leant in through the window. 'It's only a small suitcase worth. I'll be about half an hour.'

I went in and bought some food while she was gone, then borrowed a *Yellow Pages* from Customer Services. Half a dozen numbers got jotted down on the piece of paper an astoundingly pretty Asian girl on the counter gave me. I was just sticking my shopping on the back seat when Carol showed.

'No one's been around,' she said. 'Just a message for him on the answerphone. No name, but the guy says he'll call back.'

She didn't sound too worried about putting people off. I shoved the case across with the groceries. When I straightened up, she was standing a few inches away.

'Any other time, I'd ask you back,' she said. She leant in, pressed her lips on mine and her tongue danced inside my mouth. She'd cleaned her teeth and tasted of toothpaste and a little of cheap wine. I pulled away slightly, then gave in and moved with her. After a minute she disengaged, and without another word she was gone.

As I say, Carol was OK.

The first two service flats I called wanted payment by banker's order and plenty of references. The next two sounded vaguely promising, and I said I'd ring back. I nearly gave the last one a miss, it was that close to bandit country, but I liked the easy sound of the woman who picked up. A nice *I mind my own business* sort of easy. And secure parking. I said I'd be round in ten minutes.

Allness Road runs through Whalley Range to the borders of the Moss. It used to be well upmarket, all merchants' houses and tree-lined avenues. It still houses a few straight members who keep up appearances, but it's mostly pretty crap these days. I was after a detached pile straddling the main drag and a side road. It looked pretty solid and respectable, given the venue. I locked the car, went up the drive and rang the bell.

I was in a couple of hours later. For a service job, it was the business. Newish furniture, thick carpets, decent kitchen and bathroom. Not cheap by Whalley Range standards – the best part of £800 a month – but as Rosie the landlady said, the deal was she kept the problems of the area from coming inside. She had two dogs who dwelt in the kitchen. They weren't vicious, but sounded as if they might be.

'I'll introduce you if you take the place,' she said.

It turned out the hounds were called Hale and Pace. I didn't think that was very funny, to tell the truth. But then nor were Hale and Pace.

14

I turned the shower jets off about eight the next morning and went to the bedroom for towels and aspirin. As I looked in a drawer for both, Leon's alarm clock went off. Piss it, I thought. I should dump that. If I got a tug over his murder, some smart-arsed busy who'd been at the scene might just notice the clocks were twins. That didn't mean anything until court, where any number of things that mean fuck all on their own can be made to add up in the eyes of a jury. Sod it.

I got dressed quickly and went out. There was a skip a few streets away and nobody about, so I dropped Leon's clock down the side, between a tangle of woodwork and the metal edge. It rattled down a bit, then settled. That was it, then. He never knew how important he was. Best mate, first teacher – my wife's lover. Should have told him when I had the chance. But then you never expect someone to go out like a light, even in our game. I bought milk and bread at the shop on the corner. Back in the flat, I made toast and tried not to think about a life where a cheap alarm clock has to be chucked away in case it sticks you on a murder rap for your best friend's death.

I finished and went to the freezer for dough. After the usual check for moodies, I drove to the bus station, swapped motors and took the renter back. Finally, I drove the Rover out to Cheadle Village. I'd picked it up from Amy's the previous evening, then had a quick meet with Casey to give him the dough for the minders and bring him up to date on what Terry had been up to. Then I'd found a quiet phone box and called Monty about the grass Pearson.

'He's onside,' he'd said. 'And hot for it.'

'Is he expecting a call?'

'Lunchtime tomorrow, in his office. That pub. To sort a meet out. Be lucky, uncle.'

The move against Pearson was what had brought me to Cheadle Village. The place was as quiet as you like that time of day. There was a phone box outside a jug on the main drag. Directories gave me the number of the Shakespeare, the boozer where Charlie Pearson had his office. The voice that picked up said hold on. I heard shouting and a 'No idea' in response. Then he came on – deep, confident and very Manchester.

'Charlie speaking. Who's that?'

'Charlie. You met my pal at the fights. I believe we could do with a meet?'

A beat.

'Yeah, yeah, whenever you like. Drop round here now, if you like.'

Oh, I think not. Keep him waiting, the cunt. 'Not sure of the timing at the minute.'

Silence.

'Later would be better. You'll be in the office tonight, will you?'

'Yeah, that's fine. I'll be in here six till seven. No later though.' Now he wanted to sound busy himself.

'I'll speak to you later then, Charlie. Ta ra.' I hung up, my heart pounding. I'd finally spoken to the grass and he'd stood for me. He wanted to do business. Fine. We'd do business.

A woman was waiting outside, clutching a child by the hand and looking at me like I was an idiot. I held the door open and they shuffled in without a word. Back to the motor for the bag and I started walking for Parrs Wood and the Galleon Hotel. It started to spit thinly. Collar up and walk faster. By the river, it was doing it in sheets and I was running with the bag across my back. I skated across the car park and into the hotel just as the sky gave it the first roll of thunder.

The warmth hit me like a slap, as did the musak oozing out of hidden speakers: it was, I think, a samba version of *Are Friends Electric?* Lightning cracked and hailstones bounced off the glass door. I was dripping.

'Can I help you, sir?' A German-accented functionary in piped blue blazer had shimmered up out of nowhere. His manner was servile, but his tone suggested *Hit the road, Jack*.

'Health club,' I said.

'Downstairs, sir,' he said, and shimmered off again.

The girl behind the counter looked up as I pushed open the door and flashed ideal teeth. 'Hello,' she said, and handed me a folded white towel. 'Here, dry your face.'

'Thank you. I've come to renew my membership.'

She tapped my details into her machine. She was about five and a half feet tall with streaked blond hair to her shoulders, gold earstuds and a Persil-white T-shirt. The toned muscles in her forearm rippled as she pushed the card across to fill in. Her handwritten badge said her name was Andi, with a big circle over the i.

'If you renew for a year, you get four guest passes.'

I snapped out of it. 'Then I will.'

The locker room was pretty empty for a weekend. I changed, worked out, swam, and lay in the sauna. I felt pretty fit and I'd need to be for what was coming up. I swept sweat off my chest and saw it hit the wall next to me, then lay back and thought about the call I had to make. About half five, I showered, left the club, and found a payphone. Then I rang the Shakespeare. Pearson came on.

'Me again, Charlie, from lunchtime. Do you know the Galleon Hotel in Parrs Wood, opposite the school?'

'Yeah, yeah, I know it, mate, but it's a bit off my plot, can't you come in a little closer than that?'

'Sorry, Charlie, no. Can you do tomorrow afternoon, between three and four? No need to bring anything other than yourself. It's just for a chat, to arrange details.'

'All right. Make it three sharp.' He didn't sound happy.

'OK then,' I said. 'I'll be sat on the first chair on the left in reception.'

'Yeah yeah yeah.' He hung up. As I say, he didn't sound happy. He'd be a lot less happy by the time I'd finished with him, the prick.

Later that evening I called Monty and told him Pearson had bit. We made our own meet in Birmingham a couple of days later. Then I drove back to the service flat and went to bed. I slept immediately.

I was sat first seat on the left in the Galleon reception by ten to three the next day. The gravel had crunched wrong as I walked up the front, the sun had shone too hard and the plate glass walls on reception were too dirty to see through. And there were too many gardeners on the plot. The woman vacuuming a few feet away from me now didn't look too comfortable with the hoover, swinging it around like she'd never used it before. And the concierge's blazer looked a bit small on him. Maybe it wasn't his.

There was movement across the foyer and I saw Pearson step inside, five minutes early. He really was huge. Well over six foot with shoulders like truck spoilers; his body had a silhouette like a war memorial. He looked around and moved towards me, stooping slightly at the hip.

'Charlie?' I rose as he nodded. 'You know who I am,' I said.

We shook. His fingers were oddly thin for his size, but his clasp was firm, a little too firm. Trying to be top dog by crushing the other fella's hand. Fucking schoolyard trick.

'We'd best go straight downstairs,' I said. 'Out of the way.' I held out one of the guest cards I'd got the day before. 'Show this. If anyone asks.'

For a split second I thought he'd kick off, but he took it. I led the way downstairs, nodding at the Eurasian girl on duty. Charlie was a few steps behind as I pushed open the double doors and then turned right into the mens' locker room, which was empty. Each box had a key with a thick numbered elastic band. A twenty pence piece freed the twirl. I took two coins out of my pocket and gave one to Pearson.

'No offence, Charlie, but I'm careful where I talk these days. There's a stack of clean towels over there in the corner. The sauna's just through the door on the right. I'll see you inside as soon as you've changed.'

I stripped off as I spoke, rolled the bits up and stuck them in a locker. Then I pulled a pair of trunks out of my bag and stuck that away too.

I dropped my twenty in the slot, slammed the door, grabbed a towel and made for the sauna. Empty. Good. I clambered on to the top shelf and lay down. A few minutes, and I started wondering where Charlie had got to. If he hadn't done bird for a while, my sudden nakedness might have thrown him. Maybe he'd fuck off. Depended on how bad him and Hamilton Jacks wanted me. I waited.

The door clicked open and there he was. Towel twisted round his waist, he shuffled across the boards and perched on the lower tier a couple of feet away. I sat up. His body was almost hairless and he had the kind of undefined anchor cable muscles you get from labouring, not working out in a gym.

'All right, Charlie?' I swung my feet on to the deck, took the couple of steps to the door and gripped the handle firm. With a bit of luck, people would get the message and leave us alone. Even so, I spoke quickly.

'Sorry about the theatrics Charlie, but I know a few people doing serious bird for talking business without taking precautions. Nothing personal, but no one ever got nicked for being too careful.'

He just sat there, staring at me. I went on.

'I've spoken to Monty. The deal is this. The gear will be up here in a few days. Won't be tomorrow, won't be the day after, but it would be handy if you could keep the next couple of days after that free. The meet, the first meet that is, will be at the Copthorne Hotel at Salford Quays. I'll ring you on the day and give you the time. Me and you on that meet, no one else. I'll be there before you. The gear will be someplace nearby and your dough will need to be on call as well. We'll discuss the actual terms for the handover then. You've had a sample and Monty's given you a figure, but just to remind you: the price is a non-negotiable one hundred thousand pounds.'

His mouth stayed shut. Perhaps he thought the silence was intimidating. I let go of the handle. 'I'm going to have a shower and a swim now, Charlie. If you want to talk about football, or whatever, then stay around. Otherwise, I'll be in touch. Be seeing you.'

With that, I left him to it.

*

The next morning, I was driving the Rover south down the M6 for the meet with Monty and thinking that Charlie Pearson was not a man I'd care to play poker with. He'd been gone from the locker room when I got back from the pool.

Nothing as I left the place, except for a woman with two teapots in the back and a bread van. Even this I'd given a good coat. The filth can call on butcher and baker all day – not to mention the gas company, florist, undertaker. You name it. But being on your feet makes it harder for them. It means they've got to have their wheels crawling – which is a right giveaway – or go on foot themselves. I'd spent an hour going round the houses this morning before I nosed the Rover on to the motorway and I still didn't intend going directly to the meet. Another hour of the usual pissing about and arse-watching had me fetch up at the Metropole Hotel next to the NEC just after one. The old guy was already in the bar when I arrived, wrapped round a large gin and tonic and scowling at a newspaper. He said he was dwelling in the centre.

'Hundred a night, room the size of my bog.' He nodded at the restaurant. 'You ready?'

The cavernous dining room was sparse of punters, but we still asked for a corner table away from the rest.

'Of course, sir,' said the maitre d', in a tone that suggested we'd asked for Madonna on toast. 'No problem.'

In the end, our table was so quiet and tucked away it was an isolation ward. As we ate, I put Monty fully in the picture. He wasn't too surprised at Pearson's Easter Island act. Haşim had filled him in.

'Silent but very handy,' Haşim had said. 'Pearson's a very dangerous man. And he's killed. At least once, so the story goes.' I thought of Leon slumped up against the wall, reached out and closed his eyes again. 'Anyway,' said Monty, 'I think you got him hooked.'

'You sure?'

'As fuck. Listen.' He pushed his plate to one side and wiped his mouth with his napkin. 'It's like you're selling him money. If the deal was straight, he could sell it on two minutes later and make a good profit . . .' A waiter drifted past and he stopped, watching the lad's back move away.

Then he went on. 'But if he sits on it and waits for a famine and then cuts it and ounces it out, then he'll be talking telephone numbers for his whack. And the cunt's well enough connected to do it in relative safety.' He leant back and took a mouthful of wine.

'No, he'll come on the meet all right,' he continued. 'And he'll bring the hundred grand. A straight villain would come. But he's a grass and grasses serve their masters. He'll go to Hamilton Jacks all right. Thanks.'

The last word was to the waiter who'd come for the plates. When he'd gone, Monty swept a few crumbs off the cloth and put both elbows on the table.

'Where are we going to call it on?'

I gave him a broad outline of my plan. 'I still need to check a few things out,' I said.

'If he's straight, he'll be well minded outside the door. Old Bill will be there, of course, but they won't come in until the charlie arrives. That'll give us the time to move on Pearson.'

'Getting out's the main problem,' I said.

I didn't want Monty on the work, though I wasn't going to tell him that now and have a row. I said I'd call him on when I was ready. 'I'll try to make it the next few days.'

'If you can,' said Monty. 'I've got things to do. I've got to start giving something a serious look soon. OK?'

In truth, I'd plotted the sting on Pearson a lot further than I'd let on. I'd sorted the place and most of the rest in my head already, but I did need to confirm some details for the offmans. I stopped a couple of times on the drive back to Manchester trying to raise Carol and finally got through while I was filling the motor at a service station. She said I could come round. I made her gaff at ten thirty and she showed me into her front room in a flowing white dress and bare feet. A widescreen TV in the corner was showing the news, loudly.

'Didn't expect to hear from you so soon,' she said, reaching down to a long fat leather sofa and scooping up a remote. 'How's Terry doing?' She killed the sound. 'Go on, sit down. Don't wait to be asked.'

The sofa looked like it might swallow me up. I sank into it with a creak of soft leather.

'Can I get you something?'

'No thanks, Carol. And Terry's fine. He's tucked up and calm, someone's trying to get him off the gear. Has anyone called for him?'

'No.'

'OK, good. Glad to hear that.'

'Is this a social call, then?'

'No, it's kind of business. I've actually come about something else, Carol. From your Midland days.'

'I left the hotel years ago.' She perched on the other end of the sofa. 'You know that. Why aren't you on Terry duties any more?'

I told Carol as much as she needed to know. That Terry had been mixing it with some bad faces and that one of those faces was a slag and a grass. And that I wanted to sting this grass for dough before I declared his name to the crowd.

'I want to do the business in a hotel room, Carol. But I need a very tricky offmans.' I drummed the soft brown leather between us. 'A few years ago, I remember you telling me something about the Midland. An angle you'd worked out.'

'I brought you a lot of angles on the Midland. Most of them went on the back burner. Which one are you talking about exactly?'

I reminded her. She clicked her tongue.

'I thought we were saving that stroke for our pensions. Or when there was a jewellers' convention in town.'

'I know. That's why I'm asking.'

'If this happens, will it be good or bad for Terry?'

'Good, in the end. There's a lot of shit flying around, Carol. I need to sort it out.'

She sighed and flicked out a neat little thinking tattoo on her teeth with her thumbnail. Then she shrugged

'Oh, well. If it's that serious. OK.'

She gave me the room numbers and a couple of other details to do with layout. Twenty minutes later, I stood to go.

'Once you get out into the staff corridors, you'll be OK,' she said.

'Thanks, Carol.' She shooed me out to the front door. 'Give Terry my love,' she said as she opened up. 'He's a nice lad, really. He just went wrong somewhere along the way.'

I stepped out and the door closed behind me. No kiss this time. I shrugged and made for the motor. I had to do the Jacks tapes later, so I needed to burn an hour or two. And I was hungry. I kerb-crawled down the Wilmslow Road, a neon stretch of ruby houses with callers every few steps trying to reel you in with rhetoric. I slipped into one, ordered a couple of plates with mineral water and split at half twelve – though you wouldn't have guessed the time; cars, bikes, people and noise. I cruised a little, then drove the mile or so to the copper's manor before parking a few blocks away and walking in. The boozer and the copper's pad were in complete darkness as I swapped the tapes and reburied the machine.

I listened to the cassette in Whalley Range an hour later and decided to marry Grundy and have his children. The call that had me muttering Hail Marys was the last of twelve and I'd played it again and again.

'Has he got back to you yet, Charlie?'

'No. I said I'd be in touch as soon as he did.'

'You haven't naused him off, have you, Charlie? He should have been back by now. You didn't fucking put him off, did you?'

'He said a couple of days, Keith. That's Wednesday, that's Thursday, maybe Friday.'

Keith and Charlie. How cosy.

'He hasn't gone somewhere else with his parcel, has he Charlie?'

'From what his mate said – '

'What, London?'

'Aye, London. Doesn't sound like the kind of trade he wanted to advertise.'

'Make sure you don't fuck him off when he comes back. Give him whatever he wants. Just make sure he stays hard for it.'

'He's acting double paranoid. He'll be covering all the angles.'

'They're all double paranoid, they all cover all the angles. Doesn't make any difference.' The line went quiet for a moment, then the copper went on. 'Hope you're not losing your arse on me, Charlie.'

'I'm not losing me bottle. I'll bring him in.'

'Well, make sure you do. I want him boxed up like a kipper. I don't care what time he gets back to you. Home, office, mobile. You find me. I'll ring this time tomorrow if I haven't heard from you.'

Then Jacks hung up. No goodbye or see you or how's the wife, Charlie. He just cut the call and left the grass with the dialling tone for company. I took the cassette out of the machine. It was just gone two.

Sometimes you can plot up a piece of work for weeks and sometimes you know the time to go is now. I thought of the twins packing their things up to leave the house they'd lived in most of their lives, stuffing the last bits into the back of Sara's Fiat and fetching up in a cold bed and breakfast somewhere in a city they didn't know. Walking into a new school with the term already started, lives torn up and put down again. Tomas dead and Hamilton Jacks blacking me up to my wife and kids.

Five hours kip would be enough. I'd go today.

15

I switched off the wipers. I could see well enough for now.

It was just after eight and I was sitting in the Rover opposite a private nursing home in Cheadle with a gravel drive, disciplined bushes and a manicured lawn. A few minutes before, I'd seen motors pull in as staff arrived for the day shift. No movement now, so I got out and nipped across the road into reception. It stank of heavily lavendered polish and the desk was vacant for the minute. Flapping the water off my jacket, I crossed the hall and schlepped down a short corridor before stopping to tap on the first door. An end-of-Empire voice came from the other side of the wood. 'I'm all right. I don't come to breakfast until eight thirty. That is my programme every morning. Thank you.'

I tapped again and opened the door. Tom unrolled his body from a high-backed chair by the window, snapping down his *Racing Post* as he straightened. Tall, white-haired and sharp-featured, he looked like he came from a family born to rule. Then he squinted hard and the irritation dropped off his face.

'Well, bloody hell. Come on in, chief.' He grinned at me and gestured to a chair opposite. I crossed the room and we shook.

'Sorry to bother you so early.' I nodded at his paper. 'Probably before you've sorted out the winners as well.'

I met Tom in an open nick fifteen years before – he called himself a 'proper old-fashioned kiter'. There'd been nothing to guarantee a cheque in the old days, he said, so a kiter had to sell himself. He'd been the Duke of Westminster, Saudi princes, film directors, judge and jury. He spent hours moaning at me how any mug could go out with a piece of plastic these days. All the style, he said, had gone right out of the game.

'Don't be daft,' he said now. 'Always a pleasure. Especially since I haven't seen you for a while.'

'I've been away. Eighteen months.'

'Ah.'

'How's the home treating you?'

'One hundred per cent comfortable. Coming up to six years next month. Couldn't be better.' He cleared his throat loudly. 'It's like a decent hotel. Waited on hand and foot, plus the medical assistance. I got a good price on my flat, which I didn't declare, of course.' He paused, and his eyes flicked across me like he was looking for something. 'Eight o'clock's a bit early to socialise.'

'Yes, Tom.'

'So, talk to me.'

'Bit of work, Tom. Needs doing a bit lively. Like today. Like now, if you fancy it.'

He dropped his paper on the deck and linked fingertips.

'I need you to come down to the Midland with me, suited and booted. I need you to book me a room. For today. Tomorrow will do at a pinch. But it has to be a particular room: 518. That will make it safe.'

'And if 518's not available?'

'Then it's off. Just come on out and we'll do it another day.'

'That all?'

'No. The room's to be used for a swindle. Old Bill will be involved. On the plot. I know I don't need to say this, but you'll need to think about your appearance, and your handwriting and dabs on the registration card. Wages before with honours to follow if the coup comes off.'

By now he was up and ushering me to the door. 'Yes, yes, yes. We'll sort all that out. Give me fifteen minutes.'

'I'm outside in a blue Rover. Other side of the road.'

He pushed me out. I walked down the corridor, nodded at the girl who'd just come on in reception and went out to wait. It stopped raining. I wound down my window for the air.

Bang on the fifteen minutes, Tom slipped out the front and strode down the gravelled drive looking dapper and carrying a rolled brolly. He crossed the road and slid in beside me. I pulled out for town and gave him the details.

'The main thing,' I said, cutting across a black cab, 'is that the law will almost certainly put a ready-eye on the work. I don't want them to know you've asked for a particular room. Not before the work's on, anyway.'

'I'll play it by ear depending on who's on the desk. Do you reckon I look the part?'

I flicked a glance at him. Cream suit, check shirt, red tie and a floppy trilby hiding most of his face. 'Just right, Tom.'

'I can still cut it, son. I may be sixty-eight, but I can still cut it.'

He'd nicked nearly ten years off his age. Well, they were his to nick. We went on in silence for a while. The traffic was crap and the going slow. Tom started chatting, he obviously wanted me to lighten up.

'If I'd had more notice, I could have fixed myself up with a bird to take in.'

'A what?'

'Don't sound so surprised. Old people have sex lives as well, you know. They're all at it in the home.'

'What, with each other?'

He turned his head and shot me a glance. 'One hundred per cent. And the staff. Since I've been in the gaff, I've had it with half a dozen widows, two cleaning ladies, a cook and a physio.'

'Go on.'

'It's the waterhole.'

I slowed down at some traffic lights. 'What do you mean?'

'In the jungle. All the animals go to the waterhole to drink. They all need water, so if you want to hunt, you go to the waterhole as well, am I right?'

The lights changed and we moved off.

'So if young women have the horn for older guys, they'd sort themselves out with a place at the waterhole where the older guys drink. I'm not saying all the birds who work in the gaff are up for it. But some of them are. And they come looking for you.'

We were approaching St Peter's Square. I wiped my nut of the OAP orgies I now imagined were a nightly feature of Tom's evenings in, and started to look for a place to park. Tom rustled around and chucked an orange disabled card on the dash.

'Nicked from the home. Thought it might come in handy.'

I swung off the main drag and stuck the Rover on the double yellows at the Mount Street side of the hotel. He unbuckled his belt.

'Martin Stollit, I think,' he said.

'Stollit?' I gave him two hundred in tens.

'Stollit,' he repeated, opening the door and getting out. Then he bent down and stuck his head in the door. 'Stollit. Stollit. Stole it. Oh, please yourself.' He shut the door and strolled off.

I watched his back in the rearview mirror, then glanced at the dash clock. Nine thirty five. The next bit was important. Having made up my mind to pull the coup today, it now felt very important it wasn't postponed. The sun came out, and for some reason I thought of Italy. At the start of the last bit of bird with Terry, I'd thought about going over for a little break when I got out. Life had seemed pretty straightforward then. Get nicked, do your time, learn some lessons, then pick up your life again. This train of thought tripped over to Leon and the depression started in.

'Out,' I said aloud. 'Just fuck off out of it.' I hissed in a deep breath, rubbed my eyes and face and looked at myself in the mirror. 'You're on work,' I told my reflection. 'That's all you've got room for. Concentrate on that, step by step.'

In the mirror, I saw Leon on the back seat. I twisted round.

'Leon?'

'All right, mate.'

'How long have you been there?'

'Few minutes. Long enough to hear you talking to yourself. Are you going mad or something?'

'I'm talking to you. I'm talking to you, now.'

'Well you are fucking mad, then. I'm dead.'

With a sudden movement, he pulled up his sweater and showed me his stab wounds. Then the sun shone brighter and filled the car with light, and he was gone.

Tom was knocking at the window. I didn't remember locking up. I stretched across and flicked up the button. 'You all right?'

'Tom. Yes, I'm fine.'

'You look as white as a sheet.'

'Thought I saw someone I knew. Gave me a bit of a surprise, that's all.'

'Well, we're weighed in chief, and at a canter.' He tapped the dash clock. Nine forty nine. Not been gone fifteen minutes.

'Got the twirl to 518 and the key card with my signature in case you want room service. Classy looking bird receptionist. Too full of herself to remember my boat for more than two minutes. She goes off at midday, anyway. So as long as you don't declare the number to the opposition before then, they shouldn't have any means of tippling to the fact we asked for 518.'

I slid the car into drive and we moved off. Tom gave me the key card.

'How did you swing it?' I asked.

'Told her that my wife and I had that very room at the Midland thirty years ago, and that we were back in Manchester for the first time since then, and could we have bollock bollock bollocks. She wasn't bothered, anyway.'

I dropped him at the cab rank and gave him a twoer for his wages.

'And I'll give you a day at York next spring, for the races.' I said as he eased himself off the seat.

'That would be a pleasure. Best of luck on the work.'

Nine fifty-six. I needed to ring Monty. No matter how it went this afternoon, he needed to be off-show for a couple of days until we knew which way the wind was blowing. So he had to know that today was the day. I found a phone box and Noriko picked up. 'He's not here.'

'I'll be round your office at half ten.'

'OK.'

I drove for Dud's garage. He was on his back under a jacked-up white Transit when I showed. Two more legs next to his.

'Come about that wing for the wife's Mini. Can I use your phone while I'm waiting?'

'All right,' his voice was muffled from underneath. 'Put the kettle on. Be along in a minute.'

Noriko picked up in the call box at Belsize Park.

'Bit pushed, Noriko. Can you give your man a message?'

'Yeah, yeah.'

'Just let him know the horse is running this afternoon. He should act accordingly for a couple of days.' Even though Monty wasn't going to be involved in the day's capers, we were connected. So he should still watch his arse, in case it came on top.

'He's already away for a couple of days, actually. I'm ringing him tonight. I'll pass the message on.' Then she said something in Japanese.

'What?'

'It means be lucky.'

Dud came into the office wiping his hand on a rag. It was about six inches thick in paint already, but that didn't seem to bother him. Without preamble, I told him that I needed a tool, explained what it had to do and asked if he could put one together in the next hour. I didn't give him the full SP, but I said the kit might end up in the hands of the busies – it had to be made out of materials that you could find anywhere. And he should wipe it for dabs before he laid it on me. He rubbed at a thumbnail with the rag.

'Give me a minute,' he said. He took a couple of paces back and swung out of the office.

The kettle boiled, I brewed up the tea and was just pouring out a couple of mugs when he showed again.

'I've got the bits. I can do it in an hour.'

'Thanks.' I handed him his mug and split, leaving mine untouched. Ten forty-five.

It was clouding over again when I made the flat. I'd dropped off at an old-fashioned mens' shop on the way and picked up a set of overalls. These went into a holdall along with a pair of turtles, some spare bits of clothes and a couple of screwdrivers. Also a tyre lever I'd got out of the boot. Then I went under the sink and into the bathroom and added a couple of sticking plasters and a penlight.

I washed and changed into a collar, tie and smart jacket. One last thing. Out of habit – in case things went wrong on the work and the next people through my front door were the Old Bill – I had a quick look round before I left. Just to be sure. Cupboards open close, look under the bed, kitchen drawers, all the rest. I never speak to the filth. Strictly name rank and number if nicked. They'd never get this address from me. But you never know how badly a piece of work can screw up.

Eleven forty-seven and the flat was clean. I picked up the bag and made for the car, scooping a *Yellow Pages* up in the hall. I sat behind the wheel and looked for the address of the shop I was after. Not there, probably changed its name again. If they didn't have it I'd have to try another, but it would make time even tighter. I chucked the book onto the other seat and drove for the garage. Dud was alone and the tool was wrapped in a bin-bag by the door. He told me how long it was and the weight it would take. I put four fifties down on a workbench. 'Thanks, Dud.'

'Well, all right, mate.'

Back in the car and check the clock. Twelve ten.

'Don't rush mate, you're on time.'

Leon. I looked in the mirror and made eye contact. 'What are you doing here?'

'I'm always around. Today, I mean. I'm around today.'

I turned the key in the ignition, pulled out on to the main and looked again. 'Leon.'

'Yes?'

'Do us a favour. Don't pull that stroke with your jumper again, eh?'

'It's why you're here, mate. Not for the dough. For the revenge. I'm calling for it.'

'Calling for it?'

He sighed loudly. 'I can't do it myself, now can I?'

'No.' I drove on in silence for a few seconds. Then I said, 'Am I right, Leon?'

'What do you mean?'

'Am I right? Is it all connected?'

He didn't answer, but he was still there.

'Who killed you, Leon?' I took my eye off the mirror to glance at a changing set of traffic lights. 'Leon?'

I looked back and he'd gone. I drove on to the shop alone.

Twelve twenty. The place I was looking for was off Stretford Road in Old Trafford. It had been Sven Books, but was now called Naughty Old Hector's. Windows blacked out and a big 'RU18?' over the front. There was also a lucky space outside, so I parked up. The front door was jammed open, with a black-painted plasterboard wall blanking the shop off from the main street. I flicked through a set of red and white plastic ribbons hanging ceiling to deck.

The walls were covered with porn. There were a couple of punters flicking through the mags and a jump at the far end. I ferreted around in the 'restraint' section, and bought a pair of plastic tie handcuffs for a score. I split for the pavement, saw a phone box on the corner, dialled the club and asked for Kaluki Ken. He was in, as I'd expected. There was a thump and rustle as he picked up. Did he fancy a fare that afternoon? 'It'll be your indoors money sorted out for a month or so.'

'Done.'

I gave him the time and the place. 'Wait twenty minutes, no more, Ken. If I don't show, fuck off. You'll get your dough, anyway. OK?'

'Sure.'

I hung up. Twelve forty.

Now to the last. Charlie Pearson. According to form, he would be in his office now, the Shakespeare in Fountain Street just off Piccadilly. I needed to talk to him, but there was no way I was putting myself on show. If his drinking pals were one tenth as snide as he was, they'd be queuing up to go into the box against me in the event of a nicking. He was going to come to me, or not at all. I drove for the centre and a short stay carpark near the old Grand Hotel. Then I walked quickly up Portland Street and into the Britannia foyer and a phone booth. I called the Shakespeare and asked for the grass, hearing the shout out and a muffled answer. About half a minute later, Pearson came on.

'Know who this is, Charlie?'

'Yeah.'

'All right. I'm on the plot, but I've just seen a face go in your pub who I wouldn't want to see me with you. Are you there, Charlie?'

'Yeah, yeah. I'm listening.'

'It's time to do business, Charlie.'

'No fucking chance. Who do you think I am?'

'Now or never, Charlie. Meet me at the southbound metro stop on Mosely Street. I'll be there in five minutes and I'll wait another three.'

I hung up and made for the metro. Two minutes past one.

Now we were on for real and I was about to lay down the rules of engagement. Either he followed them or there'd be no trade. Under normal circumstances, he'd be entitled to stamp his feet. Dealing is a two way business, and by not giving him a shout in the arrangements, I was treating him like a mug. But I was banking on what Hamilton Jacks said on the tape. The cozzer wanted me bad, and doing the trade would bring me to him. He was pulling Pearson's strings. All this meant that in theory, it had to go down. This meet – in public, on Mosely Street – was particularly dodgy; it would be one of the few times that I was giving anyone a chance to log me and Charlie together. But the Bill only had five minutes to get weaving and Charlie would waste two of them phoning Hamilton Jacks, so I made myself favourite. For the moment.

The lunchtime crowd was thick on the street as I made the tram stop. He used up a minute of the deuce I'd allowed him, crossing Mosely Street and moving swiftly up from the left. Then he was in front of me, blocking out the sun. I turned to the board, pointing at the figures like I was sussing buses, and laid the SP down to Judas boy.

'All right, Charlie. Here's how it goes. I want you to bring the dough to room 518, that's five eighteen, at the Midland for two thirty. I'll wait ten minutes after that, then I'm off and so is the trade. You can bring as many minders as you want to the hotel, but there's only you who can walk through the door. I'll be on my own in there and not tooled up. You can come in without the dough if you want, to check. Have you got that, Charlie?'

I flicked my eyes left. He barely nodded, but I had his attention.

'I can't go anywhere from that room, it's on the fifth floor and there's no communicating door. You can check that as well. I'll be spinning you for a tool, then I'll check the dough. When that's done, I'll call the tackle on. Did you come alone now Charlie?'

Pokerface almost reacted. 'I'm on my tod.'

'All right. When the gear shows, it'll be brought by one guy, a guy you know. I'll call him on when I've checked the dough's kosher. When he shows, and it won't take him long, you can call one of your boys in to even things up.'

I flicked another glance at him. Over his shoulder, a couple of broad-shouldered dark-suited men were studying an A to Z. New in the last few seconds. Maybe they were the watchers.

'I told you I'm paranoid, Charlie, so that's the way the trade's got to be. In your favour, I'm paranoid all round, so me and the other geezer will be clean; you've only got to make sure that your end will be the same. That's the deal, Charlie. Room 518, two thirty. Hope we can do business.'

I walked away. It was ten past one.

There was enough in that conversation to get me double figures on a conspiracy charge. But as I'd made such a point of ensuring that Pearson wasn't wired up on the first meet, I fancied the odds were against him trying it on this time. And the filth wouldn't have time to get cameras or wires into place at the Midland before I got there.

In other words, all they would have against me if it ever came to court would be Pearson's statement. And that would mean him coming to court and getting named as a grass. They'd also have statements from any copper who might see me going into the Midland, but that didn't amount to much.

This means they have to nick you on the work, you prick. So the place will be swarming with filth. A hundred grand of police money and a grass to protect, it'll be all hands on deck.

I'd got to the motor now. I pushed the voice down and stood, hand on the doorhandle. I had intended to take the car but now I sussed it would piss time I didn't have. That's what comes from slapping work together on the hoof and on a hunch that it was the right day. I jogged down to the attendant and, yes, a short stay could run over into a long one without being clamped – it would only cost me pound notes. I took the work bag out of the car, stuck the parking ticket behind the sun visor and locked up. I pulled a black cab cruising up Aytoun Street.

'Midland Hotel and fast as you like.'

'If the lights are with us, three minutes. Five if they're not.'

We pulled out into the traffic. The driver started kvetching over his shoulder.

'You're in a hurry, mate, you should slow down. You're a long time dead, you know. That's what my mum used to say, God rest her.'

He banged on all the way down. I sat and stared at my watch in the back. We got to the Midland in four and a half minutes flat. It was starting to rain again as I pushed through the revolving doors into the lobby. The chill wet of the street slid away and in came a low hum of chatter, the smell of warm expensive perfumes and the buzz of milling sales reps. A grey-moustached Nazi in blue uniform was showing a nervous blond lad braided into similar kit how to fold newspapers and lay them out on a desk. I could almost see the slipstream as I passed through the straightgoers for the lifts. There was a car waiting. I got in alone and hit the button.

One twenty-five.

Hamilton Jacks only had fifteen minutes to get me clocked entering the hotel. The odds were still in my favour but they were starting to even out a bit. In an hour or so, with Pearson to beat inside and God knows how many filth on the outside, I'd have to mind my work well to keep ahead of the game.

I let myself into room 518, dropped the bag on the deck and gave the gaff a quick coat of eyes to familiarise myself with the layout. It was particularly spacious, just as Carol had said. The two beds were king-size and covered with thick blue throws. It was ten paces from their feet to the wall, then a desk and chair in the corner by the window. A dark blue sofa, two matching easy chairs and a telly were grouped like a sitting room in the other corner. There was even a coffee table with a few complimentary magazines.

I went to the window and pulled back the nets. The rain was much heavier now, and I had to wipe the mist away. The clock on the G Mex centre across the way said one thirty, dead. It was a hundred-foot drop straight down to the pavement. The windows were the type that only open a few inches, for air. No way out here. For anyone. I let the net drop and went into the bathroom, checked the light was working, then came out and leant on a chair.

'I think you're in nicely enough, mate.'

Leon was perched on a bed. He was dressed like when I found him, but with his sheepskin on top and the buttons done up.

'Now all you've got to worry about is the offmans.'

'I was just about to check the tools.'

'Go on, then.'

I bent down and unzipped the holdall. Something struck me. I looked up at him again. 'Is Hamilton Jacks in the hotel?'

'He will be. He'll arrive just before Pearson. Now check your tools. Then the offmans.'

I was alone again. I reached into the holdall and spread the contents out across the carpet. Then I went over each stage of the plot and checked I had the particular tool for that part of the job. On a screwer, to be in and well tooled-up usually represents seventy-five per cent of the work. But this wasn't a burglary. Not for the work and not for the bird it carried, either. And it wasn't my game, and – to pile it on a bit more – there was a guaranteed ready-eye being put into place this minute.

We were ready-eyed on the work. The law was there, fucking waiting for us. How many times had I heard that in the nick? Most bits of work, even the worst-prepared, most ill-thought-out and badly-staffed, have some chance of getting a result. The only result you're going to get on a ready-eye is a lesser sentence than you were afraid of. And if you were heavy duty and being plotted up on by nervous and trigger-happy filth, you might get a bigger turnout at your funeral than your reputation warranted.

And here you are, you fucker, I thought. Walking right into one.

There was still time to walk out of the door. Still time to cut it all and do Pearson in the more traditional way of dealing with a grass. And then plot up on another move to sort Hamilton Jacks out.

Then Leon hissed in my ear. 'What are you doing sitting there, you mug? This is going to go, get on with the fucking work. Move!'

Dud's tool had to vanish first in case the grass gave the room a proper spin before he brought in the dough. The Phillips got the bath panel off easily enough and I stowed what had to go in there. Getting the fucker back on was fiddly and nicked more time than it was entitled to, but it went back neatly in the end. The cuffs and the Phillips had to be handier. I unfolded the sheets and cover carefully from the bottom end of one of the king-size twins. Then I used the Phillips to rip a gash in the mattress skin, big enough for me to stuff the cuffs and the screwdriver inside. I snapped the covers back, made the bed and stood up.

Two minutes past two. Time to check the offmans. Time to check the fucking offmans indeed!

I felt it like a slap on the back of my head. I was well out of my depth.

Why the fuck didn't you check Carol's knowledge before you put the tools away? You shouldn't be here.

'There's still time,' I snapped. 'There's still time.'

The bathroom was big, about fifteen by eight. Big shiny bath, toilet, basin, the usual neutral colours. For a second, I imagined the cleaner scrubbing it all up that morning. There was a buttress to the left of the door, like a chimney breast. It held a mirror and a cabinet. I leant on it and knocked.

Solid.

I knocked again.

Solid. Still fucking solid. The offmans was a fucking no no.

You've left it too late to get out of here. Ten past two and the place will be crawling with cozzers now.

The tools alone would get me a five before they started to fit me up on a drugs conspiracy.

Your head is up your arse, mister. You should have used Monty. Who the fuck do you think you are?

I hissed 'fuck off' at myself and tried to think. Sweating hard, I ran my fingertips along the surface. It had to be the front panel. Knock knock. Sounded better, but still solid. The middle, try the middle. Knock knock.

Knock knock.

That wasn't me. Not a fucking echo either.

More knocking. I swung round and felt the sweat shoot off my forehead. It was coming from the main door. Then a muffled voice, someone speaking quietly. Answer, from in here. I opened my mouth and a tiny croak came out. The other voice got louder.

'It's me. It's Charlie. I'm a bit early. Don't want to hang around. Come on.'

Think quickly. 'Two minutes, mate. You've caught me halfway through a pony. Don't go away.'

Rip the karsi paper and crumple it, he can't hear, but it keeps to the timetable. Think. Flush the toilet.

Why's he fucking early?

Unfasten your belt, drop your strides, pull them up. Fasten the belt. Think.

Pearson or the filth with him are showing you, telling you, that this meet won't be going entirely as you laid down. They're trying to throw you. They know you can't call a trade off because the other guy turns up early. Let him in.

Out and across. Head down and squint through the spyhole. Pearson was a pace away from the door, hair wet and hands outstretched and empty. He must have seen the spyhole go dark.

'I'm on my own and I'm carrying nothing. Just this.' Finger and thumb opened his mac to show a pocket, the other hand half showed a mobile phone. He let it drop back and pulled the coat across. 'When I've looked inside, I'll call my parcel up and bring it in. It's just downstairs.'

My hand went for the door handle. It didn't belong to me any more. I turned the knob and heard – or felt – the metal tongue click back inside the mechanism. I opened the door halfway, keeping my profile behind it, and extended my hand in a waving welcoming move. 'Come in, Charlie, come in.'

The grass slid through the gap. I glanced at my watch. Two thirteen.

As Pearson walked past me into 518 and crossed to the bed, I suddenly felt ice calm. Like a lot of thieves, I can get worked up on the waiting, but when the work's on it's different. And now there was something else. It took me a moment or two to pin it down.

Pearson smelt.

I got it as he came through the door, and now I got it again. And as I walked towards him with my arms up and outstretched in crucifixion stance, I got it strong. Pearson smelt. He was sweating badly.

Well, well, well. The bastard's bottle was twitching, despite his size. He was taller and probably three stone bigger, but he was still shitting himself. And despite that, despite the fact he knew the law was outside and onside, the guy's arsehole was going. I felt a whole lot better. Time for me to take charge again.

'Better get this over with, Charlie,' I said, stepping a little closer to him than I fancied he'd prefer. 'Give me a spin, because I'll be giving you one. No offence, but I told you I'm paranoid. I'd rub my brother down if I was meeting him to do a trade.'

I kept my arms up and the snide patted me down, but half-heartedly. He'd have done his homework on me and Monty. Neither of us were known as fuck-goats. Pearson knew that this was going to be straight from our end. That's why he was only playing now. He didn't expect to find anything.

This close up, he smelt rank. I decided to press my advantage and unsettle him a bit more. He hadn't been comfortable with stripping off in front of me in the sauna, so I stepped back, maybe a foot at most, undid my belt and dropped my strides around my ankles. My shorts followed, and for a second I looked straight into the bastard's eyes. I was beginning to enjoy this.

'Puts you back in reception, Charlie, I'd imagine.' I smiled. 'I'll squat if you want, but don't worry, I won't ask you to do the same.'

He gave me a tight non-smile back that involved mechanically pushing the corners of his mouth up towards his ears for a count of two seconds. Win or lose today, I was making this arsehole earn his pieces of silver.

I bent down and pulled my strides up, then motioned for Pearson to check out the room. He started to look around, half-heartedly again. He waved at the turtles on the bed. 'Doing a bit of screwing later, are you?' He cracked the half-smile again.

'They're for counting the dough when you bring it. Never handle anything from work till I've got it home. No one ever got nicked for being too careful. No one I've heard about anyway.'

Pearson finished his inspection with a cursory glance in the cupboards and bathroom. Then, without looking at me, he made for the window and looked out. There was a gust of wind as he lifted the nets and the glass rattled some. He would see there was a long drop to the deck. A couple of seconds and he let the curtain fall, turned on his heel and nodded at me, apparently satisfied. He reached inside his jacket and pulled out the mobile.

'Hold up, Charlie. My turn, before you make that call. Better move away from that window, though. Don't want a button-boy sent up here looking for a flasher.'

The grass did his snide smile again, but he didn't see the joke.

Fuck you Pearson, you're forgetting who's in charge here.

I gave him a very good spin that finished with him dropping his strides. *Get them down, you dirty toerag, get them down for your master's work. You'd let Hamilton Jacks fuck you up the arse if he was that way inclined.* By then I was sure the slag wasn't wired up. And I had the added bonus of seeing what little composure Pearson had pissing away. When I was done, he pulled his trousers up and turned back to the window with the phone.

The grass was talking. 'Yeah, things are sweet here. You can bring the other up. I'll open the door when you knock. Don't go too far away, though. I want you hanging around for when the other guy shows.'

The last words sounded like more of a plea than an instruction. Please, Keith, please, Mr Hamilton Jacks, keep me safe and sound.

This was the part of the deal that had worried me when I'd offered him the clause. If the deal had been kosher on both sides, then the last thing that either of us would have wanted was something as moody as a minder hanging around a hotel bedroom while some class A was being traded inside. I knew that. The opposition should have known that as well, and got nervous. But between the copper's horn to give me a good nicking and the grass's willingness to bark at the sound of his master's voice, the question had been overlooked.

Pearson went and sat on the edge of the bed nearest the door. I leant against the wall to be behind the door when it opened.

Two twenty-six.

The grass sat staring ahead, I stood and watched his staring. Considering they'd turned up for the meet early, this wait for the dough was a bit odd. Then I tippled. A hundred grand is a lot of dough in anyone's language. Jacks would have had to get a lot of his filth superiors to sign a lot of fucking forms to take it out on the streets. They must be double-checking all the possible offmans now, before the dough went out of their sight.

Two thirty-two. Someone knocked at the door.

The sound made Pearson snap round like his head was on elastic. Then he looked at me. I reckoned his silence was a card that he wouldn't want another player to use. So I just nodded. Charlie stood up, moved to unlock the door and stuck his arm out through the gap. When it came back, he was holding a plain black canvas bag. He closed up, moved to the bed and upended it. Bricks of new fifties fell on to the bed like Lego.

'You'll find there's twenty stacks there,' he said. 'A hundred fifties in each. They've all been checked for snides, but,' he added in what was now an openly hostile tone, 'I'm sure you'll be my guest.'

I straightened up casually, crossed to the bed and sat, then reached over to pull the gloves on. I smiled at Pearson again and reached into my own bag, pulled out the two sticking plasters and held one up in each hand. 'Nearly forgot.'

His eyes followed me as I went to the door and stuck both over the spyhole in a cross, one on top of the other.

'Don't want any chambermaid getting an eyeful, do we Charlie?'

The grass said nothing. I strolled back to the bed, sat down and picked up a bundle of the cash.

'Thanks, Charlie.' I smiled widely. Tiny muscles twitched in his jaw.

I counted every note in banking style. Each bundle took about a minute and a half to reckon. When I'd done, I took another ten to pull notes out at random and crumple them near my ear. I've been around a few snides in my time and I knew what to look for in the count. The turtles made feeling for fakes impossible, but money has a sound to it as well as a feel. This lot was kosher.

Five past three.

I stacked the bundles into the bag they'd come from. Then I walked to the window, pulled out my phone and punched in the number for a firm of briefs I didn't like. The switch answered.

'Will you tell the clerk that the papers are ready to be signed, please?'

'Who's calling?'

'Twenty minutes, that'll be fine.' I closed the cover and stuck it away. If there was to be a nicking out of today, that move would get a few heads scratched. Time to gamble a bit.

'You heard that, Charlie. Should be twenty minutes. To the minute. The geezer will need to get knocked over crossing the road to be late. So why don't you phone your man and get him to be ready at the stroke. They can come in together, one after the other. Then we can get done and get home.'

I knew the filth would be edgy about the dough by now, and they had no way of knowing their man was OK. Letting him call should make everyone think it was safe up here.

The grass lightened, faintly. He rang and went into the bathroom where I heard him take a long piss. I was unlocking the minibar as he came out.

'I'll open this, Charlie, in case anyone wants a swift one for luck, when the trade's done.' I pulled out a half-bottle of Moët et Chandon from the fridge. 'That'll be about right, Charlie. What do you reckon? Appropriate, or what?'

This time, the crack in his face actually resembled a smile. He was starting to relax. 'Yeah, why not?'

His phone was lying on the bed where he'd left it. Opening his coat, he bent down to pick it up.

I suddenly and deliberately thought of Tomas as he had been as a kid, and then his dead and decomposing face in a wooden box six foot under Southern Cemetery, Leon taking a knife in the guts chest shoulders and neck, blood pouring out of him as he sank to the ground. But what I said was, 'Is that the new Nokia, Charlie? I was offered a good deal on one of those last week. Chipped up for a month, unlimited calls and no comebacks. Mind if I have a look?'

I took a step towards him, holding out my left hand. Then I took another step and smashed him good and hard right in the middle of his gut. He snapped at the waist and I twisted and slammed my whole upper body forward and headbutted him solidly on the bridge of his nose. I heard bone crack and he dropped to the floor gasping for air. Trouble was, I was gasping too. I put my palms to my temples and took a couple of burning deep breaths. My head was ringing, my eyes were gushing and Pearson was starting to shift.

Fucking move.

I threw myself across the nearest twin, pulling on the gloves as I rolled, ripped down the cover and grabbed the bolster, tore off the slip and threw myself on the deck next to him. I snapped the slip round his jaw and lips, yanked hard and tied it behind. Robbed of easy air through his mouth, he started to thresh. Fuck this. I sprang up and kicked him hard in the bollocks. He folded again with a muffled squeal. I knelt and stuck my mouth right up against his ear.

'I'm going to wrap you up now, grass. That's all I'm planning to do. Lie still and I'll do it fast and easy. Struggle, and I'll hurt you again. Either way suits me.'

I stood up, ready to kick his head in. He squeezed his eyes shut and I saw his nostrils flaring in snatches. I went for the other bed and snapped the cover back to get at the Phillips and the plastic ties. I had his arms twisted round his back and the cuffs on and tight in seconds. Then I tore the sheets off the bed and wrapped him up proper. Straddling his waist, I pushed a corner under his back and pulled it out the other side. I did this a couple of times, then tied the two ends tightly together. Now all he could do was roll. And to stop that, I tied the last sheet tightly around his ankles and the leg of the bed. It was a heavy unit. Pearson wasn't going anywhere for a while.

Three sixteen.

I stood and breathed deep for a second, then I said loudly, 'Nice drop of wine, eh, Charlie?'

I counted three.

'No, I couldn't say. I'm not that much of an expert.'

And into the bathroom. One thing was for sure now. There was no point in any more knocking. Either the offmans was there, or it wasn't. I shot the bath panel off and pulled out the tyre lever. There was going to be noise, but please God it would be one quick wrench as the panel came away. I needed cover. Back to the bathroom door.

'Charlie, do us favour and turn the telly on. I've got a bet on in the three thirty. Might as watch the race while we're waiting.'

I padded across the bedroom and punched the TV on, horses in the paddock, chuck the remote on the bed and back. I stuck the tip of the bar into the casing, worked the tool around and out. Same at the top and the middle. There was a definite gap now, enough to slip in a wedge.

The mags in the bedroom, back and grab a couple, bend them over and cram the bastards into the gap. The bar went in again, I leant on it, leant harder, gave it my full body weight, come on, come on, come on . . .

The gap widened to a brick wall.

Fuck. The knowledge isn't kosher, Carol. I'm going fucking nowhere and now I've got a GBH to go with the tools and the plotting.

'Of course there'll be brick at the edge. Leave the bar in the bottom, run a tap, pull the karsi and then rip the panel off with your hands.'

'Thanks, Leon.' I stretched and twisted the tap, then flushed the toilet and swung back to the panel.

It's coming now, it's noisy, but it's coming and there's air. Pull, pull, there she goes and there it fucking is. *Carol, you are a fucking diamond.*

This was what Carol gave me. Before the Midland was converted, each floor used to have a pantry on it, for room service. And running down, from here to the ground, was a pulley-operated dumb waiter to haul the food. 'The pantries are gone now,' she'd said, 'but the shaft is still there, it runs behind the bathrooms covered up with panelling.'

Three twenty-four. About five minutes before Jacks and his mob got itchy.

Into the bedroom. Pearson's eyes were open and he was rasping horribly through his nose. Good enough for a grass who'd taken second prize and was about to lose a hundred grand of Old Bill dough. Over to the bed and the bags. I pulled the bits out of mine, tipped the dough on to the kip and stuck the lot in my bag with the clothes and stuff on top. Then the mobile, Phillips and bar. Into the bathroom for a wet towel and whip round the bedroom, wiping every surface I could have touched.

On the box, the runners were going behind the stalls. Three twenty-seven.

Bag into the bathroom and drop it by the skirt under the dumb waiter. Then into the bedroom for a final coat. Rattle and slam as the stalls opened and the horses shot off across the turf.

Three thirty.

Pearson's eyes were closed. I squatted to check his breathing. I didn't give a fuck if he lived or died, I just didn't want a murder charge a few weeks down the line. Fuck, the bastard had corpsed – I saw myself nicked and wrapped up, pulled out of a car into a cop shop, then kicked up against cell walls by the filth until my head was the size of a beachball. He opened his eyes and looked straight into mine. I sensed him flex against the ties and the rest of the wrappings. I leant in right in and hissed, 'You had this coming. Right down the track at you since you started fucking me. Be seeing you, Charlie, be seeing you.'

I straightened up. His eyes flicked up to follow me and I held his gaze for a second. Then I turned on the spot and went back to the bathroom.

Three thirty-two. Hamilton Jacks would be starting to sweat.

I stuck my head down the shaft. Black. Faintest suggestion of light a long way off. I swung round and went back under the bath for Dud's tool. This was a solid steel bar he'd bent round at one end into a tight hook. The other end was twisted into a circle and had a short length of thick chain attached. There was a length of nylon rope wound round and into this chain, tied and double held in place by thick steel wire welded solid into the metal itself.

I squatted and fed the hook round the toilet wastepipe, pulled the rope after it for a foot or so, then fed the hook round again and gave it a good wrench. I stood up, leant back, and put my whole weight on it. The pipe never shifted. It felt safe enough. No choice, anyway.

Three thirty-four.

Across to the shaft and I slung the coiled rope into the black. I wiped the wet towel round the pipe, then wrapped it round my neck.

Three thirty-five.

Cold sweat down my spine. I picked up the bag and hung it round my neck. Heavier than I'd expected. The penlight came out of my pocket, I switched it on and hung that round my neck as well.

Three thirty-six.

I stepped to the shaft, bent and swung one leg over the edge, kept the other foot on the bathroom floor and twisted the rope round my arm a couple of times. My head went in, dust coated my nose and throat in a breath. Steadying myself with my free hand, I stretched out for the opposite wall. And just grazed it with my toe.

Jesus fucking Joseph and Mary. The shaft's too wide.

Calm it down, I told myself. Just shift your crotch over a bit, try again. This time, I got my sole on flat. Thank Christ. Now I took the rope in both hands and brought my foot back to the near side, finding a tiny ledge to rest it on sideways. The most dangerous part was coming.

Pulling tight on the rope, I let it take all my weight and swung my right foot up and over into the shaft. My left swivelled in time till just the toe was on the ledge. I waved my right foot around and found the same edge. Then I slid a few inches of the rope through my hands and leant slowly out till my back hit the other side, flattening my feet as I made contact. I untwisted the rope from my forearm and eased my weight on to the far wall. Still holding the rope, I straightened my legs as far as they would go. Everything felt solid. I let go and slapped my arms against the shaft wall. The bag was resting on my stomach, the penlight hung to the right. The rope sat on my lap for a second, then slid off and hung straight.

I slid one foot a few inches down the wall, keeping my weight on the other leg, then shifted the other sole and slid my back down to follow it. Braced on all sides, I could slide my feet and back down, but slowly. Again, left foot, right foot, back. I twisted my head up at the light spilling into the shaft from the bathroom. No sound yet. I reckoned Jacks would give it fifteen, twenty minutes before he went in. He probably had a minder with his ears up against the woodwork right now. They'd hear the telly and think we were watching the racing while we waited for Monty to show with Charlie's charlie. I hoped.

I went quicker after the first few feet but I couldn't go too swift, otherwise the bag would slip off and strangle me. But I had to move, I was running against the hotel timetable. The shaft came out close to the back office. The early shift clocked off around half three, said Carol, and I meant to slip out with them. The place would be crawling with filth, whether they'd gone in to 518 or not, and I needed the cover.

I slid on down. Fourth floor. Each move stirred up dust and dried my throat. Just breathe as lightly as you can. The further down, the worse the air.

Someone was taking a piss on the other side of the wall in front of me. My back was starting to hurt badly and the sweat was building on my forehead, running into my eyes in rivers. This was far harder than I'd imagined. The bag was getting heavier with every inch. It flicked through my brain I wouldn't make it.

Fuck that.

I rammed the possibility of defeat right out the front of my skull. Focus on the hate. Tomas, Leon, Sara, Lou, Sam, Jan, Steph. Dead, running away, hating me. All down to fucking Pearson and Hamilton Jacks. No way I wasn't going to make it.

The sounds of afternoon sex. Screams and moans as some bird climaxed with the deeper bass grunts of a man across her. I got an image of a fat bald bloke with a moustache and a much younger woman, him panting with each stroke, sweat dripping down on her face, her turning away to stop it falling into her eyes. That made it the second floor.

Keep going. Don't think of the drop. Don't think of anything except the next move. Right foot, left foot, back and arms. Right foot, left foot, back and arms. Voices told me I was level with the first floor. Nearly fucking there. Nearly fucking there.

I felt a ledge under my right heel. Gasping for breath, I focused on the wall just below me and saw the outline of the door. Sounds behind it. A long way off, but behind it. Ground floor. Must be. I slid my left foot over the ledge, pressed it against the door, felt it slide and slip, then I fell, and as I dropped . . .

What if there's a basement level below you and another twenty feet to go? You'll break your fucking back and then –

I fell feet first and I fell about six feet. No basement level. Just a dull shock up my legs and dust in my face. I dragged the bag up and over my head and bent over gasping, something like fresh air was coming in the gaps round the door. I pointed the light at my watch.

Three forty-six.

Carol said the door led out into the old pantry, now a storeroom. I jammed my eye up to the keyhole – boxes, trolleys, metal cases, hotel stuff. The lock felt loose. I kicked and the door scraped a couple of inches. Something the other side. Christ, I was trapped. No, I pushed harder and felt something slide along the floor. The gap was just enough to let me through and in. Stacks of boxes, crates and other junk near the door, and I saw I'd been fucking lucky.

Three forty-nine. Any minute now, Hamilton Jacks and his mob would let themselves into room 518.

I tore open the bag and pulled out the boiler suit. Then I saw the state of my hands, dropped it back and snapped the towel off my neck. Dust black one side, other side OK. I smeared the dust off face and mitts, the overalls went on in one move, light away, zip the suit up the front. A baseball cap came out the bag and got jammed on my head, the towel got rolled and stashed and I closed the bag up. The rasp of the zip sounded like a line being drawn, a signal the work was over.

Not yet. I gave the door a tug. Locked. The Phillips came out, I prised the lock off and pocketed the screwdriver, then opened up a couple of inches. It gave on to a corridor going right about ten yards down. I couldn't hear anything. No footsteps, voices, rattling trolleys.

'Jesus fucking Christ almighty!'

The shout bounced down the shaft. I imagined the cozzer – whoever it was – leaning out into the pitch black from the bathroom. I saw the filth swarming into room 518, taking in the telly and Pearson wrapped on the deck, then fanning out and one of them ending in the bathroom, seeing the hole in the wall, looking down the shaft, putting it all together.

The corridor was empty. Moving as fast as I dared, I got to the corner and round. Buzz of chat from a few yards down, round the next corner. I walked fast, fixing my brain on the filth upstairs. One of them would leg it to the lifts for sure, another would be at the stairs by now, taking them two, three, five at a time. Someone would be on the radio, screaming the rest down here top speed.

I turned left, saw half a dozen guys walking in a loose group a few steps ahead. Young lads, black trousers and baggy jackets, waiters knocking off. I speeded up, got myself a few steps behind the one at the back. He had his head down, looking at something in his hand. 'They've done me on emergency tax again.'

Another lad glanced back without breaking his stride. 'So get them your bloody code, and they'll sort it out, you pillock.'

Fresh air on my face. A double door at the end of the corridor, swinging slowly shut, daylight beyond. We passed another set of doors on the left, stairs through the glass.

When they come, they'll come through that.

One lad was at the door ahead, starting to push it open. There was a crash behind us. All six of them swung round, and I forced myself to turn with them. Two suits and a button boy nearly fell into the corridor, hotel geezer with them shouting something I was too strung out to hear, and all four legged it down for the storeroom.

One of the waiters shouted behind me, then all six shoved past after the filth and sprinted for the corner. I turned and walked calmly through the street doors straight on to the pavement. It had stopped raining, and a watery sun had come out. And there was no one running towards me. Men and women, kids in prams, teenagers, students, shoppers, old ladies with shopping baskets. Just walking or strolling. No one running at all. That was the most important thing.

I crossed the road and turned into the street where Ken was waiting in his black cab. He saw me coming, folded up his paper and started the motor as I slid on to the back seat. We pulled out into the traffic and he looked at me in the driving mirror. 'All right?'

'Yeah, all right,' I said.

16

Ken didn't ask where I was going, he just concentrated on putting some distance between us and the Midland without drawing attention. We hit the far end of Deansgate about three minutes later.

'Where to?'

'South. Just got to make a quick call.'

He swung left in the direction of Old Trafford. I dialled directories, punched in the number I got and a guy called Ray Sergeant picked up. I told him I could do with a shower and a change of clothes. 'And are you still my size, after your holiday?'

'I reckon, yeah.'

'Thanks. How's your dad, Ray?'

'He won't mind you coming up. He hates 'em anyway. Number sixty-two, yeah? One very light ring, I'll know it's you.'

I pressed off and glanced out of the rear window. Ken must have clocked the action in his mirror. 'We're alone.'

'Thanks. Hattersley estate, Ken.'

I knew Ray Sergeant from Foston Hall and since. His dad was dying and needed looking after, so it made Ray certain to be at home. I ducked down to strip the overalls off and stuffed them in the bag. A few minutes and I slid back on the seat.

'Ken?'

'Listening.'

'Couple of things. Suppose someone saw me get into your cab?'

'I'm not paid to clock people, just to drive them.'

'If they push, say you dropped me in Hattersley. It's right bandit country, they won't know where to start.'

'OK.'

'Second, your money. Can you make a meet at three tomorrow morning? All night garage on Withington Road? I'll settle up then and there's something else needs doing at the same time, if you can.'

'Fine.'

He dropped me at Hattersley station about twenty minutes later and I walked on to the estate to look for Ray's block. Sixty-two got the swiftest of rings and he buzzed me in. I took the steps two at a time and his door was open.

'Thanks for the silent routine, mate.'

He looked very tired and he'd lost a bit of weight. As he dubbed up behind me I saw his dad stretched out on the couch in the lounge, apparently asleep. Propped up on pillows and cushions, he was in pyjamas and dressing gown with a blanket up to his waist and his skin was grey as metal.

'In here,' whispered Ray.

We moved into the kitchen and he pushed the door half closed. There was a full-length mirror stood in the hall showing his dad on the couch.

'They reckon he's only got a few weeks left now. But he likes waking up to a familiar room and having me here.'

I nodded. He checked the mirror, turned back and whispered again.

'How can I help you, mate?'

'Change of clothes and a shower,' I whispered back. 'Also, I'd like everything I've got on and with me cut up and got rid of.'

'Go and strip off in the bedroom. I'll get you a towel.'

I was going into the bathroom a couple of minutes later when I caught sight of Ray in the mirror. He was sat by the couch, stroking the old guy's hand. Then he raised it to his mouth and brushed his dad's fingers with his lips, one by one.

There were strides, sweater and socks on the bed when I came out of the shower. Ray had already Stanleyed my work kit into a pile of strips on the deck next to a new-looking sportsbag and a pair of trainers. A board squeaked in the corridor and he bobbed in with a mug of tea.

'If you empty your stuff into that bag, I'll stripe up your holdall while I'm at it.'

I took the cup and nodded. I didn't like to speak in this flat unless I had to. I dried off, swapped the dough and got dressed, wincing if I stood on a board with a voice. When I was done, I walked along the corridor gingerly and joined him in the kitchen.

'You got wheels?'

'I was dropped off, Ray. I'll ring a cab from a pub.'

'I'm going to the chemist for him anyway, next door comes in if I'm out. I'll drop you off and stick your stuff on the dump in Hyde while I'm at it.'

'Thanks. I'll send you a drink in the next few days.'

'That'll be handy. I won't be going to work until the old boy's . . . you know. I could do with a few quid.'

We sat with his dad for a few minutes before we left. He didn't recognise me, but he seemed interested by the new face. He managed a few words about United and his other kids while Ray knelt on the floor beside him, then dropped off to sleep again mid-sentence. I left Ray to settle him and went to check the bedroom.

Amy was getting ready for bingo when I rang her doorbell about an hour later. I took the stepladder up the stairs and stowed the bag and the prize in the loft. Then I dragged some exes out from under the dog's basket and left the mobile, switched off. I'd have to get a new one later. For now – on show in my own city and after a piece of work that Old Bill knew had my name on it – I needed to be as clean as a whistle, just in case they got lucky and clocked me. I told Amy I'd call in the morning, walked into Withington Village and found a box.

'Hello Noriko.'

'Everything OK?'

'Fine. Have you been to the office yet?'

'Uh uh.'

'When you go, tell him that horse won, would you? And I'll see him at the halfway house for lunch tomorrow, if he can make it.'

'Half an hour and I'm back.'

'Thanks.'

I took a bus to the centre and got off a couple of blocks from the Rover. I was starting to feel very tired now. All that burnt adrenaline and the physical effort of wrapping Pearson up. He should be feeling a lot worse. I called Noriko back from a box on Portland Street.

'All OK for tomorrow.'

'Thanks.'

'You sound tired. You're all right, yeah?'

'I am and I am.' A yawn forced its way up. 'Better get some kip. Thanks, Noriko, bye bye.'

I went looking for a new mobile, drove back to the flat, put it on charge and forced myself to eat. The tiredness was starting to overwhelm me. I creaked into the bedroom, set the alarm for two next morning, stripped and lay down. I turned over and crashed out before the springs stopped moving.

Two minutes to three, the all-night garage on Withington Road buying fags. At three exactly, Kenny pulled up at the parade of shops on the next block. I got into the cab and he drove. He'd been at the Kaluki table since six, he said. Gone a monkey in front, but the rest of the school had started chipping back at him and he'd been glad to leave while he was three and a half hundred to the good.

'Don't you ever sleep, Ken?'

'Not if I can help it.'

I pushed an envelope through the divider. 'Fifteen. Don't spend it all at once.'

He dropped it to his feet and kicked it back under the seat. 'You said there'd be something else.'

I gave him Hamilton Jacks's address, he took me one corner down and into a quiet side street and killed the lights and engine. I leant forward. 'I've got to make a quick visit to a garden round the corner. I don't expect any trouble but if there is, I'll only come back if the opposition is more than two turns from the motor. If I'm not back in twenty minutes, just split. And if anyone asks . . . '

'I'm just having a quick forty winks.'

'You got it.'

I opened the nearside door, clicked it shut behind me very slowly and walked lightly down on to the main road. It was cold as you like with the odd loop of mist lolling round the streetlights.

The Midland coup hadn't made collecting the tape any more difficult – it would still be a slap on the wrist at most, if nicked. But stick in a conspiracy to rob the filth, cue in the grass Pearson giving evidence in court from behind a screen – and topping his injuries right up, no doubt – it became a different matter altogether. A serious piece of work and as sinister as the prosecution could make it look. Endgame could be fifteen plus. All this put me right on my toes.

I crept round the side of the pub car park where there was cover. The mist made the pole invisible till I was a few feet away and it was thick enough to shroud me from passing cars, but I stood and listened for a good five minutes anyway. Anyone hiding in the bushes would have been waiting a long time and there'd be some noise. So I stood there and strained. Nish.

I moved across and squatted at the pole, slid my fingers behind Grundy's wire, then stood and yanked sharply out and down. A thin ribbon of cable snaked down at me, I scrabbled in the soil for the recorder, bundled the lot up into my jacket and shot down the side of the pub into the road. A quick shufti for any cruising uniformed – a runner would get a serious tug this time of the morning – and I tore down the main, only slowing to a trot as I hit the street where Ken was parked. Pursuit always brings noise, plenty of it. Nothing. I trotted up and slid on to the back seat, he started up without a word and dropped me at the corner of Withington Road and Mayfield, just round the corner from the service flat. I stuck my trainers in the placcy bag with the wire and prodded it through the gap.

'Do you think you could dump this for me, Ken?'

'You don't want it burnt?'

'A skip on your way home will do. And thanks for everything, Ken.'

'Pleasure. Be seeing you.'

My feet got soaked in the couple of blocks to the flat. I ran a bath, made tea and lowered myself into the water. Then I rewound the tape and pressed play.

The first call was from the copper's wife confirming a theatre date for that evening. I gathered it was yesterday, about the time I was dealing with Pearson by the metro stop. The next was number one son sorting out more porn. Early evening, I guessed. Then an incoming from Hamilton Jacks, saying he'd be late and sounding deeply pissed off and another from some copper asking if the guvnor was back yet. Mrs Jacks again talking to the woman from earlier. This time she sounded pissed off herself, saying they'd have to cancel the theatre that night. Then several outgoing from Jacks – orders and shouts to various subordinates. The last call was from another copper called Dave. Dave was calling from the hospital. When it finished I got out and made more tea, then put on a robe and sat down in the lounge to listen to Dave and Hamilton Jacks one more time.

Dave sounded as shagged out as the other coppers, but he wasn't as nervous of his boss as the rest. His tone suggested that maybe he'd been the one – and there's always one, on any work – who hadn't fancied the coup.

'Spoken to the old man yet, guv?'

'On the way home.'

'And?'

'He fucking loved it, Sergeant Craze . . .'

Dave Craze, Harry's john. Only eight people in Manchester.

'Hundred grand down, what do you think? We're all in his office at nine sharp tomorrow morning. Now what have you got for me?'

'Pearson, guv.'

'That prick.'

Sounded like Charlie wasn't exactly flavour of the month right now.

'Doctors say he can't talk to us. They've got him sedated.'

'Did he say anything before?'

'Just gabbling. He wants protection.'

'Gabbling what?'

'He's going on about everyone knowing he's a grass now. He wants protection off us, guv. Him and his wife.'

'Fuck Pearson.'

'Guv?'

'I said, let the fucker sweat.'

'What?'

'No one knows what happened in that hotel room today but us, Dave. And that's the way I want it kept. No fucking ringing up the *Manchester Evening News* like some of you usually do.'

'I think he should have someone to stay with him, guv.'

'Is there anyone on him at the moment?'

'DC Webster and DC Hardy.'

'Take them off.'

'Guv?'

'Send them home. Send a uniform out.'

The line crackled for a couple of seconds.

'I don't think that's a good idea, guv. Do you think he was in on the swindle or something?'

'No I don't, but don't tell him he's not in the frame. Let him stew for tonight. And let him stew about someone coming for him, it'll do him no harm.'

'Guv . . .'

Dave sounded very uncomfortable. I almost liked him.

'I'll make him a fucking target, Dave. He fucked up. Take the suits off and put a uniform in.'

'Guv, I'm not – '

I wondered how much Dave spent on Harry in a month.

'Fuck Pearson, Dave. I'm not wasting any more time on him. I want every man we've got after the money. There's too much to do without playing nanny. I want that hundred grand back. I want some fucking movement, now.'

He was almost screaming, but Dave still came back at him. He had some bottle, this Craze. 'He needs to make a statement, guv. There should be someone there. For when he comes round.'

'No. Leave that as well. He's had some promises off us, promises not in the book. There'll be an internal on this – ghost squad, you name it. I need to talk to Pearson, before he talks to them or puts anything down on paper.'

A beat. I could hear a telly on in the background somewhere.

'You promised him, guv. And I didn't know about the money until it went off.'

'Yeah yeah yeah. We'll have a look tomorrow, but for now he's neither use nor ornament. In the meantime, the absolute priority is getting that hundred grand back. That'll buy us a dozen Charlie Pearsons. Get back to me when you got something.'

He hung up. I pressed stop and drew on my stub. No talk about forensics or physical evidence, most importantly no mention of CCTV or other film. Nothing on me, just a continued scream-out for the dough. That made me feel comfortable for now, but it was early doors yet. And there was still the grass and his eventual statement to think about.

It had just gone five. Too early to make the calls I wanted, too late for the kip I needed. I compromised by slinging the duvet cover on the couch and setting the alarm for seven. Two seconds later I swung my feet on to the deck feeling like a bag of shit, stuck my head under the cold tap and poured coffee down my throat. Then I got suited and booted and staggered out the front door with last night's tape and the player in a plastic bag. Fortunately, Casey was an early riser. I belled him with my new mobile and we made a meet for the hospital car park at eight. I got there early and sat reading the *Guardian* report on United's midweek fixture to kill time.

Casey's Landcruiser. He drew up the other side and got out and walked across, thank fuck. I unlocked the door and he bent and adjusted the passenger seat as far back as it would go before he slid in.

'You look like shit,' he said cheerfully.

'Thank you. How's the boy?'

'As of last night, his methadone intake had come down a fair bit. Stevie says Terry is pretty much free of the physical symptons. He also says that Terry has put up the notion of a week or so at a private clinic. He asked to get the message to you that he'd pay the bill.'

'That's big of him. He's lucky that money is all this is going to cost him. Is he well enough to make a phone call?'

'A normal phone call or a special one?'

'A special one.'

'Do tell.'

'I need him to bring someone on to a moody meet. Terry's plugged into him, if he calls the other guy might come. If not, we'll have to leave it for now.'

'We?'

'I could do with one of your lads on minding duties, if they're up for it.'

'I'm beginning to enjoy all this strutting around. Makes me feel like Reg Kray. Who is it?'

'Guy called Nathan Chambers.'

'Why him?'

'Chambers is working with the grass Charlie Pearson. Chambers propped Terry in Strangeways, told him that I was a grass. That's where all my grief started. I want a word.'

'Just a word?'

'Just a word. I've got a tape to play him, tape of a conversation between Charlie Pearson and his handler DCS Keith Hamilton Jacks.'

'Blimey.'

'Yeah, blimey.'

Casey tugged at his beard for a moment. I noticed there was a patch just below his chin on my side where it didn't grow.

'Don't bother with Terry,' he said. 'He'll only mess it up. I think I know Nathan Chambers' cousin, if it's the same guy. Bloke called Ernie. Do you want me to bring him on?'

'Can you do it?'

'I'll just tell him I've got a parcel that might interest them. Ernie's the greediest little bugger I've ever met. I'll get him to turn up with Nathan, say it might interest him as well. If it's not the same guy, I'll call you and we'll have to use Terry.'

'Thought you weren't frontline.'

'I told you, I'm starting to enjoy all this. Now, when do you want them?'

'If you can get Terry into the clinic this evening, then after. After he goes, at the flat.'

'I'll try. Where can I reach you?'

'Number you got on your screen just now.'

'All right, I'll call you.' He gave me the address of the flat. 'Go home and get some sleep.'

'I wish.'

He split and I drove for Amy's, stopping at a box to tell her I was on the way. Nine fifteen and I was sitting at her kitchen table with a pile of breakfast the size of Ayers Rock in front of me. She banged on about bingo wins and the woman next door, I ate and said thanks, stashed the tape and the player, collected the Midland dough and left.

Manchester to Brum is usually ninety minutes top whack. Today I had a hundred grand of almost certainly marked police dough in the back, so it was mirror-driving, back-doubling and arse-watching all round and I didn't make the Metropole bar till half twelve. Monty was already on-site, drinking coffee at the counter and reading the *Telegraph*.

'Hope the short notice didn't put you out, Monty.'

'Nah. The work I'm looking at means clocking a van around the nine o'clock mark and then again a few minutes before five. Sorting when's the best time to have it. As long as I leave the city by three, I'm sweet.'

He hardly glanced up from the paper as he spoke. He flicked a page and turned it, then smoothed it out in front of him, still not looking up. Obviously waiting for me to say something.

'You all right, Monty?'

'Yeah yeah yeah. Tell me how things went yesterday.'

Not without purpose, the way I told the tale made it seem like a mid-afternoon doddle. I knew Monty wouldn't be happy I did the graft on my tod. Now that I'd come down to do the chop-up, I also knew he'd feel a bit defensive about taking his corner. Hence the pissed-off routine.

'I've got the hundred here. I haven't checked it. I know it's straight, but that's it. They'll certainly have the numbers, and maybe they marked it a bit cunning. Can you change it for me? You can take your corner out while you're at it.'

'What do you reckon my corner is, mate?'

'Same as it ever was – three ways. You, me and Leon. His goes to his mum, obviously. Apart from the exes, that's it.'

'What have I done to earn my corner? I set up the slag, and that was it.' He folded his paper and slapped it down on the counter. 'We were meant to plot this up together, with me backing you up on the swindle itself. But you fucked off on your own. Now I'm sat here feeling like an old ponce.' He stared into his cup, then threw back the dregs.

'I now realise Noriko has the patience of a saint,' I said. 'Listen, when I came down to see you, my head was up my arse. All I wanted to do was get a gun and shoot someone. You helped me out. You got the knowledge, you dreamt up the plot. So a third is yours, all right? Just as it should be. Now will you please change the dough up?'

Two and a half hours later, I was driving back up the M6 with sixty-five grand in used tens and twenties locked in the boot. Monty had stopped moaning and gone to make a phone call to his Turkish-Cypriot-Brummie pal Haşim who owned a few bricks in a local casino and made use of them for money-laundering purposes. We took the Rover to the centre and I waited in the Holiday Inn while Monty did the trade. Turned out the dough was marked. Every note had a series of minute pinpricks which only showed when they were held up to a strong light. The Turks had charged ten grand for the service – which was a bit steep as it happens. Monty had phoned to say he could probably get it done for five per cent in London, and what did I think? I said we might as well do it now and told him to go ahead.

When he got back, he was giving orders again. 'I'll take twenty-five,' he said. 'Then twenty-five for Leon's mum and twenty-five for you. You take the exes out of the fifteen that's left, then spend the rest on a holiday. And if you don't do as I say, you can stay in a fucking hotel next time you come down to see me and the girl.'

'Whatever you say, Monty. Whatever you say.'

By five thirty I was coming off the M6, steering with my right hand and punching out Casey's mobile when the phone rang and it was him.

'I was just calling you, Casey.'

'Felt it in my water. Got some news.'

'I'm listening.'

'OK, Terry's booked into the Priory. Detox, therapy, TV, all the trimmings. And at their prices, naked ladies. It's four grand a week, cash up front. A snip.'

'Well, he's paying.'

'They're expecting him half eight tonight. One of the lads will take him along in case he has second thoughts.'

'Thanks. Any luck on the other matter?'

'Called on for tonight at the flat, around eight fifteen. Through his cousin, it was the same guy and as I said, the greediest little bugger in the north. They think they're coming for a pick 'n' mix of silver I can't shift up here. I'll be there and Stevie – he's the larger of the two you met the other day – will stay to hang about in the background and flex a bit. Now is that enough, or do you want some more muscle?'

I thought of Jack's Beretta buried in Amy's front garden. 'Not if you're there, Casey.'

'Let's hope I've got the time to put him in a neck-lock, then.'

'I'll be there at seven. Thanks, Casey.'

I clicked the phone shut and tossed it on to the passenger seat. He'd sounded a bit strained. Maybe the meet had been difficult to sort at such short notice. And despite the fact he was a handy lad, I suspected he didn't want a ruck with Nathan Chambers. He was a big hard-looking guy according to Terry. But Chambers was coming on to this thinking it was a straight, friendly meet. And it would still be two against three, so we should be all right. I hoped.

I drove to Amy's and she waved the dog out into the garden for a bounce round. I lifted its bed and the boards, counted a few quid out and stashed the rest of the Midland money in the bag behind the joist. Then I stuck the Hamilton Jacks tapes one and two in a carrier with the player. She made me a cup of tea and I put a grand on the table. She riffled the notes and created a bit, but I got her to take it in the end. She wasn't ever in it for the dough, she just liked to be part of the game.

There were explosions as I rang the entryphone in Benchill a few minutes later. Bonfire Night, I'd forgotten. Casey buzzed me up and met me at the door. As I stepped in I saw Terry down the corridor in the kitchen with one of the lads, apparently drying dishes. Casey led me into the lounge: two sofas at a right angle, a couple of armchairs and a portable telly on a box. The other lad was clearing up, putting papers and emptying ashtrays into a bin liner.

'You remember Stevie.'

'I do. Thanks for all this, Steve.'

Stevie came and stood a few inches away so he could speak in a low voice. With Casey on the other side, I felt like I was on a day trip to some standing stones.

'Terry's been all right today. He ate a proper breakfast this morning, then we had a game of cards and watched some telly. He talks about you a lot, and his dad, how you used to work together.'

'Anything about the guy we're seeing tonight, Chambers? Or a face called Charlie Pearson?'

'Not that I've heard.'

'OK, thanks Stevie.'

'All right, mate?' We turned and saw Terry in the door, drying his hands on a dishcloth. His eyes were brighter and his skin was clearer. But his smile was nervous as well as friendly. 'Come to see me off?'

'I'll speak to you in a minute, Terry. Go into your bedroom, I'll just finish up here.'

'All right.' He turned and trotted off obediently. The other lad filled the door. Casey reminded me this was Wayne. I paid him and Stevie the rest of their dough and gave Wayne the clinic money.

'Where's his bedroom?'

'Second on the left,' said Wayne. 'Opposite the front door.'

I excused myself and went down. A couple of rockets shrilled and burst outside. The door was ajar, with light coming from a lamp on the deck. Aside from that, an upright chair with some clothes and a single divan with blankets and sheet twisted and tangled across it, the room was empty. Terry was watching some rocket splashes and he turned as I clicked the door shut and met my gaze. He held it longer than I expected him to. For a second, I saw his father standing at his shoulder.

'All right, Terry, I'm only going to say this once.'

And what was I going to say, anyway? That he was lucky to be standing here at all, lucky I was still looking after him. That most other people would have leathered him or worse by now, father or no. Or that I'd failed with him, just like I had with too many other people in my life. Maybe I'd just stick to the facts.

'This is the way it's going to be. Wayne will be taking you to the clinic and he'll be paying the bill. He'll make certain you can't pull any of it back. Whether you stay there or not is up to you.'

He nodded.

'I'm going to take Chambers off your back for you. If you end up going back to him – or even the law – that's up to you as well. But Chambers won't come looking for you.'

I gave it a beat.

'The money for the bill and the money for the lads here will be coming out of your whack of our last parcel. What's left will stay with me and will only be returned to you – in small instalments – after you've had a negative piss test. Those will be arranged by your mother, who won't lie to me about the results. After maybe six months of negative tests, you'll get the rest of the parcel. That's all that's on offer. No plan B. If you fuck off from the clinic, or fail a piss test then it's no dough. You're leaving in five minutes, Terry. Make sure you're ready.' I turned for the door.

'Is there anything I can do to make this better, mate?'

My fingers were resting on the door handle. There were mucky dabs on the paintwork. I wondered if they were his. Maybe he'd got lively and they'd had to lock him in here sometime over the last couple of days and they hadn't told me. If I didn't look at him I wouldn't be reminded of his dad. 'Sometimes it's just too late, Terry. Get your stuff together.'

They went at quarter to eight and the three of us remaining went over the game plan for Chambers. Then I set up the tape machine on the floor by the telly and we waited. Casey spent some time winding Stevie up about supporting City. I stared out of the window and counted rocket bursts.

The buzzer went at twenty past eight. Casey went to the front door, spoke into the entryphone and pressed to release the door catch downstairs. 'We're on,' he said. 'Starting positions please, gents.'

I moved into Terry's bedroom and stood so I could see through the gap at the hinges. A few moments and there was a quiet knock on the main woodwork. Casey opened up and two guys came in. The first was short and in his forties, the second was Nathan Chambers, just as Terry had described him. Big sod, grey hair and hands like hams. Casey muttered something about the lounge and they shifted out of my line stage right. I counted sixty and crept down the corridor. Stevie had left the door a few inches open as agreed. I moved up and listened: low chatter and Casey's laugh. It sounded good and relaxed, just what we wanted. Then I leant on the wood and pushed it open.

Chambers was sat on the sofa to my left, Ernie was on the other and Casey was sat just down from him with his long pins stretched out in front. Stevie was just inside the door at the right. Ernie and Chambers looked up and then a lot of things seemed to happen at once. Chambers lunged at me screaming and shouting, Stevie crossed and punched him once and he went back down on the sofa, Ernie and Casey stood, Casey laid his palm on Ernie's chest and sat him gently back on his butt with a two ton push. Now Chambers was curled over nursing his shoulder and looking at me, and he looked like a man about to get shot. Then he flicked from Casey to Stevie to me, obviously weighing up the odds to go again.

'I wouldn't if I were you, Nathan,' I said.

'You, you fucking grass. You fuck.' He snapped his nut at Ernie. 'It's a fucking moody, your fence mate's a grass, him as well.' He flicked his eyes round at the three of us. 'What's this? A fucking bunch of grass. Go on, then. Get on with it.'

'If we were going to do you, Nathan, we'd have done you at the door,' I said. 'We don't want any more aggro.'

'I'm afraid your Nathan's right about one thing though, Ernie,' said Casey. 'This is a moody. There's no silver, sorry.'

Ernie stayed schtum. He was a little guy and didn't look the type for a row. But still.

I nodded at his cousin. 'Are you carrying anything, Nathan?'

'No.'

'No gun?'

'No.'

'A blade, anything?'

'I said no. This was meant to be a friendly meet over a bit of silver. Not a fucking grasses' convention.'

'Well, keep your hands where I can see them, anyway.' I looked across. 'You too, Ernie. Then there'll be no need for any more treatment. Casey?'

'Thanks. Like I said, Ernie, the meet's a moody and I apologise but we had no choice. My mate wanted a word with your cousin, and this was the only way. I reckons he deserves it as well. Seems like your Nathan nicked a few months off him recently.'

Hands held out away from my sides and fingers splayed, I moved to the tape machine on the deck and eased down slowly into the chair next to it. Chambers was staring at the floor, still rubbing his shoulder.

'Thing is, Nathan, you've been calling me a grass. And I want to know why.'

'Because you are a fucking grass – '

'Shut up.'

Chambers snapped his head up at me, but he was one puzzled heavy by now. He knew I was right about them not copping for it early doors. In his world, you did the damage first and wrote the script later. He threw another glance at Stevie, who'd gone back to leaning against the wall.

'It's not in our interests to hurt you any more,' I said. 'So why not just get comfortable for a moment, eh? Then we can get done and go home. OK, I've got a couple of tape recordings I want to play you. Then there'll be a bit of Show and Tell. Clear?' Neither of the guests spoke.

'Listening, Nathan?' Nothing. 'I'll take that as a yes, then.' I pressed start and eased back, nice and slow.

'The first voice is a jock from the Regional,' I said: 'A DCS by the name of Hamilton Jacks. The second voice, we'll talk about in a minute.'

There was some buzz and crackle, and the first tape came on. Unless Chambers had trained at RADA – and not too many Manchester robbers have had that advantage – Pearson's voice gave him a shock. A few seconds in, he stopped rubbing his shoulder and wrapped his big left hand round his chin. Then he shook his head and closed his eyes for the rest. Even without my intro, it was quite obvious that Pearson was a grass and Jacks was his handler. When tape one was done, I played the second, where they were plotting on the cocaine. It finished, I rewound and let it click stop. Then I looked over at Chambers.

'Big pal of yours, Charlie Pearson, isn't he?'

'He is.'

'I know you plotted up on me. I know you turned Terry against me and had him grafting for you. Well, Terry's dealt with now.'

Alarm flicked through Chambers' eyes.

'He's alive,' I said, 'and probably better than when you last saw him. You're not here for a row. I've already said.'

'Then what?'

I lit a cigarette, for punctuation. 'Hamilton Jacks and your mate Pearson are talking about me on those tapes. They thought they had me on a ready-eye at the Midland Hotel, but I beat the trap. I'm telling you this because the Old Bill already know it was me. So my first question to you is this: would the filth and a grass plot up on another grass?'

He shook his head.

'I can't hear you.'

'I don't know.'

'Yes, you do. Do the Old Bill go to war on a grass? Yes or no?'

'No, they don't.' He looked like he was in the dock on a guilty plea.

'Listen,' he began. 'I've known Charlie Pearson for years. I can't take that in.' He nodded at the tape. 'I was drinking with him two nights ago. I'd know his voice anywhere.' He looked down for a moment. 'I got Terry to plant the brown in your cell.'

'I know.'

'Pearson told me you were a grass. I had no reason to doubt him.' He stopped for a second. 'If I was in your shoes, I'd be letting a gun do the talking.'

'Well, you're not. And the next: why did Ricky Yatnick call you about my nephew, when he was shot?' I was taking a punt here.

'How do you know about Ricky?'

'I've got a lot of friends. Why did he call you?'

Chambers shook his head again. 'Charlie wanted to know what was going on with Tomas. I told Yatnick to keep me in touch. He called me and I called Charlie.' And Pearson called Hamilton Jacks and the copper bundled down to the Infirmary I thought, and remembered Sean the baghead lying on his face in his Moss Side pit. 'And you knew he was my nephew, how?'

'It just came up. He used your name for credit and Yatnick put it in front of me. I thought Charlie would want to know, and he asked me to lay him on. I thought you were a grass. I've known him for years.' He looked at the machine.

'Did Pearson say why he wanted Tomas laid on?'

'No.'

'And you didn't wonder?'

'Why should I? I was doing him a favour, why not?'

'What was it, some kind of plot to make sure my nephew ended up a proper baghead? Was that how you were going to get to me? Do you ever think what happens to the people you sell smack to, Nathan, how they feel when they're sick, crawling up the walls. I said: do you ever think?'

And there it was again, he shifted, he twitched. The guy was frightened of me. 'I don't force them.'

'Oh no, you don't force them. You just turn things so they force themselves.'

He shifted forward, rubbing his palms against each other like they were sweaty. 'I'm sorry, I've known him for years, I was doing a favour. What would you have done?'

'I don't know, I don't sell smack.'

'I said I'm sorry.'

'Sometimes it's too late, Nathan.' Terry and his dad danced in my head. I ground my fag out in a saucer on the telly. 'All right, here's the deal. Terry's away, now. When he comes back – if he ever comes back – you stay away. You don't go near him, you don't have anything to do with him. If he tries to make contact, you fuck him off. Go near the boy again and it won't be slaps next time. Understood?'

'Yeah.'

'And no more grass calling. Not me, anyway.'

'All right. Where's Charlie now?'

'I don't know. But you leave him to me, anyway.'

He sat quiet for a few moments, still rubbing his hands together like he was trying to dry them. Then he looked right at me. 'Look, I've treated you bad. I'll try and make up for it.'

'Don't bother.'

'I'm going to make a couple of calls. I'll get back to you tomorrow.' He nodded at the tapes. 'Can I take those?'

'No, I don't have spares. I can arrange another performance later. Or make some copies. I think you better go now.'

The tiredness was rushing over me in long sweeping waves and I was losing the strength to follow through. Chambers and Ernie were up against two now. I couldn't have fought a flea. Speaking was a struggle.

'Go on, go and make your calls. If you've got anything to tell me, get back to me through Casey.'

Chambers nodded. He stood and stretched out his hand.

'Don't expect me to shake.'

They left. Stevie gave them a minute to clear the landing and followed them out. I heard the front door close and I slumped. I was wiped.

'Think he's on the level, Casey?'

'I reckon.'

'Yes,' I said. 'So do I.' I sank back into the chair heavily. 'He's still a piece of shit, though. He's off my Christmas card list for sure.'

There was noise in the hall and Stevie reappeared. 'They had a BMW and a driver. Nutter from Hulme, name of Danny.'

I glanced at my watch. Five minutes since the meet had ended, time enough for Chambers to blow the whistle if him and Pearson were at the same stroke. Time we were gone as well. 'What's happening here?'

'Quick ten minutes and out,' said Casey. 'No one's using the place for a while anyway. Stevie?'

'The guy opposite will let me know if anyone's sniffing around looking like trouble. It'll be fine.'

'You go home, mate,' said Casey. 'Tell me all the rest another time. We'll finish up here, you get some sleep. You still look like shit.'

Two things when I woke up the next morning. One: it was too hot for me in Manchester and I should be getting out today, and two: I ached from tiredness. It was eight fifteen and the night's kip hadn't made any difference. Pay everyone off, get across to Leeds to see the kids and I could go tonight. Better get moving then.

I creaked out of bed, took a hot then cold shower and went out to ring Amy. Yes, she said, the café could be open for breakfast.

She was feeding me half an hour later, then split to take Krypto the wonderdog for a walk. I went into my stash in the floor, collected the rest from the loft, did the washing up and sat down at the kitchen table to cut up the dough.

Two parcels of twenty-five grand. A couple of padded envelopes

I'd bought on the way took fifteen hundred each – Tom for booking the room at the Midland and Ray for sorting me after. A last wrap of five thousand for Carol for looking after Terry and the knowledge on the Midland.

I slung the lot into the bag I'd brought with me along with the bin liner of Leon's cash from the Wilmslow Love Nest and remembered I'd left the Hamilton Jacks tapes back at the service flat in Whalley Range, bugger. I'd have to get them later, and the gun. I couldn't leave that knocking around in Amy's garden while I went away for unspecified days. I hung on for twenty minutes, but she still hadn't showed and time was short. I'd have to call her later. I split, pulling the front door shut behind me.

I was sitting opposite Leon's cousin Ronnie in his office half an hour later. He was telling me the inquest had been set down for the following Monday. I asked if they had a date for the funeral yet.

'Week after next, providing the coroner gives the OK.'

'I won't be coming.'

Ronnie didn't really look surprised.

'Could you tell Judith that I'm keeping my head down right now?'

'Whatever you want.'

'And this.' I pulled out the twenty-five grand wrap and laid it on the desk. 'Can you give her that from me, please?'

'What is it?'

'Money.'

'She's got plenty of money.'

'It's Leon's.'

'How far away from it was he when he died?'

'It's not mine, Ronnie. It's hers now. And this,' I said, passing the other bundle across, 'is some dough that Leon had lying about. It's Judith's as well.'

Ronnie was resting his chin on his hand, the look on his mug said he couldn't wait for me to be out of here. 'I'll give it to her. Any other message?'

'No more than I've already told you.'

I stood to go. He shook my hand, but didn't get up as I left.

As I walked out the building, I glanced up at his office. He was at the window, staring down at me. I could still feel his eyes on my neck as I walked round the corner to the Rover.

I drove till I found a phone box and called Carol and said I wouldn't mind calling round. She said fine. I stopped off at a post office and sent Tom and Ray Sergeant their cash, registered.

'He's been off the gear for a week, now.'

I was in Carol's kitchen drinking tea.

'But you won't be seeing him again?'

I didn't answer.

'But you still sort him out. Boy scout.'

'What?'

'Running around, looking after people. Even people like Terry. What's all that about, eh?'

'I knew his dad,' I mumbled.

She picked up the teapot and waved it at me. I shook no and she poured herself another cup. 'I'm glad to hear about Terry though.'

'He'll get the best help. If he wants to stick to it, that is.'

'I might go up and see him.'

'Well.'

There was an awkward silence. I made myself busy in my jacket pocket. 'Here,' I said, holding the envelope out.

'What's this?'

'Five grand. For expenses.'

'I don't need paying.'

'You did me a couple of favours, Carol. Over Terry, and over the Midland knowledge. Now I'm doing you one, simple as that.'

She took the envelope.

'Right little boy scout,' she said.

I left Carol's at one fifty. Deansgate, across to Suede Hill, then Rochdale Road, Middleton and the 62. With a good run across, I could be in Leeds by the time the kids came out of school. I punched in Lou's mobile, got voicemail, and left a quick message saying I'd be at the bus stop at half three.

I'd been waiting fifteen minutes when they trundled down the road and stood by the shelter. The Rover was across the street and half hidden by a van a few feet in front, so they didn't see me. I sat and watched them for a bit. They'd changed even in the short time I'd been in the shovel.

I remembered the first time I'd gone in after they were born. Sara red-eyed and angry on her first visit, all *You said you wouldn't do this again, what's going to happen to the kids with their father locked up?* Then something like, *I will not bring them to see you here, or any other prison, do you understand?* Me pleading with her over successive visits, her finally relenting and bringing the two of them – just five, then – padding wide-eyed and anxious as they followed her into the visiting room. Then the screams from Lou as the visit ended and screws stamped around shouting, *That's it, time up, I said that's it, time up.*

Why can't Daddy come with us, Mummy?

I felt ashamed and guilty even now. I got out of the car and walked towards them. She saw me coming and they ran to me and the misery lifted off.

'Is your mother at home?'

'She said she'd be out and we were to get our own tea.'

Lou was next to me and Sam was in the back, leaning over his sister's seat.

'Will she be long?'

'Seven. We're going to the cinema. Together.'

As a family, I thought. I said, 'All right. Take this bag, love.' I handed it across, zipped up. 'Put it somewhere safe. In the loft, if you've got one. If not, take the panel off the bath and put it behind there. Anywhere a burglar won't find it.'

'There's a lot of thieves about,' said Sam.

'Do you want to come out with me for a bit?'

They looked at each other conspiratorially.

We went shopping. Lou had said (very casually, of course) that she'd quite fancy a trip to Harvey Nichols. I wouldn't have been seen dead in the place without someone else's plastic for ammo, but the pair of them seemed quite happy to pay blood. Or rather, to watch me pay it.

When we'd done, we cruised up to the Headrow to an Italian. I had their schoolbags and the holdall which I wasn't about to leave in the motor, and they had a couple of shopping bags each. They crushed these out of sight and under chairs in the restaurant. I kept the holdall between my feet. We talked over the food about what they'd been up to, what their new school was like, how they were settling in. I could tell they were dancing round the subject of . . .

'Tomas,' said Sam out of nowhere. 'What happened?'

I moved the salt cellar forward and right like it was a knight on a chessboard.

'All I know,' I said gently, 'is that Tomas died over an argument to do with drugs. He probably owed someone some money. Do Jan and Steph still think it had something to do with me?'

'They did at first,' said Sam. 'They believed the police. I don't know about now. We left them a message last week. They didn't call back.'

None of us spoke, and I slid the knight around again, thinking of Alice. After a few minutes I said, 'How did your mum take Leon?'

'How did Mum take it? How about us?' said Lou. She was staring at her plate, pushing a few berries around. I could see her eyes starting to fill with tears. 'I was upstairs and I heard her screaming. She'd read it in the paper. Then she cried for a few hours. I had to sleep with her in her bed that night. Do you want to know more?'

I shook a brief, guilty *no*. I'd run out and hadn't called them. I hadn't been a good enough father here.

'I'm sorry,' I said. 'Whatever happened,' I said, 'it won't come back on me.'

I could see they didn't believe me. I think it was the first time I'd lied to them that day. They didn't ask about Leon or Tomas again.

I drove them home, telling them things were clearing up for me in Manchester, but that I was taking a few weeks off, having made some moves which required my absence. We drew up a few streets away from where they lived and I let the car idle, taking out the note I'd scribbled to Sara and tapping it on the steering wheel. Neither of them showed any sign of moving.

'I never wanted to leave, you know.' I'd said this before, let me say it again. 'It was between me and your mother.'

'We know,' said Sam.

'It nearly killed me when we split up. I was leaving you two as well as her.'

You can only beg fortune when you divorce and there are kids involved. You can only try to make them understand that the leaving has nothing to do with them. You can only tell them that you love them.

'I love you both.'

They both hugged me. Lou from the passenger seat, Sam from behind. I was engulfed in sudden affection. Awkwardly, I fished two fifties out of my pocket and gave them one apiece. They were good kids, and could do without. But they wouldn't have been kids if they couldn't find something to do with a few quid, when it came.

Dear Sara,

There's twenty-five grand in the bag I gave Lou. Use it to pay off the mortgage on Buckingham Road, or do whatever you like with it.

There's been a lot to sort out, but I'm getting there. The brown in my cell had nothing to do with me, but I know why it was put there. You know I had nothing to do with Tomas and I don't know why Leon was killed. I loved him and I won't let it go, you know that. You won't have anyone come looking for you over that, over me, or over anything else. It's sorted now. Almost.

Please tell Jan and Steph that Tomas wasn't down to me. I don't know if they'll listen right now, but try and make them understand that when you think the time is right.

I still want to be part of Lou and Sam's lives. Please don't make that difficult for me. I'm sorry I screwed up.

Good luck in Leeds or wherever you go.

I'll miss you.

I cried for someone as I took the road for Manchester. I wasn't sure who.

The traffic was bad, so I only hit the city about half nine. I pulled up to ring Amy. She said to drop by before eleven as she'd be going to bed then. I hung up and dialled Benny, yes it was OK to come round now. The Alex was shifting into full frontline mode when I turned up, with dealers moving around the houses and picking up their Es and whizz to service the club trade later. Benny was watching some DVD of United's Top Hundred Goals when I rang his bell. I asked him if he'd heard or seen any good villainy on the local news the last couple of days.

'Oooh,' he wheezed. 'Let's have a think.' He listed a bunch of robberies for me, then burglaries and a murder, but nothing about the Midland or anything close to it. Good to know. When he'd finished, I gave him a monkey. 'What's this?'

'The baghead Sean. I earned on the knowledge you gave me. So you've earned that five hundred, Ben. More than.'

Bemused, he looked at the cash in his paw.

'Oh well, if you're sure.'

I saw myself out, checking the telephone directories as I passed. The two hundred quid I'd left for him last time had gone.

Ten past eleven. The traffic had been a bit thick on the way across, and I'd only just made Amy's. I sat across the road and drummed the steering wheel. I didn't want to stick around tonight, but I didn't want to wake her either and all the lights were out. OK, I'd hotel it locally and drop in for the dough first thing tomorrow, but I'd get the gun now while it was dark. The street was deserted. I skipped across and darted up the path behind the bushes. The Beretta was buried under her front window next to a mini rose bush. I scraped down about six inches with my hands, hit the bin liner twisted round the box and filled in the hole in a couple of minutes.

I got back to Whalley Range at midnight. For the moment, the gun stayed out of sight under the passenger seat and I went inside to get my stuff together. And discovered that I only had about three quid left in shrapnel. Nothing for a hotel.

'Sod it,' I said aloud.

I had intended to pack up, drop the twirls through the letter-box and phone Rosie the landlady tomorrow. She had my deposit, so she'd be in front. Now I was stuck here till breakfast time at least. On the other hand, Benny had just told me there was no scream. And nobody knew where I was. Hotels mean people and earwigging, here I was on my own. And I was very tired.

I hung up my jacket, opened a bottle of wine, rolled a joint and smoked it.

Then I showered and lay on the sofa wrapped in towels to kill the booze. I found a jazz station on the radio and had a last cigarette to an old Bessie Smith number. The recording made me think of the tapes I'd forgotten to dump at Amy's. The pelmet on the curtains had a lip on the inside, they could go there for the night. The coffee table was solid enough to take a chair, so I climbed up and tucked them out of sight.

I jumped down, falling heavier than I expected. I really was dead beat. I set the alarm for seven and went to bed.

Dark shapes grouped noiselessly outside the door. Someone smiled and gave the nod, and someone else slid a key – no, not a key, some part of a long bony finger, almost transparent and tapered at the end – into the lock. A gentle slide as a choir sang quietly on the landing and in the street outside.

I was dreaming. I turned over comfortably, feeling my feet stretch and find themselves another warm piece of bed to dwell in. There was a low click and I tried to place where it came from inside my head. Then I felt shadows around the bed.

This was called lucid dreaming, and if I was clever, I could control it. I decided not to open my eyes.

The noise of men roaring in unison had me snap bolt upright, blinking furiously as the light was turned on, heart racing, cold sweat prickling across my palms. I took a second to focus on the three men in black flack jackets stood round the bed, arms extended beyond the barrels of three big revolvers. A clear voice came out of the fog: 'Blink, you arsehole, and your wife will be your widow. Don't fucking move.'

This was no dream. I froze.

The face directly in front of me was young and spotty. It was also tense, hyped up and very frightened. There was a bead of sweat running down his left temple. I was sacred shitless that this prick was going to let one go. Believe me, I didn't blink.

Two more of them – how many-handed was this mob? – moved in from the side, grabbed a shoulder and arm apiece and pulled me forward over and off the bed on to the deck. I was spreadeagled in front of the other guy, who was still covering me with his gun. I nosed dust and carpet as they twisted my arms behind me. The cuffs pinched, tightened and cut into my wrists. Someone screamed out, 'He's nicked!'

Then they pulled me to my feet and bundled me out of the bedroom. As we passed through the living room and out of the door I saw at least another half dozen filth starting to rip the place apart. My crew pulled and pushed me down the stairs, forced me down on to the deck again, then grabbed my legs for the run to the car. They lifted and jogged me to the motor, then dropped me on my knees. A big meaty palm slapped the back of my neck, pushed down with a grunt and shoved me in bent double, one busy either side of me.

You stupid fucking prick, how many bells have to ring before you listen? The night before last and all day yesterday, and still you dwelt. You'll fucking dwell now all right, you mug.

It was on top. It was fucking well on top, as on top as it ever fucking could be. I was in a cop car on the way to a nick, armed filth up my backside, bent double and chickened up. There was a scam with my signature on it, a grass waiting to spill his guts, and a detective chief superintendent I'd ripped off for a hundred grand waiting to sink me.

To fucking top it off, I was wearing my boxer shorts and fuck all else. They hadn't even let me grab a few scraps of fucking dignity when they hustled me out to the fucking car.

Fuck. Fuck. Fuck.

17

Head crushed down to ankle height and with a noseful of dust and carpet shit, I tried to follow the tug and lurch of the motor.

A right as it rolled off the plot from Allness; a left on to the main drag. Then a straight run, which meant the city. I lost my way as the motor spun and turned at short intervals, but when we swung a fast right and then a left before slamming to a stop, only seconds after starting the slalom, I figured that we had to be in Bootle Street, the old city centre police headquarters. They threw a blanket over my head, dragged me out of the car and hustled me across the tarmac. There were prodding hands all around me, but at least my back wasn't twisted double this time.

I heard and felt our journey through double doors, single doors and along corridors, then keys in heavy locks as they hustled me into what I knew was a peter. There was a muttered conversation going on just out of earshot, then quick decisive strides from the corridor. The steps came into my space and a clipped tone said, 'Take that off, and the cuffs.'

The blanket got snapped off by a man smelling of bacon, another one who didn't wash ripped my arms up and unlocked the bracelets. I didn't rub eyes or wrists, I just looked. Six of them, five plainclothes and a uniform. The blue was standing directly in front of me holding a piece of paper, the rest of the mob gathered loosely around him. Two of them looked ridiculously young. Uniform's stance and manner made him favourite for head boy. Now he started rapping; my name first and asked me to confirm it, along with my date of birth. I ignored both. He glanced round at the others before continuing. One of the YTS boys turned and left the cell.

Uniform then read on that I'd been arrested on suspicion of being involved in two separate conspiracies: one was with persons unknown to commit two murders, between certain dates in the city of Manchester.

Murders? What the fuck was this?

The second, between another two spots on the calendar, conspiring with Montague Lee, and unnamed others, to supply class A drugs to one Charles Pearson, again on the manor.

Then he went pratting on about PACE and how long I could be detained, before being put in front of a beak and what my rights were during that period, allowed phone calls and all that style. Then, surprise surfuckingprise, he switched to how those rights could be curtailed or body-swerved altogether on the nod of an officer on or above the rank of inspector, providing that officer was satisfied implementing those rights would obstruct the investigation.

The prick had the grace to look towards his shoes when he added he was that inspector, and the nod had been so given.

Murders, what were they talking about here? Yes, they could talk to me about Leon through association alone, but what was the bunny about the two? Did they think I was mug enough to hold my hands up to the coke, in return for the dropping of cobblers homicides? How old did these pricks think I was? Fifteen? I didn't say any of this, I just stayed quiet and let him finish.

'I said, did you understand all that?'

I looked round the box, the government-green tiles, the wooden bunk, the regulation black mattress and the piss-stained karsi in the corner.

'Is this a nick then? You do surprise me. I thought it was a McDonalds. I thought you were going to tell me to have a nice fucking day.'

One of the younger lads started a snigger, then thought better of it.

The YTS boy reappeared. He was holding a white paper boiler suit and had a cellophane parcel tucked under his arm, what looked like a pair of slippers. He lobbed both on to the bunk, and the gang of six moved as one towards the door, slamming it shut behind them. And locked it. Then footsteps away and silence. I sat down on the bench and leant against the wall to think. I'd fucked up by not going. What had this done to the others?

Short of being nicked for something unconnected, Monty was safe. All they had on him for the Midland plot was Pearson's word that Monty first propped the trade to him and gave him the sample, that night at the fights. And that was worth fuck all. So he was probably OK. Amy was safe; she wasn't known to anyone, so she could go out of my mind as well.

This was important. Right now, the filth would be dancing around in double-quick time. The days after they lift a suspect are crucial to them. Having secured the body, they now have to find the evidence to secure the conviction.

Ray Sergeant was sound, and the Midland evidence was stripped and stuck on a dump days ago. Stevie and Wayne the minders would be fine unless Terry had gone bandit again, but he was tucked up in the Priory. If Chambers was a grass, he had the address of the flat in Benchill and he knew Casey's name, but that was it. Where would that get them in terms of the Midland coup or Leon's death, anyway? The mobile with all my recently phoned numbers was down at Amy's, so they couldn't even go on the ring round. Casey's number was on the new one, but he could live with a knock on the door, he'd had enough in the past. Picking up a fare ain't a crime when you do it for a living, so that was Kaluki Ken out. Carol, Benny and Harry were all unconnected.

So this mob would have to rely on what they'd got, plus anything they'd found at the service flat in Whalley Range, which was zilch, apart from the tapes.

The tapes. Why hadn't I fucking buried them properly?

Because you were tired. Well, you'll have plenty of time to sleep now, you mug.

The tapes put me in trouble, no point in trying to get around that – though I fucking would, come my day in court. For the moment, I had to accept that they would count as a big chunk of evidence towards a conspiracy. Bad enough my not pissing off last night when every instinct told me to go. Doing the prosecution's job for them by leaving evidence around was unforgivable.

Jack's gun.

Bastard, sod it, sod it. They'd find the Beretta in the Rover soon enough and then I'd be charged with that. Illegal possession, five years without the option. That was a baby's mistake. At least I'd not unwrapped it – but my dabs were probably on the box. My only chance would be screaming a fit up. But that wouldn't amount to much with all the rest on the sheet.

The best I could do right now was distract myself. Put the gun and the tapes away and concentrate on the here and now. Start by winning the mind game on the table.

These turkeys with their pointed guns, blanket over the head, no phone call, no brief and no clothes. All done to soften me up. Fuck 'em. Seventy-two hours in a police cell was a doddle compared to some time I'd done. How about solitary, the seg unit, prison block, the nick within the nick, getting grief from the full-time sadists, the ones that stamped up and down the wings with their slash peak caps and their Nazi books. Dragging you down the block for a beating, bouncing your head off the stairs on the way, then you'd be weeks away without seeing a friendly face.

That was hard time.

Strangeways, Walton, Armley, you name it. Right back to Foston Hall. I went in through the punch, the piss bed, felt the wet flapping cold pissed-through sheets wrapping themselves around my bare legs again, then I saw the two screws coming in and heard the pissboy dirty little pissdog routine and fast-forwarded it this time down through the block and Jack Keane and me pressing our lips up to the crack in the doors and Christmas Day and . . .

Then I smelt the peter I was in now and remembered Lou and Sam at the bus stop yesterday, how they'd changed in the eighteen months I was away on the last one. And now I was looking at five on the gun, minimum. Maybe ten if I went down on the Midland. Even doing all the courses and getting the earliest parole on the shortest sentence imaginable, I was going to be away for seven years. They'd be twenty-four, twenty-five when I got out. I'd miss university, driving tests, maybe weddings. They'd go from kids to adults. I could easily do a ten on this lot, then I'd be nearly fifty when I came out, maybe a grandfather for God's sake.

I had two battles to fight – the one they could see through the Judas hole, and the one inside my head. I kept up the front – anyone who looked in would see I was still in the boxer shorts, first lying on the bunk calmly, then on the deck doing a fierce workout for an hour or more. I ran on the spot, did press-ups against the floor and against the bed. Then I did sit-ups until I'd lost count and my abs were shouting *Enough!* Then I lay down for a rest, then went again. Sod your slippers and boiler suits, I can do without them. Think you can soften me up? Forget it.

But as I worked out and lay on the bed, all I could think of was Lou and Sam aged five, coming to see me for the first time and being dragged away screaming. And Sara shouting at me for ripping their father out of their lives. Some time that day, after rewinding and fast-forwarding in my nut and chopping up the facts and the lies and the stuff I'd use in my defence, I decided to pack it in. If I went down on this lot, I would finish with crime. I'd stop being a villain. Not for me, but for the twins. I didn't know what I'd do for money, but ten years would be plenty of time to prepare. And if Lou or Sam came to see me in the shovel, I'd promise them this would be the last one. I'd never made them that promise before, and they'd know I meant it, and I would mean it. I wouldn't ever let someone take me away again.

I asked no one for nowt that day, and when they looked through the Judas or brought me food, the cops saw I didn't give a toss about them or their cell or their charges. They couldn't look inside my head, but I'd already won the battle there. When night came, under a single blanket and using the second as a pillow, I slept well.

Breakfast came the next morning, a sergeant opened up for the tray an hour later. 'You smoke?'

'I can take them or leave them,' I said.

He took a packet out, lit up, and offered me one. I took it. I knew his game – he wasn't playing for the CID, he was just fucking nosey. A lot of uniformed have the hump with detectives. They think they watch too much television, that they're a bunch of posers. This guy felt left out of what was obviously a big operation centred on me. He tried chatting me up, but sod him. He gave me another snout and went. In the afternoon, another button boy came in with a towel and soap.

'Wash up. Don't hang around, we might change our minds.'

'Please yourself. It's you who'll get a noseful.'

He took me down the corridor. Two other uniforms in attendance, but I wasn't shy. Off came the shorts for a stand-up bath. Play your games all day, you turkeys.

At ten o'clock on that second night, a big move came. I knew it was ten because the CID who opened the door told me. He also told me my brief was here. He stepped aside and in came John Carlisle, rumple-slacked and loose-sweatered, looking like he'd just got up from watching the TV at home. His briefcase looked businesslike enough, though.

'You can lock the door.'

The filth stayed put.

'I'll ring the bell when we're done.'

CID shrugged and split. John came and sat next to me on the bunk. After two days in the peter, I was pretty sure it was clean. Even so, I spoke quietly. 'How did you know?'

He threw a glance at the door and whispered back, 'I had a call from another solicitor at home.'

He glanced again and leant a bit closer. I smelt the tang of coffee on his breath.

'I was in front of the box watching the match. He said he'd been called by a client who gave him my name and yours and wanted to know if you'd been arrested. And if so, where were you being held. The other solicitor had a contact in the force, apparently. He told me where you might be. So I came down.'

'And where are we?'

'Didn't they tell you?'

'I didn't ask.'

'Bootle Street.'

'I wasn't sure,' I said. 'Go on.'

'So anyway, I showed up and asked to see you.'

'When?'

'Few hours ago. I've been waiting ever since. They seemed to think I'd give up after a while.' He stood up and took his coat off, folded it on his lap and sat down. 'I was very sorry to hear about Leon.'

'He was a good man.'

He nodded. 'Anyway, half an hour ago, I was called into an office. There was a Detective Superintendent Lickorish there. He's in charge of the murder inquiry into Leon's death.'

'Lickorish. Is that his real name?'

'Yes.'

'Did you ask him why he hadn't changed it?'

'What?'

'His name.'

'No.' John looked confused.

I shrugged. 'Go on,' I said. 'About Leon.'

'Well. He told me he's now Senior Investigating Officer into the three matters they're holding you for. They want to interview you tomorrow morning at seven. That's an hour before the PACE time runs out. They're probably going to charge you with one or all of the offences they have in mind. Then they can get you in court in the morning. That's two murders and one drug-dealing. And they found a gun in your Rover, they'll be charging you with unlawful possession of a firearm as well. Are you taking all this in?'

'Yeah. Go on.'

'The rules mean they had to give me the gist of what they want to ask you about. In two of the matters, they want to ask you about people you know and your whereabouts at certain times on two certain days, one a few weeks back, another very recently. On the third inquiry, they're talking about two tapes which they found at a service flat where you've been living recently. Under a false name according to them.'

'Have you brought any cigarettes, John?'

'Yes. I forgot, sorry.' He pulled a pack and a lighter from his pocket and handed them over. I lit up. He didn't smoke.

'They're a bit cagey on the contents of the tapes,' he went on. 'They just say it's connected to a drugs deal at the Midland, a few days back. That's it.'

I inhaled deeply.

'They've said fuck all to me.'

I blew out and watched the smoke curl for a second.

'Why are they talking about three matters? Obviously, I know about Leon's death.'

'It was in the paper.'

I put my mouth right up to his ear. 'The tapes may fit in with a trade at the Midland. What else are they on about? Leon was my best pal. Full stop. If they want to charge me with his murder on that basis, then let them. But what's this other murder? What the fuck's it got to do with me? Do these pricks think I'm some kind of serial nut or what?'

John looked at me without speaking for three enormous seconds.

'Don't you know about the other guy? The guy on Thursday night?'

'What other guy?'

'The guy in the Royal Infirmary. Side ward, he had a uniform guard on him. But it was low key, and the blue was off chatting up a nurse. Someone came in wearing a white coat and put four bullets in him. They nicked the guy in his motor twenty minutes later, he had the gun in the side pocket. Game set and match. Your problem is, they're trying to tie you up in it.'

I'd been about to spark up another cigarette. I clicked the lighter shut and took the fag out of my mouth. 'The man who got killed,' I said. 'Did they give you a name?'

'No.'

It didn't matter. I knew his name all right. An execution in the Royal Infirmary hospital. An execution that I was tied into.

Charlie Pearson wouldn't be doing any more talking to the law. Charlie Pearson wouldn't be talking to anybody. Jesus H. Christ. I stuck the cigarette back in and snicked on the lighter. Another huge second, then I said, 'John, can you do me a favour? Will you slip off for a coffee or something, and ask this firm whether you can come back in, say, half an hour? I need to think. Do you mind?'

The brief made a face, but he nodded.

'Leave the snout and the lighter, please. I'll say I nicked them off you if they get found.'

'All right.' He stood to go.

'On the drugs deal, John. Who's running it?'

'I heard the name Craze. But I think he's just minding it for now. I got the impression it was pro tem.'

'No one said anything about a superintendent called Jacks?'

'Hamilton Jacks?'

'You know him?'

'I know of him. I've not heard his name today.'

'OK. Thanks. One other thing – how did United get on?'

He picked up his coat and threw it over his shoulder. 'Nil nil. Newcastle came for a point and they got it.'

'Never mind. Can't win 'em all.'

'No.' He rang the bell and someone opened up for him.

I stretched out on the bunk again and closed my eyes. The call to John from the other brief must have originated from Monty, and that meant Monty knew the full SP, and that meant he was safe for now. The Pearson thing was far more pressing.

The fact that the shooting went off only hours after I'd declared Pearson a grass to Chambers and his cousin made me very uneasy. A picture flashed up of Chambers walking into that side ward and shooting Charlie Pearson. This was very bad news, very bad news indeed.

With an effort, I moved on. Hamilton Jacks was apparently off the Midland, and Harry's john Dave Craze was holding the reins. Presumably Hamilton Jacks's superiors weren't buying his excuses about where the hundred grand went. But Craze, or whoever finally took on the responsibility for the Midland, would still be up my arse anyway.

So, back to the matter in hand – the likelihood that I was going to be charged with two counts of conspiracy to murder and one of possession with intent to supply. And the gun. It didn't really make any difference that – from what I knew – there wouldn't be enough to hang a cat on either of the two killings. With four counts like that and a shooter on site, no jury would give me a complete walkout.

No smoke without fire. The police can't have got it wrong on four cases.

I could hear the words in the jury room already. They'd hand down a guilty on at least one, and with charges like that, one was all it took.

I had to do something before the charges were laid. Once that happened and the process began, the train wouldn't stop until it got to the crown court. I had a chance on some of it. Time to play the only card I had.

A couple of minutes later, there were heavily booted footsteps and the jingling of keys. The cell door opened and John showed with two polystyrene cups.

'This is what passes for coffee round here.'

The door slammed behind him. I sat up and took the cup, then patted the bed next to me. 'Come on, don't be shy.'

He sat and pulled out a yellow legal pad from his briefcase, clicked it shut and rested the case on his knees like a desk. Then he smoothed the top sheet and pulled out an expensive silver pen which he clicked.

'First off,' I said. 'Is Lickorish still on site?'

'Yes.'

'Is that really his name?'

'Yes.'

'What's his first name?'

'Brian.'

'Fucking hell.' By now I was speaking almost normally. If the peter was bugged they'd have my message soon enough anyway. 'Bizarre. OK. Here's what I want you to do. Go to Lickorish, tell him I had absolutely fuck all to do with Leon or the other murder. Got that? Nothing.'

'That's it, is it?'

'No. You can also tell him I haven't ever plotted to trade in a class A drug.'

'And?'

'If he wants to charge me with any of those offences then it's up to him and the CPS. But there's more to this than they're letting on to you, John.

'The guy shot in the Infirmary was called Charlie Pearson. He was a long-time grass of theirs, they'd had him on the payroll for years. Those two tapes they told you about are phone-taps of Pearson talking to his handler. The cops used Pearson for a sting at the Midland Hotel which went wrong and ended up with Pearson screaming for protection because he'd been outed as a grass. The cozzer Hamilton Jacks was Pearson's handler.'

John's left eyebrow twitched.

'The problem for the filth is this. There's a third tape, far more damaging. This third tape has Hamilton Jacks talking to the copper you mentioned before, Dave Craze. Craze tells him Pearson is in hospital, can't be moved and he wants protection. Hamilton Jacks tells Craze that he wants to make Pearson a target. And that's what's happened. Pearson's dead because of them. Let them explain that to a jury. And let them think on what that will do for future informant recruitment figures.' I tugged at my fag again.

'One more thing. They needn't think they'll get away by claiming public interest immunity bollocks. There'll be no immunity certificates when it gets into the papers. And I will make sure it gets into the papers, John.'

He looked up. 'Is that it?'

I nodded. He closed the pad and stuck it back in his case. We were silent for a beat or two.

'OK. You know your own mind. I'm not going to change it. I will change the wording a little. Make it sound more like a declaration of intent rather than an ultimatum. It's probably better coming from me than from you, anyway. Saves them a bit of face. They'll still get you on the gun, though. Prints or no it was in your Rover, down to you.'

I flicked some ash on to the deck and shrugged.

He went on. 'I just hope you know what you're doing, that's all.' He looked at his watch.

'Twenty past eleven. I may as well kip down in the cell next door, if they'll let me. Don't want to be late. I'm sure they'll rent it me for the night.'

I forced a grin.

'I'll get back for six. Oh. While I think of it.' He went into his case again and took out a sheaf of Legal Aid papers, spread them out on his case and handed me his pen. It felt very heavy. I knew where to sign.

'Thanks.'

He stood and rang the bell. As the footsteps came down the corridor, he looked down at the bed. 'Sleep well. Be seeing you.'

'And you.'

The door opened and he slipped out. I heard movement away and the mutter of conversation fading.

I threw my fag end into the karsi and lay down on the mattress, paper boiler suit rustling as I laid my head on the rolled blanket, pulled the other up to my neck and stared at the ceiling. A few seconds later, the main bulb clicked off and I was left in a soft red glow. The only bit of white light was what came in through the door flap.

I turned my head to the wall and closed my eyes to think.

I'd be charged the next morning. Old Bill would ask for and get a remand in custody. That might mean another few days in police cells, or a straight move to jail. Strangeways again. At least in the nick, my physical conditions would improve. If they were sticking to the murder bollocks, then I would go on the book. That would at least guarantee me a single peter and I drifted into sleep thinking of who was in the shovel.

About the same fucking mob when you walked out a few weeks ago.

It seemed like I'd never left.

My cell had no windows. That meant no visible difference between night and day. But this was a police station, and the building's routine sounds indicated the time as well as any light change. So when the two young coppers unlocked my door the next morning, I'd been awake for a few minutes. I don't like being walked in on while I sleep.

A blond-haired kid said that it was six fifteen and that I was being interviewed at seven. Would I like a wash and a cup of tea? Of course I said yes. The two uniforms led me down the corridor to the sink, where I performed the full strip routine again. Then they put me back in my box and brought me two polystyrene cups of very strong sweet tea. Halfway through the second brew and the fag I was having with it, the door opened and they let John in. He looked like a brief this time, fully suited and booted.

'Did you get much kip?' I asked.

'Three or four hours. I set the alarm for half five. And I booked an alarm call. Three in fact. I was paranoid about sleeping on.'

'I know the feeling. Pistols at dawn.'

'What?'

'How they nicked me. Coppers round my bed with guns. I'll bet Sue was happy about you jumping around first thing.'

'Well, she's pretty much adjusted to the job by now.' He sat on the bunk and dropped his voice. 'I'm a bit puzzled here.'

'What do you mean?'

'There's something going on. Lickorish was waiting for me when I got here, stood next to a uniformed inspector. The button boy wants to know if there's a reason you couldn't have been staying at your place in Chorlton. He wants me to ask you.'

My instinct was to tell them to fuck off and mind their own business. 'Tell them to fuck off and mind their own business.'

'Can't we try something else?'

'Like?'

'I don't know. You should, though.'

I shrugged. 'Oh, all right, tell them I'm thinking about moving house and I was – I was staying in Whalley Range for a bit to see whether I liked the area or not.'

John raised an eyebrow.

'You're raising an eyebrow, John.'

'Well. Seeing if you liked the area?'

'Not a crime to be eccentric.'

'All right. I suppose facetious is an improvement on unhelpful. I'll go and talk to them. I'll be right back.'

He didn't come back at all. When the door opened next, about ten minutes later, it was the young blond copper. Two things odd here. One, he was on his own. Before, there'd been a couple of them at least, every time they opened my box. The second was that blondie was carrying a sports bag that looked familiar. He took a couple of paces and laid it on the deck near my feet. 'This is yours,' he said. 'From the flat where they picked you up. We fetched you some clothes. They want you to get changed and come to the interview room.'

'What's wrong with the Hugo Boss number?' I plucked at the paper suit. The button boy laughed and looked even more like a teapot. Then he left me to get changed.

I picked up the bag and tipped it on to the bench. Socks, shirt, strides, trainers. If I didn't know better I'd have said they were letting me go.

I rang the bell when I was ready and blondie ambled me down the corridor. Now I wondered if I did know better.

These fuckers are letting me go, no way are they going to let a suspected double murderer and class A dealer walk through their place with a kid who's hardly out of school. I'm going home. They've got no fucking evidence, it's as simple as that. What about the gun?

Blondie led me into the charge room. The desk sergeant was there, freshly on by the look of him, all tidy and efficient. Stood around were a uniformed inspector and a podgy plainclothes in his fifties I took to be the man Lickorish. In a corner, foot against the wall and looking triple chuffed, was John Carlisle.

By now the warm relief flooding my body was almost sexual. So much so, that when the desk man started reading out my address – having got the nod from me as to who I was – I swear I got the beginnings of a hard on. And halfway through the rest of the spiel – after the explanation of section twenty nine police bail – I could have asked him if he was ready for me.

And when he finally asked me to sign for the twirls of the Rover, telling me they'd brought it in to search and it was now in the compound outside, I seriously felt like giving him a wet kiss on his lovely bristling moustache. Tongues and all.

Fucking bloody hell.

Neither of the other two coppers spoke a word during the proceedings. John strolled over and said about them informing him if they wanted to question me about the 'further inquiries' on the bail sheet. The sergeant muttered back the usual, then John said, 'Can we go, then?'

For a twelve-month second, the desk sergeant sat scribbling and blanked the question. During this wait, I had a crazy flash that caused me to do something even crazier. I pinched myself. I grabbed a fold of skin on the back of my neck and gave it a good crunch. If this was a dream, finish it now, don't wake me when I'm through the fucking door. What about the gun, they're going to nick you for the gun when you walk out the door, what about the fucking gun?

The desk sergeant looked up.' Yeah, you can go whenever you like.'

We schlepped out and down the corridor. John was rabbitting to me quietly as we made for the exit, but I wasn't listening. All I knew was that the filth had no evidence. Sure, they'd have been on the plot when I met Pearson in the health club, but so what? With the grass lying dead in the morgue, there was no fucker to say what the meet had been about. And they'd obviously drawn a forensic and ID blank with the Midland. I thought of the description the hotel receptionist would have given of old Tom. That would have the fuckers scratching their heads.

What about the fucking gun? They're going to nick you as soon as you step outside.

I noticed we'd stopped walking. John was saying hello to a guy parked up on a bench. Poncey shoes, tasty kettle and flash all over. Had to be a brief.

John beckoned me across. 'This is Paul Shapiro.'

I knew the name. He had a reputation as an expensive bail jockey. Shapiro nodded. I nodded back. 'All right?'

Then I stood away and let the two of them rabbit, drifting away again to think about the result I'd apparently just had.

'Up in front of the stipe this morning,' Shapiro said, 'about as much chance of bail as I have of making President of the Law Society.'

Then I knew one hundred per cent they were talking my business.

'Royal Infirmary,' said Shapiro. 'He looks like he's in trouble.'

He was about to say more, but he'd clocked my interest. Nathan Chambers. I needed to hear him say it.

'Your client,' I said. 'Would it hurt to tell me his name?'

Shapiro looked at John. Glancing at me, John said, 'He was pulled in on something else, but the business your man was nicked for was mentioned.'

The other lawyer was silent, but I could read the way his clock was ticking. I'd had a tug over the same villainy that his client was dubbed up for. I was going home, his man was going nowhere. That could mean I was bad news for his client. He looked at John and could see that he'd also fingered the entrails.

'My client's been in here since early Friday morning. He's not said a word to them. You can take my word for that, Paul.'

Shapiro relaxed a couple of notches. 'Normally I couldn't, but they've already given my man's name out, it'll be all over the papers, local TV and radio too. So there's no harm. Jack Keane.'

I felt slammed in the gut. A dozen questions shot up in my head. My impulses told me to get knowledge, there and then. Find out what's been happening. Get this Shapiro to pass a message to Jack.

This guy's a brief, and he's Jack's brief, not yours.

Also, Shapiro was a bail jockey and popular with the faces, but that didn't bring him onside. Plenty of lawyers stick as many in as they get out.

'I'll be outside, John. Need some fresh air.' I nodded at Jack's brief. 'Nice to meet you, Mr Shapiro.'

I spun on my heel and made for the door. The echoes of my past clanked and rattled and came with me. I hoped neither John nor Shapiro could hear them.

There were double doors at the end of the corridor. I pushed through them to the car park and felt a feeble winter sun across my face. I took in portakabins, a few cars, the skyline. None of it looked right. I knew nothing would look right for a while. A couple of lungfuls of cold air, then the doors opened again and John Carlisle said, 'What was all that about? Do you know his client or something?'

'Yeah.' I scanned the car park. Couple of button boys getting out of their jam butty, nothing else. I looked back to John. 'I know him. The long story I promised you. It may be even longer. Why aren't they doing me for the gun, John?'

He looked at me like I was an idiot. 'Very funny, ha ha. You could have told me yesterday. Made me look like a right pillock.'

'What?'

'I said: you could have told me yesterday.' Then he stopped and it was like someone had wiped a sponge across his face. 'You didn't know, did you?'

'Know what?'

'The Beretta they found in your Rover was a replica. Looks like a gun, feels like a gun, but it won't fire. It was a rep for gun-nutter collectors. Very good one too, the button boys couldn't tell the difference. Wasn't until they sent it to forensics the armourer saw it. He didn't know before he'd started to strip it down. Who sold it to you?'

I pulled out my keys and jangled them as a distraction. 'Do us a favour, John. Walk to my motor with me. See me off the plot. Just in case they've got something in mind.'

'Who?'

'Police. You know their style.'

We crossed to the pound. I forced something out as we walked.

'What do you reckon to my position?'

'You know as well as I do, you've got them by the bollocks.'

'The tapes?'

'I don't think the tapes were the deciding factor. If they'd had the evidence, they'd have said do your worst and you'd have been off to Strangeways. Question now,' he said as we reached the Rover, 'is will they get any evidence?'

We were at the car. The twirls were out of my pocket and in my hand. Very deliberately, I held his gaze.

'Well? Will they find any?' he persisted.

Did you look someone in the eye when you were telling the truth or trying to cover up the fact that you were lying?

I shrugged and slid the key into the lock. 'It's possible they might be able to come up with something on the Midland caper. If they want me for Leon, they'll have to go for a blatant fit-up.'

As it happened, I had no intention of hanging around waiting for them to dig up anything fresh on anything, but it was neither the time nor the place to declare this to my brief. I stuck my hand out instead.

'Thanks for everything, John.' Hang on. 'Oh John, could you do me a favour? Could you lend me a few quid? I'm right out.'

He dug out a couple of twenties, nodded and turned away. I got into the motor, fired it up, and pulled out on to Bootle Street. At the service flat, Rosie the landlady was feeding the dogs in the kitchen at the back. She seemed surprised but quite pleased to see me. I apologised for any fuss my nicking had caused, telling her that it had been a misunderstanding, now – of course – cleared up.

'I was going to be leaving about now, anyway,' I said. 'As the police have done my packing for me, I might as well go. Keep the deposit, Rosie.'

'Your stuff's in the living room,' she said, leading the way. 'They woke me up and asked me some questions about you before they crashed in. I just told them you were a quiet guy who paid his rent.' She knew what I was.

'Thanks, Rosie.'

She'd packed what the filth had left into a couple of laundry bags.

'Sorry again for the inconvenience.'

'Don't worry about it, love.'

I drove back to Chorlton feeling bits of my story over the last month finally slotting into place. Jack Keane knew the difference between a rep and a real Beretta and the knowledge made me sick. All this time and I'd never seen it in front of my face. I remembered Foston Hall, Christmas Day all those years ago, shouting through the gaps. I could feel the flakes of paint on my lips.

The flat was rubble. Old Bill had given it a right seeing to. Carpets up, bed and chairs dismantled, the lot. At least they'd used the twirls on the Rover key ring to get in, rather than their favoured method of taking a sledgehammer to the door.

I spent the morning clearing up and trying not to think. My head was firmly up my arse and I needed activity to get normal again. I did laundry, bought food, went to a call box and called John Carlisle. He'd spoken to Monty's brief, and Monty was fine. We agreed I'd drop round his office the next day about three. Later I drove to another box and rang Noriko, then I rang Casey on his mobile and filled him in.

'Did you get a visit?'

'Not yet, but I'll be double careful for a few days. Ernie called with a message from Nathan Chambers. He wants you to know he'll be keeping out of the way for the while. He assumes you'll understand. Do you?'

'Charlie Pearson.'

'Did you know Chambers was connected to Jack?'

'We do now.' I hung up and drove home, turning my options over in my head. When I walked out of the police station that morning, my first impulse had been to keep walking. Now I wondered if I wasn't making the same rick as a few nights before.

One, was I really in the frame for Leon's death? Pick that to bits: OK, we were known to be close, and most murder victims are killed by people near them. My smudge had probably been hawked around the plot where Leon went from day one. They'd found no one to place me at the scene so far, so it was unlikely they'd do it now.

Two, the Midland coup. This was a lot fresher. However, the odd lot had known before the event that my name was on it, and yet this morning – days later – they were still going nowhere.

I stayed at Chorlton that evening. Mostly on my bed, drinking and thinking.

The next morning, I was driving along Upper Brook Street in a twelve-month-old Frontera. I'd needed a renter for a couple of days now that the Rover was blatantly down to me. I couldn't raise Laurie at his car shop so I'd dropped into the club on the off-chance. The motor belonged to Fat Len, a ticket tout and general wheeler dealer from Moston. He'd been into a good game when I pulled him and asked about wheels. He said I could have his for the day for fifty.

I stopped at a box and rang Noriko in London. She thought I was returning her call; she'd left a message on the answerphone in Chorlton a couple of hours ago. Mr Alexander would be where we last met by six that evening.

'Will you be speaking to him before tonight?'

'Yeah, yeah.'

'Then tell him I'll see him.'

'OK.'

I hung up, then stuck some more coin in and dialled my flat. A tap into my answerphone told me I'd got new messages. This I knew. I pressed in the code and listened. Noriko first, then: 'It's me. Harry.'

Harry?

'I need to see you urgently. Please call me.'

I played it again, heard the time it was left and looked at my watch. She'd only rung ten minutes ago. One more listen.

'. . . urgently. Please call me.'

There was an edge to that *please*. More trouble. More coin. She picked up immediately.

'It's me. What's happening?'

She breathed out fast over the mouthpiece. Magnified, it rushed in my ear like wind. 'I need to see you, fast as you can.'

'What is it?'

'Not over the phone. Can you come over straight away?'

'Behave yourself, Harry, I'm on my way.'

I hit the Mancunian Way three minutes later, doing eighty. Her voice sounded like it was on top. My mind flashed back to the busy Craze as I made Chester Road. Was he on the run round for his master? I swung left on to the M60, surged up above ninety, slipped across Sale and down Brooklands Road. A couple of minutes later I was walking up to her door blimping around for anything moody – Old Bill or villain. No one parked up and it didn't feel like a mousetrap, but still.

I buzzed the intercom. 'It's me, Harry.'

I took the stairs two at a time, but something jerked me up as I made her landing. It was the smell. Man's scent, full on, aftershave. Crisp-edged cologne.

I thought coppers, Hamilton Jacks.

If they've hurt her, I'll kill them.

I heard a door hinge and she was there, standing at the top of the flight.

'What's going on?' I took the last few stairs.

'It's OK, it's OK.'

'Has anyone hurt you?'

'No. I'm fine. Come in.' She took my arm and led me through her hall and into the lounge. As we went in, a man rose from the couch. He turned as he stood and looked at me. The scent got stronger as I got him full face on. Well, fuck me.

'Who are you here for?'

'Mr Webster.'

'John Webster?'

'I never learnt his first name.'

The Asian smiled widely. 'Jack told me you'd be on time. On the stroke, he said. Come in.'

Harry was at my shoulder.

'He phoned as a client. Then he told me he wanted to speak to you. He let me pat him down. But I knew he wasn't any danger to you. He isn't any danger to me either, but he didn't know that.'

'No,' I said.

'Jack told me you'd be on time. On the stroke, he said. Come in.'

Sonny Jim was stretching out his hand to me.

I said, 'It's quite all right, Harry. Sonny and I are old friends.'

I didn't take his paw, I walked round him instead. He revolved on his heel to keep me in sight.

'Why don't we all sit down,' I said.

Sonny lowered his arse back on to the sofa.

'I did OK, didn't I?' said Harry.

'You did fine, Harry.'

I hadn't taken my eyes off Sonny, but Harry was right. This man was no trouble to either of us.

'How's Jack?' I said.

'I don't know.'

'Where's Jack, then?'

'In a cell. As you know.'

He'd put on weight since we'd last met. And he'd aged badly too.

This man did his bird hard.

'I had to make this move with the lady to get to see you. I thought you might go for me if I fronted you up.'

'Tea?' It was Harry.

'Yes please,' I said. 'You?'

He shook his head and she headed for the kitchen. Now I swung my legs either side of a hardback chair and sat.

'I don't know how much you know.'

'A little more than I did yesterday.'

'Well, anyway.' He stopped and sighed loudly, then looked up at me like a sheep. He had soft brown eyes.

He wants me to like him, I thought.

Sonny began to stumble some words out. 'Jack and I hooked up in the nineties. We were introduced, I was looking for somebody to – he did me a favour.'

Wonder who got hurt?

'We did bits of business, but the plot he wanted you in on, that was the first really serious bit of work.' The words 'bit of work' sounded very odd on his tongue.

'I see.' I reached for my fags, moving slowly so I didn't alarm him. I offered him the pack. He shook his head.

'No. Gave up inside. Only good thing that came out of it. Hard time otherwise. I got fucked for a lot of dough while I was away.'

Halfway through lighting up, I nodded. It happens.

He went on. 'He spoke very highly of you, kept on at me to cut you in. We don't need him, I said, he's worth it, he said, keep on, keep on, keep on. In the end, I couldn't say no. So after all the kicking and screaming, I couldn't believe you turned us down on the deal. It was a lot of money. And you trusted Jack.'

'I did. I just don't trust heroin, that's all.'

Harry came in with tea on a tray. She gave me mine first, then handed him a cup, even though he'd said no. 'I'll be in the kitchen. Phone's off the hook. Shut up shop for an hour.' She closed the door behind her.

I looked back at Sonny. He had the cup to his lips, using both hands to steady it. As I watched him, I realised someone had been singing at me for weeks. I'd heard the melody: Jack's Beretta replica taught me most of the words, but they were still muffled, bits missing. I'd never heard them clearly. Until now.

'How much did you know about?' I said.

'Most of it.'

'The smack in my cell? Putting Terry on a string? All the rest?'

'I knew.'

'Whose idea was it?'

'No one's. Everyone's. Jack and me got nicked, we were in the same cell at Walton. What else could I think? Only him and me knew the details, and then it was on top. They caught us with the first shipment, the whole firm got wrapped up a few days later. And you were away. No contact with anyone. He wouldn't have it, but I kept on at him.' He looked down at his cup. 'I'd never been in prison before. It was a bad time.'

'How long before he believed you?'

'I don't remember. It took a long time to come to trial. Months. Almost a year.'

'But in the end, he believed you.'

'Yes.'

After all those years. I wanted to blame Sonny, but Jack should have known better.

'Did Charlie Pearson know about the heroin trade?'

Sonny's chin sank into his chest a couple inches more. 'Not from me. But Jack used him for most things. And we were all looking the other way.'

'Tell me the rest.'

'Jack put the word out around a few people. After a while, it came back about your nephew being on the, on the . . . '

'Being on the gear.'

He looked up worried. 'The idea was to keep tabs on you through him, maybe work something out. Later it came back you were working with Yoda's son Terry. Then it fell into our laps. You both got nicked and ended up in Strangeways with Nathan. Nathan's a mate of Charlie Pearson.' A tiny smile flicked along Sonny's upper lip. 'He was only on remand. And he walked.'

'Finish it.'

'We thought you were a grass. I wasn't sorry then, but I am now. That's why I came. I didn't have to.'

I sighed. 'We're not done.'

'That's it. I'm going. I don't know whether I'm in the frame for Pearson, but I'm not hanging around to find out. I still do business with Jack, you know. We're connected.'

'You have to finish. Tell me. Did you know before? About the shooting? About Pearson getting shot?'

He licked his lips. 'Few nights ago, Jack came round to my place, storming like a lunatic. He'd done a lot of charlie. I live in Whitefield, you know,' he said, as if it meant something. 'He was screaming about the tape you played to Nathan, Pearson having it with the police who nicked us, Pearson having us over. I live alone, you know.' He wiped his mouth. 'He said he was going to kill Pearson. Showed me a gun.' He shook his head.

'I told him he was mad. We could order it done, if it had to be done at all. Or he could, anyway.'

'Yeah.'

'Then he started slagging me off. Paki this and nigger that. Then he left, still screaming.'

'And what did you do?'

'Packed a bag, made some arrangements. I'm going away now. I won't be back for a while. Until it's cooled down.'

'When did Jack start calling me a grass?'

'There was something else. The copper who nicked us dropped a hint with your name on it. Jack wouldn't have it at first. But then he never heard from you.'

'This was eight years ago, wasn't it? I was on my toes.'

'I know that now. But then I was sure. And Jack told me no one else knew about him and me.'

'Except Pearson.' I wanted to hear it from his lips. 'What was the name of the copper that nicked you?'

'Keith Hamilton Jacks. Jack knew him from before, long time he told me.' He shifted on the couch. 'I ought to go.'

'One last thing. The phone calls to my ex-wife and kids. Whose idea was that?'

He shook his head. 'I didn't know about them at the time. I only heard later. And I said it was out of order.'

I believed him. It didn't really matter now. Heavy with the years on my back, I stood and held out my hand. 'All right. You did the right thing in coming here. Sonny, or Jim. Whatever they call you.'

He nodded. 'I'm sorry.'

'The time's done,' I said.

'All right.' He looked towards the kitchen. 'OK if I say goodbye to the lady?'

A minute or so later, they came out together. She walked him to the door. He turned his head at me. 'By the way. It's Anwar.'

'What is?'

'My name. It's Anwar Sidiqi. But Jim will do. Goodbye.'

'Goodbye,' I said, to his back.

I sank on to the couch and listened to the front door click shut. I heard Harry move into the bedroom and a couple of minutes later, she came back into the lounge. She'd changed into a pale blue housecoat and her hair was down, long and shining. 'I heard some of that. It sounded very heavy.'

'It was.'

'Is it over for you, now?'

'I think so. But I'm going away for a while. Like him. There's some dust that needs to settle.'

She took a few paces across to me. I felt and smelt her perfume rush towards me as she pulled my face towards hers and kissed me on the lips. We stayed like that for a few minutes, then she stopped and pulled away.

'He paid me, you know,' she said. 'Just now, in the kitchen. A lot, way over the top. But then I don't come cheap. Where are you going?'

'Italy.'

Her smile dropped. I'd never seen her so lonely.

'Are you all right?'

'Fine. You'd better go. It's time for me to open up again.'

Something was going to happen between us there. Now it never would. We went into the hall. She slipped the latch.

'Have a nice time in Italy.'

'I'll see you, Harry.'

I turned at the bottom of the stairs, but she'd already gone inside and closed up. I went out on to the street and walked slowly to the motor.

I sat in the car for a couple of cigarettes, thinking about Jack Keane and Foston Hall. Calling to each other across the corridor in the seg unit, mouths pressed up to the gaps in the door. Christmas Day twenty-five years ago, Jack shouting he wouldn't go up on to the wing unless I went with him. I felt the flakes of paint on my lips again.

I fired up the motor and went looking for a call box and rang Marcus in his furniture shop. I was lucky, he said tonight was the night for the meet I had in mind. He gave me the address, the time and a few other details. Then I got back into the Frontera and drove down to the centre and bought a ghetto blaster in Argos at the Arndale, the sort that dubs tape to tape. I called Amy, drove across and said I'd like to come round again about five. Then I left the ghetto blaster, grabbed some dough from under the dog's bed and drove down to John Carlisle's office off Deansgate.

'They don't seem to be looking that hard for Leon's killer. They've got Jack Keane for Pearson. The Midland – well, probably least said about that the better, far as they're concerned.'

John's desk was piled with files and papers. He tried to stand his mug on a stack by the phone then thought better of it.

'What about the bail?' I said. 'What happens if I don't go in on the requested date? Will they issue a warrant?'

He thought for a moment. 'Well, if I ring up first and sound them out, and they aren't going to proceed, then they'll probably be happy for you not to go in. It'll save them a bit of face.'

I wasn't worried about jumping police bail. It was hardly a hanging matter. But I'd answered my bail on the last one, which meant I now had a bail record. You never know when one of those will come in handy.

'Ring me a couple of days before the date, and I'll find out the state of play.'

I finished my coffee which was vile, stood and dropped an envelope among the papers in front of him. He made a *What's that?* face.

'Just a drink, John. I put you to a lot of trouble.'

There was two grand in the parcel, as it happened. That meant there'd be a bit of change from a drink, but I felt sure John would come to terms with that. It was one of the reasons he was my brief.

I drove back to Amy's and spent twenty minutes copying the third Hamilton Jacks tape while she got ready for bingo upstairs. I listened to the cozzer hanging Charlie Pearson out to dry, stashed the original, grabbed some more dough and tuned the radio to Classic FM. Then I shouted up there was a little present for her on the table and split before she had time to argue. I drove the Frontera to the NCP in Portland Street, bought a padded envelope at a newsagents in Piccadilly and called Mr Alexander at the Britannia. Monty was in for the night now, he said.

'And I've eaten,' he said. 'In the carvery. Must be the only carvery in the country overlooked by a swimming pool. Fucking crazy.'

I rapped his door a few minutes later. As soon as I was inside, I said, 'Jack Keane's been nicked for Pearson.'

'Yeah, I know.'

'And it was Jack Keane behind all of this,' I said. 'Not Hamilton Jacks.'

'Jesus Christ Almighty.'

I told him about Sonny Jim and also the meet with Chambers in the Benchill flat. I must have spoken for half an hour. Monty didn't interrupt once, something of a first. Nor did he speak for a few minutes after I'd finished. And then it was measured for a change, instead of his usual machine gun rattle and phlegm delivery.

'What an arsehole.' He lit up. 'So, nine years ago, Jack Keane offers you a heroin trade which you turn down. Then Pearson shops Jack and his firm in. The cozzer Hamilton Jacks drops your name in interview, partly to draw attention from Pearson but also from mischief because of the Turk a couple of years previous. He knows the Turk was down to you because Pearson told him. Then this Sonny Jim convinces Jack you must have grassed. You're away on your toes, so eventually he buys it.'

'Which he shouldn't have done.'

Monty's face twitched irritably. 'Yeah, yeah, yeah. But he does. So they start plotting up on you. They get Terry onside via Nathan Chambers who's working for Charlie Pearson. The boy plants the smack in your peter and gets you nicked so you do another eight months. Thus giving them time to plot up with the boy before you walk.'

'Jack's come out in the meantime and he's now running things through Charlie Pearson.'

'They know about Tomas because Nathan's a couple of rungs higher up the food chain from his dealer. So they know when Tomas gets shot, and that night Pearson rings Buckingham Road and puts the frighteners on Sara and the kids. They move, and you come out and start looking for them.'

'Which keeps me looking the other way while Jack Keane mixes me a bottle – as well as giving me a headfuck.'

'Yeah yeah. Something I still don't understand: what was their next intention?'

'Once they'd got me really shook up, I think they were going to lift and kill me, but that's a guess. It started to come undone when I called Jack asking for a gun.'

'What?'

'You wouldn't get me one Monty, and I still felt unsafe round town.'

'All right, go on.'

'I call Jack up, we meet and I tell him what's been happening, and he sees I'll get to the truth soon, even though I'm barking up the Hamilton Jacks tree now, instead of his. He must have got on to Charlie Pearson as soon as he split, and they sent Terry in the next day. Whatever the plan was, Jack wanted it scrambled there and then. Then Terry fucked up with the matchstick . . . '

' . . . we lifted Terry, and Terry gave us Nathan Chambers. You play the Hamilton Jacks – Pearson tapes to Chambers, and he goes running off to Jack Keane who pays Charlie Pearson a visit.'

'And goodnight.'

'Yeah. Goodnight.'

'The gun Jack gave me turned out to be a rep. That's when I knew it was him,' I said. 'Hamilton Jacks was on a separate track. But he knows I'm Tomas's uncle because Pearson told him. He still wants me for the Turk, and Pearson is caught right in the middle.'

'So the Midland coup was a blow in the wrong direction?'

'Yes.'

I poured another cup of coffee and drank it in silence. Monty said nothing either – another record.

'Yes,' I said. 'The first blows didn't come from Hamilton Jacks, they were coming from Jack Keane. The cozzer was just on a watching brief. Pearson probably nudged him a bit in the hope of getting me off the scene, which would suit him. Charlie was working for both sides, which we knew. We just didn't know he was working for both sides against me.'

Monty tugged at his lower lip. 'Apart from that it's been a quiet night.'

He slurped from his cup.

'Wonder what it was like for Charlie Pearson? Jack Keane's got him running around after you, then suddenly so has his master Hamilton Jacks. And it's in Charlie's interests to stitch you up, because if Jack ever props you direct about the grassing, he might believe your story and that would have him looking for who actually done it. And the nomination list for that particular fucking gong is extremely short and includes Pearson himself.'

'It all goes reels when Charlie Pearson walks onstage for the Midland coup. Because his existence depends on being a behind-the-scenes man,' I said. 'We got the right result for the wrong reason.'

'It's all down to Jack Keane, you know. If he really thought you were a grass, he should have come to you. Or for you. But the smack planting and doing Sara like that makes him a twenty-two carat arsehole. End of.' He stood up and reached for a brandy bottle and two balloon glasses. As he poured, he said, 'What are you going to do about him?'

I took the spliff he passed across from a leather case. 'They'll make an example of him for Pearson. It was premeditated, the judge will call it an execution. And he'll be told on the QT that Jack's a hero to some of the younger villains in town. He'll get life with a twenty rec. At least. That'll be plenty of time to regret what he did to me.' The brandy burnt at the back of my throat. 'On the other hand, if he swims the channel, I'll think again. But for now, that'll do.'

'Can't trust no one,' said Monty.

'No,' I said. 'I don't suppose you can. Why are you up here, anyway?'

'On the way to Glasgow. There's a trade going down, the London firm involved want me to mind them while the business is done. But that's work. I've got some knowledge for you.'

He told me that he'd had a long meet that morning with the London face with the line into Old Bill up here. There was some good feedback – direct, said Monty, from a detective working on the Pearson murder itself. Monty didn't know who this detective was, but I didn't think there were that many bent coppers in Bootle Street. I'd now put serious money on it being Dave Craze. You didn't go seeing a high class girl like Harry once a week on a sergeant's wages.

Monty's news was this: Hamilton Jacks was in deep shit. It turned out that when he'd persuaded his superiors to part with the hundred grand flash money, he'd told them it was never going to be out of his sight. He'd obviously thought the coup would justify the means. There was a lot of black swirling around because of Pearson's murder, but they didn't have much solid against him.

'There'll be an inquiry,' said Monty. 'He's suspended for now, and he'll be done for all this, that's the word. Sideways move. Maybe even back into uniform.'

Not enough, I thought.

Monty had no knowledge on how the filth had found me in Whalley Range, just guesses. 'Our man confirms Hamilton Jacks had the full scream out for you.'

'So?'

'So some ponce who knew you – probably someone you hardly know, some fucker off the wing in Strangeways or whatever – they just saw you going into the service flat at Whalley Range, and phoned it in.'

I ran through everyone it might have been in my head, but I gave up. Too many faces and too many names.

'More coffee?'

'Please.'

Monty picked up the phone and ordered more. We sat in silence. A couple of minutes and there was a tap at the door. Swift. I moved into the bathroom and washed my hands. No need to be seen together, even by the floor waiter. Pity you didn't pay more attention to the broader aspects of your security, I thought, as I dried up.

The room door clicked shut and I went back in. Monty poured us more of both, then went on. 'Leon,' said Monty. 'Louie Fenton. He's still away.'

I thought about the chip from Leon's phone. 'Right.'

'And the Bill have statements from two witnesses, one the postman and one a neighbour. They both saw two men leaving the flat.'

A beat.

'Together, around eight. Neither of them look like you, mate. One was a shortarse and bald.'

'Sounds like Louie. And the other?'

'Pretty crap. Tall and that was it. Wore a suit. Postman said grey hair, the neighbour said dark.'

'Louie knows dozens of faces in Manchester. Wonder why they didn't use those two statements as an excuse to keep me in, though.'

'Only Hamilton Jacks really fancied you for it.'

I wanted to talk about who the second man was. But there wasn't much to talk about.

'Maybe it had nothing to do with you,' said Monty.

'I don't believe that. Neither do you.'

He lit another fag and shook his head. 'That slag Pearson must have felt like he was walking on death row every fucking day of the week. Good enough for him.'

He went for the brandy again and drank, staring at the carpet. I thought about Charlie Pearson, dead. Leon, dead. I hoped they wouldn't meet wherever it is that dead villains go. Then I decided that Leon's sins were only venial, but that Pearson's were mortal. They'd not meet again.

I noticed we'd talked ourselves out. The silence got longer. We both knew we were thinking about Leon. Monty spoke first, avoiding the subject. 'What about the future. What's your next move?'

'For once, I'm going to take your advice and go on a long holiday. First thing tomorrow, I'll drive over to Leeds and see the kids again. Then I'll take the rattler down to London. I'll leave the motor for Sara to knock out so that she and the kids can have a holiday as well.'

I stood up and took my glass to the window. From the fifth floor room, moving traffic and a thousand spots of light spread out before me. So familiar. Time to move on.

'I'll take a ferry from Dover on a day ticket and train to Paris. Sleeper overnight to Rome and hire a motor. Then I'm going to drive south and stay there until I feel ready to graft again.'

'Drive south? To Naples, you mean.'

'Yeah, that's right.' I thought of the first time I'd been there. Sitting at a red on the highway around midnight, I'd glanced up as an ancient lorry jumped the lights. The driver was grimy-faced with a cloth cap jammed down on his nut and a fag hanging out the corner of his mouth. He was about twelve.

'Are you going to see her?'

I looked round. I'd forgotten Monty knew. 'Yes. If she wants to see me.'

'You told me she looks like a young Sophia Loren.'

'She does.' I turned back to the window. 'I'll keep in touch with the brief while I'm away and see what the SP is up here. If it's still iffy, I may come back to your end and graft. Give this place a right body-swerve for a while. What do you think?'

'If I was twenty years younger, I'd come with you. I'd like to meet this Sophia. As it is, I've got to keep working on my pension fund. Can't go on forever. Don't get any easier this game, as you know.'

I left Monty at half seven and drove the Frontera up to the address Marcus had given me. The salvage yard in Failsworth was dubbed up, but I could see lights on inside and there was a Toyota 4x4 parked up just outside. How blatant could he get. I parked a few yards down and it came on to rain. I turned off the lights, checked the tape in the envelope on the passenger seat and sat. Twenty minutes, thirty. Maybe Marcus was wrong and this wasn't his night after all. Then movement, and he came out alone. The streetlight was good enough to see him clearly. Short hair cut right close to the scalp, about twenty-five, stocky, a kid. Black strides and DMs, short black jacket done up to the neck against the weather. PC Jim Stefanowitz, the bent copper who answered the call when Tomas got dumped at the Infirmary, crossed the pavement and jumped into the 4x4. I swung my door open, jogged over the road and tapped on his window. He cranked it down.

'You are James Stefanowitz and I claim my ten pounds.'

'What?'

'OK, you're too young to remember the *Daily Mail* money girls. I've got something in my car for you.'

'Fuck off out of it.' He started to crank up again, looking worried.

I rested my hand on the edge of the glass. 'Get out of your car and walk across the road, Stefanowitz. If you don't, I'll let everyone down at the station know what you've been getting up to in there.' I had his attention. 'Out.'

I stood back and let him see my hands were empty. Then I turned and walked for the Frontera. I heard his door open and the bleep as he locked it up. He followed me, just as I knew he would. I got in and opened the passenger door. 'Don't be shy. Get in.'

He sat next to me, breathing lightly. I'd made sure I'd parked out of direct street amber, but I could see his face clearly. He was frightened all right. 'Are you ghost squad?'

'No, James. Not ghost, not internal investigation. I'm just a man who wants a package delivered.' I chucked the envelope with the tape into his lap. 'Give that to Dave Craze at Bootle Street. He'll know what to do with it.'

'What the fuck should I do that for?'

The last month screamed at me – Sara, Lou, Sam, Tomas, Leon, Jack Keane. They all leapt up in my head, shouting and clamouring to be heard. I couldn't speak. Instead, I leant across and pushed inside his jacket and tore out the wad of money I found there. It fell into his lap on top of the envelope. Must have been three hundred quid.

'Is your mother proud of you, Stefanowitz? Your father? Come to your copper graduation, did they? See you march up and down, get your licence. Pose for the class photograph with all the rest of the coppers? Something to be proud of, isn't it, your uniform? And what are you doing now? Running around on earners for the salvage boys.'

'Who are you, talking to me like that?'

I moved further back into the shadows. 'Who am I? I'm John Drake. And I'm John Mason, Andrew Dawson, Danny Warden, Joseph Doyle, maybe someone else. Tomorrow I'll have another name. And you'll still be tramping up and down on earners for villains.'

I tugged two hundred quid out of my pocket and dropped it with the rest. 'There's another couple of hundred for your trouble. Go and see Dave Craze.'

He looked down at the tens and twenties and the envelope. Then he scrabbled the cash together and got out of the car. I reversed and U-turned and went before he'd crossed the road.

I left the Frontera in the NCP on Portland Street, stuck fifty in the glovebox and left the keys on the near back wheel out of sight. Then I called Fat Len at the club and told him where, took a cab up near the M&S in Altrincham and walked the rest of the way to the Rover. The answerphone was flashing when I got in at half eleven. Two new calls.

Sam first, to say they were off school for three days. The background hum and echo on the second made it a nick during association. It was Don Beattie: face in his forties doing a six in Strangeways for travellers' cheques. Didn't know him that well, but here he was asking me to visit him – and in a hurry. Next day in fact. *Urgent*, he said. *Would I mind?*

'The visit's already been booked for half ten tomorrow morning. All you got to do is turn up. Big favour, I would appreciate it.'

I wiped the tape, wondering what he wanted. A prop, a bit of work that couldn't wait till he walked? And so hot, the niceties had to be bypassed. Come to that, how did he get my number? You normally check before you give a face's phone out, and no-one had come asking me. It was a pain in the arse, but you don't blank people inside. I'd see him in Strangeways at half ten and leave after. Too bloody late to argue the toss with myself now.

The ringing was a drill in my chest. But I knew if I did nothing, it would go away. Maybe it was the phone.

Now I opened my eyes and heard it as the doorbell. Someone's thumb was stuck on it, holding it down. I was still half asleep. I tried to bring myself round. The red numbers floated in the dark. Twenty to one, I'd hardly been in bed for half an hour. The noise stopped and I rolled over and grunted, *Imagined it.*

It came again, continuously for about half a minute. Fuck this. There was a fair bet the Wessons would have been on to it by now, and they could do without it.

Naked and angry, I got out of bed, went out into the hallway and took the few paces to my front door and the intercom. There was an orange glow from the street lights. I jabbed angrily at the pad. 'Who the fuck is this and what do you want?'

Crackling and buzzing, then –

'It's me, you cunt. And it's you I want, so open this fucking door.'

'Who the fuck's me?'

He must have stuck his mouth right up to the box. Now I could hear the pure Glasgow poor. 'Detective Chief Superintendent Keith Hamilton Jacks, you slag. Let me in.'

I shot into the living room. One car I didn't recognise out front – a dark saloon, blocking the drive.

Since when did Old Bill come for me in one motor? Come to that, when did they ever ask to come in? What the fuck was going on? Monty had said Jacks was suspended. Two strides and I was back at the door. 'If this is a nicking, Jacks, then break the fucking door down like you usually do. If it isn't, then fuck off.'

The cozzer went snide on top. 'What's the matter, sonny, not feeling brave without your smart-arse lawyer to hide behind?'

Who did he think he was? I hit the pad again. 'The door stays shut to you, Jacks, but I'm getting dressed and coming down. You stay where you are. You want a fucking row, you've got one.'

Back to the bedroom and snap some clothes on. Dave Craze had faster footwork than I expected. He must have called Jacks at home and told him he was going to turn him in for Pearson. Harry said he was ambitious. So now it was right personal for Jacks, as personal as it gets.

I slid my keys out of the lock and pulled my door closed. The stairs and hallway were in darkness. The porch was lit. When I got down

I'd be able to see out, but Jacks would be blind to my coming until I declared it. I crouched for a clear view of the front door. A body in outline through the frosted glass. Hamilton Jacks.

I spread out against the wall and moved down the stairs on the balls of my feet, ducked at the bottom to keep out of his view and edged along the passage to the fire exit. I knew the bar was always kept well oiled. I leant on it and glided out into the back garden. Dead. If this had been a nicking, the filth would have it covered. Hugging the wall for shadow, I slid right, down the side return and crept down the grass verge to the two small trees at the corner. They hid me but I could get a good blimp of my front door. A single figure on the top step peering inside. He was alone there at any rate. That only left the motor. There was a little wind to help the swishing and hum of traffic from the main drag so I crept for the car, still scanning the plot for opposition. Nish. Jacks was single-handed all right.

He was in a late Vauxhall and the driver's window was open. I stepped into the road, opened the driver's door and rapped the horn lightly. The cozzer twisted, saw the shape at his motor and took half a dozen swift strides down the path. He paused at the bottom, seeing me clearly now. I let him take a good look, then closed the door and lost the light. The cozzer stayed put.

'Just wanted to check you're not mob-handed. Not used to dealing with your lot on these terms.'

Jacks made like he had a bad taste in his mouth. 'I don't need a team. I've been locking your kind of rubbish up for years.'

He moved out into the street lights. Big bastard – three or four inches on me and fuck all excess fat. I saw the truncheon too late. He lunged at me. The cosh gave him extra inches and he whapped me in the gut. I went over gasping for breath. Then he slugged me on the nut and that should have been it, but he half lost his balance and staggered against the side of the motor. This gave me enough to whip out and round the pavement side and grab a few breaths in. He came after, truncheon up. Head down, I slammed into his gut. He doubled up with a grunt and the cosh jumped out his hand and chunked off into the dark.

Then we fought properly, standing up.

I smashed his windpipe – but he was fit and when I tried to follow up he went for my bollocks, missed and did my thigh, fuck. But the move had put him off balance, so head down again full on his chin. Bastard back and down, I go down on top of him, fucking hard slap in the face. Fucker stuck me in the mouth. Don't feel it – just hit him harder down and down again, hammer into his face. His fists become palms, he's done.

He started coughing, and the noise startled me into realising we'd fought in total silence.

I stood up and looked round. No lights, no movement, no noise. A quiet south Manchester cul-de-sac. Just me and Hamilton Jacks. Just like he'd said. I crumpled against the bonnet of the motor, breathing very hard and wanting to spew.

The copper pulled himself up. I gasped in and waved at his motor. 'You want to get in and scream, I won't stop you.'

He stood, swaying slightly. His hard rasping breathing sounded even louder than mine. The amber showed me his face was a mess, one eye half closed already.

'As far as I'm concerned, this is between you and me. But I think you're done now, Jacks. Here, and as a copper. But I tell you . . .' I rasped in some more air. 'Go near my family again like you did before, and I'll fucking kill you. And if I get lifed off for doing it, I'll do every day with a smile on my face.'

I wiped my mouth and held his eyes for a second. Then I brushed past him and up the garden. Inside the flat a few seconds later, I heard the sound of his motor cough into life. He pulled off and I listened till the noise faded away. Then there was just the distant buzz of the main drag and the light movement of the trees in the breeze.

All the strength went out of me and I slid into a squat against the front door. After a few minutes of heavy breathing and heavier nausea, I straightened up and went into the kitchen. Sleeping pills, painkillers and brandy went into a mug. I slung the lot down, filled the sink with cold water and tugged my sweater up over my head.

Fuck.

The move seemed to rip my scalp off. I pulled a couple of towels out of a drawer, took a deep breath and stuck my nut under the water. And again. I dabbed off with one towel, soaked the other and pressed it gently against my nut. Fuck, again. I filled the mug with more booze and staggered to the bedroom, dropped on the bed and used the free hand to drag my trainers off. Socks and strides were a job too much. They wouldn't bother the filth if they came crashing in.

This last thought made me laugh. That stabbed me everywhere that could hurt. I decided not to laugh again for a while.

I lay under the quilt with the dripping headgear still in place and I thought about reaching down for the brandy. The tiny tensing of my muscles sent the scream up again. No chance of moving at all, then. I pulled the wet corner of towel away from my nose, with the vague thought I might drown if I wasn't careful. The last bits of my brain were closing down. I remembered I'd set the alarm for seven.

'That's all right, then,' I thought. 'Everything's all right. Let 'em come. Fuck 'em, fuck 'em all.'

18

No one came in the night.

I dragged my eyes open at the radio. There was a knotted rope being pulled tight round my skull and too much light.

Christ.

My insides were promising to chuck up if I moved an inch. Perhaps if I lay very still and waited, that would go away. I lay very still and waited. A wave of nausea swept over me.

Everything hurt. Head, face, arms, thighs, belly, balls – everything he'd hit, and most of the bits in between were out in sympathy. I slid to the edge of the mattress and every shift was a slap. My head was pounding so loud I couldn't hear the news clearly, it was just a muffled beat like a generator a few floors away. I hooked my legs off the bed and on to the deck, felt the impact from knee to neck and shuffled to the bathroom like a ninety-year-old. Cold water, three painkillers.

I needed a ladder for the shower tray. The hot water sent scarfs of pain across every inch of skin. I tensed and twisted the handle to cold, gasped and stuck my head through the curtain for a few deep breaths. Then I folded back in and stood there, letting it numb my nut and cool the rest of the cuts and steak-size bruises down my thighs and ribs.

I noticed the bedroom stank when I came back from the shower so I opened all the windows and stripped the bed. The sheets and the gear I'd had on last night got stuck in a bin liner and slung in the hall, clean underwear and razor went into a carrier bag. And *Through The Looking Glass*. That was my packing. Almost there. I got dressed and dragged a bin liner round for rubbish, bathroom, lounge, kitchen. I necked three mugs of water at the sink and went round again closing the windows, then out into the hall and locked up behind me.

There was a letter from probation on the mat downstairs saying call asap. Old Bill would have worded Pam post-Midland, she probably wanted to know what the hell and why. Well, I was fucked if I was going to walk into any probation office right now. I'd bell her from London. Say I was shit scared down to being nicked on a moody for two murders and the drugs deal and that I was keeping away for a bit. And if it eventually meant a couple of weeks in the slammer while John Carlisle argued the toss with the Home Office, then fine. I opened the street door and jammed the rubbish bag into the bin. The move sent an electric storm up my right arm and whapped the back of my neck.

If there were watchers, I wouldn't have looked like a man about to leave town and split for Europe as I walked down the garden to the motor. And if they had a tap on my line, the listeners would know I was headed for Strangeways already. I drove on the mirror anyway.

I dropped the clothes at the laundry, drove for the centre and made the Ramada about nine fifteen. I ordered coffee and gave the lounge a quick coat, then split for the karsi and its wall to wall mirrors. Apart from a split lip and a bit of bruising round the cheekbone, my face didn't look too bad. And I was dressed smart, not too much like a face. Have to do, anyway.

I found a telephone off the lobby and dialled their number in Leeds, hoping they'd be in and alone. The answerphone picked up, Lou's voice: 'Hi there, we can't come to the phone right now. You know what to do.'

The machine beeped and I left a message saying I'd call at the weekend. I wouldn't see them before I left. Christmas break was a few weeks, I'd ring them from Italy. Maybe ask them to come across and join me for a while. Maybe.

Same crew in the lounge when I got back. Otherwise I'd have taken every single credit-carded, suited-up, travelling-in-biscuits sales man and woman to be a nailed-on busy of a certain rank or over. The girl brought my tray across. Cigarette, coffee, almond biscuit. There was a café in Naples I used to go to, down on the roundabout by the Piazza del

Plebiscito. The tables were a few inches from the road, vans and buses churned up the dust as we drank, little kids used to come in pairs and beg for money or food. I was a right easy mark, she used to try and wave them away but they ducked under her arms and snatched whatever I held out for them. They should have been in school. So should she, that day. Teaching her class, not bunking off to grab an afternoon with me. I thought of the first time I saw her, reading alone in a café. A mass of curly black hair with clear olive skin and long eyelashes, big hoop earrings and a deep green designer jacket thrown over her shoulders. She looked like Sophia Loren at twenty, and she looked like another man's woman.

I waved the waitress over and gave her a tenner. 'Do you think you could get me ten coins for that. Maybe a few fifties if you've got them?'

She smiled. Either she liked me or she was new. 'My pleasure.'

Back at the payphone, I dropped in five quid. It rang four times and the message clicked on, first in Italian, then in soft accented English:

'Hello and thank you for calling. If it's urgent, you can ring me at the university on 081 253 1111. Otherwise, leave a message at the tone and I'll get back to you.'

She was still there. My hand stopped juddering.

'It's Wednesday the eleventh. I'm coming down to Naples, I'll be leaving later today. Don't call me at home, I'll try you this evening. OK. Bye.'

I hung up. The rest could wait.

I got out *Through the Looking Glass* at my table and flicked to what's almost the final chapter, the one where Alice becomes a Queen. 'Everything was happening so oddly that she didn't feel a bit surprised at finding the Red Queen and the White Queen sitting close to her, one on each side.' I used to read it to her in the afternoons when we were lying on the grass out in the hills. She could never understand why Alice wasn't more excited when everything changed for her. 'Alice knows no one ever really changes,' I'd said.

The painkillers were starting to wear off as I made the motor. I'd be staying sore for a while yet. Fine. I wanted my mind clear for the meet with Don and then the leaving of it, all of it.

I drove past the cathedral, under the bridge and the prison tower came up. Up Southall Street, hang a sharp right and park. I'd never felt less like going to prison as a free man.

With a few minutes to spare I lit up a fag and drifted up and down the pavement. I thought of coming out, Terry dancing at the gate and everything he'd brought with him.

Exactly one month and one day ago. To the day.

I could still blank Don, and now that seemed the best thing to do. He wouldn't know I'd got his message. I looked up at the prison. I'd know I'd blanked him.

The screw on the desk asked for my name and Don's. He checked my ID, looked at his list and waved me on. I emptied my pockets into a tub a second screw held out. He took my jacket and gave it a feel, then dropped it on to the conveyor belt which took it through a machine like an airport luggage scanner. I walked through a metal door frame without a squawk and a third screw patted me down, gave me the dough back, put the rest of my gear into a locker and handed me a small metal key.

I made for the lift. A few yards away, there were about nine hundred men in single cells and twoed up. Playing pool, writing a letter in their peter or getting someone to do it for them, buying a bit of snout, mopping down the floors, sticking photos on their wall with dabs of toothpaste, queuing for the phones, queuing for a rubdown before visits. There'd be some down in the seg unit waiting for a beating, or recovering from one. All the buzz and chatter and shouts and echoes filled my head and the images swam around and made me giddy with their colours and their drabness.

Two mums and two kids and me. We shuffled in, a screw in the armour-plated ops room saw us on the camera and threw a switch. We whirred up in silence to the main waiting room where we shuffled out and gave our names to yet another screw at a table.

This room was warm with bodies. Some of the faces said it was their first time, some of them made it their thousandth. There was an argument going on at a window between a screw and a tired blonde girl over something she was handing in for one of the lads. Lou'd had similar arguments over me, I knew. Same nick, same window. Maybe the same screw.

A list of names was shouted out, Don Beattie was one of them. We shuffled through a door and up some stairs for the main visiting area where a woman screw with a security stamp pressed an ultraviolet number on the back of our right hand.

This was part of the new Strangeways and it was huge and cavernous and broadly L-shaped. Big windows and powerful lights, to make sure the banks of security cameras hanging from the ceiling and corners got a good picture. Near the door where the cons came in was a raised platform with a couple of tables. This was the screws' station, wired up to the watchers in the camera room. The Cat A section was beyond this – a handful of tables roped off from the main with another set of screws to do the watching. Two tables gone – a Chinese guy and a white guy, both strangers.

Just then, I saw Don come in the cons' door. I waved and mimed lifting a cup to my lips, went to the counter and got a couple of teas and coffees. The prisoner could take his pick. I slung some sandwiches and chocolate on the tray as well. If Don wasn't hungry, there's always plenty of bored kids in visits who kill time by grazing off other people's tables.

I saw someone on the way across – Tony Walcott out of Ardwick, sitting at an empty table a couple of rows down and not showing out. I knew his story. Only a few months out after a ten for smuggling hash, he'd organised another boatload from Morocco and sailed it to a quiet little cove on the coast of Wales – straight into a Customs ready-eye. Tony was looking at double figures again, and his visitor still hadn't shown. I rested the tray on his table.

'Back already?' He nodded at my face. 'What happened there?'

'It's nothing. Tell me about you. How's your head?'

'I'm going to toe the line, do all the courses and work myself into a Cat C nick. With luck I'll do that in a two stretch. Then I'll consider my options.' Which meant, go over the wall.

'You know you can rely on me, Tony. Just send the word.'

We shook, and I got the same sense of fracture I always get with visits; the feeling of being with them, but not of them. For a second, I'd experienced that peculiar intimacy that prisoners feel. And for that second, I could share his burden. Then we both remembered I'd be walking out in an hour or so, and it became awkward. I nodded and went across to Don.

'You OK?'

'Not bad. Thanks for coming.'

I emptied the tray on to the table. 'You still working out?'

'Not much else to do in here. What happened to your face?'

'Nothing.' I sat and he followed me down.

We talked jail talk for a bit. Don assumed, as cons do, that everybody's life revolved around prison politics. But he seemed nervous on top. As we talked, he fiddled with his cup and his eyes jumped around. If he wanted a favour he was probably plotting a lead-in. I cut the chat.

'Listen, Don, we don't know each other well, but I know you're straight. If it's a favour you're after, just tell me.'

He looked at me and away again and it was like someone pulled a curtain down and daylight poured in. My trouble meter turned right on. Seven or eight on a bit of work means I start looking for the offmans. It was tapping nine plus already. I had the sudden urge to stand up and walk out and keep walking.

'What's happening, Don?'

He twitched left and right and wiped his mouth.

'I said, what's going on?'

'Listen, mate, the visit's a moody. I didn't call it on. I was asked by someone in here who's in deep shit. He's on the book. Table over there.' His head jerked to his right. Same place his eyes had been dancing before.

'His visit's just sat down. It's his brother, about your age. In a minute, when I give him the nod, the brother will go to the tea bar. If you'll stand for it, you're supposed to go over there with him.' He glanced right again.

'The guy's just given me the office. The Cat A screws have been straightened. If you walk to his table and his brother comes here, there'll be no scream. It's sweet. The guy's a mate of yours. And he's sound.'

I twisted round at the Cat A section. There was another screw at the table now; the third prisoner must have come in while I'd been talking to Don, but all I could see was the back of his head, shaved. Then a gap opened in the scrub of faces and bodies as a woman got up. As she moved, the new man turned to look at us.

It was Jack Keane.

I snapped my head away so fast it hurt. 'Who put you up to this, you cunt?'

Don fell back in his chair, bewildered.

'What the fuck are you doing booking me a visit for Jack Keane?'

'Oh Christ. I'd no idea. Not a clue.' His shoulders dropped and he started gabbling.

'He came in on the book a couple of days ago. I got a stiff from him with your number. Cat A wouldn't normally get a visit this quick, but he's got the screws straightened. The stiff said phone you, but not to mention his name. It made sense to me, what with him being on the book and everything. He's a straight face. So are you. Anyone would have done the same.'

No, that wasn't it.

'What's Keane got on you, Don?'

He slumped forward on the table and delivered it up. 'My brother's on another wing. He's on the gear and he pulled a stroke on a firm from the Moss. I offered them dough to cool it, but they want revenge. They're going to cut him. Jack Keane told me that if I got you to walk across, he'll turn the Moss gang off. If you don't change tables, the cutting goes ahead. I'm sorry.'

Keane knew I wouldn't put it on Don by walking out, there was no point in being angry at him any more. I sighed and shook my head. 'Give Keane the office. I'll go and see him. Then think about what you're going to do the next time your kid pulls a stroke.'

I stood and offered my hand. He took it, then looked down at his own before rubbing his eyes. His voice was tired too. 'Yeah, yeah. It's a fucker, innit?'

I brushed Tony's table on the way back. His wife was sitting opposite him, crying quietly. She'd done the last sentence with him, and now she was starting all over again, the same as he was. Or maybe she'd had enough and it was goodbye.

Get two coffees and teas at the bar. And biscuits. Tea or coffee for my old friend Jack Keane who'd decided I was a grass and gone about wrecking my life. Why didn't I just walk? So that Keane the stroke-puller gets himself a result? Until the next stroke. Who wrote these fucking rules and why was I following them?

A tap on my arm, the brother. Same stocky build as Jack but a beard on top. Time to play musical fucking chairs to the tune of this crazy fucking game. I noticed my head had stopped banging.

I took the tray and knocked past Keane's brother. There were three screws on Cat A now, including a ginger one who must have come in with Jack. They were all sat looking at a wristwatch that Ginger was holding. The cons' passports were open on the table, photographs face up.

Jack watched me move across the room. I laid the tray on his table and forced myself to sit. He took a tea and sipped at it, using the cup as a prop. We sat there for about two days and nothing happened. Then I heard myself speak. 'Why did you do it, Jack?'

He looked surprised.

'Why did you do it?'

'You ask me that, son?'

'Why?'

He put the cup down and his hand went up to his chin, voice through fingers, visiting style. 'Look, son. I spoke to Nathan before this . . . ' He waved his cup in the air. 'He told me about the tape, Charlie and the copper. When I heard it, all the pieces slotted in.'

'If you thought I'd grassed you, why didn't you come to me?'

A beat. Then he settled and leant forward. 'Try and hear me out, son. When Sonny and me got nicked on the heroin, you were away, you were on your toes. That's the way it looked. I never thought you, but Sonny kept on at me. And look why – only you, me and him knew where the gear was. No one else even knew I was doing business with the guy. Who else was there?'

'Pearson?'

'Then, at the end of one of the interviews, that Hamilton Jacks drops your name. All snide, divide and rule, that kind of style. I wouldn't have it, but Sonny kept on at me. How I shouldn't have brought you in before you said yes, and he was right. It was a rick. And then Sandra fucks off, and it was the beginning of a fucking long stretch, and I thought, who else? So I put the lot on you. I thought it must have been you who grassed us.'

'So why didn't you come to me?'

'When Nathan told me about the tape, well. Pearson knew about the gear and where it was. I just hadn't counted him.'

I sucked in some tea. It tasted like piss.

'Charlie was more like a dad to me, he was closer than family, that's why he never came in the frame. But he knew all right and he obviously knew that fucking Hamilton Jacks. Pearson put me away for eight years – and him and Jacks would have plotted up to mark my card about you. They fitted us both up, you and me, mate.'

He reached for another cup, tea or coffee, he wasn't tasting; he drained it and put it empty back on the tray. Then he took the third and nursed it.

'Listen, son, you know what I'm nicked for. That cunt Pearson ain't ever going to get anyone else put away. Nathan told me everything about the Midland, and you've had the copper over as well. They've both been paid out. In full.' He paused. A long one this time, I could feel the pitch rolling in his brain.

'Don't go to war on me, son. Pearson's dealt with and the copper's taken a second prize. There's no call, is there?'

I kept schtum.

'Listen. I'm not asking you to fall in love with me. Things have happened. You're entitled to have the needle. But we're in the same game, me and you – it's called getting a pound note while you're out there. And then if things go wrong, we stick together, try and minimise the damage in court and after. Like we did with the Turk.'

His voice got stronger, though not perceptibly louder. I knew the play. He was on about observing the code. Playing the straight face.

'For fuck's sake, I'm in deep fucking trouble. I'm virtually bang to fucking rights for killing Charlie. You don't think I planned to go into the Infirmary and empty a piece into his head, do you? But I was fucking furious and I'd been doing a load of coke.' He leant further in.

'You must have done a lot of work on that Hamilton Jacks to tape him up. I need all I can get on the police, on Pearson, any sort of shit to muddy the prosecution's water. Talk to my brief as a start, eh? With enough background, he reckons we might have a shout at an entrapment. Maybe get it down to manslaughter, temporary loss of, all that style. Sentence in single figures, at least one I could see the end of. You'd do it for a normal straight face, I know you would. The fact that I've made it a bit personal with me and you, it shouldn't keep you from doing what's right.'

My silence was pissing him off. He started to flick between anger and persuasion. He was losing it.

'For fuck's sake, if you won't do what I'm asking under the old pal's act, I can promise you there's plenty of dough on the table if you come onside. Surely you can swallow your pride for a serious earner? Or maybe . . . ' He went even lower, I had to lean in to hear.

'Maybe you could do something like you did for the Turk. For me. That's another option.' He sucked a couple more gulps from his cup. 'Unless a miracle happens in court, I'm looking long, long term here. Twenty rec at least, maybe twenty-five. You get to work on your plot – as well as talking to my brief – and I'll put fifty K up front now, wherever and however you want it, with another hundred to follow when you get me out.' Now he leant back in his chair and stared at me.

For fuck's sake, say something.

'OK, I made a big rick but I've squared it by putting Pearson in the morgue. And now I've asked for your help and I've offered you very serious money up front. You've had my best shot.'

Go on, Jack.

'Friendship in this business means asking for and giving favours. If I ask a man for help when I'm in trouble and that man blanks me, then he's against me. You know what I'm saying? Now I've said my piece, it's time for you to say yours. So fucking say something.'

It had been a good performance. Never mind his best shot, he'd tried every shot, and a crawling sickness coming up through my body told me that some of it had worked. I'd hated him when I sat down. Now, guilty as he was, and as ruthless and scheming as he'd been in saying his piece, I felt the change. Jack Keane was playing part of the tune I'd been dancing to for my entire criminal career.

Most of our rules are open to loose transaction. But there are a few chipped in stone. One of them says that when you're out, you don't pile more shit on a man who's in. Despite everything, I was starting to see Jack Keane as another lifer in the system.

Then there was the dough. A hundred and fifty grand is a lot of money. If I pushed him, he'd probably double it, treble it, whatever. He'd cough up anything to beat this one. If he did the time they were promising him, he'd be a pensioner when he came out. Whatever was left of his life on the outside wouldn't be worth a tanner. His mates, the family that still visited him, they would all have moved on. Years on the book, years without sex, without a night in the pub, a meal out, a walk when he fancied it. Years on Cat A, then working down to Cat B then C or D. Maybe twoed up with a sweaty sick farting old man like he was starting to become, then lights out and the sound of the other snoring and fitting and sobbing his way through the night or taking an hour to wank himself to sleep. And when he finally gets out in twenty fucking years time, God knows what the world's going to be like. Even the money's going to be different. Christ, what a life.

My heart was banging hard. Jack saw he'd made an impact. He knew what was going through my brain. He was gambling on it.

That dry throat. Balloon forcing its way up, trying to get out. Last drink's over there, in front of him.

'Jack.'

Hurly burly.

I was croaking.

Hurly burly early.

'Give us your cup over here. I'm dried out.'

With an almost imperceptible nod, he pushed his cup across to me. I lifted it to my lips and took a gulp, mouth and throat went soft again. I took another sip and looked down at the cup. It was half-empty now. I swallowed and looked across.

Hurly burly.

And held his eyes with mine. I felt the blood pounding in my head and ears. I opened my mouth slightly. He leant forward.

Slowly and deliberately, I let the saliva run out of my mouth and collect on my lip. Then I spat in his cup and pushed it back across the table.

'I hope you do every day of your twenty years, Jack. You killed Leon.'

Hurly burly coming.

'Louie Fenton. He had a meet up here and he asked you to come with him, didn't he? And you went. Why, Jack? In the middle of all that plotting and betrayal, why did you go? What did you want from Leon?'

Keane's face was sinking in on itself.

'You went to prop Leon, didn't you, Jack? Told him I was a grass, thought you could get him onside because you'd found out he was having it with Sara, had to be something wrong there. But you got him wrong didn't you, Jack? You got him wrong.'

His mouth cracked open, a fleck of spit came on the corner.

And just like Tomas, I saw it all. Jack calling me a grass, the shouting and now Leon knows everything. Louie screaming at Jack to cool it, Leon telling Louie it was bollocks, and all it takes is a few seconds. They don't see Jack go running into the kitchen and coming out with the knife. And then he loses it, just like he did with Charlie Pearson and at the fights, and all the way back to Foston Hall. And now Leon's dead.

Keane was nearly gone. He was tasting the start of the twenty.

'You think killing Charlie Pearson evens the score? You just did him because he got you eight years, no other reason. Talk about friends and enemies – I was your friend and you betrayed me. From start to finish – my wife, my children, Tomas, Leon, everything. Go back to your cell and rot, Jack. Rot in here and then rot in fucking hell.'

I looked at him for the last time. The years ahead were lying on his face already. He was dead. Then I stood and turned my back and walked away.

I'd just heard Louie's message clearly for the first time.

I'll be coming or jacking it in.

I'll be coming.

I'm coming.

I'm bringing . . .

I'm coming and bringing Jack Keane, Jack Keane.

I'm coming and bringing Jack Keane.

Louie Fenton knew plenty of people in Manchester. And one of them, I'd just heard, was Jack Keane.

My hand got checked with the ultraviolet and I staggered down, leaning heavily on the rail. The prison noise, its lights and lines, were wrapping themselves around me. I entered and left the lift in a thick shroud and got my stuff back at reception. Didn't help. My identity was shattered. I went through locked and unlocked and locked doors, and joined a group at the gate. The screw let us out: two mums with kids, a couple of teenage lads and a white-haired old girl, grey coat and ankle boots against the cold.

It was eleven fifteen when I got out of Strangeways. There was a sharp wind, it cut my face. But there was no one waiting for me this time. It was a start.

'Excuse me.'

The light Scots accent made me look round, then down. The old girl was a step below me, looking up. Her eyes were watery pale blue and she looked lonely and anxious and poor.

'I came to see my son. I took a bus from the station, but now I don't think I can remember the way. Do you, do you know how I can get back?'

I took in her frail body, the thin fingers clutching at her collar against the wind, and her sad beautiful eyes. My gaze flicked away as I remembered some other mother, some other prison. Then I looked back at her.

'I'll take you,' I said.

ACKNOWLEDGEMENTS

Firstly, maximum thanks go to Leslie Gardner for all the help, encouragement and advice as *The Last Straight Face* was conceived, nurtured and done.

Thanks also to everyone who gave up their time to read, comment on or otherwise help out on the book. The guilty people here are Tommy Allison, Matthew Birchwood, Tony Burrows, Cammy and Madge, Chris and Agnes, Anna Cocozza, Dan Dennis, Nigel Foster, Gabriella Francis, Michelle Gribbon, Simon Heath, Rae Howells, Jo Johnson, Barney Lynch, Richard MacAndrew, Ian O'Donnell, Diane Toland, Melissa Weatherill and Steve Williams.

Thank you to everyone one at Old Street – especially Becky Senior, Ben Yarde-Buller, Francesca Yarde-Buller, Sam Duncan and Sam Carter – for all the hard work and for making the whole publishing process generally enjoyable.

Lastly, a very big thank you to Julie Klavens, whose insights, input and understanding were incredibly helpful during a period best described as grim.